FATEFUL PATHWAYS

A STORY OF THESEUS

BILL HIATT

Edited by
LEWIS POLLAK
Cover by
PETER O'CONNOR

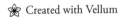

To all the leaders who put the needs of their people above their own

PROLOGUE: VISITED BY A GHOST

MILTIADES WAS ALONE in his tent as he often was on the night before a battle. This particular night, though, he might have welcomed company. He might have walked around the camp and spoken to the men as they huddled around the flickering flames of the campfires. But he had already done that once tonight. Doing it again could have made him seem nervous—and a nervous commander made for nervous soldiers. He might not sleep tonight, but if none of them did, the odds of winning would be even worse than they already were.

So he stayed alone in his tent. No, not entirely alone. Phobos, fear incarnate, that pale-skinned, wild-eyed son of Ares, was with him, whispering in his ears and gnawing at him with long, knife-sharp, icy teeth. Every footstep was the sound of an approaching spy or assassin. Every cry of the screech owl was some dire warning from the gods. Every hint of movement near his tent was the beginning of a surprise attack.

Miltiades cursed his weakness. He was no stranger to war. His heart should not be beating so fast. His hand should not be twitching toward his sword. His eyes should not be riveted to his tent flap as if a horde of enemies might rush through it at any moment. But never had he faced a single engagement that could so change his life—if he survived.

The Persian empire had far greater forces at its disposal than the

Greeks. It also had a unity they lacked. Despite occasional alliances, the city-states would just as soon fight each other as stand together against the Persians. And while the warlike cities squabbled among themselves, the Persian lion gobbled them up, one after another. Now it waited, salivating in anticipation, as it neared Athens, the city Miltiades now called home. The lion had whetted its appetite on the Aegean islands and Eretria. If it could win here, at Marathon, it would be ready to pounce on Athens.

There would be no saving his city then—not even if the gods themselves took the field.

Though there was no wind, Miltiades felt a chill, and the tent flap rippled slightly. At first, he saw nothing, but Phobos stopped gnawing and tore into his flesh with cold claws as a blur that at first looked like mist became a human figure right before his eyes. It could not be a man, for no man could appear from nothingness. Besides, the stranger was translucent. Miltiades could see the tent wall right through him.

Was this intruder a god, come to punish Miltiades for the unintended blasphemy of his thought? Or was he a Zurvanic, one of the Persian priests or magi, as the Romans called them, sent to cast some fatal spell upon him?

Miltiades's hand moved toward his sword hilt, but for the first time in his military career, he had no idea what to do next. Raising a blade against a god would seal Miltiades's fate. But if the stranger were a magus, the only way to avoid death would be to cut him down before he could weave his fatal magic.

"Rest easy, friend," said the apparition. His Greek was flawless, but Miltiades didn't recognize the accent.

"Who are you?" The leader tried to sound fearless, but to his shame, a slight tremor in his voice betrayed him.

The apparition smiled—a warm smile, despite the chill that accompanied his presence.

"In life, I was called Theseus. I have come to help in tomorrow's battle—if you will have me."

Miltiades's eyes narrowed as he studied the stranger's translucent face. In the dark tent, it glowed slightly, but its features told him nothing. Olive-skinned, handsome, his brown eyes intense and deep as the sea, the stranger could have been Theseus, but Miltiades had no way to know for sure. He could just as easily be a magus's illusion. Nor was the newcomer's body, muscled like that of a warrior, any help. Even if it were not an illusion, Miltiades had no idea what Theseus had looked like.

"You hesitate," said the stranger. "Perhaps I am in the wrong tent. I took you for Miltiades, one of the ten strategoi of Athens. But such a man, threatened by overwhelming odds, would certainly not reject an offer of help from one who is a friend of Athens."

"I am Miltiades. But what proof have I that you are Theseus?"

The stranger smiled again, more sadly this time. "Is it not evident that I have come from the land of the dead? Or do you so commonly receive ghosts as guests here that you think I am someone else's ghost?"

"Why did you not seek out Callimachus with your offer of help?" asked Miltiades. "He is the polemarch. I am but a lowly strategos under his command."

"A strategos isn't so unimportant, as any Greek would know," said Theseus, frowning slightly. "Did you take me for a Persian? Callimachus voted to break a tie in your favor, but you formulated the battle plan. You are the leader who best understands strategy and particularly how to defeat the Persians. You would also most appreciate how much I could help morale by encouraging the troops. They are every bit as apprehensive as you are."

"I'm not—"

"You are. Your face betrays you. Even if it did not, only an idiot would remain unconcerned when faced by an enemy as formidable as those fierce warriors from the east."

"How are you able to be here? You pointed out yourself that it is not common for the spirits of the dead to walk the earth."

The stranger sighed. "Though I am dead, the ways of the gods are still a mystery to me. But this much I know—they intervene less than they used to. You will not see them take the field themselves, as they did at Troy. That does not mean they do not care about the outcome. I imagine some of them persuaded Hades to let me offer what help I could."

"How do I know you aren't some Persian trick? It is said the magi are skilled in the magical arts."

3

The stranger looked down at himself. "Enough to create me? Enough to make me speak Greek better than they can themselves? If they had such power and such skill, the war would already be over.

"Yet I cannot fault you for having doubts. My offer is…unusual. A good commander is ever wary of offers that seem too good to be true." Theseus nodded as if agreeing with himself. "Yes, that's it. I should have expected such skepticism.

"I hesitate to ask you to lose sleep on the night before battle, but if I were to tell you my tale, with all the knowledge of Athens and of the rest of the Greek world that it contains, would that persuade you that I am not some Persian deception?"

"I doubt that I will sleep much tonight, anyway," said Miltiades. He took his hand off his sword hilt. "Sit if you will, and tell your tale. Someone as wise as Theseus will certainly be able to convince me."

The look the stranger gave him hinted at suffering beyond anything Miltiades had endured.

"I am not as wise as you think. When you have heard my story, you will know that. Maybe I am here, not because I am some virtuous sage but because of all the times when I fell short of that ideal. Maybe I am here to give me a chance to undo some small part of the damage I have done."

THE MEDDLING WAYS OF MEN

FOR YOU TO UNDERSTAND MY story, you must know something of my mother, Aethra. I will speak of events that occurred before I was born and when I was just a child. What I am about to tell you I learned from my mother when I came of age. She was an honest woman, and I believe every word she told me, even though I wanted to disbelieve some of it with all my heart.

In the early part of her life, Aethra seemed destined for happiness. She was a granddaughter of Pelops, which made her a descendant of Zeus himself, and she was every bit as beautiful as you might expect a woman with such ancestry to be. As her son, you might expect me to be unable to judge her looks. Are not sons universally of the opinion that their mothers are beautiful, yet at the same time, obligated not to think of that beauty in the same way other men might? Luckily, when I was young, I stumbled upon letters from her once-numerous suitors. To describe her appearance, I will rely on phrases they used.

Her olive skin shone like highly polished stone. Her eyes were the rich brown of earth warmed by the sun. Her hair was dusk-colored, suggestive of both the sunset that precedes dusk and the starry night that follows it. Her body was as shapely and alluring as that a model a sculptor might look to for inspiration before carving a statue of

Aphrodite. Thus wrote those suitors, and had you been able to behold her in her prime, I am sure you would agree.

But beauty was far from her only asset. Her father, Pittheus, was legendary for his wisdom and knowledge. Aethra had understanding befitting the daughter of such a man and a fine environment in which to develop her gifts. Troezen, the city he ruled, was certainly no Athens, but it was of good repute, well-governed, and prosperous. Though there were cities powerful enough to have made war against it, their leaders restrained themselves. The advice Pittheus could give them was more valuable by far than any benefit that a ruler could gain from conquering little Troezen.

As an adolescent, my mother had dreams of love, as all girls do. She envisioned the prince as handsome as Apollo or Hermes, who would come to make her his wife and love her as much as any man had ever loved any woman. She had her share of offers for Pittheus to sift through. None of them were quite godlike, but she was still young, and Pittheus was in no hurry to see her married off. He wanted to find the best match possible—even though he thought in terms of position and advantage more than love.

My mother would not have been difficult to love. Her beauty was complemented by her sun-bright smile and a laugh that would bring joy even to the most miserable creature who walked the earth. And as I've said, she had wit enough to appeal to any man who appreciated the value of a wise woman. Perhaps she would not have found the lover of her dreams, but she would undoubtedly have found someone who would make an excellent husband.

Indeed, it did not take long for a suitor to emerge upon whom Pittheus and Aethra could agree—Bellerophon.

He was the eldest son and heir of Glaucus, king of Corinth. At least, that was the public story. Men whispered that Eurymede, the king's wife, had lain with Poseidon.

Pittheus didn't care which version was true. Either way, Bellerophon would one day make his daughter queen of Corinth. Always looking to the future, Pittheus knew the marriage would eventually bring a grandson of his to the throne, perhaps even unite Corinth and Troezen as one kingdom. He nodded his head in satisfaction. It would be a good match, a good match indeed!

Aethra didn't care much about the identity of Bellerophon's father, either. Like the son of a god, he stood out among men—tall, broad-shouldered, well-muscled, more handsome than the norm. But something more important than his body also set him apart. Glaucus's face was sharp and hard, his eyes cruel. Bellerophon's face was softer, his eyes kind. Aethra could look into them and imagine that she had known him for years.

In those days, it was not hard to find men who were fathered by gods —or at least claimed to be—but many of them were evil. Glaucus himself claimed to be a grandson of the titan Atlas on his mother's side. On his father's side, he could claim descent from three other titans. That did not prevent him from becoming so obsessed with perfecting his chariot horses that he fed them on human flesh, an offense against gods and men.

No, Aethra wasn't drawn to Bellerophon's ancestry—she was drawn by his nobility of spirit. She would be proud to love him. And he would truly mean it when he professed his love. He was awkward around her, having had little experience with women, but that made his sincerity all the more apparent. He didn't care about the politics of their marriage. He cared about her as much as she cared about him.

Aethra was officially betrothed to Bellerophon in a spring ceremony, though the actual marriage would not take place until winter, during the moon sacred to Hera, goddess of marriage. To Aethra, her betrothal day was the happiest day of her life.

She had no way to know then what tragedy would flow from it.

It was not customary to complete the betrothal so long before the marriage, but Pittheus was taking no chances. After all, Bellerophon was quite a desirable match, And Glaucus was not the most trustworthy man. Once the couple was betrothed, the marriage contract could only be voided by mutual consent. That should be enough to prevent Glaucus from reneging later should what he saw as a more desirable offer present itself.

Even someone as wise as Pittheus could not anticipate every possible problem, however. He was as surprised as everyone else when Bellerophon killed his own brother, Deliades.

Much later, when I was king of Athens, I tried to enforce the idea that intent should be a factor in determining guilt. Yes, Deliades had died by Bellerophon's hand, but it was an accident. Bellerophon was no deliberate murderer and should not have been treated as such. But the law in those days—and for a long time after—was harsh and unyielding in such a case. Regardless of intent, Bellerophon was guilty, and Glaucus would have to exile him.

Pittheus found himself caught in a trap of his own making. Bellerophon might well convince someone to purify him of the blood-guilt. Indeed, he had already gone to the king of Tiryns to seek such a cleansing. But that would not necessarily allow him to return to Corinth —and an exile could never assume the throne.

My grandfather asked Glaucus's approval to cancel the betrothal, but Glaucus, thinking only of himself, refused. Obsessed as he was by his horses, he still wanted at least one grandson, who might be able to rule Corinth eventually even if Bellerophon could not. Stained as Bellerophon was by murder and exile, he was no longer a sought-after match. If he did not marry Aethra, it was unlikely any other princess would become his wife, either.

My mother cared nothing for such complications. She knew in her heart that Bellerophon was no murderer, and she would have married him in the winter, just as she had promised to do. She was loyal and not at all reluctant. She still loved Bellerophon with all her heart.

But Bellerophon did not come for her. No doubt, Pittheus would have barred the door against him, but perhaps Aethra could have won her father over to the idea. She was sure she would succeed if only fate would give her the chance to try.

It did not. Perhaps Bellerophon was too ashamed to face her. Maybe he was waiting until he was purified, a much longer process than he anticipated. The wife of the king of Tiryns tried to seduce him, and when she failed, she accused him of rape. Having already accepted Bellerophon as a guest, the king was unable to kill him himself, so he sent Bellerophon to his father-in-law, a Lycian king, with instructions to kill the young man.

Bellerophon survived, despite being required to perform several quests, any one of which could have killed him. Eventually, the Lycian king learned enough of Bellerophon to realize that the rape story was false. But by then, years had passed.

One sunny day—yet among the darkest in Aethra's life—word reached Troezen that Bellerophon had married a Lycian princess. At first, my mother refused to believe the news. She had waited for him all those years, for she doubted the rape story every bit as much as she doubted the murder. Surely, he would have waited as long for her.

But, no, Bellerophon had not waited. When my mother could deny the truth no longer, she made excuses for him. He must have thought Glaucus and Pittheus had canceled the betrothal. He must have thought she would never take him back. Every woman in Troezen, from the slave girls to other members of the royal family, nodded their heads as they listened to her weave a tale of pure love lost by ill-luck. But they nodded because she was the princess, not because they believed her—and in time, she knew that. She stopped retelling the tale of Bellerophon and kept her broken heart, sharp-edged and still bloody, to herself.

As for Pittheus, his heart wasn't broken at all, though he feigned sympathy for Aethra and stretched his face to show a sorrow he didn't feel. From the moment he had heard of the murder and exile, his strongest desire was to see Aethra married to someone else. Guilty or not, Bellerophon was damaged goods in his eyes. Even the stories of extraordinary heroism trickling into Troezen didn't move him. Not even hearing that Athena had given Bellerophon the right to fly on Pegasus—proof that Poseidon was the prince's father—did not change Pittheus's attitude at all. After all, what good was a god's son if stained by scandal and without the ability to make Aethra a queen and Pittheus's grandson king? He rejoiced in Bellerophon's marriage every bit as much as Aethra sorrowed in it.

Yes, Pittheus's judgment of Bellerophon was hard as stone. But at least Aethra was spared being forced into marriage with someone else.

The sad truth was that no one would have her. As long as the betrothal had remained in force, other kings doubted she could be legally married to anyone else, despite the bizarre circumstances. Glaucus himself died—eaten by his own horses, or so the story went. But the betrothal, unmoving as a mountain, remained as an obstacle. That stumbling block was not removed until Bellerophon's marriage—and by then, it was too late to matter.

By that time, there were whispers that my mother was cursed in some way. Why that would have been, no one ever said. Any idiot should have recognized that Glaucus was the cursed one, for he was a notorious sinner, long out of favor with the gods. Did not his grisly death prove that?

But one of the harshest goddesses of all is Pheme, goddess of rumor. Harshest—and least concerned about the truth. Aethra was cursed in the minds of men, if not in reality.

However, my mother was resilient. She still cherished the memory of her brief relationship with the unlucky Corinthian prince, still dreamed of what they could have had together. But the edges of her broken heart dulled with time and bled less. She was not the sort to throw herself into the sea and drown. No, she was too strong for such a fate. Instead, she would endure.

She would not take another man as her husband, however. It was not hard to stay firm in her resolve when marriage was impossible, anyway. But even if the rumor that she was cursed faded over time, she had a way to evade the possibility of marriage. The goddess Artemis welcomed women who chose not to wed into her hunting parties. Under her protection, no fatherly authority could force Aethra to take a husband. Even better, the goddess frequently hunted near Troezen. Aethra could approach her in person when the time was right.

Only later did my mother realize that Pittheus suspected what she was thinking. Aethra, never interested in hunting before, would find excuses to tag along with one of the hunting parties when it went into one of the nearby forests. Pittheus also noticed a change in how she spent time when she was alone. Before, Aethra had spent long hours at her window, gazing out to sea as if expecting a ship bearing Bellerophon to appear on the horizon. Now, she was still at her window, but her eyes stared into the forest instead of at the ocean.

Nor were these the only signs. Aethra had offered frequent prayers and sacrifices to Hera and Aphrodite as she waited for Bellerophon. What better goddesses to appeal to than those representing marriage and love? But then Aethra's devotions to them tapered off, replaced by prayers to Artemis. It wasn't uncommon for young, unmarried girls to pray to the virgin goddess who was a protector of the young, among other things. But Aethra was a bit old now to offer that kind of prayer.

At some point, Pittheus must have decided he needed a way to thwart her plan—for her own good, he would have told himself. The fact that it was for his good as well would have been a pleasant coincidence.

My mother would have been happy as the wife of Bellerophon. Of that much, I am sure. What would have happened if she had become a huntress of Artemis, I cannot truly say. She would not have been the first woman to have found peace in such a way.

Pittheus, overconfident in his assumption that he always knew best, robbed her both of that peace and of any possibility that she might find happiness with another husband.

Because Pittheus was famed for his wisdom, kings from other cities frequently visited to ask him for advice. One fateful day, the king who came to visit was Aegeus, king of Athens.

Athens was not quite as important as it is today, but it was even then one of the most important Greek cities, certainly more prestigious than Troezen. Pittheus was naturally eager to help the Athenian king with whatever he needed. He was even more anxious when he realized that he could use Aegeus's question to solve Pittheus's worries about Aethra.

Aegeus was well into his second marriage but remained childless. Fearing that he might have somehow incurred the gods' displeasure, he had consulting the oracle of Delphi, who advised him not to drink wine until he returned to Athens. What good that would have done, I'm not sure. Sometimes, oracles are answering a different question than the one posed to them. But whether or not that advice would somehow have solved Aegeus's problem, no one will ever know because the oracle had shrouded her meaning in poetic language. Aegeus could not help but wonder if there was some symbolism he was missing, some hidden meaning potentially more important than the obvious one. Since Pittheus was known for his skill at interpreting confusing oracles, it was natural for Aegeus to seek the advice of the king of Troezen before returning to Athens.

Pittheus at once saw an opportunity to exalt his family and his city far beyond their current prestige. If Aegeus became the father of Pittheus's grandson, that grandson would eventually become heir to both Troezen and Athens. The two kingdoms might even become one, just as Pittheus once hoped would happen with Corinth. The difference was that Athens was an even greater prize than Corinth. With the proper management, Athens united with Troezen could end up as the most powerful kingdom in Greece.

There was one obvious problem—Aegeus was already married. He could never be Aethra's husband. But that difficulty, which would have seemed a boulder in most men's eyes, was transformed by Pittheus's ambition into a mere speck of dust. The oracle had shown him the way. If Aegeus became drunk, Pittheus could get him into Aethra's bed easily enough. A man desperate for an heir, as Aegeus was, would certainly take an heir born outside of marriage in preference to none at all.

After assuring Aegeus that the oracle's words were not literal and providing him with some contrived alternate meaning, Pittheus offered the king of Athens one cup of wine after another. Aegeus, ready to celebrate the son the oracle had foretold, was easily persuaded to keep drinking.

Once the king was utterly drunk, Pittheus came to my mother.

"A princess has certain duties, my daughter, certain acts she must perform for the good of the realm."

Aethra feared another marriage offer had finally arrived, but she lowered her head obediently. "What may I do to serve the kingdom, my father?"

"You must bear a child by Aegeus," said Pittheus. "This very night, you will allow him to lie with you."

Aethra's cheeks reddened. "But Aegeus cannot become my husband. And if I sleep with him—"

"We will find you a husband who will understand," said Pittheus, knowing full well there would be no such husband. But it was likely there would be none, anyway. At least this way, Aethra could become a mother and give him the grandson he craved.

"Through Aegeus, you will have a son who will one day unite us with Athens."

Despite the warm fire burning in the hearth nearby, Aethra felt a chill like death settle upon her. A marriage would not have happened immediately. She would have had the time to join Artemis in the forest. But this idea, that would so suddenly take the virginity she had guarded so faithfully, would allow her no time to make her escape.

"Sleeping with the king is wrong! How will Aegeus's wife feel about such a thing?"

"She will accept it, for she has borne him no son. She will understand."

Aethra was not so young that anyone could fool her easily that easily. She doubted any woman would accept a breach of faith by her husband, whatever the cause. At that moment, she wanted to scream her protests so loudly that everyone in the palace would hear.

She wanted to—but she hesitated. Her father had seldom said a harsh word to her, and even now, faced with her refusal, he was still smiling at her as if it were his birthday and she had just given him a thoughtful gift. But she knew too well how the world worked. A father had authority over his daughter. A king had even more authority over his daughter and subject. She could refuse to sleep with Aegeus, but Pittheus would be within his rights—legal if not moral—to imprison her until she complied or to disown her and send her out to beg on the streets.

Would he have been so heartless? Aethra looked into his eager eyes and didn't know. That her father could be so cold seemed impossible, though. And if he proved himself the tyrant the law allowed him to be, she would still have the time to reconsider. Even such a father would accept repentance rather than insist on punishment.

"Father, I cannot sleep with the king. If I could marry him, I would do so, but this—I cannot."

Of course, she didn't mean the last part. But it is easy to promise to do something you know is impossible.

She allowed herself to feel relief for a moment. Her father's smile faded, but he did not rage at her, much less threaten her with dire consequences. He seemed still to be the reasonable man she had always known.

Then he spoke again, but his words, meant as consolation, were like salt in her wounded heart.

"I would not even ask if only the welfare of Troezen was involved," said Pittheus. "We have survived this long without the support of Athens. I'm sure we will endure. But Aegeus is a decent man—wouldn't you agree?"

"I know little of him," said Aethra cautiously. "But I have heard he is a good man and a just king."

Pittheus nodded his head vigorously. "He is all of that—and more. It is for his sake I make this request, though he knows nothing about it."

"For his sake? I do not understand. Surely, there are other women—"

"This is no idle matter of sexual pleasure," said Pittheus, hunching slightly as if the weight of the world were pressing down on his shoulders. "Childlessness is a source of grief for any man. But childlessness in a king? It endangers his very life."

Aethra frowned. "I do not understand. There have been childless kings before. Not all of them have come to a violent end. I know my history better than that."

"Aye, you know it well. But Athens is in a precarious condition. You have read, no doubt, of the numerous Athenian kings who have been overthrown by usurpers. Aegeus still faces many conspiracies: that of his brother, Lycus, that of the sons of another brother, Pallas, and that of the sons of his Uncle Metion, a former usurper. There is hardly a shadow anywhere in Athens that does not hold at least one assassin, each ready with an eager knife, hungry for Aegeus's heart.

"Nor is that the extent of the danger. Far to the south, on the island of Crete, Minos, son of Zeus, reaches out an oppressive hand toward the mainland. He has already taken Megara, once Athenian territory ruled by Nisus, another of Aegeus's brothers. And he has forced Athens to pay tribute. If Aegeus looks weak, Minos will not hesitate to darken the sea between Crete and Athens with his navy.

"You see, more than Aegeus's life may be at stake. For if Minos invades, he will paint the streets of Athens with the blood of its people. Your virginity is no small thing—but is it larger than all the lives that might be lost?"

Aethra's heart was beating too fast, and her stomach was so uneasy that she feared she might vomit. "But what does this have to do with Aegeus being childless?"

"Men see a king who cannot father a child as less of a man," said

Pittheus. "This is true even if his wife may be at fault. And a king without a son to succeed him has a harder time retaining his people's loyalty.

"His life is not in immediate danger. His second marriage is still recent enough that there may still be some hope of a child from it. But if Aegeus is still childless some years from now, he will be as good as dead."

Aethra would rather her father had threatened her with prison, even actually thrown her into one. At least then, she would still have had a choice. Prison offered hope of reprieve or even escape—and she could still go to Artemis after.

However, Artemis wouldn't take her if she were no longer a virgin. That path would be forever closed to her. But how could she live with herself if she refused her father's request and Aegeus died because of it? And what if his was not the only death?

She had never seen a battle, but it was easy for her mind to conjure up a lurid scene of blood, severed limbs, and devastation. She beheld Athens in flames as Minos raced through it, hacking to bits every living thing he saw.

Her ever-wise father was right again—how could she weigh her virginity against such carnage?

She lowered her eyes. "Father, I will do as you ask—for the sake of Aegeus and the Athenians."

Pittheus patted her on the arm. "You are as wise as you are virtuous. You will not regret the choice you have made today."

As it turned out, she did regret it at times. But at that moment, she felt a momentary lightness of heart. After all the pointless misery of her separation from Bellerophon, the gods had given her purpose. It was not the one she wanted, but at least it was not the broken heart whose emptiness had plagued her.

Would she have felt differently, I wonder, if she had known the gods were prepared to ask far more of her?

THE MEDDLING WAYS OF GODS

AUTHOR WENT TO HER ROOM, and it was not long before Pittheus knocked at the door. He was too old to be maneuvering a drunken man the size of Aegeus around, but this was not the kind of task he could entrust to any servant, not even the most trusted.

My mother helped Pittheus get the king of Athens into her bed. The scent of wine was as heavy upon him as if he had been celebrating with Dionysus himself for days, rather than the hours he had spent with my grandfather.

"He is barely conscious," said Aethra, more to herself than to her father.

"I offered him a bed companion for the night, and he accepted," said Pittheus. "I just didn't mention that it was you. When he realizes he is not alone in bed, he will do what comes naturally," Since Pittheus was never anywhere nearly this drunk himself, Aethra had no idea how he could be so sure. And given her own innocence, she had no idea of how to encourage the king.

"All will be well," said Pittheus, putting his arm around her. If he felt her trembling, he made no mention of it. "The gods, particularly Athena, have an interest in the well-being of Athens. They will bless what you do this night, and you will bear Aegeus a son."

Pittheus offered a few more words of encouragement and then excused himself. Aethra looked down at Aegeus. His closed eyes and slow breathing suggested he might have fallen asleep. On top of everything else, she would need to wake him.

He was no Apollo, nor even a Bellerophon. He was older than she, and his body bore the scars of battle, white and twisted, stark against his olive skin. His brown hair had strands of gray. Even in sleep, his face was tense, lined from the burdens of kingship. In his youth, though, he could have been handsome. Even now, she could look at him and believe that he, like Bellerophon, was descended from gods, though more remotely.

Aethra sighed. She didn't think she could ever fall in love with him, but at least she was not repelled by his appearance. And he was a good man. Everyone agreed on that. To save his life, she could get through this night.

Despite herself, she giggled. Pittheus had inadvertently conjured up an image in her mind—the gods looking down from Olympus at all she and Aegeus would do. She knew she was being silly, but she felt as if there really were many eyes fixed on her. Was Athena smiling to think that the son Aethra was about to conceive would save Athena's favorite city? Was Hera frowning at the planned adultery? Was Artemis looking down with disappointment? Aethra doubted the virgin huntress would approve of her choice, whatever the others might think.

But it was fruitless to dwell on such fantasies. The gods were surely too busy to spend time leering at her and Aegeus. And if some among them disapproved, what of that? She was following her father's instructions. If what she did was wrong, he was at fault, not she.

Though she didn't really believe that—she would not feel so nervous if she did—she undressed before more visions intruded into her mind and crawled into bed next to the king.

She was afraid at first to wake him. Pittheus had said Aegeus did not know he would be sleeping with Aethra. What if he were shocked to find the princess of Troezen in his bed—or, more correctly, to find himself in hers? What if he cried out in alarm and threw her out? The servants would hear. What would they think? Would he think—would they think—that she was some wanton girl who would sleep with any man she could get her hands on?

She pressed up against him. His body felt warm against hers. He stirred, and she knew he was not quite as asleep as she had thought.

The ever-wise Pittheus had predicted the outcome well. Aethra didn't have to take the lead. Aegeus, drunk though he was, knew exactly what to do.

She had heard from older women that the first time was often painful, and she braced herself to endure what she must. Yet Aegeus, though she couldn't understand how he knew what he was doing, was surprisingly gentle, not at all the rough drunkard she had expected. Perhaps the gods, appreciating the sacrifice she was making, had blessed their coupling after all.

"Chalciope," he whispered. Aethra froze at the sound of his wife's name. Was his use of it now an accusation? A message from Hera, perhaps? If so, it came too late.

But no, she quickly realized that it was neither thing. Not too drunk to perform sexually, but drunk enough to have forgotten where he was, Aegeus imagined that she was Chalciope. That was why the situation wasn't awkward for him!

His example inspired her. If he thought she was Chalciope, could she make herself believe that he was Bellerophon? She tried for a while, but the young man who had haunted her, awake and asleep, for so many months, picked this one night to be elusive. He was like the touch of the slightest breeze, here for a moment and then gone. Perhaps even a phantom of him conjured up by her own mind could not bear to see her with another man.

Gentle as Aegeus was, his lovemaking continued for far longer than she would have liked. When at last it was over—even someone as innocent as she was had been taught by the older women what to expect—he tried to hold onto her, his hand gentle but insistent.

"I have done what I must," she whispered to him. "I will do no more." More alert than he was, she slipped away from him and out of bed. Putting on her clothes as quietly as she could, she crept from the room, quiet as a ghost—or an imaginary Bellerophon. She lay down near the hearth in the main hall, and there she slept. She feared the dreams she might have, perhaps of a wronged Chalciope pointing an accusing finger at her, but the gods spared her that. However, she was troubled by a different and unexpected dream.

In the dream, Athena was standing over her. The goddess's armor and spear glittered in the moonlight. Her gray eyes looked into Aethra's as if the goddess wished to learn what was in her heart. Though Aethra could not make out Athena's face, she felt the goddess's grim mood and shuddered.

"Your family has neglected the rites they must perform at the tomb of Sphaerus," said Athena. "You are not to blame for that negligence," she added in response to Aethra's horrified expression. "But you are the best person to correct it. Take wine to the island of Sphaeria and pour the offering on his tomb. Do this now, for his spirit is restless, and he deserves far better."

Haven't I done enough for one day? thought Aethra. But even asleep, she had better sense than to say that to the goddess.

"I will do as you have commanded."

Athena nodded, and the dream ended. Aethra found herself back in the great hall, shivering even though the night was not that cold. Moving as quietly as she could, she found an appropriate wineskin.

Lest you think the goddess was asking for the impossible, the "island" of Sphaeria was more like a sandbank and so near the shore that Aethra could easily wade to it. Still, it was the middle of the night. The goddess must have thought the princess was one of her owls.

The guards at the gate naturally raised eyebrows when she told them of her errand, but they didn't try to dissuade her. It struck her as odd that none of them volunteered to accompany her, but she was in a hurry to be done. The distance was short, the area regularly patrolled and free of bandits. Why would she have needed an escort?

The seawater felt icy as she made her way across the narrow patch of sea that separated Sphaeria from the mainland. The monument to Sphaerus, clearly visible in the moonlight, felt peaceful to her. If his spirit was restless, she saw no sign of it. Of course, she was no interpreter of the ways of ghosts—and she was no horse. The spirit of Sphaerus, Pelops's charioteer, was reputed to be a horse scarer. Gamblers would sometimes invoke his aid when they wanted to influence the outcome of a race.

Though the distance was short, Aethra was cold and tired, and her legs felt heavy as lead. She couldn't help but be a little grumpy. That Athena would use her to mother a future king of Athens she could understand, but why use her as an errand girl?

For that matter, what did Sphaerus care about his little fake tomb near Troezen? His ashes had been buried on Lesbos, after all, far, far away from here. Yes, he had been a faithful charioteer, and yes, Pelops had felt responsible for his death. The poor fellow had died following an overly rapid ride in Pelops's new chariot, a gift from Poseidon, crafted by the gods and pulled by winged horses. But was that enough to justify performing rites in every city which had a ruler descended from Pelops? Even then, there were a lot of them. And what did dead Sphaerus do with wine, anyway? It was not as if ghosts could get drunk.

Of course, there was another possibility that chilled Aethra more than the seawater. Sphaerus had never fathered a son. Perhaps he, too, needed her to be a mother. The idea was ridiculous. Ghosts were insubstantial and could never father children. But she had a hard time shaking the thought once it had occurred to her.

By the time Aethra set foot on the tiny island, she was in a foul mood. She stood have stayed in bed with Aegeus, where at least she would have been warm.

She blinked as she stepped toward the monument. Was it a trick of the light, or was there a figure standing just out of reach of the moonlight in the shadow cast by Sphaerus's tomb?

Aethra saw movement in the shadows—and out stepped Athena herself, not a dream, but the actual goddess in the flesh—or what served for flesh among the gods.

She was less grim than in the dream and even more beautiful. Even if Aethra were a newcomer who hadn't heard the goddess described a hundred times, she could not have mistaken such a radiant being for an ordinary mortal. Lit not just by moonlight but by her inherent divinity, her face glowed. Her gray eyes were as bright and hard as diamonds, and, as in the dream, they seemed to look right through her.

But her beauty was the only thing that gave away her gender. She wore the helmet and armor of a man and carried a spear with a death-sharp point, all no doubt fashioned by Hephaestus, blacksmith of the gods. If the stories were true, she was a better warrior than almost all of them. Even the savage war god, Ares, was no match for her.

Even as long ago as my mother encountered Athena, it was far from being an everyday occurrence for a god to appear to a mortal. Stiff as Aethra's legs were, she fell to her knees before Athena.

"Goddess, I have come to do your bidding. Are you here because you require something more? Let me know, and I will gladly do it."

Gladly was on her lips but not in her heart. The words she really wanted to speak were more like a curse than a submission. But she knew better than to curse a goddess. No good could come from such defiance.

"I do have need of you for something else," said Athena. "I thought it was better to speak to you in person. No dream should stand between us now. Our common purpose of saving Athens unites us. If you do what must be done, you will save it."

Aethra didn't know how to respond. Hadn't she saved Athens already?

"I see you are puzzled. Your father, Pittheus, so wise in so many ways, has made one mistake this night. The case of Aegeus is the case of blaming the land for not growing a crop when it is the plowman who is to blame."

"I don't understand."

"Aegeus is incapable of fathering a child. Have you not wondered how a man twice married over a reasonable number of years has not had at least one child already? Could both women be barren? Either he is truly unlucky—or, as is the case here, the fault is his."

"Goddess, I do not wish to seem irreverent. I will do whatever you ask, but some questions burn within me."

Aethra lowered her eyes, but she could still feel the goddess's eyes upon her.

"It is usually not wise to question the gods," said Athena slowly. "But I am the goddess of wisdom, and wisdom grows in part through questions. You may ask what you wish."

Aethra, realizing she had been holding her breath, exhaled as softly as she could.

"You may also rise and face me if you so desire. I would not have appeared before you if I had wished you to look only at the ground."

Aethra rose and looked up, but not all the way up. She could not yet bring herself to meet the goddess's gray eyes.

"If Aegeus must have a son but is incapable, why do the gods not simply make him capable? Then he could have a son by his wife."

To her surprise, Athena laughed. "I wish we gods could do what must be done as easily as mortals believe we can. Sadly, the universe is more complex than you can know, and even we immortals can see only imperfectly through the shadows thrown by fate.

"Aegeus's condition is not natural. It was brought upon him by the curse of Aphrodite. What is done by one god or goddess cannot readily be undone by another."

"But cannot Zeus order Aphrodite to remove the curse?"

"Zeus orders when he must, negotiates when he can. He would not see Athens destroyed or brought so low that it cannot play its destined role. Even Aphrodite herself would not. But there are ways to avoid such a catastrophe without lifting the curse."

"By sacrificing my virginity. Goddess, I have done what I must, and I will do what you ask of me. But I cannot pretend that I lost my virginity to Aegeus with joy in my heart. You have kept your own virginity intact. Surely, you must understand how I feel."

Aethra lowered her eyes to the ground again, afraid she had gone too far. But she knew she would not regret speaking what was in her heart. She would have remembered this night over and over, and each time anger at her silence would have cut her like a blade. No, better to face the possibility of the goddess's wrath for a moment than to face the certainty of her own inward-directed wrath.

"Aethra, look at me," said Athena. The words had the unmistakable edge of command to them but no anger. Aethra did as the goddess told her.

"You speak the truth when you say I am a virgin and would not be otherwise. I do understand why a woman would feel the same way.

"I would not have asked you to make such a sacrifice if there were a better way to save Aegeus and Athens. There is not. I will tell you what more I have to ask of you, and I will explain why that is the path you must follow."

"Your will be done," said Aethra, though in her heart, she meant exactly the opposite.

"It was necessary for you to lie with Aegeus, for he, who believes the curse is on his wives and not himself, must believe your son is his. Otherwise, he will not accept that son as his heir, and your sacrifice will have been for nothing."

"My son?" asked Aethra. She shivered from the cold—and from the feat that ate at her heart. She was no oracle, but she could guess what Athena would say next.

"To provide Aegeus a suitable heir, you will lie with Poseidon."

"Why with him?" whispered Aethra. The sea surrounded them, shallow as it was in this area. Poseidon might hear her.

Nonetheless, she had to ask. Poseidon's sons tended to be monsters—in human form or otherwise. Bad as her situation was already, to be the mother of a savage, bloodthirsty child would make it far worse.

"I am sure that Hermes or Apollo might have been more to your liking," said Athena. "But Apollo has discerned as much of the possible outcomes as he could. The nature of the gods plays a role in the nature of the children they father. Your son by Hermes would have likely been a thief. Your son by Apollo might have been a poet or musician. Neither would have been an ideal king for Athens.

"I know what your real question is, the one you fear to ask. Poseidon's sons are often…difficult, but the son he will father by you tonight will not be."

Will father?

She shivered again. Was her fate as chiseled in cold stone as it seemed?

"You should not be surprised at such a thing. Your love, Bellerophon, was fathered by Poseidon—and in less favorable circumstances."

"Bellerophon? Then the stories were true?"

"They were. And the situation is similar in one way. Glaucus, too, was unable to bear a son because of one of Aphrodite's curses."

Aethra should have known. Bellerophon's touch had been like a calm sea at sunset. His whisper reminded her of the sound of the waves lapping against the shore.

"But was Bellerophon supposed to become king of Corinth? Because that's not what happened."

"Would that it had," said Athena. "That would have been much better for Corinth—and for him. But mortals are wrong when they think of fate as one path. The path of fate has many forks, and most mortals reach at least one of them during their lifetime.

"Bellerophon could have been the king of Corinth, but when he reached a fork in the road, his moment of wrath against his brother sent him down the wrong path. Once he had started down that road, *Ananke* —necessity—would never allow him to retrace his steps. So it is that mortals make their own fates without even realizing it."

"What will prevent my son from taking the wrong path?" asked Aethra.

Athena smiled. "You are showing yourself to be every bit as intelligent as I had hoped. The answer is simple—you will.

"You have not yet asked why you had to be the mother of Aegeus's heir. The woman chosen would have to be a princess—an unmarried princess, lest Aegeus think your son could be another man's.

"But these two qualifications, though essential, are far less critical than your qualities. You are wise, as your questions show—wise enough to help your son find his best path. You are courageous as well, and strong. A weaker woman would never have had the nerve to question me as you have.

"Mothering this child might not be what you would have chosen, but at this moment, there is none better suited for it than you."

Emboldened just a little by Athena's praise, Aethra took another risk. "But if I am as wise, brave, and strong as you say, is being a mother the fate that enables me to contribute most to the world?"

Athena looked at her with those piercing eyes. Her sacred bird was the owl, but Aethra wondered if a hawk would have been a better choice.

"You would happily have been both wife and mother if you had married Bellerophon. Aethra, there is no way for you to have that life now. Some women there are whose best destiny is to hunt by the side of

Artemis. You are not one of them, and in the end, such a life would make you unhappy.

"You may not be aware of this, for Pittheus has raised you with an easy hand, never commanding until tonight, but men seldom let women fulfill their true potential." Athena stared out across the sea, her look so stern that she seemed to be saying to Poseidon, "Not yet!"

"If I had created the world, there would have been only one gender, and mortals and gods alike would have been able to reproduce without sex. Instead, we have a world in which there are two genders, the female oppressed more often than not by the male.

"In such a world, women have not as many paths to choose as men. I scraped out my place on Olympus by proving I was just as wise and strong as a man. Even as a goddess, that was a hard road, and it is rarely possible for mortal women.

"Hera took a different road. Instead of avoiding marriage, she embraced it, thinking to use the marriage contract as a lever to advance her own position. Indeed, she is a queen, but the stories speak the truth when they point out that the path she took has made her bitter. Even among the gods, being the king's wife is not enough to give a woman equality with men. In the mortal world, some few have managed to achieve influence that way—often fighting every inch of the way with their husband. You would not have had to do that with Bellerophon to be queen in name *and* authority, but few men are like him.

"Aphrodite took yet another road—gaining power through the manipulation of the sexual appetites of men. Ironically, she does not crave power. If she did, she could rule Olympus—in fact if not in name. Her goals were more modest. But she is a goddess with unmatchable power in that area. Mortal women may try the same path, but only with constant effort. Even then, the results of such a strategy are mixed at best. The approach is ill-suited to your temperament.

"Artemis took a road opposed to that of Aphrodite and Hera—separation from men. Aside from her brother and the occasional male hunting companion, she has little use for men and associates with gods only as much as her duties require. She is happy enough, but no mortal woman, except one under her protection, can follow that road—the men will simply not allow it.

"But there is one path you can choose that is well suited for you *and* for the future—motherhood. This is the path goddesses such as Demeter have chosen, and though it has brought her suffering, it has also brought her joy.

"Raising a child is an important task," said Aethra. "But—"

"But you do not see how it enables a woman to take a more significant role in society. Think of motherhood as the seed. As your son's mother, particularly since he will not have a mortal father getting in your way with his own ideas of childrearing, you can raise your son to have a different idea of the role of women. Eventually, that seed will grow into a flourishing tree. Think of it! A king of Athens who believes that women are more than property. He will not overnight change other men's attitudes, but he can help his city—and perhaps others who learn from his example—begin to look at the world in a new way. The process will take time, but through it, you will be able to influence countless women's lives.

"And there is also the salvation of Athens to be considered. You will save thousands of lives that way—and even more in centuries to come. The path Athens travels under your son will be quite different from the one it takes if Aegeus has no heir. The revolts, the senseless violence— even someone as accustomed to battle as I am trembles to think of all the suffering."

And there it was again. Aethra twitched as she felt the weight of the world descending on her shoulders. She was just one woman. It wasn't fair even for a goddess to demand so much of her.

Yet Athena had told the truth in at least one way. Aethra no longer had a multitude of paths in front of her. The doors that closed when Glaucus sent Bellerophon into exile would never open again. She had now only the stark choice between accepting the role Athena had crafted for her and defying the gods.

Some risks she would take. And if it were a choice between Bellerophon and the solitary mothering of this child, she would have dared even the wrath of the gods to have the man she loved.

But risk everything so that she could—what exactly? Live out her life as Pittheus's old maid daughter, tucked away securely in a palace that would be both her sanctuary and her prison? And that was assuming no god chose to curse her for her disobedience."

"I am ready to do what I must," said Aethra slowly.

"As I knew you would be," said Athena. "I have asked Poseidon to be gentle."

Apparently, she had not asked Poseidon to be patient, though. Aethra felt his overwhelming presence even before she saw him. When she turned her eyes away from Athena, there he was, holding the shining trident it was said could bring tidal waves when it struck the sea or earthquakes when it struck the ground. Mortal though she was, she could feel the power of the weapon roaring like a storm in his hand. Why would Poseidon bring it with him? It was hardly a romantic gesture.

Nor was the god of sea himself someone Aethra could ever have loved, at least not in the way he chose to present himself. There was no denying the physical appeal of his hard-muscled body. He looked as if he could have wrestled a sea serpent without working up a sweat. And his face, though thickly bearded and wearing the look of early middle age, was handsome. But beneath these features was a power untamed as that of the trident. In his eyes, she could see storm-tossed seas, filled with restless energy. He smelled of seawater the way Aegeus had smelled of wine. Some women would have found his savage energy appealing. Aethra did not.

"Gentle," reminded Athena. "You agreed, Uncle."

Poseidon nodded. "Your name is Aethra, is it not, princess?"

She tried not to be intimidated by the sound of the ocean depths in his voice. "It is, lord of the sea."

"You have no need to fear me, Aethra. I can be furious, but I can also be gentle, as someone such as yourself who dwells near the sea must surely have noticed."

Aethra nodded, not trusting herself to speak. She didn't want her voice to crack before him.

"Perhaps it would be easier for you if I assumed the form of someone you knew. We gods can appear as we wish. From what I've heard, my son's form might please you."

Despite herself, Aethra gasped when Poseidon shed his fierce majesty and donned the gentle form of Bellerophon.

Aethra felt disoriented, as if Poseidon had somehow turned back the flow of time to the very day on which she and Bellerophon had been betrothed. His son had the warmth of the rising sun reflected in ocean water. He moved as gracefully as a fish swimming effortlessly through the depths.

More than anything else, she wanted him to make love to her now, to give her the wedding night she had never had and never would have, except in this way.

But even as she shook with desire, her heartbeat surging like the open sea, she knew it would be one of the worst mistakes of her life to let Poseidon take her in the form of Bellerophon.

Poseidon didn't love her, though she had no doubt he could convince her he did if that was what she wanted. He could play Bellerophon to perfection. But that was all it would be, a play such as an actor might perform during the festival of Dionysus.

The actor might play a king or even a god—but underneath, he was still an actor, and to that identity, he would return the instant the play was over.

No, Poseidon would never love her. He would pretend to be Bellerophon, but just this once. She might know ultimate bliss—only to spend the rest of her life feeling nothing but its absence. Even if Poseidon did love her, or come as close to that feeling as he could with a mortal, it was beyond credibility to imagine that he would return every night, or once a week, once a month, once a year, and be Bellerophon again for her. Once in a lifetime—that, and only that, was what the god offered. And it was not enough. It would fill her, only to leave her empty. It would break her. She would be no fit mother to her son, and then all her sacrifice would have been for nothing.

"Mighty Poseidon, I thank you with all my heart for such a gesture, but since I must be separated from the real Bellerophon forever, I fear such a union as you offer would give me more grief than joy. Can you allow me to sleep deeply enough that you can make me a mother without my experiencing anything more than dreams?"

Puzzlement twitched across the false Bellerophon face. Had Aethra offended Poseidon? His temper was legendary, and Athena had slipped away.

"I do not mean to seem ungrateful. I am honored you have chosen me, unworthy as I am. I am sure countless women pray to be chosen in just this way. But I love your son, and being with you—in any form—would be awkward. I would only disappoint. Let me sleep, and while I sleep, let me fulfill the purpose for which you and Athena have selected me."

Aethra had never needed before to massage a male ego. She was relieved to discover she was good at it.

The sea god, still in Bellerophon's form, nodded. "It shall be as you wish, princess."

Aethra sensed another presence, but it was like the barest breath of wind, no more. Perhaps Poseidon had summoned Hypnos, the god of sleep, soft of step and gentle of touch.

* * *

WHEN SHE AWAKENED, she was not on the cold island nor back in her bed with Aegeus, which was a relief. Someone—Poseidon or Athena perhaps—had carried her home and laid her next to the hearth fire in the great hall.

While Poseidon had planted his seed in her, she had slept as deeply as she asked. She had dreamed of Bellerophon, and in that dream, they had made love. But the experience had all the blurriness of a dream, and she had dreamt in that way many times before.

Poseidon had kept his promise to be gentle. If not for the faint smell of saltwater, she might have thought her encounter with him a dream as well.

Pittheus was standing over her, looking concerned. "Daughter, uh—"

"It is done," she said, trying to manage a smile for him. "If the gods blessed us as you thought, I am sure to bear him a son."

She would tell him soon that son would really be Poseidon's, but she would not tell him yet. She was too tired to explain all that she had been through. Tomorrow would be soon enough.

"Excellent news. I—"

Before Pittheus could finish, Aegeus, still smelling of wine, eyes bloodshot, stumbled into the room. As soon as he saw them, he lowered his eyes to the floor but kept walking. When he got close enough, he fell to his knees and grasped the knees of Pittheus in supplication.

"My friend, I ask your forgiveness, for I have committed an unpardonable offense against you—"

"You have no need of forgiveness," said Pittheus quietly. "You have realized what happened last night, have you not? I was not sure you would. Know this: all was arranged with my full permission in fulfillment of the oracle. Rise now. Approach me not as a supplicant, but as the king you are."

Aegeus looked confused. Staring into his reddened eyes, Aethra could imagine what he must have seen when he awakened—her bedroom rather than his own, and sheets red with just enough blood to serve as mute testimony to her lost virginity. "But...how can you have consented?"

"Rise," Pittheus repeated.

"If it is allowed, I would speak to your daughter in private."

"If that will put you at your ease, I'm sure my daughter would not object," said Pittheus. He left the room, though Aethra had the feeling he was standing just outside the door, listening.

It didn't matter. What Aegeus would say, Pittheus must already have guessed. What she had to say to him would be the same whether Pittheus stood right next to them or as far away as Egypt.

Aegeus still had not stood. Awkwardly, he crawled to Aethra and took her by the knees.

"I did not intend to take advantage of you. I have been with many women in my time, but never in such a way. Never without knowing who she was...knowing what her circumstances were."

For a moment, he seemed as innocent as her poor, dear Bellerophon. She would not have him feel such pain. There was no point in it. Certainly, it did not lessen hers.

"My father spoke the truth. He told me how much you needed to have a son to reign after you. And he told me of the oracle. All I did was give you what help I could—what help the gods themselves would have me give.

"There is no blame here, for you or anyone else. Please rise, and know that I hold nothing against you. I came to you willingly."

"Truly?" he asked.

"Truly. Now rise as my father bade you before. We should discuss what will happen when your son is born."

He was still clumsy from so much drinking, but he managed to get to his feet. "You seem most confident, princess. Are you so sure you are pregnant?"

She nodded. "Whatever the gods' will must come to pass."

Even if the way it had come to pass would have horrified Aegeus. But that part he would never know.

"I know I cannot be your wife, for you have one already," said Aethra. "But when your son is born, I ask that you allow me to come with him to Athens. I could be his nurse. You do not need to introduce me as his mother if such a thing would give your wife pain."

"My son will need to stay here with you until he is grown," said Aegeus. "It would be too dangerous for him—and perhaps even for you —otherwise."

Aethra opened her mouth, then closed it again. She had no idea how to respond. Pittheus had said Aegeus needed to have a son to keep Athens stable and himself alive. What good would her son be for that purpose if he Aegeus kept him hidden in Troezen?

"Please allow me to explain. If I had my choice, I would parade him into Athens the moment he was born. But he will not be the son of my legal wife, and you are not an Athenian. Many will regard our son as a foreigner. People will not at first want to accept him as my heir."

"But...but I thought...my father said your very life might be in danger unless you could quickly father a son!"

Aegeus looked puzzled, but only for a second. Then he managed to force his face into a neutral expression. "Indeed, my life may depend upon having a son—at some point. But I am safe for now. And a son born...in these circumstances would not be welcomed, just as I said. Fear not, for I will acknowledge him when the time comes."

"And when…and when will that be?" Aethra had to choke the words out.

"When our son is in the first flower of manhood, he will be able to prove his worth. An infant is easily dismissed. A young hero would be far harder to ignore."

"You would put our son in danger?"

"If he is a spirited young man, he will doubtless put himself in danger," said Aegeus. "But not too much," he added quickly in response to her dismayed look. "In any case, I did not mean to suggest some ghastly ordeal.

"What I propose instead is this: before I leave, I will dig a hole into which I will place my sword, my shield, and my sandals. Over them, I will place a heavy boulder, such as only a few men could lift. Between your divine ancestry and mine, our son should be stronger than most. All he needs to do when he has come of age is lift the stone and retrieve the gifts I have left for him.

"Be careful that you do not tell him who his true father is before that time. A child could not be trusted with such information and might blab. Any hint of who he really is could spell his death in his early years. When he is ready to lift the stone, he should be strong enough to defend himself. It will be safe to tell him then.

"Once he has passed the test, send him to Athens to meet me. I will acknowledge him as my son and name him my heir the moment I see who he is. This I swear upon my very life."

Aethra hardly knew him, but she believed him, anyway. Even then, she was a good judge of character. She knew he was a good man—and knowing that made the next few years more bearable.

A CHILDHOOD BY THE SEA

FOR THE FIRST few years of my life, I had no idea of what my mother had endured to bring me into the world. I would not have understood the story then, even if she had tried to tell me.

All I knew was that my mother loved me. She may not really have spent all her time with me, but I can't remember any time in my childhood when she was out of my sight, and usually, she was right by my side.

When I was old enough to realize that my family was different from others, I asked my mother where my father was.

"Your father is a good man. He would be with us if he could. He is staying away to keep us safe." Her voice was closer to a whisper than I had ever heard it, and her usual smile was missing. I was too young to pick up on those cues, though.

"But where is he?"

"I will tell you when you are older," she replied. "For now, know that he is thinking of you and wishing to see you as much as you wish to see him."

We were at the beach. Back then, we spent at least a part of every warm day near the sea. I loved the feel of the sand between my toes, I loved the salt smell of the air, and I loved the feel of seawater against my body, not minding when it was cold. I cannot remember a time when I did not know how to swim.

Aethra could see I wasn't satisfied with what she had told me. "Your father is that way," she said, pointing out to sea.

I looked out across the waves and smiled. I thought my father must be a sailor. That would have explained why he was not around, for sailors sometimes spent months at a time away from home. He would return someday, and we would be together.

Only later did I realize that my mother might have been pointing at the sea rather than to some distant boat. Or she could have been pointing to distant Athens, not visible from where we stood, but reachable if one sailed across the Saronic Gulf. These mysteries were still beyond my grasp.

Nor was I old enough to understand the tension between my mother and grandfather. He was affectionate to her and never refused her anything, at least not that I ever saw. She was always respectful to him and appeared at all court functions where the presence of the resident princess would have been expected. But she never laughed in his presence, and when she smiled, it was only a mouth smile. Her heart just wasn't in it. While she was with him, her every move conveyed a sense of duty, not of joy.

No, I understood none of this, but I saw, for children see in ways that adults do not. I also saw the way Pittheus treated me. He was always attentive to me and never spoke even one harsh word. Yet his love for me, if that was the right word for it, was not the same as my mother's. He looked at me as he looked at a prize horse. He spoke of my great destiny, but always in vague, impersonal terms, as if he were talking about how much the commerce of Troezen would grow in the future.

One day, a guard muttered, "bastard," as I passed by him in the hall. I asked my mother what the word meant, and she answered evasively, just as she often did when I asked about my father. She would tolerate no evasion from me, however. I must tell her who had spoken that word. Not realizing the significance of the question, I answered it.

I never saw that particular guard again. Nor did I hear the word again. However, I was a clever boy, and it was not long before I figured out what it had meant—my mother had not been married to the imaginary sailor I still thought was my father. How could such a thing be?

Pittheus might have handled Aethra's pregnancy differently and spared both of us much grief. He could have sent her somewhere, perhaps to the island of Skyros, where we had relatives. She could have given birth there and returned with a story about being married and widowed somewhere in the east. Working out details that would sound plausible and not easy to prove false would have been a formidable task, but not one beyond Pittheus and his fabled wisdom.

Yes, he could have done that. But he didn't. To ensure that Aegeus would accept me as his son, Pittheus had to prevent any man's name being linked to my mother's. That way, Aegeus would know that no one else could possibly be the father.

Yet, as painful as it was for me, and infinitely more painful for my mother, I do not fault him. Perhaps that kind of face-saving story would have sowed doubts in the mind of Aegeus and made his life much worse. Pittheus believed at the time that it would have led to the Athenian king's death. And in one way, the course Pittheus adopted brought pain to him as well. He would have liked nothing better than to brag that his grandson was the son of Poseidon—but that he could never do. His lips stayed closed as if they had been sewed shut.

At least Pittheus knew the truth himself. I didn't have that comfort, for Pittheus was right that children chatter about things they don't really understand. I might have given myself away and ruined my chance to be Aegeus's salvation. Or I might have revealed my connection to him and become a target to his enemies.

Still, it would have been better if I had known the truth and been able to hold my tongue. By the time I was little more than a toddler, it was obvious that I was different from any of the other boys I knew. Though I was human, I was also the son of a god. Such children tend to grow faster than normal, and so it was with me. During most of my childhood, I looked at least three years older than I was. But it was not just my appearance that hinted at the secret of my birth. I was a far better swimmer than boys my age, a far faster runner, a far stronger wrestler, even a far faster learner.

Boys that far above the norm attract followers and rivals, but hardly ever do they make friends easily. Who feels friendly with a boy who can beat him at—well, virtually everything—without even really trying? My excellence was a joy in some ways, but it left me isolated. I longed for at least one companion I could call friend, someone like me, but there was no such boy in all Troezen. I was tutored with the sons of well-to-do citizens of the city, but, though we sat in the same room for a growing number of hours as we got older, our physical proximity was the only thing close about us.

When I was about seven—but looked ten—Troezen went into a social frenzy over a visit by the great hero, Heracles, come to consult the all-wise Pittheus. The hero asked not to be honored with any great banquet, a request that led to a great deal of moaning from those who might have been invited, but even that caused only a momentary dip in the excitement. People plotted and schemed for weeks about the best way to ensure they could catch a glimpse of him. His very presence was said to be a good omen, and it was whispered that those who actually touched him would be blessed, indeed.

I was excited, too. Heracles was a son of Zeus, after all. With an irony I didn't perceive until much later, I longed to meet the son of a god. I knew the stories of my family, knew that Pelops, my mother's grandfather, had himself been a grandson of Zeus, which made me a distant—but direct—descendant of the king of the gods. But there were many men, even in Troezen, who could claim some remote connection with one or more gods. Sons and daughters of gods, though, were much rarer. Each of them was someone special.

Of course, I didn't know then that Heracles and I were cousins. As far as I knew, aside from my distant descent from his father, we were only related by marriage. Pelops had fathered many children, and four of his daughters had married into the house of Perseus, making them in-laws of Alcmena, Heracles's mother. That wasn't much of a connection, either. But, young as I was, I perceived that our lives had some similarities.

Heracles had been even more of a prodigy than I was. It was said he had strangled two serpents in his cradle. Even when he was not much older than I was, he was called the strongest man on earth. And, from what I knew, he had many admirers, even a few worshipers—but far fewer friends. In that way, his life was like mine, though on a much grander scale.

Also like me, Heracles had known unhappiness. As with his strength, it was far greater than mine, though in my childish mind, somehow related. However, his sorrows had a much more well-known origin than mine.

Zeus's wife, Hera, enraged by his many adulteries, delighted in finding ways to torture Heracles, Zeus's most famous son by a mortal woman. It was said to be she who had sent the serpents to kill him. Much later, she had driven him mad, causing him to kill his own children. His wife survived, but she wanted nothing more to do with him. At the time of his visit to Troezen, he was in the midst of his labors, imposed on him as a way to atone for the bloodguilt, even though it was insanity, not him, that really killed his children. Even at the time, I found it hard to blame someone for acts committed while insane. If anything, he was Hera's victim, not a murderer of innocent children.

Imagine my disappointment when Heracles wanted to meet with Pittheus alone. I ached to meet him, but my grandfather was firm in his refusal.

"He comes to speak of grave matters," said Pittheus. "What he and I will say is not for the ears of children."

I went to my room and sulked. It was the first and only time my grandfather had refused me something. I could understand why I must not hear their talk, but surely, it would have done no harm if I had been allowed to greet him. Much later, it occurred to me that his inflexibility might have been born of caution. Could the children of gods recognize each other in some way? Would Heracles unwittingly reveal the secret of my birth and prevent me from being acknowledged as the son of Aegeus? Pittheus was not prepared to gamble with that.

Aethra, seeing how unhappy I was, offered a trip to the beach, but for the first time, I had no desire to go. Maybe I could at least catch a glimpse of Heracles as he left. Maybe Grandfather would even relent and let me meet him. I could not risk leaving the palace.

My mother did persuade me to go play with my schoolmates. At least that would not take me away from the palace, and I agreed, though the thought brought me little joy.

The other boys would play with me. I was the grandson of the king, after all, bastard or not. Their parents must have insisted they play whenever I wanted to. So they accepted my invitation with as little enthusiasm as I gave it, and for a while, we tossed a ball around. I could see them thinking, counting the minutes until they could be rid of me.

I was thinking, too, but not about them. An idea was forming in my mind.

In those days, nobody would tell a prince not to throw a ball indoors. Skillful as I was, it was not hard to toss the ball farther and farther away from where we started, shifting my own position enough each time to force my unwilling schoolmates to shift theirs. Bit by bit, I moved us farther away from my room, closer and closer to the great hall, where Heracles and my grandfather were discussing matters unfit for the ears of children.

As I had gotten older, my mother was still at my side most of the time, but she kept her distance when I was playing with my schoolmates. I suppose she thought that they would tease me if my mother seemed overly protective. Little did she know their preference was to ignore me as much as possible. In any case, the same parents who shoved them in my direction would have punished them for teasing me.

But at that moment, the only thing that was important to me was that my mother wasn't around to see what I was doing and stop me. Nor was there anyone else who might do so. Pittheus had deployed the guards mostly around the entrances to the palace and the outer wall. The idea was to keep overly agitated citizens, eager for even a brief glimpse of the hero, from trying to sneak into the palace. It didn't seem to occur to Pittheus that anyone *inside* the palace might try something. He certainly wouldn't have expected his own grandson, who was mature for his years and had always been respectful, to defy him.

Even the all-wise are not always wise.

When we reached the hallway that ended at the great hall, the guards looked our way but said nothing. We weren't yet close enough to make them nervous, and they recognized me as the prince.

I turned to my school mates and spoke to them in a voice too low for the guards to hear. "Do you want to see Heracles?"

"We cannot," said the tallest one among them. "It is forbidden."

"I think I can get us in," I said, my voice more confident than I was. "Don't be afraid. If something goes wrong, I will take all the blame myself. I am the prince, remember? I will accept responsibility under oath, and my word will be taken."

I could read their thoughts on their faces. Can he really do this? Would he take all the blame for us?

Their expressions weren't exactly friendly, but they looked at me with new interest. They may have wondered if their parents had been right. Being a companion to the prince might have its advantages, after all.

"It is worth the risk," said one of them, which one I no longer remember. I almost laughed. Of course, it was worth the risk now, for it was not they who risked anything.

"Follow me," I said. "When we get close enough to the door, throw the ball to me—hard. I will miss the ball and follow it into the room. I can move faster than the guards, weighed down as they are with armor and weapons. Once I'm in, I will beg the opportunity for all of you to come in and meet Heracles."

In truth, it was a stupid plan. The guards were well-chosen for their jobs, and the ones guarding the great hall during important meetings were among the best. But I was desperate to see the hero and pleased that I might finally win some approval from my schoolmates.

The guards tensed as our game of catch moved closer and closer to the doorway.

"That's far enough, boys. You will disturb the king and his guest."

"Now!" I mouthed to the boy holding the ball. He threw it as I had asked, and it flew right past the guards. At that point, though, I realized I was too far away. The guards were moving to block the doorway. Fast as I was, I would never be able to slip past before they had blocked me.

But what was that I saw behind the guards? It looked like—no, it was—a lion! How had the creature invaded the palace? How had to gotten past the guards? I didn't have time to answer any of those questions.

Heracles could easily stop such a beast, but he hadn't seemed to notice it. It might be able to harm someone before he did.

"Lion!" I yelled, charging the door. "Lion!"

The guards looked at me as if I had lost my wits. However, they were surprised enough that they hadn't completely blocked the doorway. That, and my faster-than-average speed, enabled me to push through the gap between them.

The lion had frozen, but its stare was fixed on me. At any moment, it might spring. I had no idea how to fight it.

One of the guards had a small ax at his belt. Without thinking twice, I grabbed it, leaped in the air, and plunged toward the lion. I was shocked when the blade bounced off, not having even nicked the beast. Even more surprising, the lion didn't budge.

"What are you doing?" shouted Pittheus.

"There's a lion—"

Then I realized my mistake. The lion was not alive at all. It was just a lion skin with something underneath it, a footstool perhaps, that made it look at first glance like there was still flesh beneath that skin.

Why had I not remembered that Heracles wore the skin of the Nemean Lion as armor? I had made a fool of myself in front of Heracles, in front of my grandfather, and in front of my schoolmates, looking wide-eyed at me through the gap between the two guards.

"Who is this young warrior?" asked a deep, resonant voice.

Red-faced with embarrassment, I looked up and saw Heracles walking in my direction.

The stories about him were so incredible that it would have been easy to doubt them, but the moment I saw him, I knew they were all true. He had more muscle than any man I had ever seen. His arms and legs looked to my young eyes as big as tree trunks, his chest as massive as a great boulder. Each muscle stood out as if carved by a master sculptor from wood and stone. Pittheus, though an old man, was still more muscular than average, but his arms and legs looked like mere sticks compared to those of Heracles. No wonder the son of Zeus had been able to strangle the lion with his bare hands. The poor beast never stood a chance!

His face I'm sure the women would have regarded as handsome. He was at least three times my age, his look far more mature, but his smile made me feel like I was his friend, even though we had never met, and I must have seemed no more than a child to him.

"This is my grandson, Theseus," said Pittheus. "I beg your pardon for this interruption. I promise you he will be punished for it."

Heracles looked at him as if he had said something foolish. "Please do not punish him on my account. He has done no harm—and it does my heart good to see such heroism in one so young. How old are you, Theseus?"

"Seven, sir."

"Seven! You look ten, if not more. Come here, boy."

Despite Heracles's manner, my plan, which had seemed so clever a few minutes ago, now made me profoundly uncomfortable. I looked at Pittheus for guidance. He gave me a grudging nod.

As soon as I got close enough, Heracles swept me up in his arms, and my discomfort faded away. Was this hug what it felt like to have a father? I knew Heracles wasn't really my father. Surely, there would have been no reason to keep such a thing from me. But for just a moment, I imagined what it would be like.

I hardly noticed the spark of electricity that passed from him to me like the tiniest thunderbolt ever. Heracles noticed it, though. I could see Pittheus over Heracles's shoulder, and Grandfather noticed it, too. He turned pale.

"Who are those boys at the door?" asked Heracles.

"My...my friends," I said. The word felt strange on my tongue, but I had promised to get them a glimpse of Heracles. Perhaps, I could do better than leaving them standing in the doorway.

"Ah, then they should come in!" said Heracles. "Uh, if it is all right with you, Majesty."

Pittheus nodded stiffly. He was too much of a politician to refuse such a simple request from an honored guest, but I could tell he didn't like the idea.

The guards stood aside, and my schoolmates walked in timidly, eyes still wide.

Heracles continued to hold me as if I were his own son, but he took the time to talk to each of my schoolmates. They now looked at me with genuine appreciation.

After a while, Heracles turned to Pittheus and asked, "How long has he been training in the use of arms?"

"He is only seven," said Pittheus. "He has not yet begun."

"Amazing!" said Heracles. "He handled that ax as if he had been practicing with such a weapon. And what courage! He faced what he thought was a lion without hesitation. Only a born warrior would be brave enough for that."

"But it's only the skin," protested one of my schoolmates.

"But someone might not know that at first glance. Have you heard that Eurystheus, King of Mycenae, ran and hid when I came to present this skin as proof of the completion of my first labor?"

Even Pittheus chuckled a little. The idea of the ruler who claimed precedence over all Greek kings being more afraid than a seven-year-old was bound to evoke some laughter.

"I hope I will grow up to be a hero even half as great as you," I said to Heracles. He smiled even more broadly, but there was sorrow in his eyes.

Young as I was, I knew what that meant. He was remembering his own children, lost to him forever.

"Better," he said. "You could be better. For heroism is not measured solely by the battles that one wins or the monsters that one slays. Oh, you have the strength, the speed, the heart to conquer your enemies. That I can see as clearly as a lightning bolt against the night sky. But being truly great means having the wisdom to make the world a better place in other ways, as well. Your grandfather is known throughout Greece for his wisdom, and I have heard your mother takes after him. Learn wisdom from them, Theseus. Learn it well, and be a better man, a better hero, than I have been."

Pittheus was looking much more at ease. I don't know where all the stories about Heracles being a stupid lout came from. It was obvious even to a child like me that he was at least as much of a diplomat as my grandfather. Besides, it was said Athena favored him, and she valued wit in a man at least as much as strength.

"Would you like to marry my mother?" I asked, so caught up in the exhilaration of the moment that I did not realize how complicated a question I was asking.

Pittheus went pale again. "I'm sure he meant no offense, but—"

Heracles laughed and held me more tightly. "How could I be offended by such a fine offer? What better wife could I have—and what better stepson?"

I knew Heracles was being diplomatic, but he was the first man who ever laid claim to me, whether he spoke literally or not. I could not remember ever feeling so happy—and indeed, there were few times in my later life when I even came close to such joy.

"Theseus, I would make a poor husband and father now, for I could spend too little time at home. I must decline your generous offer, but I thank you for it."

Of course, I didn't really have the authority to offer my mother's hand in marriage. That right still belonged to Pittheus, and Heracles knew that. But he treated me as an adult when he spoke to me. That kept me from feeling too sad when I realized that he would be gone by tomorrow.

Would I ever see him again? I hoped so, but there was no way to know.

"Now, if you gentlemen will excuse me, the king and I must conclude our business," Heracles said to my friends and me as he put me down. They expressed their thanks for his willingness to meet him, and they looked at him with wonder. At me, too. The praise Heracles had given me would ring in their ears for a long time. They didn't feel any better when I inevitably beat them at sports or studies, but somehow Heracles's approval of me made those things less important.

At Heracles's suggestion, Pittheus started my arms training, even though I was younger than any other trainee. That, too, made me happy. The sooner I became proficient with weapons, the sooner I could become a hero worthy of the praise Heracles had bestowed on me.

I might have remained content for some time, except that unexpected news arrived, and I found my mother crying in her room. I had seen her sad before, but I had never seen her tears until this day.

"Mother, what's wrong?" I asked her, putting my arm around her.

"It is nothing," she said. "I am being silly."

"Tell me," I said. "If I am old enough to hold a weapon, I am surely old enough to know what troubles my own mother."

Aethra looked at me and wiped her face. "I was once betrothed to a man named Bellerophon."

"The hero who rode Pegasus?" I asked. My voice was filled with wonder even though I knew it was the wrong time.

"So I have heard. He had to leave me when he was forced into exile. He killed his own brother, you see, though he did so accidentally."

How had I not heard that a hero like Bellerophon was betrothed to my mother? It made me wonder how much else might have been kept from me.

"His efforts to expiate his bloodguilt were complicated," said Aethra. "He stayed in Asia Minor long after he should have been able to return. Even after his expiation was completed, still he did not return. Some time ago, I heard that he married a Lycian princess. He thought...he must have thought that our betrothal had been canceled. At that point, I knew I would probably never see him again. But I...I still wished him well, of course, still thought of him fondly. And now I hear that he is dead, thrown from the very back of Pegasus while trying to fly to the top of Mt. Olympus, or so it is said, anyway."

"Was...was Bellerophon my father?" I knew it was the wrong time to ask, but I couldn't help myself.

Aethra forced her lips into a smile and kissed me on the forehead. "I have often wished that he were and that he had been here in Troezen with us the whole time. But no, he was not. The day is coming, Theseus, when I can reveal who your father really is."

"How will you know when it has come? I don't want you to miss the day somehow."

Aethra laughed. "I cannot miss that day, my son, for there will be an obvious sign."

An omen that would announce when I was to know my father? Could the gods be so interested in my family business?

"What will the sign be?"

"Do you remember the big stone I have showed you many times?" I nodded. "Underneath that stone, your father placed three gifts for you. When you are strong enough to lift the stone and receive the gifts, it will

44

be time for you to learn the truth of who you are and journey to meet your father."

Despite myself, I frowned. The stone looked so heavy. Heracles could have lifted it, but me? Would I ever be strong enough for that?

I would have to be. It was my destiny to be. I knew that as surely as if a god had descended in person to tell me.

Aethra was still with me most of the time, and when she wasn't, I was busy with my tutors or arms instructors or perhaps playing with my new-found friends. But whenever I could manage a few minutes to be alone, I would hurry to the stone and try to lift it.

The first time it budged, I wept tears of joy, but I was still a long way from being able to lift it. Had my father been a giant, that he could have lifted such a stone with ease? Whoever he was, I would prove worthy of him.

When I was twelve (but looked about sixteen), my mother caught me trying to lift it, but she wasn't angry.

"I knew you came here from time to time. I saw scuff marks near the stone."

"I moved it a little," I said, feeling inadequate.

"In truth, I had not expected you to be able to move it at all at such a young age. The day you will go to meet your father will be sooner than I thought."

Her eyes shined with tears. Why was she sad about a day I had been looking forward to for as long as I could remember?

"It is the way of things," she said, wiping her face. "Boys become men, and they leave home. This is as it must be. I can only pray that your grandfather and I have trained you to be the best person you can be."

"If I fail, it will not be because you didn't train me well." I said the words, though, in my heart, I never imagined I could fail. "Whatever shortcomings I have will be my own fault."

Aethra hugged me tightly. "I have seen you looking at some of the girls in the household with longing. Let us see if my teachings have been as effective as you claim."

I rolled my eyes. "You have been talking about such things since before I even knew what a girl was."

"Very well, then. When you wish to be intimate with a woman, what is the first thing you must do?"

"Make sure that she wants to be intimate with me," I replied, trying and failing to stifle a snicker. "The other boys use different words to describe intimacy. But Mother, Grandfather has told me something different."

Aethra raised an eyebrow. "He has? And what might that be."

"That I must be sure to obtain her father or guardian's consent unless she is a slave girl in my own household, in which case—"

Aethra's shock was evident from her sudden paleness and widened eyes. "Social custom demands the consent of the male guardian, yes, but never believe that is all you need, my son. The most important consent is that of the woman herself. And as for slave girls, they are unfortunate enough to have lost their freedom by war or other mishaps. Yet they remain people. They remain women. You may 'own' them, but even so, you must not force yourself upon them. To do so diminishes yourself and them."

She spoke with even more intensity than she had when I was younger. "Why does talking about this subject make you so emotional?"

"That will become plain when I can tell you the story of your father."

"You do not mean…did my father force himself upon you?"

She hugged me again. "No, your father is a good man. I went to his bed willingly. He is not to blame. But I consented because of circumstance, not because of love. So I know in some small measure what a woman might feel like who has been taken by force.

"Theseus, you will be king one day. When you are, you can begin to fight the attitude that women are property. But to make men be better husbands and fathers, you must lead by example. You must be married to a woman only with her consent, and you must treat her like a partner, not a servant. Do that, and the men in your kingdom will take notice."

"But what if my wife is not as wise as you are, Mother?"

She laughed. "That is a simple matter—pick one who is. She should be wise. Wise, strong, virtuous. Theseus, when you are king, there will be many women who wish to be your queen. Do not settle for a mediocre bride. Search until you find one that is as special as you are."

Seeing my self-satisfied grin, she added, "But, though you *are* special, think not too much on it. Strive instead to be humble. For hubris, the overwhelming pride that causes men to liken themselves to the gods, is an ever-present danger. Too much pride can bring ruin upon even the greatest of men."

I was still focused on finding a woman worthy of me. I had heard the lecture on hubris so many times that I wasn't really listening. Perhaps hearing it one more time would have made a difference. Perhaps not.

FROM CHILD TO HERO

SHORTLY AFTER MY FOURTEENTH BIRTHDAY, by which time I looked eighteen, I lifted the stone.

I had tried so often and failed so often that I had begun to wonder if I would ever succeed. When I finally did, my heart sped up until it was pounding like a drum. Time seemed to stop for a moment, as if the gods themselves were taking notice.

Eagerly, I ran to the palace to tell my mother, who accompanied me back, running almost as fast as I did, to see the proof of what I had told her.

Beneath the stone, I found a sword, a shield, and sandals. The sandals were ordinary, as far as I could tell, though the soles were heavy enough to accommodate a long journey on foot. The sword and shield were of fine workmanship. The shield had Athena painted in its center, with her owl on her shoulder. The sword had owls in an intricate pattern on its hilt.

I squinted at them for a while, felt them, turned the sword over in my hands. Then I looked into my mother's eyes.

"The owl is the emblem of the city of Athens, and Athena is its patron goddess."

Aethra smiled. "Yes, the gifts do provide a clue about who your father was. But there is no need to guess. As I have vowed, today is the day I will reveal the secret of your birth to you. You will know all—perhaps even more than you wish to know."

I shook my head. "It is impossible to know too much."

As so often happened later in life, I had assessed the situation too hastily.

I wanted Aethra to reveal everything to me right away, but she insisted we wade out to the island of Hiera, formerly called Sphaeria, before she would tell her tale. Much as I loved the sea, I wanted answers, not a swim.

"It is the best setting for such a story as I must tell," she said. No matter how much I pleaded, she would not speak a word more until we were on the island.

It was a small island and more crowded than I would have liked. The monument to Sphaerus had been there for a long time. After my birth, my mother renamed the island and provided for the building of a small shrine to Athena Apaturia—"Deceitful Athena." It had become a custom in Troezen for young girls to come there to dedicate their girdles to Athena before they were married.

"Wasn't the goddess offended by the name?" I asked when Aethra told me what it was.

"That was many years ago, and she has never expressed offense," she said, sounding as if the goddess would have dropped by in person to tell her. After I had heard the story, I understood.

We sat in what little space there was between the monument and the shrine, shaded from the sun as it rose higher in the sky. There, close to the very spot where I had been fathered fourteen years ago, Aethra told me the story of my birth.

All my life, I had been without a father. Now, suddenly, I had two—one a king and the other a god. No wonder I had felt so drawn to Heracles when I met him. We were cousins! If only I had known. Perhaps he did. That spark between us—was it the divine part of our natures acknowledging each other?

But my joy was tempered by sorrow. My mother had sacrificed the life she wanted to give me mine.

"And I would do it all again, even knowing everything that would come after, for you are the one I love most in all the world," she told me when she saw how unhappy I was.

The betrothal to Bellerophon had definitely ended when he married the Lycian princess, yet no suitors had come to court my mother. She was older than most unmarried women, and she had me, the mysterious bastard whose father no one could name. Not knowing the truth and fearing that she was a woman of loose morals, they stayed away.

"You have always told me my father was a good man, but he allowed you to become the object of unkind rumor and gossip. He should have done better by you."

"He could not acknowledge you, much less the circumstances of your birth, without making you a target for his enemies," she said. "What he did, he did to protect you. I cannot fault him.

"But now you can go to meet him, and when he knows who you are, he will claim you. You will be the salvation of him and of Athens, just as Athena and Poseidon wanted."

Poseidon. He was my father, too. Did he have enemies who would have killed me had he visited? His wife, Amphitrite, was not jealous the way Hera was. She would not have tormented me the way the queen of the gods tortured my cousin. Yet Poseidon came to see me not even once. For years, I played by the sea almost every day. It would have been easy for him to visit.

"The ways of the gods are strange," said Aethra. "But we know this much—they have many duties. Your father must govern the whole, wide sea, with all its creatures. He must tend to every fisherman and sailor who relies upon it to earn his bread. And he must do much else besides. Do not think he does not care because he has not been at your side. He knew you had me and Pittheus to love you and raise you. And had there been danger, he would have intervened. He watches over you. Sometimes, I feel his presence."

I smiled and pretended I believed her, but it was hard, for I had never felt his presence. If he did watch over me, he did so from far, far away. Is that the way a loving father would act?

When I had asked all my questions—and there were many of them —Aethra rose.

"We must prepare you for your trip to Athens. Aegeus will want to meet you as soon as possible. And the city is but a short trip across the Saronic Gulf from here. You will be there before you know it."

Would Poseidon acknowledge me as I sailed across his sea? I was not eager to put that idea to the test. But I had a better one.

"I will travel there by the land route instead."

Aethra shook her head. "Over the years that Heracles has been occupied with his labors, other heroes have been busy as well. Many of them sailed with Jason on his quest for the golden fleece. Many of them also joined in the hunt for the Calydonian boar that was mercilessly ravaging the Aetolian countryside. And they often faced other ordeals as well. As for Aegeus, he has had one problem after another keeping the Cretans from overrunning Attica completely.

"As a result, bandits infest many parts of the land, but particularly the road from Troezen to Athens. The bandits there are a particularly vicious lot, and even some of the local kings are not trustworthy. Such a trip would be too dangerous."

"You have made my argument for me, Mother. While other heroes have been making names for themselves, I have been a mere child, sheltered from the dangers of the world.

"What have I done to make Aegeus want to claim me as his own? I lifted a stone. I've learned from my studies that any man with the right equipment might do as much."

"It is the test he proposed," said Aethra, staring at him as if she could change his mind by sheer force of will.

"But will it be enough for his enemies? If all this time he waited until I became a hero, then should I not have more proof of my heroism than that I lifted some stone, with only my mother to serve as witness? Surely, his enemies will not be satisfied by such a flimsy claim. Surely, his people deserve more of a hero than that."

Aethra made every argument she could think of to persuade me to go by ship, but I was more stubborn than she had ever seen me and would not yield.

In desperation, she turned to Pittheus. More than my grandfather, he was still my king and could have commanded that I travel by sea. He was no more pleased with my decision than my mother had been—but he would not give the order.

"There is a risk to this course of action," he said, gesturing in my mother's direction. "Yet, if he is to be a man, let alone a king, he must be able to make his own choices. Unwise as I think this one is, how is he to learn better if he can never choose for himself?"

My mother sputtered. "But what if—"

"I doubt Athena will allow her chosen ruler of Athens to die before he even gets there. However, just as Theseus makes a good point, so also do you. Therefore, Theseus, I will require your word. You may go by land—but use your mind, not just your new sword. If the danger becomes too great for you to handle on your own, you must vow to return to us and take the sea route. There would be no dishonor in taking the more prudent course if necessary."

"I vow to do exactly what you have suggested," I said without a second thought.

My mother looked as if I had stabbed her through the heart. I realized then how wracked with grief she would be if she lost her only son. I went to her and drew her into my arms.

"Have faith in me. You and Pittheus raised me well. I am no fool who draws my sword against enemies too great for me. You have heard my oath. Is that not enough?"

"He will do much good for the people of Athens if he succeeds," said Pittheus. "Reopening the land route across the isthmus would be a help to their economy. And he is right about one thing—the more heroic he seems, the more easily he will be accepted. We gain nothing if he arrives safely in Athens, only to be assassinated once he gets there."

Now that I knew the whole story, I suspected that Pittheus was still thinking about how much my succession to the throne of Athens would improve the status of Troezen as much as anything else. The prize horse was finally going to pay for all those years of feeding and tending. But I didn't care about his motives. I cared only about being given leave to go.

"Then so be it," said my mother, pulling away from me. Fear shrouded her face, making her eyes wary and her skin pale. For a moment, I regretted the pain I was causing her. She had always been so good to me. And it would be so easy to put her mind at rest.

I opened my mouth, but before I could speak, I saw a shadow that should not have been there.

There was nothing nearby that could have cast it, yet there it was—the image of a woman with a helmeted head, spear in hand, and owl on shoulder. It could only be the shadow of Athena.

I glanced around, but the goddess herself was nowhere to be seen. Nonetheless, the message was plain. She was watching over me, even though I couldn't see her. I need have no fear in following my chosen path.

"I...I have received a sign from Athena," I said. Aethra's eyes narrowed as if she doubted me.

"Mother, I have never lied to you and never would. The goddess is with me in this."

"Well, that settles that," said Pittheus. Believing me was convenient for him.

Aethra still looked unconvinced. Yet she lowered her eyes to the floor as if afraid she might catch some glimpse of the goddess and be tempted to blasphemy.

"My son, you may go with my blessing. But take care, for if anything happens to you, I will not long survive you. This is *my* vow."

"Then you will live a very long life, Mother, for nothing will happen to me," I said, pulling her close again for a kiss.

Athena's shadow was not as good as having Poseidon rise from the sea and take me into his arms, but it was still more notice than the gods paid to most mortals. It had to mean something.

Afraid that my mother, despite her seeming acceptance of my wishes, would find some way to weaken my resolve, I prepared to depart as fast as I could. Though I had sandals of my own, I put on the ones Aegeus had left under the rock. I belted a scabbard to my waist so that I could carry the sword easily. To my back, I strapped a pack containing some food, water, and money, and over the top, I strapped my shield.

"You should ride on horseback, as befits your station," said Pittheus.

"It is easier to keep footsteps from being heard than hoofbeats," I replied. "I may need to move stealthily if I encounter someone who is too strong to beat."

"But the journey will be so long on foot," said Aethra.

"I am faster than the average man, and my endurance is greater. I will arrive in Athens soon enough."

I expected more arguments, but both of them could see my mind was made up.

"Be wise on your journey, and may the gods protect you," said Aethra, embracing me as if she would never see me again.

I didn't tell her what I was thinking, but in my heart, I knew we would meet again—and perhaps much sooner than she thought.

Aegeus was no Bellerophon, but my mother had assured me over and over that the king of Athens was a good man. We didn't get as much news from Athens as I might have expected, but I had heard his wife had died. If he was such a good man, then surely, once he had acknowledged me as his son, he would take my mother as his wife and queen.

I was too young then to realize that mortal plans often go awry. Even what the gods wish for does not always come to pass. But no one could have told me that on the day I set out to prove myself and be united with my mortal father.

FIRST BLOOD

DURING THE FIRST part of my journey, I traveled along the coast, moving northwest from Troezen. I liked the smell of the salt air and the crunch of the sand beneath my sandals.

I listened to the sound of the waves to see if Poseidon would speak to me. Perhaps he did, and I was just not perceptive enough to hear. I thought about invoking him but decided against it. The gods were not at the beck and call of any mortal, not even one of their own sons or daughters. Much as I longed to see him, I knew it was wiser to wait until I truly needed his help.

Besides, Aethra had warned me not to tell Aegeus that Poseidon was my father, for the news would break his heart and deprive him of a much-needed heir. Even though I had never met the man, I would not wish to bring him such grief.

My first stop was near Epidaurus, about two hundred and forty-five stadia from Troezen. That would have been a good seven-and-a-half-hour walk for a healthy man. I made it in less than four without a drop of sweat on my brow.

I visited the marketplace to buy some broiled fish to go with the bread in my pack, but I bought no wine. I needed to be clear-headed to face my first true test: Periphetes. I thought much about what I would do as I sat in the shade of a pine tree just outside the city and ate my lunch.

Periphetes was said to be the son of Hephaestus, the blacksmith of the gods, and a mortal woman, but no son could have been less like his father. Though Hephaestus was less handsome than the other gods and lame in one leg, he was said to be gentle, and the crafts he taught to men helped make civilization possible.

Periphetes took after his father only in the lameness of his leg. Instead of becoming a smith, he took to robbing travelers, but he didn't stop at taking their goods. He took their lives as well, bashing in their skulls with an enormous bronze club and allowing their brains to leak out upon the road.

Why would his divine father allow him to behave in such an evil way? I shook my head. I thought the question a good one—but I had no way to answer it.

Once I had finished eating, I walked in the general direction of Periphetes, but I kept to the trees as much as possible rather than walking down the road in plain sight. I wanted to see him before he saw me—and fortunate it was that I took that precaution.

After seeing a few stains on the road, all that remained of some of Periphetes's previous victims, I caught sight of him. The stories had not mentioned his size. I was tall, but he was at least two heads taller, and his arms were longer than mine as well. That, coupled with the size of his club, gave him considerably more reach than I had. The fact that he could move it so easily, swinging it back and forth as he walked, the way a child might swing a stick, suggested he was at least as strong as I was, perhaps even stronger.

Fortunately, he was as lame as the stories implied, which meant I should be able to move much faster. Not only that, but, dressed in animal skins, his hair unkempt and his feet bare, he seemed little touched by civilization. He won his battles by brute strength, and I would have bet my life he had no understanding of tactics. Swing and bash was the only strategy he knew.

Once I had assessed him as an opponent, I crept as close to him as I could get. Dodging swiftly from one pine tree to another, careful always to keep the trunk between Periphetes and me, I got to within three arm-lengths of him before he spotted me.

Rather than demanding my property, he yelled a battle cry that sounded more like that of an animal than a man and hobbled in my direction. I dodged away, but his club crashed into the last tree behind which I had hidden. The bronze tore through the bark, and the tree, uprooted by the force of the blow, fell to the ground.

I could easily outrun him, but that would defeat the purpose of my seeking him out in the first place. I tried moving closer, but each time, I ended up having to dodge another swing. I couldn't get close enough to strike with my sword, and my shield would not be sufficient protection against that club. One blow might shatter the bones in the arm behind that shield.

How did such a slow runner ever catch people? Perhaps he surprised them. Perhaps as the son of a god, he had the stamina to follow them until they tired and then pounce.

One thing was certain—he was deadly at close range.

Dodging another club swing—which missed my head by inches—I dropped to a crouch and flung myself in his direction. I intended to take advantage of the weakness of his legs to knock him over, but he was only lame in one, and he managed to stay up despite the force with which I hit him.

My first impulse was to retreat, but, close as I was, he would have a hard time swinging the club hard enough to kill me. Instead of pulling back, I head-butted him in the stomach. He was not as well-muscled there as in his arms, but all I succeeded in doing was knocking the wind out of him.

He tried to grab my throat with his left hand as he raised the right to attempt a club strike. He might have beaten me if he'd dropped the club and used both hands to strangle me. As it was, I used both my hands to tear his from my throat, bending his wrist enough to hurt him.

With no time to draw my sword or space to use it effectively, I threw punches instead. Periphetes was tough, almost like one of Hephaestus's automatons, but he was flesh, not metal, and my blows were strong enough to slow and confuse him. The club fell from his hands, but not because he had changed his strategy. One of my punches in the face had stunned him.

Reaching down, I grabbed the club. My own muscles protested, but I managed to raise it and back up enough to swing it effectively.

Putting all my strength into the swing, I shattered his skull like a melon and watched his brains seep from his destroyed head as he had watched the deaths of so many others.

Though the sight sickened me, I could not deny the justice of it. Criminals should be treated as they had treated others—or so I told myself.

Having never seen death so close before, I vomited. I worried it wasn't what a hero like Heracles would do, but I couldn't help myself. I washed up in a nearby stream, using the opportunity to clean off the club, which would make an excellent trophy.

I returned to the body, not to gloat, but to give it burial. Though Periphetes deserved no such consideration, even a fool knows that the gods abhor the practice of leaving bodies unburied. The bodies of evil-doers are no exception. We may do justice upon them in this life, but we are not to presume to dictate what will happen to them in the Under-world, where Hades determines their fate.

Though I lacked the means to prepare the body as well as I might, I buried it deep enough to keep it from becoming food for animals. In his mouth, I placed an obol with which his spirit could pay Charon, the ferryman of the dead. Otherwise, his spirit would never be able to enter the Underworld. He would be forced to wander forever, a restless spirit who might haunt me or someone else.

I left no monument for Periphetes. Who would have come to mourn him, anyway? But I did stack stones into a primitive monument to Hephaestus, his father, and, lacking a proper sacrificial animal, I mingled some of my coins among the stones. I gathered sticks, laid them on top of the stones, and lit a fire. I knelt and prayed to Hephaestus, asking for his understanding and promising to do what I needed to be purified of the bloodguilt.

I doubted Hephaestus himself would mourn his sinful son, but gods can be unpredictable that way, and I wasn't taking any chances. Bandits on the road I could face. I had just proved that. But facing the wrath of a god? That was a challenge to which I was not yet equal.

Sore from the combat and still somewhat sick, I didn't try to eat a whole dinner. Instead, I crept into one of the orange groves for which Epidaurus is still famous and ate a little of the sweet, juicy fruit. I doubted the owner of the grove, whoever he was, would begrudge me such small hospitality, but I prayed to the gods to look with favor upon him, for I wished to show my gratitude in some way.

I lay down for a moment. I was more tired than I thought, for I fell asleep and did not wake until morning.

Periphetes haunted my dreams, waving his bloody club and promising to serve me as I had served him. But he faded away like mist in the rising sun, and Athena stood in his place, praising my bravery.

I awoke to the smell of oranges. I wondered whether I had really been visited by Periphetes or Athena. I did not know the ways of spirits. Gods used dreams to communicate, but normally, they conveyed command or advice when they did so. I had never heard of a god entering a dream merely to congratulate the dreamer.

But if it were truly a divine visit, why did Athena come and not my father?

There was no point in asking such questions. Nor was there any point in lingering in the orange grove, though it was a pleasant place to be.

Walking with the club as well as the shield strapped to my back was harder, but I made good time on my trip toward Sinis, the next sinner who had earned his own death.

His lair was just a little southeast of the Isthmus of Corinth, about three hundred and fifty stadia from Epidaurus—about a thirteen-hour trip that I finished in six despite the extra weight. This time, though, my legs ached a little, but that did not concern me. I could rest as soon as I had dealt with Sinis.

Sinis was a big man and older than I, to judge by his beard, but unlike Periphetes, he was the son of a mortal father, not a god. Yet perhaps some god had favored him at some point, for his strategy was so stupid that I could not imagine why no one had yet defeated him.

Sinis, who looked much less threatening than Periphetes, asked passing travelers to help him bend down two pine trees. Why anyone would need to do such a thing I could never understand, but apparently, no one questioned him.

Once the pines were bent to Sinis's liking, he surprised the traveler, tied his arms, one to each pine, and let the pines snap back to their normal shape, ripping the traveler apart in the process.

If Sinis was muscular enough to overcome those travelers, why not just rob them? Why kill them in such an elaborate way? There could only be one answer—Sinis was the kind of man who reveled in inflicting pain for its own sake. I would see how well he liked it when he was the receiver rather than the giver.

When Sinis requested my help, I gave him my most innocent smile and walked over to help him bend the pines. I was tempted to ask why he needed them bent just to see what he would say, but I didn't want to make him suspicious.

I pretended that bending the pines was difficult for me. Just when they were almost completely bent, I struck Sinis before he could do the same to me. I did not quite knock him unconscious, and he struggled against me, but he was no match for the strength of a son of Poseidon. Using his own ropes, I tied him to the trees. Then I let them fly back up, and he was killed as he had killed so many others.

I should have given him a more ordinary death. His ending was even more sickening than that of Periphetes, but before I could take in all that had happened, I heard a scream.

Subjecting myself to such a sight was one thing, but I had not expected to inflict it on anyone else. Looking around, I realized I had done something even worse.

The woman looked no older than I. She looked as if some nimble-fingered goddess had fashioned her from nature, with hair the color of chestnuts, skin soft as roses, and eyes the vivid green of fresh pine needles. Despite that, the family resemblance was still unmistakable.

She was the daughter of Sinis—and I had just killed her father right in front of her!

I tried to make excuses for what I had done. She must have known what kind of monster her father was. Perhaps she was even complicit. I could imagine her luring unsuspecting travelers into her father's clutches.

But the look of horror on her face made me doubt my own story, so desperately constructed. She had not known—or, if she had, at least she had not been a willing participant in his evil. But he was still her father. Seeing him run through with a sword she might have tolerated better. But this?

No wonder she turned and ran, screaming as if a monster was pursuing her.

Judging from her reaction, she had no idea how her father earned their bread. She must have come here unknown to him, perhaps in defiance of his orders. She would have seen the truth about him had she come on any other day. Instead, she beheld his murder—at my hands.

There could be no question. In her eyes, I was a monster.

I didn't know what to do. If, as seemed likely, she had no brothers, the road would be no safe place for her. Yet by what magic could she ever be persuaded to go with me?

Praying to Athena and Poseidon for help—and Artemis, protector of the young, for good measure—I ran after her.

"I mean no harm!" I yelled as loudly as I could. She did not slow her frantic run. Why should she? Spattered with her father's blood as I was, how could she believe my words?

I could have outrun her easily, but I feared she might die of fright if I did so. Instead, I let her stay a little ahead of me. I yelled everything I could think of after her.

"Your father was a murderer. All I did was treat him as he deserved."

Like my earlier words, those were inadequate. What daughter would believe me? What evidence could I offer?

So on we ran. Was it better to catch up or to let her exhaust herself first? Was it better to leave her alone and trust the gods to keep her safe?

But I already knew the answer to that last question. The gods gave us life—but they did not stand by us every moment of the day to preserve that life. Even I, though son of a god, could not depend on a rescue. Perhaps if I died, Poseidon would shed one salty tear. Perhaps not. Either way, the gods expected us to take care of ourselves—and of each other.

I had grown so used to her soft footfalls, fast but otherwise giving no hint of her terror, that I jerked to a stop when I could no longer hear them. At last, she was exhausted.

I slowed from a run to a walk and looked around. It was not hard to hear her panting from her run. It was even easier to see her crouched behind thorn bushes too short to hide her.

"I know this is hard to believe, but I mean you no harm. I killed your father only to prevent him from killing others. I will swear to the truth of that by any oath you name."

Much to my surprise, she rose from the bed of rushes, where she had hidden herself. Had my words been that persuasive? No. She looked up at me with her tear-stained eyes that had no use for oaths and saw despair there. She expected to be raped and probably killed after.

"Who…who are you?" Her voice was little more than a whisper, but I heard her words.

"I am Theseus, prince of Troezen." It would not do to claim to be a prince of Athens. Aegeus must acknowledge me first—and at that moment, Athens seemed half a world away.

My name meant something to her, but she didn't look as if she believed I was really Theseus.

"What is your mother's name?"

"My mother is Aethra, daughter of Pittheus."

She still looked at me as if she expected me at any moment to lunge in her direction, bent on inflicting death or worse upon her. Not knowing what else to do, I kept talking.

I told almost everything I could think of about my life in Troezen. I left out anything to do with Poseidon or Aegeus, for it would have been unwise to speak of the sea god at all and foolish to speak of Aegeus just yet. After all, if I didn't win her over, she might try to run again, and if she managed to escape, she might seek out Aegeus's enemies and give me away. More likely, I'd catch her again and then be stuck with a captive to haul along with me. I would not—could not—kill her. Perhaps the way in which I told her what was safe to reveal made her realize that.

"You do not sound like a murderer," she said quietly.

"Because I am none. I do not wish to give you pain, but your father's death was justice, not murder."

"I suspected, you know. I have heard things. But it was so hard to believe them. Finally, I worked up the courage to see what he did during the day. Instead, I saw—"

"A sight that was not meant for your eyes. For that, I am sorry. But if you have no other protector, I can make it up to you by offering you my protection. This road is not safe for a woman alone. Young though I am, I am not without skill in combat, should such a thing be required."

"But surely, one such as yourself could not devote the rest of his life to protecting me—unless you mean to marry me." Her voice was now flat, betraying no trace of any underlying emotion. I couldn't tell if she was suggesting marriage or praying with all her heart that such a thing never occurred.

I couldn't marry her, at least, not yet. As a prince of Troezen, it would be proper for me to receive permission to marry from Pittheus. As a prince of Athens—assuming I ever got there—it would be proper to receive permission from Aegeus. Showing up with a wife would complicate my acceptance as his son.

"I do not propose marriage. Instead, if you allow me, I will take you back to Troezen. My grandfather and mother will happily look after you. Eventually, they will find you a suitable husband."

Suitable for what, I wasn't exactly sure. After all, she was not someone of royal blood. Instead, her father was a notorious killer. What man would willingly marry such a woman? Perhaps it would be better for her to become one of my mother's attendants and remain unmarried. But I could not bring myself to burden her with all those complications. I would see to it that whatever could be done would be done.

"And do you seek to be rewarded, as is the right of a protector to demand?"

Innocent as I was, I knew what she meant. Given how often my mother had spoken to me of such things, it could hardly have been otherwise.

"I seek no reward unless you offer it freely, nor will I ever. My protection is freely given, not bought."

For the first time, Sinis's daughter looked less frightened. I might have been trying to trick her, but what would have been the point? Had I been an evil man intent on taking her, there was no one around to stop me. And given who she was, no one would have tried to avenge her. The tiny, withered thorn bushes she crouched behind would have been no barrier, either.

"Then let me wash away the blood as a sign that I have accepted your offer," she said.

"That offer I will gladly accept, but first, I must know your name."

"I am Perigune, daughter of..." She had started out of reflex but could not go on.

"Henceforth, you will be Perigune, daughter of..." and then I found myself hesitating, but for different reasons.

As her protector, I might well claim her as my ward, in which case, she could properly be called my daughter. But we were too close to the same age for that to seem anything other than ridiculous.

"Daughter of Troezen, for the city itself will treat you with fatherly love."

Pittheus would scold me for making such a promise without consulting him, but it was all I could think of at that moment. If he were too displeased, we could work out something different later.

We found a nearby stream, and there, with gentle hands, she washed away every trace of blood from my body. By the time she was done, she seemed perfectly at ease around me.

No, more than at ease. Something had changed between us—and too rapidly for ordinary human emotions alone to be the cause.

The last part of the washing had been more like caresses. Was I imagining that she was fond of me, or had she suddenly fallen in love with the man she had so frantically run from not too long ago?

I knew I had both a face and a physique that could easily catch a female eye, but the circumstances were hardly favorable for a budding romance. Yet I also felt drawn to her. She was beautiful, yes, enough so to make me believe her the daughter of a goddess and not a murdering bandit. But I had a mission which I must fulfill. The very life of Aegeus might depend upon it. Doubling back to Troezen to get her to safety would take time enough without...other complications.

I had prayed to Athena, Poseidon, and Artemis to help me win the trust of Perigune, and I had been answered—but by Aphrodite.

"I must see to your father's burial," I said. "I will escort you home first."

"Shouldn't I be involved? The rituals—"

"His body is in no fit state for you to see."

"I know that. I will stay at a distance until you have buried him. Then I will mourn him, though not for the prescribed time. I just feel as if...I should do something."

Monstrous as her father was, I understood her desire to do something for him. He had not been a monster to her.

Together, we walked back to his infamous pine. I told her where to stand, and she did as I said. I gathered up every fragment I could find, put an obol with them, buried them as deeply as I could, and called her over once I was finished.

She stood next to the burial mound and chanted the funeral rites while pulling her hair and striking herself. Normally, the ritual would have continued for hours, but her performance of the Prothesis was brief. At least, there was someone to shed a tear for Sinis. It was more than he deserved.

I walked her back to her home, a small dwelling set far back from the road and hidden behind pines almost as tall as the one Sinis had used for his murders. Perigune prepared a dinner of bread, akastos—lobster in lemon oil—and wine.

The bread was like what I had in my pack. The akastos must have come from the Aegean and not one of the local streams. The lemon oil would have been made from lemons in the groves of Epidaurus. That meant that Sinis, hard as it was to imagine, must have visited the Corinthian marketplace. But murderers didn't always look the part. He certainly didn't. He would have passed unnoticed among people he would have killed without hesitation if he caught them alone on the road.

The wine was watered in the Greek manner, but it went to my head, anyway. Perhaps it was my reaction to the stress of the day. Perhaps it was the god Dionysus playing with me.

Perhaps Aphrodite had not yet given up.

I know that men often blame the gods for their misdeeds. Surely, Aphrodite has not personally motivated every man who looked lustfully at a woman. But when that lust seems wildly inconsistent with the circumstances, then one may well wonder whether a divine hand is at work.

Perigune should not have been drawn to the man who killed her father—at least not so soon. And I, constrained by urgent business, should not have been so attracted to her, beautiful as she was. Yet the fire within me, whose flickering I could see matched in Perigune's eyes, told me something would happen between us.

She took my hand to lead me to her bed, though earlier I had said I would sleep on the floor.

"Is this truly what you want?" I asked. She turned back toward me and nodded. The way she pulled on my hand was gentle but firm.

"I cannot marry you. My…father would not allow it."

She smiled, but it was a sad smile. "I need to be with someone tonight. I cannot lie alone. It is comfort I seek, not marriage."

I almost pulled away. What if Aphrodite was not truly over her conflict with Aegeus? What if she was luring me into Perigune's bed as the first step in a plan to keep me from Athens?

For that matter, what if Perigune was more like her father than I imagined? What if it were she who was scheming, not Aphrodite? What if she intended revenge?

All of these were good questions, and a rational man would at least have given them more consideration. But a man who burns with desire is never rational. I had never lain with a woman, and my desire burned like the fires of Hephaestus's forge. Reason struggled against it, but it was consumed in the flames, along with everything else.

We were both inexperienced, and inexperience breeds clumsiness. But I had one advantage—my mother's frank description of her encounters with Aegeus and Poseidon. From her, I had learned that gentleness was the key, particularly with virgins. Though my longing might have made me a lover wild as Poseidon's wide seas, I restrained myself to be more like the gentle lapping of waves against the shore.

I had heard that too much conversation during sex was not a good idea, but I asked her from time to time how she felt. Eventually, she wanted me to be a little wilder, and I was eager to oblige. Her cries of pleasure suggested that my efforts were successful. I could ask for no more than that.

Despite the horrors of the last couple of days, I had never felt so good in all my life. Lying in her arms afterward, I had visions of making this humble home my own, staying here with Perigune to raise a family. When I finally fell asleep, I dreamed of such a life, simple but happy. No kingdoms to rule, no monsters to fight—just a wife and children to love.

A DETOUR TO CORINTH

By the morning's cold light, I knew that dream could never come to pass. I could neither stay here with her nor take her with him. But a worry gnawed at my heart.

"You know I cannot marry you."

"So you have said," she replied. Her voice was neutral. Though she had claimed marriage was not her purpose, I could not tell whether or not it was what she really wanted.

"Should it turn out that you are with child, I will provide for your son or daughter. You need have no fear of being left to raise the child alone."

She smiled at that. "You could not have made me pregnant. The time is not right."

My brow wrinkled. "You have just bled, then?" I knew women did not like to discuss such things with men, but I wanted to know why she sounded so certain.

"Something like that."

Her response was as vague as the most riddling utterance of an oracle, but I did not press her.

"Think of what you may wish to pack. My business requires haste, but I will see you safely to Troezen before I continue with it."

"I would not keep you from your business. Would it not be faster to hire men in Corinth and let them escort me back?"

"Certainly," I agreed. "But I may not have brought enough coin for such an expense."

"That will not be a problem. Come and see what I have."

She pulled me into what must have been her father's room. From beneath the bed, she pulled a chest.

Even though I had been raised in a royal court, I gasped when she opened it. Seldom had I seen so many gold coins in one place.

"I know now what the source of this money is," she said, looking at it as if it were covered in blood. "I would give it back to the families of those from which it was stolen, but there is no way to know who they are. That being the case, it falls to you. Surely, there is enough there to hire a decent escort."

"There is enough there to hire an army," I replied. "I will take just a little of it to see that you are properly escorted. The rest I will recover later to ensure that you are well taken care of." I grabbed a few coins off the top. "Hide the rest for now."

Perigune didn't seem happy with that resolution, but she didn't argue with it, either. Even had I wanted to take it, I couldn't lug something that heavy around with me. It would be one more thing to worry about on a journey that had worries enough as it was.

Going to Corinth made me backtrack a little, but far less than returning all the way to Troezen would have. Truth to tell, I had long wanted to see the city, anyway. Poseidon was one of its patron gods, and it was the birthplace of Bellerophon, my mother's long-lost love.

It was silly to expect that the god would appear to me. He was one of Troezen's patrons as well, yet I had never seen him there. Still, Corinth was a bigger, more important city. Troezen was but a town compared to it.

It did not occur to me at the time that the city was also sacred to Aphrodite, she who had cursed both Glaucus and Aegeus and who might not have been well-disposed to me. I should have been more observant, but seeing the great buildings and long avenues of the city made me forgetful. Having never been far from Troezen before, I walked up one street and down the next, eager to see everything there was to see.

Perigune had been to Corinth at least once before, but she seemed content to walk with me, trying to see the city through my eyes and share in my enthusiasm.

We must have passed the temple of Aphrodite at some point, and it would have been hard to miss it. Yet I did. Was the goddess trying to hide her presence from me? The gods could hide themselves from mortal gaze easily enough. She could have been peering out at me from the shadows or even standing in the sunlight right in front of me, but to hide her entire temple from my eyes? Perhaps.

One site we did not miss was the burned-out palace at the center of the city. The charred marble façade still stood, but most of the interior had burned away completely. The fire had happened long enough ago that the citizens paid little attention to the ruin, though newcomers like me often stood and gaped at it. It was uncommon for a fire to burn hot enough to destroy a structure so thoroughly before it was put out.

"Where is the new palace?" I asked Perigune. "I should pay my respects to Ornytion, who I hear is king now."

"I have not visited the city since the fire," she said. "But my father told me it is to a little to the west of here."

I'm sure Aphrodite wasn't trying to hide that from me, but even so, I almost missed it. The building was large but considerably smaller than the old palace. Only the presence of royal guards, identifiable by the Pegasus design on their shields, told me this must be the royal residence. Otherwise, it could just as easily have been the home of one of the more well-to-do citizens.

I walked toward the guards, who eyed me suspiciously. Perigune followed a step or two behind me, as if she wished not to be seen.

"What is your business here?" one of them asked. I could hardly blame him. I had deliberately not dressed as a prince—too impractical for combat and too much of a hint to Aegeus's enemies. Yet I was armed, making me look like a common soldier, though not a Corinthian one.

"I am Theseus, prince of Troezen. Since I was passing through your city, I thought I should pay my respects to King Ornytion."

The guard hesitated, so I showed him my hand. "This is a royal signet ring that identifies my rank." It was gold set with green chalcedony into which images of Athena and Poseidon had been carved.

Slipping it off my finger, I handed it to him. "Show this to your king if you doubt me. I am content to wait until he is satisfied that I am who I say I am."

The guard took the ring, which he could see was far too expensive for a common soldier to own, and went into the palace. Before long, he came scurrying back.

"Prince Theseus, pardon me for keeping you waiting so long. The king will see you now."

We passed through the entrance into the courtyard. The king, who had been sitting outside to take advantage of the cool afternoon breeze, rose to greet us. He was a gray-haired man in his middle years, but he stood straight and needed no cane. His eyes appraised me in the same way Pittheus's might.

"Prince Theseus, I have heard much of you. It is said the gods gifted you with many abilities."

I bowed slightly. "I do the best I can to make the most of what the gods have bestowed on me, but my achievements are humble compared to your own."

Ornytion smiled. "Gifted and modest. A rare combination. And who is that who is hiding behind you?"

"Majesty, allow me to present Perigune. I rescued her from a ruffian on the road. She is why I came to Corinth. I have urgent business in Athens but came to hire men to take her back safely to Troezen."

"There is no need to hire anyone. I will lend her a horse, and two of my guards will escort her to your city."

"I could not accept such generosity."

"Nonsense! You would insult my hospitality if you did not." Ornytion looked around, his face betraying embarrassment. "I have little enough to offer these days, but what I have is yours."

He was right. I had no choice but to accept. Nor could I argue when a couple of his slaves whisked Perigune away to meet his wife. He intended to serve us food, and it was the custom for men and women to eat separately. My mother detested that tradition, but I thought it best to honor it in this case. Perhaps when I was a king, I would nudge tradition in a different direction.

Ornytion gestured me to a seat, and more slaves arrived with bread, wine, cheese, and some salted fish. I had not intended to stay longer than to exchange greetings, but the king had other plans, and once again, I could not offend his hospitality by refusing.

It soon became apparent that there was a motive beyond just the desire to honor the host-guest relationship. "Theseus, I could not help noticing that, though you are from Troezen, your shield and sword both bear the mark of Athens."

"They were gifts, Majesty. Aegeus knows my grandfather well."

"Ah, yes, Pittheus knows many kings because of how valuable his advice is. Are you as wise as he is? I ask not out of idle curiosity, but because I am much in need of impartial counsel."

"I fear I am not nearly as wise as he, Majesty, but I will offer what advice I can."

"I am glad of it, for I face a dilemma. It concerns the witch, Medea. You have heard of her?"

I nodded. How could I not have heard of the woman who saved the hero, Jason, yet had such a tangled relationship with him afterward?

"But she fled from Corinth some time ago, did she not?"

"So it would appear," said Ornytion, leaning forward in his chair. "But with witches, one can never really be sure what they are up to. With witches who are by all accounts insane, it is even harder to know. One cannot guess what she will do next. And she may not have fled as far as the Corinthian people at first thought.

"A few men have reported seeing her, but it is hard to know how accurate those reports are. To credit them all would mean that she is everywhere. One man says Thebes, another Athens, yet another Iolcus. The most frightening one is the one who insists he saw her not far from Corinth, looking upon the city with fire in her eyes, as if she would complete the job she started and burn it all to the ground."

"I know her only from the tales I have heard," I said. "But I cannot imagine she would linger so close to the city in which she committed atrocious crimes. Even a witch would surely fear that a city as powerful as Corinth might bring her to justice if it could catch her."

"*Witch* might not be precisely the right term. From her ancestry, one might wonder if she is a goddess. Her father, Aeetes, was said to be the son of the sun god, Helios, and his mother to be the Oceanid, Perseis.

Not only that, but Aeetes was said to have married another Oceanid—not improbable, since there are said to be a thousand. That would make all of Medea's blood divine, would it not? How is she then a mortal?"

"These are not questions I am wise enough to answer," I replied slowly. "If she is a goddess choosing to live among men, then she would certainly be powerful enough not to fear Corinthian justice. But if she is a goddess, how could she be insane? I have never heard of a goddess who lost her wits."

"Perhaps she is not insane," said Oryntion. I found it disturbing that he was more willing to drop the idea she was crazy than that she was divine. But it was true that mortals didn't always understand what gods did.

"The gods can be cruel—or at least seem so to mortals," said the Corinthian king. He looked around nervously as if expecting a god to appear and denounce him for blasphemy. "That Medea was cruel there can be no question, though the stories claim she was not so at first. Some say that Aphrodite compelled her to favor Jason's cause, but if so, the goddess also inadvertently unleashed some previously unseen darkness from deep within Medea."

I shifted uncomfortably in my chair. Was Aphrodite powerful enough to bend the will of someone with so much divine blood? What if my fears were correct, and the love goddess was still angry with Aegeus? If she took her anger out on me, what hope would I have to resist her wiles?

My uneasiness wasn't improved by the fact that Oryntion was trembling. The movement was slight, and he was striving to control himself, but I was close enough to see.

For a second, he looked at me with fear-filled eyes, as if he had just heard Medea call to him from somewhere nearby. Then he looked away from me, and the moment passed. When he looked back, he kept his expression as neutral as possible.

"Jason was young and full of promise when he met Medea, or so I hear," said Oryntion, his voice level but quieter than I would have expected. I had to lean closer to hear him. "And he had right on his side, at least in the beginning. You've heard how Pelias, who had imprisoned Jason's father and usurped the throne of Iolcus, sent Jason on a quest for the golden fleece, promising to yield the throne to Jason should he prove worthy. What he really wanted was for Jason to die in the attempt to retrieve the fleece.

"It is no wonder that some of the gods, moved to wrath by the scheming of Pelias, favored Jason. And Medea, who was a priestess of Hecate to whom her goddess had provided powerful magic, must have seemed an ideal instrument to enable Jason to succeed in his quest."

"Excuse me for interrupting, but if Medea is a goddess herself, why would she be the priestess of another goddess?" I asked.

"I cannot say," said Oryntion. "Perhaps if a goddess chooses to live as a mortal, she will play the role as well as she is able. Or perhaps it was the lure of combining in herself the light-giving powers of Helios with the darker powers of Hecate. Perhaps that is what makes her such a powerful witch.

"In any case, she was successful in helping Jason, first by enabling him to pass the impossible tests Aeetes set for him, then by putting to sleep the dragon that guarded the fleece when it appeared Aeetes was going to renege on his deal. Thus far, no one could fault her.

"One might even understand her running away with Jason, whom she loved as intensely as a woman has ever loved a man. However, to some, that would seem like a clearer betrayal of her father, for she had gone from preventing him from committing treachery to denying him his right to determine whom she would marry. But what followed was worse—far worse."

I knew the basic events as well as anyone, but it seemed rude to interrupt Oryntion, who clearly wanted to explain why the very thought of Medea made him tremble. He wasn't trembling now, though his skin was pale, and he was gripping the arms of his chair hard enough to make his knuckles whiten.

"Aeetes pursued the fleeing Argonauts in one of his own ships and might have caught them if not for Medea. Tricking her brother into parlaying with her and Jason, she convinced Jason to kill him. It is said the white flag of truce was reddened with her brother's blood. But even dragging Jason into such a violation of civilized conduct was not enough for Medea. She chopped her brother into tiny pieces and scattered them in the water as the Argo set sail. The horrified Aeetes stopped to gather up the pieces, enabling Jason and Medea to escape."

"That's—" I began.

"Senseless is what it is," said Oryntion, who started trembling again. "If Medea could put a dragon to sleep, why could she not have stirred up a contrary wind to slow Aeetes enough for them to escape? Even if that was beyond her powers—which I doubt—why could she not have found a solution that didn't require the murder of her own brother and the desecration of his body?

"Jason's role in that vile plot cost him the favor of the gods—so it is said, anyway, and I doubt it not. He might yet have atoned, though. When he returned to Iolcus with the fleece, the people, not knowing of the murder he committed, were still on his side. He might yet have had the throne that was rightfully his. He could have been purified of his bloodguilt.

"Pelias was still scheming, though. Medea was determined to stop him, but, as before, she did so in the vilest way imaginable—by tricking his own daughters into killing him.

"That was too much for the people of Iolcus, who rejected Jason. The young man so full of promise became an exile from the land which he should have ruled. All of his heroic efforts were undone by the unspeakable acts of the witch."

"You sound...almost as if you knew them," I said.

"Jason did bring the blood-stained woman here to Corinth, but I give thanks to the gods, who led me elsewhere. I was then ruling in Hyampolis, which I had saved from the Locrians. I should have been king here after the death of Glaucus, my brother, but my family was then most unpopular, owing to my brother's excesses and to our descent from the deceitful Sisyphus. Instead of calling for me, the fickle populace supported the usurper, Creon, son of Lycatheus, who became king in my stead.

"Little good did it do him. He offered asylum to Jason and Medea, not from any love of the murderess but out of the vile quest for political advantage. Disgraced though he was in Iolcus, Jason was still a hero to many. Creon thought he could stabilize his own grip on the throne by befriending Jason and eventually making the exile his son-in-law.

"Up to this point, Jason had stood by Medea despite the blackness of her deeds. But, offered a chance to marry into a royal family and gain a throne to replace the one he'd lost, Jason accepted, putting Medea aside even though she was already the mother of his children and had sacrificed her old life for him.

"Medea may have been crazy by then—but she was also clever. She pretended to accept Jason's abandonment of her, all the while plotting the darkest revenge imaginable.

"As a wedding present, Medea sent a beautiful gown to Glauce, Creon's daughter and Jason's future wife. Lovely as it was, it was also soaked with magical poison. The moment Glauce tried it on, it burst into flames. Her father tried to save her, but they both died in the blaze. That same blaze destroyed the old palace.

"But that was not enough for Medea. Before departing, she killed two of her sons by Jason. What mother would do such a thing?"

"I can't imagine it," I said, and I spoke the truth. My mother would have given her life to save me.

"Jason, a broken man, wandered away. It is said he still sits near the Argo, his rotting ship, dreaming of long-dead happiness and glory. Creon's son, Hippotes, would have taken the throne, but Corinthians feared the wrath of the gods. How could Creon have fallen so rapidly if the gods, angered by his usurpation, had not used Medea as a tool to strike him down? Right or wrong, they decided they wanted nothing to do with Creon's son. Instead, they sent a belated call to me, and I returned to govern the city. I came willingly enough—but now I fear I may fail the Corinthians. If Medea is indeed nearby, plotting her revenge, I don't know what I could do to stop her."

Oryntion looked nervously at me. It was unusual for any man—and even more so for a king—to admit to weakness, particularly to someone whom he had not known until today.

"This is indeed a problem that would trouble any king," I said. He relaxed a little, just as I had hoped. I had no wish to make him feel he had lost my respect. He was Bellerophon's uncle, after all. I couldn't help feeling connected to him.

"But I do not think you need to worry if your only evidence is a man whose claim to have seen her is contradicted by others. Crazy or not, I have a hard time imagining her lingering so long nearby without doing anything. If she has not acted yet, I think she must have gone somewhere else."

"But where?" asked Oryntion. "Back to Colchis to answer for the betrayal of her father and the murder of her brother? Back to Iolcus to answer for the murder of Pelias? She has nowhere to call home now.

"But she might still have the desire for revenge. One of Jason's sons yet lives, as does the son of Creon. Both live nearby. And the Corinthians may have brought her evil gaze upon them by raising a monument in honor of Jason's two dead sons.

"The one thing I know for sure is this—we have stopped receiving news from further along the Isthmus. The bandits make it hard to travel that route, of course, but my blood runs cold when I think that Medea might be the cause of the total loss of communications."

Now it was my turn to be nervous. I had enough challenges to worry about without having to worry about a possible encounter with a near-goddess witch with a taste for senseless violence.

"Much is suspected, but nothing is known with certainty—or so it seems to me, anyway," I said. "But I still think Medea would have sought revenge against Corinth months ago if that had been her plan. What is she waiting for?

"If you wished to protect the city against her, it sounds as if an army might be needed to bring her to justice—and it is hard to deploy an army if you do not know for sure where she is.

"Here is what I think—let all men stay alert. Let them watch and continue to report. Keep the city well-defended. Continue to pray and offer sacrifice to the gods. Perhaps consult an oracle to refute the idea that the wrath of the gods may rest upon Corinth."

Ornytion nodded slowly. He looked less pale and shaky than at any point since the conversation started. "You say you are not as wise as Pittheus, but your advice suggests otherwise, for it is sound. I realize now I was letting my fear tempt me toward unwise actions.

"Perhaps Medea has forgotten about Corinth, and my very efforts to protect it against her might bring her wrath down upon all of us. It is better not to take that chance."

I was glad to have made Oryntion feel more at ease, though I couldn't help noticing that the sun had disappeared behind the western side of the house. We were finished with our lunch, Ornytion had asked his question, and I was eager to be on my way—and to stop brooding over Medea. But he insisted on giving me figs drizzled with honey, and inevitably, we talked more. It was pleasant to have an afternoon that didn't involve shedding someone else's blood, but even now, some enemy might be scheming against the childless king of Athens. I concealed my impatience because I had no choice.

By the time Ornytion, who, even though he much calmer, still liked to hear himself talk, was at last satisfied, it was time for dinner, and a roast boar appeared before I could slip away. So I feasted, worried about Perigune, and ended up spending the night. Hospitality was vital, for who could travel if they could not depend upon the help of those whose towns they passed through? But I began to feel hospitality, like so much else in life, was better in moderation.

I was fortunate in one way. Ornytion offered me no slave girl to warm my bed. Even if I asked such a girl if she consented, she might feel she had no choice but to say yes. After making so much effort to accept the Corinthian king's hospitality graciously, it would have been unfortunate to risk insulting him by refusing the girl. Accepting her would have been far worse, though.

My sleep was haunted by dreams of Perigune. Had my life been more my own, I would have married her then and there. I knew I could not, but I awoke early, with the longings of the dream world still lingering with me, and wrote a letter for her to give to Pittheus and Aethra. In it, I explained who she was, why she was under my protection, and my wish to see her well married.

Once breakfast, which Ornytion insisted I eat, was finally over, I met Perigune to give her the letter and see her off.

Had I known then what I would later learn, I would not have parted from her so easily.

You see, Perigune, raised only by her father, knew little about pregnancy. She was wrong in thinking she could not get pregnant at the time we slept together. When I bid farewell to her, she was carrying my son.

I learned much later that Pittheus, knowing it would be difficult to find her a good match, all things considered, wanted to keep her in

Troezen and raise his great-grandson, Melanippus, himself. It was Aethra who insisted the boy needed a father, not just an elderly relative. She could be unrelenting when she set her mind to it, and Pittheus eventually gave in.

To his credit, once he had agreed to find Perigune a suitable husband, he used his best skills as a negotiator. Despite her lack of royal blood and the fact that she was already the mother of a child by another man, Perigune was married to King Deioneus of Oechalia. By all accounts, he treated her well.

I say, "by all accounts," because I would never see her again nor meet my son. Deioneus was generous in most respects, but he insisted on two conditions for the marriage—that he be allowed to raise my son as his own and that I keep my distance. Pittheus had little choice if he wanted to fulfill my wishes in other respects, so he agreed on my behalf.

Even though I ached to see my son, the only honorable thing to do was to keep the agreement made in my name. It was the first sacrifice I had to make, but it would not be the last.

PIGS AND HALF-BROTHERS

EVEN THOUGH I didn't know Perigune was pregnant, she haunted my thoughts. I couldn't help but visualize making a home with her. But princes are not always free to do what they wish.

Far from being reluctant to get to Athens, I moved even faster in that direction. Getting Perigune taken care of had cost me time. I couldn't escape the feeling that I was running out of time, that Aegeus was in more danger than I knew.

I might have calmed my fears by visiting an oracle, but there were none in the area. I prayed to Athena, hoping she might appear and offer me guidance. The only response I got was the feeling of a hand gently pushing me toward Athens. But was it a general push or a specific one caused by some new, frightening development? It seemed unwise to press the goddess for more, so instead, I picked up my pace.

I thought of turning back and taking the sea route. But even returning to Corinth and arranging passage on a ship would probably cost me another day—two if Oryntion realized I was back in the city. Going all the way back to Troezen would have taken even longer.

No, going by land might not have been the best choice, but I could not change it now.

Nearby lay the village of Crommyon. I walked through it, hoping someone might guide me to the monstrous Crommyonian sow, my next adversary. A few villagers peered at me through slightly open doors, which slammed shut as I approached. They would not answer my knock, however loud and persistent I was.

Otherwise, the town seemed deserted. Perhaps there were men working in the fields, but I wasn't sure they'd be much friendlier. Their womenfolk were certainly scared out of their wits. I could smell their fear on the breeze. I could see it in the brief glimpses I got of their eyes.

Did the sow rampage through town? That would have accounted for their actions, but I saw no sign of the beast, not even any tracks.

I didn't really have time to search for it, but the way it had taken hope and life out of this place told me I must at least try. I ventured into the nearby woods. The beast was too big to run where the trees grew too densely, but it was not hard to find paths that, even though partially overgrown, were wide enough for such an animal to pass.

Sure enough, I found broken branches—lots of them. Enough to suggest a large animal had come crashing through. I could also catch the scent of pig on the air and see tracks on the ground. Unsheathing my sword, I followed the tracks, trying my best not to make much noise. I wanted to see it before it became aware of me.

Such a large beast might be strong and fierce, but it could not easily be stealthy. I heard it crunching branches as it lumbered in my direction.

Even though I had heard of the sow, its appearance still shocked me. It was nearly as large as a horse, and its eyes stared into mine with far more than porcine intelligence and with the ferocity of a bear or lion.

As I braced myself to meet its charge, I noticed behind it an old woman with hair of purest gray and eyes that showed as much malice as the beast's. This had to be Phaia, the witch said to have created this monstrosity. I prayed to Athena and Poseidon for protection against her magic, but I could do no more right then. The beast was almost upon me.

It knew enough not to impale itself on my sword, but it seemed confused for a moment. I guessed it had been long since anyone had challenged it, and in the time that followed, it had become fatter and slower. It dodged enough to keep my blade out of its brain, but I scored a hit on its shoulder deep enough to gush blood.

The beast screamed in pain and fell backward so fast that it pulled my sword from my hand. I reached back for Sinis's club, but the sow changed direction, throwing itself at me with all the force it could muster. When it struck me, it threw me off my feet. I hit the ground with bone-rattling force, and it was upon me. Its mouth gaped open, revealing un-pig-like fangs, ready to chomp off my head. The hand that had reached for the club was pinned under me, as were both club and shield.

Just before it landed on me with its full weight, I managed to roll enough that it thudded on the ground rather than on me. I couldn't get up fast enough to grab my sword, still protruding from its shoulder. Instead, I had to roll again to avoid being trampled.

In the background, I heard Phaia muttering a spell. At the same time, I rolled again, only to become entangled with a mass of vines that spread across the ground. They had thorns that bit into my flesh. Worse, they made it impossible to evade the sow or to rise up far enough to grab my sword.

Clawing desperately at the soil beneath me, I pulled loose a rock, which I flung straight into the monster's left eye. It screamed again, and instead of landing on top of me, it tried to draw back. The resulting awkward stumble brought it crashing down right next to me.

My sword hilt was now in reach. Tearing away from the thorns, I grabbed the hilt with both hands and pushed with all my might. The sword plunged far deeper into the beast's flesh, and blood sprayed in all directions.

The sword must not have been positioned well for a direct plunge into the heart, or perhaps it just wasn't long enough to reach it. Either way, the creature tried to pull away. This time, I held onto the sword and kept pushing as hard as I could.

The blade was all the way up to the hilt now. The beast, crazed by pain and weakened by blood loss, tried to run but fell instead. I pulled loose the blade and brought it down just below the beast's head. The blade bit into its neck, spraying me with more blood and drawing another scream from its convulsing mouth.

I pulled the blade loose and swung downward again. Once, twice, three times. The third time, as people say, was the charm. I cut deeply enough to sever the beast's spine. It convulsed, covered me with blood, and then lay still.

I could not say the same for Phaia. She was screaming at me, incoherently at first. But as I stood and watched, wondering if it was right to kill such an old woman, witch or not, she got hold of herself and stared at me with more hatred than I have ever seen. Then she began to speak words I knew were part of a curse. My hair stood on end, and I could feel the power, dark and disgusting, that radiated from her.

Before she could finish, I lunged at her, and with my blood-soaked hands, I strangled her to silence. I was not proud of that, but it had to be done. If she survived, she would have created another monster and started all over again.

And I would have been cursed besides. I had enough problems without having to carry the malice of Hecate around on my back for the rest of my life.

As the blood dried to a rusty crust all over me, I buried her with the traditional obol, prayed to Athena and Poseidon for protection again, and prayed to Hecate to forgive my killing of one of her witches.

To make myself as safe as I could, I built a small altar nearby. I severed the head from the sow's body. Then I divided the body into three parts, one for Poseidon, one for Athena, and one for Hecate.

Getting a fire going was difficult, and the beast's flesh didn't want to burn. I feared that was a bad omen, but I persisted. Eventually, the fire caught, and my three sacrifices were consumed by the flames. The cloud that rose toward the heavens smelled more of unnatural magic than pork, but if the gods objected, they gave me no sign. Had I wanted to haul the carcass to the nearest marketplace, I could have raised a fair bit of gold for it, if only because of the novelty. I doubt even the bravest man would have wanted to eat it, but once cleaned, the bones would have made a memorable trophy.

I carried the head back to Crommyon and laid it gently in the middle of the town square. None of the women came out to greet the man who had saved their town, but I did not blame them. Saturated with blood as I was, I must have looked more like a monster than the sow had.

My responsibility to the town fulfilled, I found my way down to the sea and let the pounding of the surf help cleanse me of the blood.

I wanted to talk to my father then—but I was afraid my words would be greeted by silence. The sea was as comforting to me as it had been when I was younger. That would have to suffice for now.

By the time I finished, the sun was close to setting, but I wanted to take care of the next threat before surrendering myself to sleep. The sow had taken too long to deal with, and I still had that feeling of time slipping through my fingers.

It would have been more sensible to rest. According to all the stories, my next challenge was even more formidable—and family as well.

Sciron was said to be the son of Pelops, which would make him brother to Pittheus, but he was no old man. Other stories called him the son of Poseidon, and like many of Poseidon's sons, he was said to be both strong and violent. For all I knew, he might be as strong as I was. I should be cautious.

If I challenged him to fight, there was always the danger that I might lose. In such a case, far more would be lost than just my life. I could not allow that. This was a time to use my wits if ever there was one.

As I approached the cliff where Sciron was said to live, I hid most of my gear among the rocks near the seashore, praying to Poseidon to keep my belongings safe. I left myself disarmed, but my weapons would have given away the fact that I was no ordinary traveler. The sword and shield were both expert work, far too expensive for someone who wasn't royal, or at least close to it. And the club of Sinis could have been forged by the hands of Hephaestus himself. No ordinary person would own this kind of gear.

The last redness of sunset was fading on the horizon, but I made a lot of noise as I passed by Sciron's cliff. Pretending to stumble in the darkness and then cursing loudly to get his attention, I hoped he would think it worthwhile to rob one more person before the night descended completely. If he didn't make a move, I would be able to do nothing until the next day. No one, no matter how brave or foolish, would climb the path up his cliff in darkness without knowing the terrain. Nor would any random traveler, such as I was pretending to be.

"What's all this noise?"

I should have seen the light from Sciron's torch, but I'd been so occupied thinking of different ways to make noise that Sciron had sneaked up on me. I turned to face him, but I didn't take a stance like a warrior readying for combat.

He was taller than I, and even by the dim fire from his torch, I could see how his arms were corded with muscle. A woman might have found his face handsome, but his expression was hard, and his eyes looked at me without a trace of humanity in them.

Yet I could sense the kinship between us. Just as proximity to Heracles had given me a spark of Zeus's thunderbolts, Sciron's presence was accompanied by the smell of salt air. Though he lived near the sea, this scent was not the result of that. What I smelled was something no ordinary mortal would have. Sciron *was* a son of Poseidon—no doubt about it.

"I beg your pardon, sir. I fear I have become lost."

If Sciron had realized I was a son of Poseidon like him, he gave no sign. Instead, he sneered at me.

"You have disturbed my rest. Come to my humble home, and we shall discuss this matter."

Under normal circumstances, his last sentence might have been interpreted as an invitation, but I knew better. Sciron did not honor the customary hospitality that was the duty of a host to a guest. Nonetheless, I followed him, doing my best to appear meek and unaware of what he had in store for me.

There was a crude path, more rock than soil, that climbed steeply up the side of the cliff. I could barely see where to put my feet by the torchlight, but I managed to follow him. His confident stride made it clear how often he'd made this trek. At least some of those trips must have been in the dark.

His cave, sparsely furnished despite all the people he'd robbed, was at the top of the cliff.

"Since you've disturbed me, you need to make amends by washing my feet," he said. He set a basin and a stool near the edge of the cliff. Then he sat down on the stool and lifted his feet. He looked at me expectantly.

I walked over, grabbed the towel from the edge of the basin, and knelt next to the basin as if readying myself to do his bidding. His leg muscles tensed, making his intent clear. He would wait until I started, then kick me to send me tumbling toward the cliff's edge. Before I could recover, he would push or kick me off, and I would fall to my death.

Except that I was ready for him. Instead of reaching over to take his feet, I threw the towel in his face, grabbed the basin, and tossed it at his head. Caught by surprise, he froze—just for a second, but that was enough.

I was behind him before he got the towel off his face. He was starting to rise, though. That suited me just fine. I gave him a powerful shove, and he stumbled. Before he could steady himself, I kicked him in the back of the right knee. He screamed, and his knee gave way, almost causing him to fall. I kicked the back of the left knee, and he went down.

Kicking him all the way off the cliff would have been more poetically just, but he wasn't in a good position for that, so I settled for grabbing him by the tunic and heaving him over the edge with all my strength.

I heard several clunks as he hit the rocks jutting from the cliff on his way down. At some point, his fading scream stopped completely. A faint splash might have been his body hitting the water.

Rumor had it that his victims had been devoured by a giant sea turtle who haunted the waters in that part of the isthmus. Perhaps it was so, but the darkness was too great for me to see if such a creature came after the body. The sounds of the waves continued, their rhythm unaffected by the addition of Sciron's corpse.

It wasn't until after he was gone that I realized I might have erred. This time, there was no body to bury, and while I didn't think he deserved a peaceful rest after all the people he'd murdered, others might disagree—including our father, Poseidon.

Carrying Sciron's torch, I descended as rapidly as I could down the side of the cliff. Once at the bottom of the path, I rushed to the shore. There I prayed to Poseidon. I told him if he wished me to bury the body, he needed only to send it ashore, and I would give it an appropriate burial.

If the ruler of the sea heard my prayer, he gave no obvious sign. The ocean breeze continued to chill my skin. The waves continued to lap at the shore. The moonlight caused silver flashes on the water as it moved. But no body washed ashore. Nor did a giant sea turtle appear from the depths. All I could do was take the fact that no tidal wave surged up to drown me as a good omen and depart.

I found a safe place to camp among the nearby trees and fell asleep pondering the strange ways of the gods.

KINGS

I AWOKE DETERMINED to reach Athens within the next two days. I had killed the last bandit on the Isthmus of Corinth. The remaining two threats were close to Athens, anyway. With luck, I could defeat them both in rapid succession.

Unfortunately, I had to lose some time by going off the main road to avoid Megara. Once an Athenian city, it had been conquered by King Minos of Crete. The Athenian workmanship of my sword and shield would not make me popular there. I might even be thought a spy and imprisoned. Avoiding the jails of Megara was worth a little detour.

I knew the next challenge I faced was the most dangerous, for Cercyon was not only yet another son of Poseidon but a king as well. Cruel as he was, both to his family and to his subjects, I could not predict how they would react when I killed him. Jail might be the least of my worries then.

Eleusis had recently become one of Demeter's favorite cities when she had stayed there during her search for Persephone, and though the Telesterion, later to be the largest temple in Greece, had not yet been built, her worship had become popular. Already the Eleusinian Mysteries, celebrated in her honor, had many initiates.

But Poseidon was still the city's patron god, and in those days, his temple was second in splendor only to the royal palace. On impulse, I went in to pay my respects.

By now, I should have known better than to expect any kind of acknowledgment by the god himself. His statue was as magnificent as the temple, but the eyes that stared down at me were made of stone, and its face remained expressionless. If Poseidon heard my prayer, he gave no sign.

As I walked through the streets, I could not help but notice the somber mood. The place had a great natural port, shielded from harsh weather by the island of Salamis. Many ships passed through that port, and the lands around were fertile, thanks to Demeter's blessing, giving the city much grain to trade.

But the prosperity didn't put smiles on people's faces. If they had any expression at all, it was a slight frown. They went about their business in a rush, seldom stopping to make small talk and only barely acknowledging their friends. From time to time, they stole cautious glances at the palace. Did they wonder what went on there—or did they know?

Once or twice, men paused long enough to take notice of me. The sword, shield, and club on my back marked me as a warrior, but they looked neither curious nor frightened. Instead, they looked sad, as if they were thinking, "Here goes another young man to a senseless death."

When I reached the palace, the guards asked me my business, and I told them I was there to accept the king's challenge. Even they looked sad, but they didn't try to dissuade me. Perhaps they didn't dare. Instead, they led me down long hallways and into the throne room to greet King Cercyon.

He looked so much like the statue of Poseidon that I wondered if he had been the model for it. He had the same calm pose, the same long, flowing, carefully-trimmed beard—and same cold eyes. Though they were not stone, they stared at me with the same lack of feeling.

He was old in years, perhaps nearly as old as Pittheus, but like many children of gods, he had aged slowly. There was nothing remotely grandfatherly about him. His royal robes did nothing to conceal his massive muscles, the biggest I had yet seen on my journey. Sinis and Sciron both looked scrawny compared to him. Only Heracles boasted a more manly physique.

For the first time since leaving Troezen, I felt the chilling touch of doubt. The stories about Cercyon's strength had not done him justice. How was I to defeat him?

One of the guards gave me a shove. Cercyon eyed me expectantly.

"Majesty, I am Theseus, prince of Troezen. I have come to accept your challenge." I thanked the gods that my voice remained steady.

"You look a little road-worn for a prince," said Cercyon. His voice was deep and confident. "And I am told you arrived here on foot and without an escort. Still, your precise background matters not at all, for my challenge is open to anyone."

Open was a generous way to put it. Cercyon had been known to force visitors to accept his challenge, a violation of civilized conduct. That was my reason for wishing to serve him as I had served the bandits.

"Are you aware of the terms?" the king asked, leaning forward on his throne.

"We wrestle to the death. If I win, I receive your kingdom."

Cercyon smiled at me with all the warmth of a snowstorm. "Yes, exactly. Since I have no pressing business at the moment, I can take up your challenge immediately."

My heart beat faster. I hadn't expected such a quick response. But I supposed it made little difference. I would be no readier tomorrow than I was today.

The guards led me out of the palace and through the streets. We traveled quickly, for the people walking on the streets immediately made way for us at the sight of the royal guards. Fear was in the eyes of most of them. It was said that citizens guilty of minor infractions were sometimes used in practice matches with Cercyon. As in the actual event, the matches were to the death.

During my martial training, I had practiced wrestling using the same form, pankration, that Cercyon knew. I liked it because of its more open rules, which allowed both wrestling and boxing maneuvers. As today, only eye-gouging and biting were prohibited.

But I had never fought to the death during such practice. The very thought would have been repugnant in Troezen—or in Eleusis prior to the reign of Cercyon. Killing in war is one thing. Killing in sport is quite another.

The guards led me to the running track, the center of which was used for the king's pankration matches. An audience had already gathered. As in other places, rumors traveled on swift feet in Eleusis. Some may have come for the sport, but even from a distance, I could see the fearful fidgeting of others. There were more guards than I had ever seen for an athletic competition. Their spears gleamed in the sun as they pressed close to the spectators. Perhaps attendance was not voluntary.

The king wanted as big an audience as possible to see his triumphs. The ground on which I stood had been cleaned, but not well. The dried blood from previous encounters stained it in several places. There had been many triumphs.

The referee carried the customary large rod to intervene in the event of a violation of the rules. Since there were so few rules in pankration, the referees normally had little to do. But it was obvious this referee was just here for show. He looked old enough to have needed a cane more than a rod of office, and he was barely able to lift the one he had.

Of course, who would have been able to enforce rules against a king, anyway? And against one as brutal as Cercyon, it would have been unwise to try.

The guards gave me a belt and a loincloth to put on, for in those days, wrestling was not yet done naked. They also gave me wrappings for my hands. They took my clothes and weapons, just as I expected.

"Take good care of those," I said. "I will expect them back when this is done."

All of the guards laughed heartily. "When this is done, you will have no need of them. Ask Hades for a new set," said one of them, sneering.

I turned away from them and finished wrapping my hands. There was no point in arguing with them. The fight would be my argument.

Cercyon walked onto the field, looking even more formidable without his royal robes. I could not hope to win with strength. If I were to win at all, it must be through speed and cunning.

Since there were only two of us, there were no lots to draw, but I prayed to Zeus as was customary before the drawing in a normal competition. For good measure, I added Poseidon and Athena.

I could smell salt water there, but that was Cercyon, not some favorable omen from my father.

Cercyon didn't bother to pray. Custom mattered nothing to him. Whatever else he was, he was no respecter of the gods.

In a barely audible voice, the referee announced the beginning of the match. Cercyon rushed at me with a mighty roar. I dodged, but he halted his charge quickly and spun around to charge again—or so I thought.

This time, he moved more warily. He couldn't judge how much stamina I had and didn't want to run the risk that I might wear him down. I had no choice but to back up, watching him carefully in case he made a sudden move. If he managed to land a solid blow, he would at least stun me. And if he got a firm grip on me, I might never escape it.

The crowd started to boo, and I did my best to ignore them. Some of those boos might have been elicited by a quick spear poke from one of the guards, but my strategy would have looked unmanly to the audience. "Too afraid to face Cercyon," they would mutter—or perhaps even shout.

They were close to being right, but that didn't matter. I could not now withdraw my challenge. There was no withdrawing from a fight to the death.

Cercyon followed me close to the edge of the wrestling grounds. If I crossed that boundary, my life would also be forfeit. However, I could run along near that edge without forfeiting, and I did so, forcing Cercyon to chase me.

"Is this a footrace?" yelled one heckler.

Soon, I would have to make some kind of move. I had thought to wear Cercyon down, but he showed not the slightest sign of tiring. Anyway, there was no reason to think his stamina was any less than my own.

The heckling, increasing in volume, echoed around the track like the baying of a pack of hyenas. I felt shame and wanted to attack Cercyon right then. But if I did so without a proper strategy, I would surely die.

The pounding of Cercyon's feet on the ground drummed relentlessly in my ears, somehow audible even over the roar of the crowd. He was getting no closer, but, despite my speed as a runner, he wasn't falling too far behind, either.

My earlier thoughts had depended on the king being slower than I was, but he was nearly as fast. What other advantage could I invoke?

I had always respected the gods. He had not. A priest would have told me such a difference would lead inevitably to my victory. Yet I saw no sign that that was the case.

It was said that, when Bellerophon's life was threatened by the Lycians, Poseidon caused the plain of Xanthus to flood behind him. And when he needed to fly to beat otherwise undefeatable enemies, Athena gave him the secret to riding the winged horse, Pegasus.

Was I of so much less worth than Bellerophon? Where was a flood to protect me? Where was my winged horse to fly me away from certain death?

The bitterness of my thoughts threw me for a moment off-stride, and Cercyon got closer. I had to focus—and I had to stop blaming the gods for my predicament. I had chosen this path with no guarantee of divine aid. And letting the gods win for me would have done nothing to prove my worth to Aegeus or the people of Athens.

I turned as quickly as I could, crouched, and lunged low at Cercyon. We were both trained not to maneuver in this way because of regular wrestling. Victory went to the wrestler who could three times force his opponent to touch the ground with any part of his body other than his feet. Low-to-the-ground moves ran too much risk of a ground touch if they went awry.

However, touching the ground meant nothing in pankration, where submission—or in this case, death—was the only way to win. Cercyon saw what I was doing and started to crouch to counter my lunge, but not fast enough. I struck his legs with my full weight. Thick and muscular as they were, they gave, and he toppled to the ground with a loud thud.

The crowd fell silent. Under normal circumstances, at least some of them would have cheered—but the guards' spear tips gleamed in the sun, and they remained silent.

I didn't try to grapple with Cercyon at that point. Instead, I struck him with my fists as hard as I could in the face. At a disadvantage, he at first had trouble with blocking my blows. I landed three good punches, and his nose began to bleed.

On the fourth, he grabbed my right fist with both hands and pulled so hard that I started to lose my balance.

I saw a flash of what I took to be my future. Falling upon him, being squeezed to death in his massive arms, failing my mission.

Except that wasn't what happened. Cercyon lost his grip on the sweat-covered wrappings on my hand, and instead of falling on top of him, I used my momentum to fly over him, hit the ground, roll, and get to my feet. He was on his feet as well, but he hadn't gotten up fast enough to attack while I was still positioning myself. I might yet hope for victory.

But I couldn't fool him twice with the same strategy.

I looked into his eyes and saw rage but little calculation. He was letting his anger at being bested, if only momentarily, get the best of him.

He charged me like a wild bull. I stood braced as if I intended to meet him head-on, but at the last minute, I jumped to one side. This time, his momentum carried him forward, and he stumbled when he tried to stop. While his footing was unsure, I struck him as hard as I could in the side. I heard a snap like the cracking of a rib, and he clenched his mouth shut to keep from screaming.

Cercyon was stronger than I was, but pain would slow him down, and I was strong enough to lift him. I grabbed him by the waist, hoisted him into the air, and dashed him to the ground with as much force as I could muster.

The blow must have worsened the rib pain, and he seemed groggy from the impact. Again, I heaved him into the air and crashed him against the ground.

He was so stunned by that point that he couldn't fight back effectively. I crashed him into the ground three more times. After the third, he lay still. I watched him carefully, but he wasn't breathing.

The audience was even more silent than before. It was as if they, too, had stopped breathing, as if the entire world had stopped in anticipation of what would come next.

When the referee declared me the winner in a voice that couldn't possibly carry far, the silence continued, but only for a second. The audience may not have heard the referee, but it could see well enough that the king had fallen.

To my surprise, the crowd roared its approval. Then I realized I shouldn't have been surprised. Such a savage king could only have ruled the cultured Eleusinians through fear. Now that he was dead, there were not many among them who would mourn him.

My belongings were returned to me by a very shamefaced guard.

"My king, I regret I spoke so harshly to you."

Tired as I was, I managed a smile. "I was not then your king. You were merely showing loyalty to the man who was. There is no fault in that."

Now it was the guard's turn to look surprised. I'm sure he hadn't expected to be off the hook so easily. Old Cercyon would probably have had him executed under similar circumstances.

Once I was dressed, a much larger group of guards showed me back to the palace, where I was greeted by the king's council, who didn't know quite what to make of me.

"Majesty, what is your will?" asked their leader, who by the look of him was in his middle years. He had the soft look of one whose only battles have been political. He eyed me not quite with fear, but certainly with caution.

"That each of you and any other officials of the city share with me the best wine from the royal cellars. Life has been hard for you, I think. This will be a new beginning for all of you as much as it is for me."

All of them relaxed so visibly that I feared some of them might become limp enough to topple over. But enough of them retained their grip on themselves to ensure that my command was obeyed.

Once they were suitably relaxed, I moved on to my first order of business. "Find Prince Hippothous and bring him here."

The councilor nearest me looked uneasy again. "Majesty, he has been in hiding. The king...the former king—"

"Tried to have him killed twice—if the stories I've heard are true. I have no similar desire, but I do wish to see him. Have heralds announce my invitation in the streets. If he is as brave a young man as I imagine he must be, he will come of his own accord."

It was not entirely unheard of in those days for newly installed kings to eliminate any possible rivals. Cercyon had no surviving sons, and Hippothous was his only grandson. These men, who didn't know me, might well have reason to expect me to slaughter the young man at first sight.

"Majesty, he is not technically a prince, for he is just a bastard."

The relaxing effect of the wine instantly deserted me. "Men do not choose the way in which they were born," I snapped. "It is their actions that should determine how we view them, not whether or not their parents were married. Is he not a virtuous youth?"

The counselor who had called Hippothous a bastard sat with his mouth hanging open, probably visualizing the headman's ax descending toward his neck. It was left to one of the others, who by his look was the eldest, to answer.

"In truth, he has not had much opportunity to be either good or evil. He has been hiding from his grandfather's wrath and has not played a public role in the city."

"Well, let us find out what sort of man he is—and quickly. I need to see him, but I have other urgent business to attend to."

Nobody asked what that business was. At that moment, they probably didn't care, as long as it didn't involve detaching their heads from their bodies or any similar unpleasantness.

I wished to meet my last challenge and go to Aegeus in Athens, but now I couldn't just run away from Eleusis. I should have thought of that before.

"If he does not at once respond, there is a reward for the first man who finds him."

Nothing speeds a man's legs more than the prospect of reward. I couldn't expect these men to exert themselves for a total stranger of uncertain motives, even if he was now their king. But add enough coins to the equation, and the job would get done. Sad, but true.

While I waited, I made inquiries about the state of the royal treasury, which had grown quite large. Cercyon was barbaric and cruel—but he was not an extravagant spender.

I summoned the chief priests of Poseidon, Demeter, Artemis, and Athena. While I doubted any of the gods had lifted a finger to help me defeat Cercyon, it is never wise to deny them credit. Aside from

Poseidon being my father, the first three had the three largest cults in Eleusis, and Athena was one of the patrons of Troezen, so they were logical choices.

When I explained to the priests the gifts I intended to give their temples, their eyes became big as plates. From their threadbare attire, I could tell that the years Cercyon had ruled had been lean years for them.

I also arranged gifts for the guards and soldiers. A wise king knows his rule is ultimately dependent upon their good will. Some of them might have enjoyed the previous regime's cruelty—but all of them needed to earn a living. They would adjust in order to feed their families.

The council, which had become much less fearful of me, tensed noticeably when a guard arrived with Hippothous.

Even without the sudden smell of salty air, I would have recognized him as my brother, though I hoped others wouldn't catch the family resemblance.

He was slightly younger than I—it was always hard to tell exact ages with the children of gods—and his eyes had a haunted look that mine lacked. He also moved furtively, as if expecting an assassin's dagger to fly his way at any moment. I had my problems, and Pittheus might have seen me more in terms of my utility than our familial bond, but at least he hadn't killed my mother and tried to kill me. No man can endure that kind of betrayal without being marked by it.

But despite our differences, Hippothous was similar in hair color, eye color, stature, and muscle. He didn't lack courage, either. He looked at me as if he expected me to kill him, but that didn't prevent him from sitting beside me, and when he spoke, his voice was quiet but steady.

It did not take me long to see he had the qualities I was looking for. Unlike me, he was not schooled in statecraft, but he was quick-witted. He would learn rapidly.

"Hippothous, it is my intent to give the crown I have just won to you. I have but one condition."

Some of the councilors gasped audibly. It was rare for a king to voluntarily renounce his office.

"That I defeat you in a wrestling match?" Hippothous asked. I couldn't tell whether he was serious or joking, but I leaned toward serious. I wasn't sure he even had the capacity to joke left in him.

"No, only that you respect the treaty agreed to after the war between Eumolpus of Eleusis and Erectheus of Athens. Eleusis will remain subject to Athens, but the King of Eleusis will still be in charge of local affairs, and the independence of its institutions will be respected by Athens."

"I'm not sure that treaty is still in force," said one of the councilors. "Cercyon did not abide by it."

"Athens does not seem to have taken notice," I said. "But fear not on that score. I am on my way to Athens to meet with King Aegeus. I have confidence I can smooth over any problems."

"Well, Prince Hippothous, what say you?"

The young man managed a smile. "I say I will accept your gracious offer, and I will happily maintain the treaty with Athens."

"Then let us drink to the long and prosperous reign of King Hippothous," I told my councilors, who were eager to oblige. Their last reservations toward me had been dispelled. In fact, I think some of them wanted me to stay. Fortunately, the young prince, touched by tragedy though he was, also made a good impression on them. Admittedly, it would be hard not to look better than a beast such as Cercyon.

It had been a long day, and Hippothous invited me to stay in the palace as long as I wished. Though I craved rest, that sense of urgency remained strong in me, and I was now so near Athens.

"I'm afraid my business is urgent."

"But it is not safe to travel at night," he said, looking worriedly out the window. "It will be dark in minutes. If you must go in such reckless haste to Athens, at least allow me to send an escort with you."

"I think you'll find the roads around here are safer than they've been in years," I replied. "There is only one obstacle now between here and Athens, and I have the means to avoid it."

I would avoid the obstacle by killing the man who created it, but it didn't seem diplomatic to say that. It would make me appear boastful— though, given my victory over Cercyon, I doubted anyone in the room would question my ability to prevail.

"Think of me as a member of your family," I said to Hippothous as I made ready to bid the city goodbye. I chuckled to myself, for my words were truer than he knew. Or perhaps he did, for his eyes had a knowing look as I spoke. But if he could sense my connection to Poseidon the way I could sense his, he remained silent about it.

The other thing I remember most vividly from my departure was how some of the councilors shook their heads when they thought I wasn't looking. They couldn't understand why a man would risk his life to win a throne only to give it up. They would know soon enough.

MURDERER

My muscles ached in protest as I took to the road once more, but I moved like a man returning to his family after a long journey—as in a way I was.

There was enough moonlight to navigate by, so at least I didn't have to worry about stumbling and breaking my neck. My tired feet told me that I should have waited until morning, but I ignored them.

Athens is over a hundred stadia from Eleusis, a trip that would take a normal man the better part of the day. My final challenge was most of the way along that road, and I was more worn down than I had ever been, as well as dulled a bit by the wine. Still, if I had survived Cercyon, the last obstacle, a lunatic by all reports, would be someone I could almost defeat in my sleep.

The house of Procrustes was really more a fortress than some modest home, but even by moonlight, I could see the obvious signs of disrepair. Why one man would live alone in such a place, I couldn't say. He would never have been able to defend it against even the smallest of armies.

That got me thinking. Why wouldn't Aegeus have taken care of such an obvious danger to travelers so near Athens? For that matter, why hadn't he reasserted Athenian authority over Cercyon? These thoughts reinforced my feeling that something was wrong in Athens.

Though it was late at night, I rapped with Periphetes's club upon the stout oak door that showed some signs of rot. I half expected to be told to come back tomorrow, but instead, the door swung open.

"The hour is late, friend, but come in, and be welcome!"

I started to answer his greeting, but the words stuck in my throat. The smell of salt air was unmistakable.

Though the stories I'd heard hadn't said so, Procrustes was another son of Poseidon. Other clues included his height, for he was taller than most men. He was also as muscular as Cercyon. He was probably stronger than I to begin with—and I was much weaker than I had been this morning.

Part of me wanted to run away, but I wasn't sure I could endure the shame. Besides, there was no guarantee that Procrustes couldn't outrun me. It was foolish of me to try to take him on without resting first, but it was too late for me to change what I had already done.

Doing my best to muster a smile, I asked for shelter for the night. Procrustes stood aside for me to enter, but his posture was stiff and his expression grumpy. I wondered how anyone would ever have stayed here, given his demeanor. His victims must have been desperate.

As soon as I had entered, Procrustes was quick to close the heavy door behind me with a loud thud.

This place didn't just look like a fortress. It must have been one at some point in the past. Its walls were mostly stone at a time when even the palace walls in most cities were limestone and sun-baked brick covered by stucco, and it lacked any kind of decoration. It didn't even have much furniture. Here and there, chairs were positioned, but their wood showed signs of rot, just as the door had. As I followed Procrustes down the hall, which was lit by smoky torches of a kind no one would ever use at home, I felt blasts of cold air from spaces between the stones.

Whatever the place had once been, it was close to being a ruin now. Why Procrustes had chosen such a place was a mystery to me.

"It is so late that you must be tired. I'm sure the bed I have prepared for guests will be to your liking."

I knew what to expect from the tales of a couple of travelers who had managed to escape Procrustes, but even so, I shuddered when the door swung open to reveal what was inside the guestroom.

The bed looked worn from rough use, as if it had been in this room for generations. But I knew it was the futile struggles of the guests that made it look so near collapse. Rusty shackles for hands and feet gleamed in the torchlight. At both the head and the foot of the bed, the floor was dark with clotted blood. Scattered around it were the tools Procrustes used to make his guests "comfortable"—hammers to smash bones and make it easier for him to stretch guests who were too short, saws to amputate parts of guests who too tall. Like the floor, they were crusted with blood.

Procrustes had learned from the successful escapes. He had positioned himself to block the door, and the room had no window through which I might jump.

I was more conversant with the sword, but Periphetes's club gave me a longer reach, so I pulled that and swung at Procrustes, catching him by surprise.

However, even though he wasn't used to such a quick response from his guests, he grabbed the club before I got up enough momentum and pulled. He threw me off balance and nearly ripped the club from my grasp.

Taking a gamble, I let go of the club. Procrustes was pulling so hard in the other direction that he fell backward. I drew the sword and lunged at him, but he managed to get the club between him and me, deflecting my blade.

He hit the floor, but he was already getting up as I lunged again, and the club knocked my blade once more, this time with enough force to loosen my grip upon it.

Procrustes now had the better weapon, and I lacked the space in which to dodge properly. If I couldn't find some way to gain an advantage over him, he would surely kill me.

I ran to the head of the bed, grabbed it, and pulled upward. The bed was heavier than it looked, weighed down as it was by the shackles, but I was desperate, and it was certainly no heavier than Cercyon. I lifted with all my might and scooted behind it, making it an awkward—but very large—shield.

That move made Procrustes hesitate. I guessed he didn't want to destroy one of the props for his horror show. I charged him with the bed between us. He had time to strike once with the club, but I was too close by the time he did to enable him to gain full momentum. The bed shuddered and creaked but didn't break. I slammed it into him. I couldn't muster the force to knock him over, though. The most I could do was drive him back a step or two. That was enough to pin him against the door jam.

He could still use the club, but at such close quarters, his blows wouldn't have enough force to break through right away. He struck once and realized as much. He dropped the club, grabbed the bed with both hands, and pulled.

This time, he was braced well enough that if I let go, he wouldn't fall back. But that strategy reduced the amount of strength he had to pull with. Taking a risk, I let go of the bed with one hand, grabbed my sword, and reached around the bed with it. I wasn't well-positioned for a sword strike, but I was aiming for one of the hands holding the bed. My stroke was clumsy, but it sliced into his hand.

He yelled, pulled the hand back, and his grip loosened. With a strength born of sheer desperation, I ripped the bed out of his other hand and rammed him with it again. He body-slammed back and nearly knocked me over, despite his cramped position. But I still had control of the bed, which I slammed into him repeatedly, putting my whole weight behind it, just as he had.

I was lighter than he was, but I had more room to maneuver. With blood gushing from his hand, he couldn't get an effective grip on the bed. If I could just keep bashing away at him—but no, he was too clever for that. My next attempt at ramming him collided with the door jam. He had slipped out the door, which was too narrow for me to thrust the bed through.

It was not too narrow, however, for him to start pounding the bed with his bare fists, rattling my bones in the process.

In between blows, I could hear blood dripping from him, his life oozing away drop by drop. But even if using his fists kept his hand wound from clotting, he would never bleed out before his blows battered the bed to splinters. And what frantic strength I had would be gone long before that. I could feel my muscles quaking.

Still supporting the bed, I eased myself far enough down to grab the fallen club. Then I listened to the rhythm of his fists as they pounded against the bed. Despite his wound, the rhythm of his blows was surprisingly regular. It wasn't hard for me to get a feel for when and where those blows would fall. Once I knew that, I forced myself to be patient.

The bed was splintering now. "Just a little more time. Just hold on a bit longer," I told myself.

I heard the crack as the wood gave against one of his fists. I swung the club as hard as I could, hitting the broken spot at precisely the moment his fist came crashing through it.

He yowled and pulled back a hand that must have had at least one or two broken fingers. I heaved the bed to one side and charged at him, club raised.

Even with both hands wounded, he could still have run away, and he tried. But he slipped in his own blood, falling against the stone wall beyond him with a thud.

My club blow to his head was too weak to be fatal, but it did knock him out.

With what little strength remained to me, I dragged him back into the room in which he had murdered so many. I replaced the now broken bed where it had been, dragged his body onto it, and chained him just in case.

"Hmmm…" I said. "You appear to be too tall for this bed. Well, we can fix that."

When I was done serving justice upon him and had finished vomiting, I staggered out into the woods to camp and rest. Wild animals weren't going to find Procrustes's body right away. There would be time enough to bury him tomorrow.

UNPLEASANT SURPRISE

THOUGH MY ENCOUNTER with Procrustes had come dangerously close to being my last battle, I was in high spirits when the morning sun awoke me the next day. Even giving his remains proper burial was not enough to darken my mood.

I had fought against the evil in mortals and won. Now I would be united with my good father, and all would be well.

After disposing of Procrustes, I cleaned my weapons thoroughly, had breakfast, and set out toward Athens, which I reached in record time.

Even from a distance, I could see that the city was bigger than Eleusis or Troezen, bigger even than Corinth. At first sight, I had the feeling that this was where I belonged. Every moment of my life until now had been a prelude for this one moment.

Because of the way I was armed, guards stopped me at the gate, just as I would have expected.

"I am Theseus, prince of Troezen, here to see King Aegeus."

The guards were as skeptical as they should have been. "Many a man who comes to see the king claims to be a prince. Few of them are."

"I have here a letter of introduction from King Pittheus, my grandfather." I wrestled the letter out of my pack and handed it to him. "I also wear a signet ring that bears the insignia of Troezen."

The guard who had spoken to me examined both carefully, then handed them back. "These appear genuine." Looking at a more junior guard, he said, "Please escort Prince Theseus to the palace."

The younger guard saluted his senior and then beckoned for me to follow him. As we walked through the bustling streets, I felt many eyes upon me, but they were just curious, not fearful as they had been in Eleusis.

"Is that Theseus?" I heard one whisper. "You know, the one who killed all those evildoers on the road—if the rumors are true."

"My cousin lives in Eleusis, and he rushed over yesterday evening to tell me how Theseus overthrew the evil Cercyon. The description he gave fits this young man," said another.

Had my reputation preceded me? Good that was, for it would make my introduction to Aegeus all the easier. It was puzzling as well, given how short the time had been for the news to travel. A few Eleusinians might have had the time to spread that part of my story, but what of the rest? I wondered if Athena had found a way to spread the rumors faster. If I concentrated hard enough, I could feel a power in the air. It was subtle, though, too faint for me to be sure what it was—or if it was even there at all. It was just as likely that my nerves were playing tricks on me.

Regardless of how the news spread, it seemed close to being common knowledge now. Whispers followed me all the way to the palace, growing louder and more numerous the farther I went. No one acclaimed me openly, though. Perhaps they were waiting for the king to acknowledge me first. That would happen soon enough.

When we arrived at the palace, one of the palace guards scrutinized my credentials and agreed they looked authentic. However, he insisted on keeping my shield and weapons for the moment.

"Pardon me, my prince, but no one goes armed into the palace without the king's express permission. When he gives us the word, your belongings will be returned."

I was reluctant to be parted from the sword and shield that were supposed to identify me to Aegeus, but I could not fault the general policy. What did it matter, really? Aegeus had been waiting for me. As soon as he met me, he would check my story, including examining the gear he'd left under the rock for me, and all would be well. The only thing that worried me a little was that I had expected the guard to notice the Athenian workmanship of the sword and shield, but if he did, he said nothing about it. I told myself there was no point in worrying about such trifles. The guard probably just had other things on his mind.

My escort led me to the courtyard. My heart was beating faster as I neared my father. In just a moment, I would be able to reveal myself again.

Then my heart froze. Before I even laid eyes on Aegeus, I knew something was wrong.

There was indeed power in the air. I could feel it much more clearly than I had been able to outside—clearly enough to know that it wasn't Athena's. It was magic not unlike that of Phaia—far more powerful, but just as dark. Was this why I had felt the need to hurry? I hoped I had not arrived too late.

I knew which of the men present was Aegeus the moment I entered the courtyard. He was clearly the center of attention, and he looked just as my mother had described him, though older. The years had been harsh to him, yet there was a smile on his face, and his eyes—

There was something wrong with his eyes. I couldn't place what. Their stare wasn't stony, like that of Cercyon. It was more like the gleam of gems—but equally lifeless.

At his right hand was a woman, dark-haired and so strikingly beautiful it was hard to imagine a man existed in all the world who would not look upon her with desire. Her eyes were lively, unlike Aegeus's, but they had the cold feeling of looking into a very deep lake, discerning its dark depths beneath the sunlit surface. Despite that, they had in them also the golden glint that distinguished the descendants of Helios from other mortals.

In her arms was a small child, barely older than an infant. His hair was dark, like his mother's, and his eyes watched me with alertness far beyond his years.

"Welcome, Prince Theseus," said Aegeus, though his voice sounded more neutral than welcoming.

I bowed, as was appropriate. "Majesty, I have long looked forward to meeting you. I come bearing important news for you."

"And I shall hear it gladly. But first, allow me to introduce the rest of the royal family. This delightful creature is my recently married queen, Medea, and our beloved son, Medus."

My heart pounded as if it might explode. Though the room was well-heated, a chill like that of death itself made me shiver.

Could any of this be true? Could I have risked life and limb to provide my father with a son and heir—only to discover he already had one?

And by Medea, murderer of princesses and kings, burner of the palace of Corinth—and who knew what else? The ruffians I killed along the road had been less evil than she.

I must have gone pale, for I saw one of the courtiers looking at me with concern. Praying that my face had not betrayed my horror, I bowed to Medea as well.

"I never hoped to have the additional honor of meeting the new members of the royal family."

"Nor did I hope to have the honor of receiving a distinguished guest from Troezen," said Medea. "We have had so little news from there of late."

"Nor have we had much from Athens," I said. And now I knew why. It was the same reason the Corinthians couldn't track Medea down, even though she was only a few days' travel from their city. She was using magic to keep her whereabouts concealed.

But surely someone in Athens must have heard of her before she arrived. If not from Corinth, then surely from Iolcus, where she had murdered the king, usurper or not, long before. Yet as I quickly scanned the room, I saw no signs of alarm, nor even of guarded feelings. These people did not know a thing. If they had heard of Medea, they somehow believed their queen was a different Medea.

No wonder I had sensed magic in the air. She must be using a great deal of it to keep herself protected from her own past.

"Prince, are you ill?" she asked in a concerned tone that didn't match her eyes. They stared into mine as if she could read my thoughts. I looked away.

The news I most longed to share I must keep secret now. I doubted Medea had any love for Aegeus. She still looked like the young girl who had sacrificed much to protect Jason. He looked old enough to be her father. A woman with her looks, not to mention her magic, could have done better if she had been looking for a man to love.

No, there was only one obvious reason for her to have married Aegeus. He was a childless king upon whose throne her own child would be placed. And I would be an obstacle to that plan if I revealed myself.

But what could I do? Attack her in front of the whole Athenian court? I would never get close enough to strike. Denounce her? Whatever magic hold she had on these people would probably enable her to have me imprisoned—or worse—even if I could prove the truth of my words.

I thought to flee from Athens and return to Troezen. But the man before me needed my help. That he was bewitched was obvious to me, if not to anybody else. And my mother, who had reason to be critical of him, had always insisted he was a good man. He deserved better. Once the child came of age, Medea would murder Aegeus. I knew that as surely as if Zeus himself had descended from Olympus to tell me.

"You seem ill to me as well," said Aegeus. "Perhaps your news can wait until you are better rested."

"I am fine, Majesty," I said, though I had seldom been farther from fine.

"In that case, perhaps you can help us, for we hear you are a hero, and we have grave need of one," said Medea.

That much was true, though certainly not in the way that she meant it.

"Although I am not as great a hero as your noble lord, I will be happy to aid you and Athens in any way within my power."

"You are aware that we have had many conflicts with King Minos of Crete?" she asked.

"Yes, Minos has treated Athens most unfairly."

"Indeed, he has. We have a matter that involves him only indirectly, but it is a delicate one that a foreign prince might be able to deal with better than our king could.

"Some time ago, Minos, eager to show that he was more than just the son of Zeus, sought to establish that he was a favorite of all the gods."

"As if being son of Zeus should not have been sufficient," muttered Aegeus.

"He wished to make clear his own right to rule Crete over that of his brothers, who were also sons of Zeus," said Medea, as if Aegeus would have required such an explanation. "Be that as it may, he prayed to Poseidon to send him a snow-white bull, which he would then sacrifice to the god.

"His prayer was answered, and a great bull arose from the sea."

Minos, whose only goal was to enhance his own prestige, received such an answer. Yet I, Poseidon's own son, get nothing?

No, not quite nothing. I got led into this trap without so much as a screech owl to give me warning.

"Theseus, is everything all right?" asked Medea, scanning me again with those penetrating eyes.

"All is well with me, Majesty. Please continue."

"When Minos saw the bull, he thought it was too magnificent to sacrifice. So instead, he added it to his herd and substituted a lesser bull for the sacrifice.

"Poseidon does not tolerate such breaches of trust. His wrath fell upon Crete in many ways, though one is of the most immediate concern. His wrath infected the bull, who became a nearly unstoppable monster and ravaged the plains of Crete.

"Heracles was sent to capture the bull as one of his labors. Minos, eager to be rid of the thing, gave his permission. Heracles defeated the creature and brought it back to Eurystheus, king of Mycenae, who constructed a prison for it."

"He never does anything right," mumbled Aegeus.

"Certainly not in this case," said Medea, nodding. "The bull broke free and wandered across Greece, leaving devastation in its wake. Recently, it found its way into Athenian territory, which it now ravages as brutally as it ever ravaged Crete."

"You want me to kill it?" I asked.

"Ah, if only it were that simple," said Medea. "I…Aegeus could have sent an army if need be to kill the creature. However, though it was intended to be a sacrifice at first, it is now considered bad luck to kill it.

It might bring down the curse of Poseidon on Athens, and right now, we have enough trouble as it is.

"We need the bull alive. You must capture it as Heracles did."

The truth rattled my bones as much as the blows of Procrustes.

Medea knew who I was. Yes, that must be it. She knew, and she was sending me out on a mission to get me killed.

But knowing that helped me little. I had already pledged my aid to Athens. How could I now refuse what I promised to give? If I did such a thing, there would be no hope of becoming Aegeus's heir. Medea would see to that, and she would still win.

Death or dishonor. Those were my choices, and failure would follow either.

"Would not Heracles, who has already captured the bull once, be a better choice?" I asked.

"Indeed—if he were available," said Medea. "We have not been able to reach him. His adventures take him to many distant lands, so it is no surprise that he is not nearby. But the longer we wait, the more havoc the bull wreaks. Will you not save us from this menace?"

Medea could probably reduce the bull to ashes with a snap of her fingers. She'd shown the ability to burn far bigger things. But if she did that, I'd still be a threat to her.

"I fear I am no Heracles, but I will make the attempt."

My grandfather had taught me to fear dishonor more than death. I'm not sure my mother would agree, but in the end, a man must follow his own heart. And mine was telling me I must do this thing.

I was able to retrieve my gear—though neither the sword nor the club would do me much good if I could not kill the beast. Riding a borrowed horse that responded to me as if I had raised it, I raced northeast from Athens toward Marathon. I had thought of writing to Pittheus and Aethra before I left, but pausing to do that might have weakened my resolve.

I did not pray to Poseidon, but in a way, I was forcing his hand. The gods were powerful, though they were neither all-seeing nor always present. But if Poseidon's wrath was within the bull, I had to think he knew what happened near it. And if I were truly his son, surely, he would sense me as I approached the bull.

I doubted I could defeat the beast on my own, much less capture it unharmed. Only a miracle could make that possible. If Poseidon wanted to save his son, he would know what he must do. If I were no son of his —no, that was unthinkable. It would mean that my mother was either a liar or a lunatic, and I knew she was neither.

As I neared Marathon, I slowed my pace. The pounding of the horse's hooves might alert the bull to my presence.

It occurred to me I should have brought a net or something like that. I could have thrown it from horseback and possibly entangled the bull. But I had no net, and my other weapons, even if I could have reached the bull with them from horseback, were more likely to kill than to subdue.

I stopped, dismounted, and tied the horse to a tree. Like it or not, I had no choice but to confront the bull on foot. Without proper gear, all I would accomplish by riding at it would be to get the horse killed.

Luckily or unluckily, I wasn't sure which, I soon heard the bull snorting in the distance. Keeping to the trees as much as possible, I followed the sound. It wasn't long before I caught sight of the great beast.

He was the largest bull I had ever seen. He was snow-white as described in the stories, but his eyes were redder than they should have been. That might have been a sign of Poseidon's fury within him. The foam around his mouth might have been the same. But what really caught my eyes were the long, gleaming, treacherous horns. It would be all too easy to be impaled on one of them.

I had thought to surprise the beast, but he already knew I was there. Only later did I learn that bulls could smell potential predators—or prey —more than fifty stadia away. Medea probably knew that, but she had no interest in telling me.

The bull charged so fast I knew it could outrun me. I might have hidden in the trees, for at some places, they grew so closely together that the bull could not have reached me—unless he used his horns to uproot them. In any case, hiding would not enable me to return to Athens in triumph. At best, I would be regarded as a coward.

I waited for the bull to be almost on top of me. Then I hurled myself right, grabbed one of the horns as the creature missed me, swung around, and ended up on his back. I squeezed with my legs and pressed down as hard on the horns as I could.

My strength would not be enough. I could feel it. The beast would toss me, trample me, gore me.

Only it didn't. I felt a moment of its colossal strength, but then it shuddered as the ground would during an earthquake. I feared it was having a seizure and might throw me. But then it relaxed. More, it bent its knees and sat, acknowledging my authority.

Perhaps it knew me, for it was in a sense my brother. Or perhaps Poseidon really was watching out for me. Either way, I dismounted without incident. The bull remained calm. It allowed me to bridle it and lead it back to Athens. It would perhaps have let me ride it, but I could not be sure. I looked into its eyes, which were no longer red. They were as deep and enigmatic as the sea, and I did not altogether trust them.

I recovered my horse and rode along next to the bull, still holding its makeshift bridal. The trip to Athens was longer than I would have liked. I was afraid if I tried to run the horse at full speed, the bull might try to break away when it started running. It made no attempt to escape at a trot, so I maintained that pace instead, though I longed to be back in Athens.

As I finally neared the city, I didn't want to risk taking it within the walls. Instead, I tied it to the biggest tree I could find and hurried back to the palace to report my success.

Aegeus nodded to me. "You have done well." His voice was surprisingly unenthusiastic, obligatory praise for someone who had not really impressed him.

I glanced over at Medea. She smiled at me, though I knew she didn't feel that smile in her heart. "What shall be done with the bull?"

"It is a symbol of Cretan power," said Aegeus. "Let us keep it and see how Minos will like that."

"Majesty, I have calmed it—for now," I said. "I do not know if it will remain so. We cannot risk its escaping so close to Athens. It would wreak havoc."

"What do you suggest?" asked Medea.

"It was intended as a sacrifice originally," I said. "I will ask permission from Poseidon and Athena to sacrifice it to them."

Aegeus looked at me as if I had just announced my intention to fly to Olympus as Bellerophon had dared to do. "Minos feared to sacrifice the beast."

"Minos lacked the courage of an Athenian," I replied.

"You are not an Athenian, either," said Medea. Was she daring me to reveal who I was?

"That is exactly why I am the one who must do it," I said. "If I misunderstand the signs, and the gods have not really blessed my idea, I will bear their wrath. None of their anger will fall upon Athens, for I am, as you say, no Athenian."

Aegeus nodded, this time approvingly. "Let it be done." Medea's face tightened as if she longed to object but had no reasonable way to do so.

Because the bull was potentially so dangerous, it took a while to set up the sacrifice. I asked Aegeus to order the people not to gather near the altar of Poseidon, where the sacrifice would take place—I had no idea how the bull would react to crowds. After untying it, I held its bridle with one hand. With the other, I gripped the hilt of my sword, though I did not draw it.

I started toward the altar, and it needed little persuasion to follow me. The trek around the city to the altar was nerve-wracking. Crowds formed behind the guards sent to keep them at a distance. If the bull decided to break away from me and I could not stop it, many people would be killed.

He looked at me and tilted his head a little, as if to mock my concerns. His steps beside me remained slow and unvarying.

By the time we reached the altar, it looked as if most of the population of Athens was pressing against the guards, pushing as far as they could in an effort to get close to the creature that had ravaged the plains of Marathon. The priests, on the other hand, stood as far back from the altar as they could, gripping their sacrificial knives in shaking hands.

It looked very much as if the usual preparations for the sacrifice had not been made. If I were not careful, what I was about to do would become mere slaughter instead of sacrifice.

Instead of waiting for the priests to find some courage, I took the lead.

"Athena and Poseidon, hear my prayer. I wish to sacrifice this bull to you, but as it is a special creature, I do not know if you will permit such an act. Give me a sign if you disapprove."

It might have been safer to ask for a sign if they did approve, but we could not safely keep the beast. Sacrificing it was the only option.

My prayer was met only by the sound of the wind blowing as it had been beforehand. No prophet emerged from the crowd to denounce the idea. Not even a stray bird flew overhead.

I doubted anyone would want to put ribbons on the bull, and I did not demand that. I asked for an appropriate veil, and a priest got close enough to toss me one, which I put on. I should also have been dressed in white, but I trusted the gods would understand that omission.

I asked for water, and the priest carrying the basin almost dropped it. Once I had it, I took one of the burning brands from the altar, dipped it in the water to purify it, and then in turn sprinkled myself and the altar with the purified water.

I didn't have to ask for the baked barley grains. By now, the priests were a little less fearful. One also volunteered his knife, though I had to stretch my arm uncomfortably far to reach it.

I burned the barley and a few hairs from the bull's head on the altar. There was no dark smoke, a good sign.

An even better one was that the bull moved toward the altar on its own and bowed its head. I heard gasps from the crowd to see the terrifying beast so tame.

I bent down and whispered to him, "Thank you. I will make this quick." Those deep eyes stared back at me, and I imagined I saw the beast nod its head, though I could have been mistaken.

Normally, I would have bashed him first with my club, then cut his throat, but I had seen sacrifices go awry if the blow to the head was even slightly off. I would not prolong this noble animal's suffering, even by accident. Instead, I dispatched him with one quick knife stroke to the neck, being careful to gather some of the spraying blood to sprinkle into the altar fire.

The priests were much braver now that the beast was dead. I cut it open so that they could read its entrails and pronounce the sacrifice accepted.

They also chopped up the bull, carefully gathered the priests' portion, and carried away the rest for the sacrificial banquet that would follow.

The sacrifice over, the crowd, which had managed to maintain the necessary solemnity, burst into applause. As I walked away from the altar, I nodded to them in acknowledgment.

Searching the crowd, I spotted Aegeus. Instead of looking happy that Marathon was now free of the bull's rampage, he was staring at me in tight-lipped disapproval. Had I done something wrong, or was it the effect of Medea's magic I saw in his face?

Guards helped me navigate the crowds, who were now as interested in me as they been in the bull before. Their fingers reached out for me. I continued to nod, but I did nothing else. I was not yet their prince, and Aegeus was dubious enough already. The last thing I needed was to appear to court more acclaim than it was my place to have.

The feeling of relief I had when I reached the palace didn't last long. I was greeted by Aegeus, who praised me extravagantly with his words, though his expression was at best neutral, and his posture was as stiff as the trunk of an oak tree. Medea was nodding and smiling at his side, her expression as warm as a snake's just before it strikes. Perhaps it was my imagination, but I felt power pulsing in the air even more intensely than before.

Between my feats on the road and my capture of the Bull of Marathon, my reputation with the people of Athens could hardly have been higher. That they would accept me as Aegeus's heir, I had no doubt. How I ached to show Aegeus the sword and shield that proved who I was and take my rightful place.

I had laid aside my weapons to perform the sacrifice, but I had reclaimed them before starting back to the palace. This time, the guard made no attempt to disarm me when I arrived. I felt the weight of the sword in the scabbard hanging from my belt. I felt the weight of the shield on my back, its design partially obscured by the heavy club hanging over the top of it. It would have been so easy to reveal the truth.

Or would it? Every time I looked in Medea's direction, I caught her watching me. She gazed as if she could see into me, even through me. Had she looked at Glauce that same way before giving her the gift that burned her to death? Had she looked that way at Jason before murdering two of their children?

It would do me little good to reveal myself only to be killed by Medea—or to see Aegeus killed. She was powerful, crafty—and, if even half the tales were true, utterly mad. How would I be able to overcome her?

We entered the great hall, which had been prepared for the sacrificial banquet. Aegeus seated me at his right hand, a singular honor, for the banquet was to celebrate my achievements as well as to honor the sacrifice. But he still didn't look happy.

Normally, the women ate separately from the men, but Medea hovered near Aegeus, and, as she was the queen, no one would question her if he did not. She fretted over every detail, particularly the pouring of the wine.

"I hope you will enjoy it," said Aegeus. "It is the finest vintage from Lemnos."

To my surprise, Medea served me with her own hands. The goblet she handed me was painted with the image of Erichthonius, an early king of Athens, son of Hephaestus and Gaia, foster son of Athena, ancestor of Aegeus himself. The ancient king, half-man and half-serpent, had been painted in such exacting detail that I could make out his individual scales.

Inside the goblet, the red wine was so dark that it appeared almost black, the most-favored wine color in those days. It had a scent like oregano and thyme. I moved the glass just enough to make the liquid inside swirl.

Medea raised her goblet. "To Theseus, the savior of our city!" Everyone around me, including Aegeus, raised their goblets and yelled, "To Theseus!"

As I raised my own goblet to drink, I looked at Aegeus, but he wouldn't meet my eyes. Instead, he looked down as if my sword, which hung from my left side and thus was plainly visible to him as I sat on his right, was far more fascinating than I was.

I hesitated for a fraction of a second, wondering why he had felt compelled to look away. Before, he might not have seemed pleased with me, but he always met my eyes. What was different now?

Lost in thought, I was caught by surprise when he knocked the goblet out of my hand. It crashed to the floor, its wine flowing out in a puddle that looked from a distance like dark blood.

The room was so silent that I could have heard a cat creeping along the far wall. I stared at Aegeus, his skin pale as ivory, his mouth hanging open. This time, his eyes met mine, but so many emotions warred in those eyes that I could not tell what he was feeling.

"The wine...the wine was poisoned," whispered the king, but the sound carried and echoed in the room. Many people must have heard it.

"Majesty, how—" I began.

Some color returned to Aegeus's face, and he pointed an accusing finger at Medea. "She...she is responsible. She convinced me you were conspiring to steal my throne. When the Bull of Marathon didn't kill you, she made me believe the only way was to poison you."

The room was silent no longer. Even the strongest partisan of Aegeus would have been shocked that the king had allowed the poisoning of one of his own guests.

This time I was not imagining the power that crackled from Medea. She looked somehow taller, and her eyes were black as night.

"This man is an enemy of Athens," she yelled, pointing to me. "If the city is to be safe, he must die."

Her words hissed like water striking hot stones. Aegeus looked at me, suddenly doubtful again. Around him, the men who had been outraged by the attempt on my life now looked sorry that it had failed.

I had no magic to combat her influence, but I could see her control was not total. Aegeus turned from certainty to struggle. He tried to point the finger at her again and failed. His face twisted as if he were trying to crawl out from beneath a boulder that was crushing him. The guards looked at me with suspicion but did not move forward to seize me. Some of them looked at the king and frowned at what they saw.

My sword was of fine workmanship—but the captured club might well have been the work of Hephaestus himself. Gambling that it was, I jumped from the chair, pulled it from behind my back, and yelled, "In the name of the blacksmith of the gods, ancestor of Athenian kings, I challenge you, witch!" To emphasize my words, I struck the table, which cracked and splintered at my blow.

Medea, her power spread thin to keep Aegeus and his men in line, took a step back. Her fear of the club told me I had chosen well.

I jumped up, landed on the table, and jumped down close to where she stood. I gave the club a mighty swing, but she was fast and dodged.

Some people had risen from their chairs, but like the guards, they were confused. Some looked at me as if I were a traitor, but others looked at Medea. None of them seemed able to move much. Medea took advantage of their positions by running between them, always a step or two ahead of me.

I had to stop her from lashing out at me with magic, but there was always someone else between my club and her. I could not strike down an innocent man to get to the murdering witch. All I could do was keep moving, forcing her to do the same. Once I struck a chair, shattering it into wood chips. Another time, I struck one of the other tables and collapsed it, sending dishes crashing to the floor. But still, Medea evaded me, swift as the wind, slippery as the snake she was.

If she evaded me long enough, she would eventually be able to attack me with magic. I had to force her to use what magic she could summon up to try to retain her influence over the people in the room.

"This is not just any Medea!" I yelled. "This is the same Medea who murdered her own brother. She manipulated the daughters of Pelias into killing him. She killed the princess and king of Corinth with magic. Vilest of all, she killed two of her own sons. Men of Athens, help me to bring her to justice!"

I could see from the facial expressions of the men nearby that they heard me, but Medea's magic was so strong they still couldn't break free completely. I didn't fear that they would turn on me, but they remained more hindrance than help.

I got close enough to Medea to swing the club again, missing her head by no more than a hand's breadth. She almost tripped. More people were struggling up, and the crowd was now as much obstruction to her as shield. I could have been wrong, but I thought I saw fear in her eyes.

I yelled loudly, jumped up on one of the tables, ran a few steps, and jumped down, coming so near here that I could easily reach her with the club. Now would be the moment. She couldn't move away fast enough. One blow would be all it would take me.

I swung with all my might, and the club struck—empty air. One second, she was trying to press her way past the people closest to her. The next, she was gone without a trace.

It is said the gods can move among mortals unseen, imperceptible. Medea must have been enough like a goddess to use such power herself. Try as I might, I could neither hear nor see her. She could be standing nearby, or she could have gotten all the way out of the room. There was no way to tell.

With her gone, Aegeus, his guards, and his courtiers were released from whatever spell she had used to keep them under her thumb. Some of them took a moment to recover from their confusion, but Aegeus, clear-headed at once, struggled his way through the crowd to stand at my side.

"Theseus!" he cried. "Forgive me!" Before, he had been reserved at best, hostile at worst. Now, he pulled me into his arms and held me tightly.

"That evil woman told me Aethra's son was dead but promised me another in his stead if I would wed her. I should have tested the truth of her words, but somehow...I don't know how...I wasn't thinking as clearly as I should."

"You know who I am?"

"When you looked at me, poisoned cup in hand, I felt a moment's guilt and could not meet your eyes. But what I looked down, the sword —it was the very one I hid beneath the rock for my son—for you. The truth helped me to resist her evil."

"This man...this man is your son?" asked one of the guards.

"Yes, yes!" said Aegeus, his eyes gleaming with tears of joy. "Left in Troezen for his own safety, he has come to claim his birthright and to succeed me as king when the time comes."

Aegeus looked around, much more alert than he had been earlier. "Medea is still a threat to us. Guards, seek her out."

I had the suspicion that they wouldn't find her, and I was right. But at least she didn't kill the baby, Medus, as she had killed Jason's sons. She took him with her instead, presumably whisking him away with magic before anyone realized what was happening.

For days, I feared she might return when we least expected it to wreak some fierce vengeance upon us. But there was no sign of her.

I would see her again, much later—but of that encounter, I will speak when I reach that point in the story.

As for Medus, I never saw him again, though he became the ancestor of the Median royal line. When the Medes were conquered by the Persians, many of them became officials and soldiers in the larger empire.

You know what I am saying, do you not? Some of Medea's distant descendants may be in the very army that faces you, ready to do to Athens what she could not.

THE SHADOW OF MINOS

DESPITE THE LINGERING fear of Medea, the months that followed were, in many ways, the happiest of my life. I had been happy enough as a boy because of my devoted mother—but now I had a father as well.

At first, we were strangers to each other, a condition he set out to remedy. He wanted to know my whole life story up to that point, insisting on any even more detailed account than I have given you. My words were like bread and wine to him, and he devoured them greedily.

Of course, I wrote to Pittheus and Aethra to tell them of my success and share my joy with them. From him, I received a short letter, but one that glowed with praise. From her, I received a much longer one, stained by a single tear she had tried to blot away.

In my original letter to her, I had suggested that she let me negotiate a marriage between her and Aegeus. After all, Medea's betrayal had left him without a wife again, and he was not too old to take another. She rejected that idea, gently but firmly.

"The time for such a thing has passed," she wrote. "I would have married Aegeus after that fateful night. I would have considered marrying him long after. But, though he is a good man, just as I told you, I never truly loved him, and whatever feelings I did have for him have faded like dyed wool left too long in the sun. I will stay as I am."

She could say whatever she wanted, but I knew the truth—her heart still belonged to Bellerophon and always would. He had forgotten her, married another, had several children. If he had thought of her at all, she must have seemed a distant dream to him, one whose details he had to struggle to recall. And now, if the tales told the truth, he had tried to fly to Olympus, been thrown from Pegasus for his presumption, and died a broken man. Yet none of that mattered to my mother, who must have been dreaming of seeking him out in the Underworld—or so it seemed to me. If that was truly her goal, she kept it to herself. I knew her better than any other man—well enough to know that she had some secrets even from me.

Jason was broken, Bellerophon was dead, and Heracles, though he still lived, had suffered more than any ten men. No, more than that— than any thousand men.

I sometimes still wondered if it would not have been better for me to run away with Perigune and live a simple life somewhere far from Troezen and Athens. For the lot of a hero so often seems to be ever-deepening misery. Would life be any better for me, cousin of Heracles, who if the fates had willed might have been son of Bellerophon and was even now his half-brother?

But in the early bloom of my relationship with Aegeus, such thoughts didn't trouble me often. I knew what it was to have a father for the first time. It wasn't that he commissioned new murals for the palace portraying my heroic exploits on the road from Troezen to Athens. Truth be told, that was embarrassing, especially since my petty accomplishments paled in comparison to those of Heracles. Nor was it the games held in my honor, though I enjoyed them well enough and won all the prizes. Not having to fight to the death, as I had against Cercyon, was far more enjoyable than adding to the blood already on my hands, justified though my killings may have been.

No, what I liked best was just spending time with him. Often, we rode together to explore the territory around Athens, which he knew well but some of which was unfamiliar to me.

"A king must know the land he rules," Aegeus told me, and he was right. But I knew what he really wanted was to create shared experiences. He had not been the one to see my first step, to teach me how to wrestle or how to hold a sword, to teach me the ways of women and how I must treat them. But he was determined to be in every part of my life from now on.

I wished I could say the same of Poseidon. Sometimes, I walked along the beach, feeling the grains of sand under my feet, as I had when I was younger, and imagined the lord of the sea rising from its depths to greet me. But he never did.

I don't really know why I even cared. I had a father more loving and attentive than I could ever have imagined. I loved him as much as he loved me. Yet I also knew another had fathered me, one who did not seem to care at all, and that irked me.

Perhaps he had so many sons that any one of us meant little to him. The fact that I was the only son of Aegeus, unless we counted the missing Medus, whom I suspected might have been conjured up by Medea's magic, seemed to make me even dearer to the king than I might have been otherwise.

But Aegeus, who wanted to share all with me, had neglected to share one thing—the terrible bargain he had struck with Crete.

I learned about it one day by listening to the slaves' gossip. Not wanting to put them on the spot, I went to Aegeus at once.

"My son, why do you look so troubled?" he asked the moment I entered the room.

"Why didn't you tell me about the sacrifice the Cretans expect of us?"

"I was hoping to negotiate a different deal this time. But Minos, immovable as a mountain, refuses to budge."

"But to send seven young men and seven young women to be sacrificed? Surely, it is an affront to the gods. Have we not been taught that they abhor human sacrifice?"

Aegeus would not look me in the eye, and he seemed suddenly much older than he had before. His hands shook slightly.

"They are not sacrificed to the gods."

"Then the tale of the half-bull, half-man monster—that is true as well?"

"I have not seen the minotaur with my own eyes," said Aegeus, looking out the window as if the familiar view had been transformed into some new horror. "Indeed, almost no one has. No one alive, anyway. But people have heard its distant roaring from the labyrinth where it is imprisoned."

"How could such a creature exist?"

Aegeus raised an eyebrow. "Was that not part of the gossip? If the tales are true, it is Minos's own fault that the creature exists.

"You remember the bull of Marathon?"

"How could I forget it?"

"Well, it is true it rose from the sea at Poseidon's command to be a sacrifice, true as well that it eventually went on a rampage when Minos refused to sacrifice it, but alas, there is more to the story than that.

"Poseidon's wrath is matched by that of very few gods. Before he drove the bull into a frenzy, he punished Minos in an even more horrible way. With Aphrodite's help, he filled Pasiphae, Minos's wife, with lust for the bull."

My face twisted with disgust. "Can such a thing be true?"

"I would not have thought so," said Aegeus. "Particularly not considering how close to being a goddess herself Pasiphae is. But she is Medea's aunt, and like Medea, perhaps she has sinned in such a way as to lose the favor of the gods. Be that as it may, it is said that she lay with the bull and became pregnant with the minotaur."

"If Minos were any kind of king, he would kill it, not feed it human flesh," I said, shuddering.

"Aye, if Minos were any kind of king," said Aegeus. "But just as Minos feared to kill the bull when it became crazed, so also he fears to kill the minotaur. That is my assumption, anyway. He worries about inciting Poseidon's further wrath. He has found he can control it by feeding it human victims. And in Athens, he has found a convenient, non-Cretan source for such victims."

"We should not cooperate with this abomination," I said.

Aegeus managed a smile, but it was like a merchant's smile, a measure of how much he wanted to make a sale, not how he truly felt. "Theseus, when a man is as young as you are, and all things seem possible, it is easy to be an idealist. As one grows older, one discovers that the world is not ideal. Many things we wish to accomplish are simply impossible.

"Could I refuse to send Minos the agreed-upon tribute? Absolutely! But far more people would die in the war that followed than will ever be sacrificed to the minotaur. If a few must die so the rest may live, is that not better than having all of them die?"

"It would be better for all of them to live, Father."

Aegeus finally met my eyes. "There is no way to preserve everyone. And if we fight, we will not win, for Crete is far mightier than Athens. Nor will the deaths end when the war does. Do you think a victorious Minos will forego the customary sacrifice? No, he will not—and every single man who died in the war will have died in vain. Is that what you want?"

I shook my head, for I could not summon up agreeable words. Feigning a headache, I asked leave to return to my room. Aegeus was willing enough to let me go. Eager, even, for the first time since he knew I was his son.

He couldn't bear to face me while the shadow of the minotaur lay between us.

I did go to my room, but only briefly. I picked up a cloak, tied it into a bundle, and moved as swiftly and quietly as I could toward the back of the palace. I longed to wander the streets of the city for a while, but by myself, not surrounded by guards. Slipping out of the palace would not be easy, but with enough patience, it was doable.

Not having anticipated such a situation, Aegeus hadn't given the guards any instructions about what to do in the event I tried to leave alone. I doubted they would let me out without checking, though. That meant leaving by the heavily guarded front gate on the south side of the palace was out of the question.

Nor would it be easy to climb the walls from inside or outside without being observed—too many guards along the bastion. And while the underlying limestone and sun-dried brick might have been uneven enough for handholds to be found, the stucco surface over them was too smooth for that. I'd have had to use the same ladders the guards did, making me even more conspicuous.

However, there was a small postern gate on the northern side of the wall, accessible from inside only through a long corridor. There were guards on the outside, but not immediately outside the gate. Since the palace was located on top of the acropolis, the only easy path to and from the postern was by the stairs carved into the stone. The guards were posted near the top of that stair. If I were quiet enough, I could slip out the gate and make my way around to the front of the palace without being spotted.

When I reached the postern, I found the gate bolted from the inside. The bolt was heavy enough to require three men to move it, as during changes of the guard. But I pulled the bolt back with no more effort than it had taken me to lift the stone that concealed my sword and shield. Then I unwrapped my cloak, which was long and had a large hood to make it more difficult to see my face, put it on, and ventured out the gate, closing it behind me.

Just as I had hoped, the guards were far enough away that they hadn't heard me open the bolt. Even from a distance, I could see them shuffling their feet impatiently as they stared down at the steps in the stone which few people ever traveled. I imagined them eagerly waiting to be relieved. Their job was the least desirable guard duty because so little happened on this side of the palace.

That was all the more reason for me to be quiet. As long as they had no cause to look back my way, they would keep staring at the stairs and whatever they could see in the distance rather than twist around to see the blank wall of the palace. But all I had to do was knock one small stone loose with one of my feet, and the sound might make their heads snap in my direction.

Praying to Athena and Poseidon to bless my efforts, I walked quickly but carefully along the palace wall. Both of them had touched this very stone with their feet a few generations back, or so the stories said.

The guards along the bastion would be more numerous as I turned the corner and continued down the west side of the palace. However, their attention was focused farther away. They wouldn't be expecting anyone walking from the north side and along the base of the wall. As long as I hugged it and stayed quiet, they wouldn't have any reason to look straight down.

As I turned another corner and was on the south side of the palace, I saw just what I had hoped to see—large numbers of people going to and from the palace on various errands. They would focus the attention of the guards, so that I could creep down the rocky slope between the palace and the road that led down from the acropolis into the main part of the city.

That descent took me longer than I would have liked. But the last thing I wanted was to lose my footing and fall the rest of the way, which would surely draw someone's attention. Once I reached the road, I blended effortlessly into the crowd. A cold wind was blowing north from the ocean, so keeping my hood up looked natural.

I hadn't freely mingled with the Athenians since I had sacrificed the bull of Marathon to Athena and Poseidon. There had been joy in their eyes then, and I hadn't been perceptive enough to see the uneasiness that lurked behind that joy. The citizens of Athens had felt the wrongness that Medea had brought with her, even if they did not know its cause.

Once I had driven Medea away, I had seen the Athenians often, but usually in the company of my father and always accompanied by guards. The people had looked happy enough, but as I walked among them now, unrecognized and largely unnoticed, I saw what I had failed to discern before. They still sensed wrongness, and their perception of it grew clearer as the time of the next sacrifice to the minotaur grew closer.

I walked slowly through the marketplace, always a good spot to listen, for people could run errands and catch up with friends at the same time. The place had been busy when I first saw it, but now the sellers had to maintain a frantic pace to keep up with the growing number of customers. Clearing the isthmian road of bandits had much improved business. That should have made everyone happy.

But behind satisfaction at greater opportunity and profit lurked uneasiness that bordered on fear. The merchants were usually too busy to express it much, but the customers had more time to speak of such things—and they did.

My hearing had always been sharp, and today my ears were daggers that dug into my heart as I heard what was in the hearts of the people.

"I'd rather lose my son to war than give him up for some beast to tear apart and dine upon. Why is our king so willing to accept this outrage?" asked one man, careful to do so when the nearest guards were too far away to hear.

"He says he saves more lives than he sacrifices," the friend of the first speaker answered. "For him, the choice is easy. It would not be so if Prince Theseus were one of those being shipped off to the minotaur—but that will never happen."

"I thought the choice was made by lot," said a third.

"Aye," said the second. "But who is it who draws those lots? For that matter, who is it who places them in a jar to begin with?"

"Aegeus," said the first, nodding. "And do you think he places in that jar a lot with Theseus's name on it?"

"And would you place the name of your own son in that jar?" asked a woman as she passed the three men.

"Of course, I wouldn't," said the second. "That's why I'm so sure he doesn't. Any man would do the same—but when that man wants others to take the risk he is unwilling to take himself, he is doing an ill-thing. Tyrants may do such a thing, but just kings never should."

My heart felt as cold as the depths of the sea. I didn't want to hear any more, but as I hurried through the marketplace, eager to reach a quieter street, I heard variations on the same conversation over and over, as if I were trapped in an echo chamber.

I had come to Athens to save Aegeus. How bitterly ironic that my very presence was undermining respect for his rule!

Once free of the crowd, I rushed back to the palace as fast as I could. By the time I reached the main gate, my hood had fallen back.

"My prince, how is it you are out of the palace and come back so unescorted?"

"I am on urgent business. Take me to the king at once."

Confused by my unexpected presence and doubtless fearful of how the king might blame them for letting me out, two of the guards took me to the great hall where Aegeus was with some of his advisers.

"My king and my father, I would speak with you at once upon most urgent business," I said before Aegeus had a chance to ask me why I was there. He looked puzzled, but he dismissed his advisers and had the guards move out of earshot.

"What is it that so troubles you?" he asked as soon as there was no one else around to hear.

I explained how I had sneaked out to walk among the people.

Aegeus tensed, but he let me finish what I had to say, interrupting only when I revealed what I had heard.

"You took a foolish risk going out alone, and for what? To listen to idle gossip? All men complain about their rulers from time to time. It is the way of things. Give it no further thought."

"No!" I said, more loudly than I intended. "This was not just idle gossip, and I heard the same complaint over and over again. Is it true, Father? Would you keep me out of the lottery?"

"There will be a lot with your name on it," he said, but I knew he was lying almost before the words left his mouth. The shifting of his eyes away from mine gave him away.

"Then reassure the people. Instead of conducting the whole process yourself, appoint men to place the lots and others to draw them."

Aegeus sighed. "I am king. My word must be good enough."

"It will not be for men with suspicion in their hearts. Perhaps even removing yourself from the process will not be enough. People will just say that you ordered them not to place my lot or to rig the drawing somehow so that it will not be picked."

My father gave me a tight-lipped smile. "You have proven my point, Son. Nothing I do now will be enough to satisfy the suspicious."

Much as I hated to admit it, he was right. Still, there was one way to satisfy even the most stubborn doubter of all.

"Then let me volunteer. I heard in the marketplace that there is a provision in the law for that."

"There is, but no one has ever before volunteered—nor will you. I forbid it!"

"Father, I came here because you needed an heir. And why? Because your throne would not have been safe without one. But if I do not go to Crete, your throne will not be safe, anyway."

"I wanted you to be my heir," said Aegeus slowly. "But it was not long before I came to love you as a son. I forbid you as a father would, not as your king would." He leaned closer to me. "In truth, I could not go on living if you died."

To my surprise, a tear rolled down his cheek. I had seen sorrow on his face before, but I had never seen him cry.

I rose from my chair. He rose from his somewhat shakily. I embraced him and felt the slight tremors running through his body.

"Father, I would not ask to do this if there were any other way."

"I thought you loved me as much as any son could love a father." His voice quaked in a way I had never before heard. "But if you will not let that love guide you, then at least let practicality do so. If you sacrifice yourself to the minotaur, then I will again be left without an heir, will I not?"

I pulled back enough to be able to look into his eyes, which glistened with tears. "Father, I said I intended to go to Crete. I never said I intended to go through with the sacrifice."

"I...I do not understand."

"Why let the minotaur rend my flesh and suck the marrow from my bones—when I can so easily just kill him?"

PREPARING FOR THE JOURNEY

NOT LONG AFTER my conversation with Aegeus, I dreamed that I was by the seashore. The dream was so vivid that I could smell the salt air and feel the sand beneath my bare feet.

I knew the gods often used dreams to send us messages, and the scenery made me half-hope that I would at long last hear from Poseidon. But the figure walking toward me on the beach was that of a woman.

It did not take me long to realize who she was. Her gray eyes, fierce and wise at the same time, told me she was Athena. The olive trees that sprung up in her footsteps spoke of the many peaceful pursuits she fostered among men, but she was dressed unabashedly as a warrior. She wore the aegis of Zeus as a breastplate, and it befit her, for it was she who had skinned the dragon Aex and used that skin to craft the aegis. I could still make out the pattern of the scales. In her right hand, she carried a spear; in her left, she held a shield decorated with a painting of the head of Medusa, the grisly trophy which Perseus had given her.

My heart was beating faster than it should have been. She had not been quite so warlike in her attire when she faced my mother. Was she angry with me?

To be on the safe side, I fell to my knees before her.

"Rise, Theseus," she said, her tone commanding but not hostile. "Rise and hear my words."

I got up and brushed the sand from my knees. "I am ready to hear you."

She raised an eyebrow. "Let us hope so, for you are fast approaching a critical moment in your life. This very night, I have visited Aegeus also. Tomorrow, he will withdraw his objection to your plan, for he now knows that it is my will that you go."

"Then my plan is wise?"

"It may prove wise or foolish, depending upon the result. Let us say that it can work out well if you are very careful."

"I...I thought the outcome of mortal acts was destined one way or the other."

Athena smiled like a tutor whose pupil has proved unusually insightful. "Fate is a force that governs even the gods—but not in every detail. And sometimes, there are different possible pathways. In this case, your actions will determine which path you will follow, though once you are on it, you will not be able to go back."

"What must I do to defeat the minotaur?"

The goddess laughed, but I didn't know at first whether I had pleased her or whether she was mocking me.

"The minotaur is stronger than the enemies you have faced before, but he is also markedly less intelligent. You will be able to outthink him without too much trouble. No, I did not come to warn you of the creature. I came to warn you of Aphrodite."

The mention of the love goddess chilled my blood. After all, by her actions against Glaucus and Aegeus, she had put my mother through great hardships. "Have I offended her?"

"Not yet, but that will not prevent her from changing your destiny. Did you not almost cast aside your future as king of Athens for the love of Perigune?"

There was no point in lying to a goddess. "I did think about it."

"Love has its place in the world, but as part of a complicated balance, not as a force that automatically prevails against all others. In your case, part of being a good king will be taking a wife and raising fine sons and daughters with her. But temper love for wife and family with duty and with reason. Aegeus is a good king. You have the potential to be a great one—but only if you maintain the proper balance in your life.

"Keep your wits about you, and you will not be devoured by the minotaur. No, it is being devoured by your own heart that you must fear."

As she spoke, a mist blew in from the sea, and I could barely see her. I knew the dream was coming to an end.

"And what of my father? When I saw the sea, I half-expected it would be Poseidon who appeared to me."

The mist parted for a moment, and Athena was once again before me, but she looked much sterner than before.

"The gods are powerful but not all-powerful. Each of us has many tasks, and, except for the few of us who choose not to marry, many children, human and divine. Be not too judgmental if Poseidon is not always at your side."

I should have let the matter go, but words pushed themselves out of my mouth. "He has never been at my side."

"That you know of," replied Athena. "The gods can walk among men and be unseen and unnoticed. This you know. What you may not know is that Poseidon has often erred, not on the side of neglecting his children and mortal favorites, but of spoiling them."

"The storytellers left that part out," I said slowly.

"Yet it is there for those wise enough to understand," said Athena. Her tone made me feel as if I had fallen short. "Why did Atlantis become so corrupt that the gods plunged it into the sea, never to rise again? Because its kings were sons of Poseidon who received every gift he had to give and still were not satisfied.

"And what of your own ancestor, Pelops? His father, Tantalus, was son to Zeus himself and much favored by the gods. And how did he repay that favor? By killing his own son and serving him to us to test our divine knowledge!

"He paid the price, and we could have left it at that, but instead, we took pity on Pelops. We put him back together with our own hands, and we raised him from the dead, an act we seldom perform for any mortal.

"All might have been well for Pelops if Poseidon had been content with what we had done for him, but instead, moved by the boy's tragic history, the sea god became his divine patron. He even brought him to live on Olympus for a while, until Zeus put a stop to such overt favoritism.

"Alas, Zeus was too late. Like you, Pelops had the potential to be great, but his hubris swelled within him until there was barely room for anything else. Among other things, he disgracefully used Myrtilus, son of Hermes, in his schemes and then betrayed and killed him. As a consequence, the curse of Myrtilus, enforced by Hermes, weighs heavily upon your whole family and will continue to do so for some generations to come. And as for Pisa, the city Pelops won by treachery, he has doomed it to sink into obscurity.

"Be thankful that with you, Poseidon chose a wiser course. But know this—the time is approaching when the lord of the sea will come to your aid. Be grateful when he does—but do not look for more than it would be wise for him to give you."

The mists rolled over Athena again, and I awoke in a cold sweat. I had heard of the curse on Pelops before, but never until that moment had I felt its weight upon me. It felt cold and implacable, like a boulder chilled by the north wind, and it rested on my shoulders like the sky upon the shoulders of the unfortunate Atlas.

But there was a way for me to avoid the fate of men like Pelops— Athena had said as much. And she was right about Aegeus. He greeted me in the morning with the news that he accepted my plan. He didn't mention his dream, so neither did I.

I was right about the public reaction. I walked alone to the market-place, this time with Aegeus's blessing. Now the talk was all about how Aegeus was a true ruler, one not afraid to suffer as his subjects suffered. There was also enough praise of me to make me blush beneath my hood. Days ago, I had been the symbol of royal privilege. Now I was the living embodiment of goodness, a prince unafraid to share the fate of his subjects. Ironically, many of them didn't want me to go through with my plan. "Such a prince would benefit us more by living than by dying," and similar sentiments echoed in my ears.

Returning to the palace, I relayed all I had heard to my father. He listened attentively and tried to smile, though his lips faintly trembled as he did so.

"Your strategy has had the intended political effect," he said. "But are you sure you will be able to put an end to the minotaur?"

"It would be hubris to say I knew for certain," I replied. "I have faith that the gods will aid me. It is for the purpose of dealing with such monsters that heroes are put are on the Earth in the first place, is it not?"

Aegeus nodded, though I doubt he was any more certain of that bit of school wisdom than I was. At this point, he knew he could not change his mind even if he wished to. He had set foot upon a path from which there was no turning back.

"The ship will depart tomorrow as planned," said the king. "There will be one change in the normal tradition. The ship will use black sails as always for the voyage to Crete, but if you take the return voyage—"

"When," I said, smiling. "When."

"When you take the return voyage, first take down the black sails and put up white ones. That way, I will know you have survived as soon as the ship comes into sight."

"I will not forget."

Aegeus put his arm around me and led me to dinner. Really, it was more like a banquet than an ordinary meal. Then as now, Greeks prided themselves on the frugality of their meals, a way of distinguishing themselves from the supposedly more barbaric societies to the east. But for this dinner, Aegeus loaded the tables with food until it looked as if they might collapse. He also invited all the royal officials, other prominent citizens, and even my former companions from school. Anyone who had ever seen my face had been invited. I was not surprised when I caught sight of King Hippothous, whom I had raised to the throne of Eleusis. He arrived right before the beginning of the feast. Aegeus rushed to greet him and hustled him over to sit at my right hand, just as I was sitting at Aegeus's.

Hippothous wasn't exactly a friend, but then again, I wasn't sure I had any true friends. The citizens of Athens professed to love me, but in general, they didn't know me. Those of a high enough social rank to be personally acquainted with me might like me—or they might be using me for their own advancement. There was no easy way to know.

Hippothous had already advanced as far as I could raise him, so he didn't need to show me anything more than polite gratitude. Yet he greeted me warmly and assured me he had offered many sacrifices to all the gods for my safe return. Eleusis was wealthy enough to sustain a large number of sacrifices, but even so, any one mortal, even a king, even the son of a god, could only ask so much from his exalted relatives. I was touched that he was willing to expend so many requests on me.

It gladdened my heart to see other signs of genuine affection from those around me, but as the evening wore on, their poorly concealed anxieties peaked out from behind their joyous facades.

The farewell feast decayed into a perideipnon—a funeral feast, just as you have today. Well, except that today, people actually wait until one is dead and buried.

As I glanced discreetly around the room, I saw the telltale signs everywhere. Unshed and almost shed tears gleamed in the eyes of the guests, though if they caught me looking at them, they managed stiff and awkward smiles. Those close enough to me that I might overhear them conversed partially in whispers, but I still caught enough of their words to understand what they were talking about.

They did not expect me to survive. I looked at Aegeus and beheld the same truth in his eyes. Athena had pushed him into giving his approval, but in his heart, he still believed he was sending me to my death. Every time I looked his way, he gave me an almost manic smile, and his movements were all too fast. The tension within him must have been nearly unbearable.

I ceased being able to taste my food about midway through dinner. When the wine was served, I would have refused it, but such a gesture would have been unmannerly, so I picked up my golden goblet and stared down into the expensive black wine from Chios that lay within it. I raised the goblet to my lips and sipped.

The beverage burned like wine uncut by water, and I realized that, just as the feast had been excessive, the wine was being served, not in the usual Greek, civilized fashion, but at its savage, full potency. Was this just an oversight on someone's part? I looked at the wine again and could have sworn that what was in my cup was blood, not wine, even though I knew such a thing was impossible.

The room was brightly lit, but by the flickering lamplight, I imagined the ominous shadows near the edges of the room were my dismal fate, moving ever closer as the oil in the lamps dwindled. Did Thanatos, death himself, lurk in those shadows. Did he whisper to me, "It is nearly time, Theseus"?

No, the whisper was from Hippothous, and it was not really a whisper, though he was speaking low enough not to attract Aegeus's attention. "For years, I lived with death. I knew my grandfather would kill me if he could catch me, yet I could not bring myself to flee far enough away to evade him forever. Eleusis called to me, the sea called to me, and I stayed nearby, knowing I was sealing my own doom.

"Yet here I am, alive, thanks to you, Theseus. Death was not what the fates chose for me. And I do not think it is what they have chosen for you, either."

Hippothous looked younger to me than I remembered him. At that moment, I realized his looks had changed because he was no longer being worn down by the weight of an ominous future. If I were wise, I would follow his example. If I were to succeed, I could not be ruled by worry.

"Thank you, you...brother," I replied. He gave me a genuine smile, as if he appreciated the irony that we *were* brothers, though no one else knew it.

Did he know it himself? Or was his smile just a display of happiness? I couldn't very well ask. But in the warmth of that smile, the shadows faded, and if Thanatos had been lurking there, just out of sight, he was gone now.

I took a couple more cautious sips from my goblet and then put it aside. I noticed Hippothous and most of the other guests nearby had done the same. Aegeus kept drinking, though, which brought his emotions dangerously close to the surface. It would not do to have the king weep before such a large assembly over a death that had not even occurred yet. With Hippothous's aid, I managed to maneuver Aegeus out of the room before he had embarrassed himself.

Once he was out of the public eye, he made no further effort to put up a brave front. Weakened by wine, he let his tears flow freely, and I comforted him as best I could while Hippothous returned to the banquet to make appropriate excuses to the guests on my and my father's behalf.

"Father, I will return to you. This will not be the end. The goddess would not send me to my death."

"If only that were true," whispered Aegeus. "The closer your departure comes, the more I doubt that dream. What if it was not from Athena at all? What if some other god, hostile to Athens, is tricking us? Or perhaps Zeus wants Minos to rule all of Greece."

I shook my head. "Minos has ruled Crete a long time already. If Zeus had wanted to hand Greece to him, he could have done it long ago."

Aegeus nodded his head, but he still looked unconvinced. However, what little comfort I could offer, combined with the relentless work of the wine, soon put him to sleep.

I was surprised to find most of the guests still in the hall when I returned. Hippothous rushed over to me like a trusted adviser and whispered to me that they had stayed to wish me good fortune on my voyage.

I could hardly refuse to give them what they wanted, but receiving all their good wishes took nearly an hour, and by the time the last had departed, and only Hippothous remained, I longed for sleep, though I doubted I would get any that night.

"I will be at the docks tomorrow when you depart," said Hippothous. I thanked him for his support, and he said good-bye, leaving me at last alone. For all the sleep I got that night, he might as well have stayed. What fitful rest I had was filled with nightmares of bloodthirsty minotaurs and angry gods.

But it was not these images that most horrified me. It was the barely audible whisper that served as a background for them. Though Myrtilus had died generations before I was born, I knew it was his whisper.

"My curse will destroy you."

I awoke with those words echoing in my ears, but there was no time to brood over them. What time I had after I dressed, I spent in prayer. I promised to make sacrifices to every god I could think of if they would bring me safely home. But I spent the most time praying to Athena and Poseidon, for they had the most interest in my success—or so I hoped.

My last prayer was to Hermes. I promised not only to offer him sacrifices but to build a monument to Myrtilus equal in magnificence to the one Pelops had built in Olympia if only the messenger of the gods would lift the curse upon my family. As with all my prayers that day, I received no obvious response.

After a hasty breakfast, I walked to the docks of Piraeus, the port of Athens. I was accompanied by several palace guards as well as by Aegeus, who looked paler than normal and more like my grandfather than my father.

I thought again of Perigune. Should I have stayed with her? How much good had I really done Aegeus? It seemed in that moment as if I had brought only suffering to him, that he would have been better off without me.

But even the favorites of the gods cannot travel back in time to undo their past mistakes. The best I could do was see to it that I came back to Aegeus. Once I had vanquished the minotaur, I would return, bringing only joy with me. That belief was all I had to sustain me.

The ship waiting for us in the harbor had no oars but only the black sails that announced its purpose. It was also small by Athenian standards. That was because Minos was strict in his instructions. He would tolerate nothing that resembled a warship, though what he, with such a massive navy, had to fear from one ship, I couldn't imagine.

A large crowd stood nearby, restrained from charging toward us only by stern and unyielding guards. Usually, the crowds that gathered to bid farewell to the human sacrifices for the minotaur were small and somber, composed mostly of relatives of the victims. But there was not normally a prince among those victims.

My ears were filled with mingled cheers and lamentations, as if a sporting event had become grotesquely entangled with funeral rites. I nodded in acknowledgment to the cheers, but that was all I could do. I longed to walk among them, reassure them perhaps, but I did not dare. Minos probably had at least a few spies in Athens, so I could not even hint publicly what I intended to do.

Leaving Aegeus was hard, particularly since he didn't want to let go of me. "Remember the message of Athena," I whispered, gently pulling away from him to prevent an overly emotional scene. People would have understood how he felt, but as a king, it was unseemly for him to show too much weakness in front of his subjects. He had already come too close to that at the banquet.

I could see the reluctance in his face, but he managed to nod, put his arms down, and stand relatively straight as I boarded the ship. The other six men and seven women whose lots had been drawn followed me. All of us took what all of them but I believed would be their last glance at family members—and, in my case, a glance and a nod to my father's assembled subjects. Then the captain ordered some of the sailors to raise anchor and cast off. In just a few minutes, we were underway.

FATHER-SON REUNION

As the ship was small, the quarters below deck were crowded at best. The captain said nothing to me about the accommodations, but the embarrassed way he had of looking away whenever I glanced in his direction told me he was disconcerted by having so little to offer his prince.

"It is a small ship because of the regulation of Minos," I said to him. "And you had to leave some space for provisions and for crew quarters, did you not?"

He studied the deck beneath his feet and nodded.

"Then worry not about the fact that the quarters are not what you think I am used to. When I traveled from Troezen to Athens the first time, I went on foot and slept in the woods. I do not need to be in a palace to be comfortable."

After that, the captain became more comfortable around me, as did the crew. My fellow sacrifices would not have felt comfortable anywhere.

"Do not despair," I told them. "The gods have ways of rescuing us even when our situation seems hopeless."

They nodded and tried to give me a smile, but I could tell that they did not believe me in their hearts. Even now, I could not risk telling them my plans. Perhaps they would have thought me mad if they had known what I intended to do.

We had a strong south wind filling our sails, so we made reasonably good time. With adverse weather, the journey to Crete might take days, especially without oars, but luck was with us—if you could call it that. I think my fellow sacrifices would have preferred to be blown off course, perhaps even shipwrecked on a small island where they might live out their days. The closer we got to Crete, the grimmer they became.

By the middle of the third day, we sighted Crete, and the captain turned the ship east toward Amnysos, the port of Knossos, the capital of Crete. Before nightfall, we would be able to land there.

To my surprise, a Cretan ship approached us before we had traveled very far. It was much larger than our craft—the very kind of warship Minos had ordered us not to bring. It had more than a hundred oars on each side, moving in an almost mechanical rhythm. Above the deck towered a tall mast from which spread an enormous sail, easily three times the size of ours. It was decorated with the labrys, the two-bladed ax that was the symbol of Zeus and of Cretan royal power.

The captain gasped. "It is the ship of Minos himself!" he said, eyes locked on the labrys. "By Cretan law, only he can use such an emblem on his sails."

"Is this customary?" I asked.

"He always inspects the tribute, but normally not until the ship has landed."

With so many oars at this disposal, Minos quickly closed the distance between us. We could not have fled even if we wanted to. The mighty warship pulled up alongside us and used ropes and hooks to draw the two ships closer. Once we were fastened securely together, some soldiers and a man who could only have been Minos boarded us.

Even had I not felt a spark the same way I had when Heracles visited, I would have known him as the son of a god. He was taller than most men, as well as more muscular, and he looked like a man in his early middle years at most, even though he had ruled Crete for close to three generations already.

His hair and beard, both immaculately trimmed, were dark brown without a trace of gray. His arms were corded with muscle that looked hard as stone. His eyes were alive with curiosity, befitting his reputation for wisdom—but they were also as cold as ice. What else could I expect from someone willing to murder innocent youths in a desperate effort to avoid the consequences of his own mistakes?

"Fear not, captain," said Minos, his voice deep and commanding. "I have only come somewhat early to inspect the tribute. It is, after all, not every day that Athens chooses to sacrifice its own prince."

No official messenger had been sent to Minos to let him know the names of the sacrifices. If I had any doubt about Cretan spies in Athens, his comment cleared up any uncertainties.

"Majesty, it is but a matter of fortune," I said, giving him a bow. I would rather have spat on him, but for my plan to work, I needed to keep my hostility in check.

Minos raised an eyebrow. "Yet I heard that you volunteered to come. Not so much a matter of fortune then, eh?"

I tensed. We sacrifices were all dressed alike in plain white attire, but he picked me out immediately. Did his spies give him very accurate descriptions, or was he able to sense my divine parentage in the same way I could sense his? Perhaps all he was doing was making an educated guess.

"It was certainly fortune that brought me to Athens in the first place," I said, keeping my voice carefully neutral.

"But not, it would appear, good fortune," he replied, giving me a smile like an executioner's. His eyes looked away from me and down the row of my fellow citizens. I don't know if they realized it, but they had lined themselves up like slaves at an auction.

Minos walked toward the end of the row, where the youngest girl among us stood, staring at him the way a field mouse stares at a hawk.

"What is your name, girl?" the king asked. His tone was more forceful than it needed to be. She was already almost too frightened to speak.

"Chloe," she said so faintly that I could barely hear over the sound of the sea.

"You will share my bed tonight," said Minos, one of his hands gripping one of her breasts through the thin, white fabric. "That will not save you from the minotaur, but it might give you a few more days before you must face it."

Every word my mother had ever said to me about how a man should treat a woman screamed through my mind. Hot with outrage, I looked to the captain, but he would do nothing. With so many of Minos's soldiers around, not to mention Minos himself, he would not dare.

"Take your hands off her!" I shouted loudly enough to cause the Cretan soldiers to reach for their weapons. Minos looked in my direction and laughed.

"Ah, so the pup has a bark."

"And a bite, too, should you force me to use it," I said, taking a step in his direction. I regretted those words immediately. Fighting him was not part of my plan, and if he chose to take my implicit challenge, he was armed, and I was not. Of course, he could just order his guards to kill me.

"The pup needs to be housebroken," said Minos, motioning for his guards to back off. "Surely, you know who I am."

"You are Minos, King of Crete—but your treaty with Athens allows you to feed us to the minotaur, not to use us for your pleasure."

"And you are going to stop me, are you?" asked the king. He was still smiling, but his voice sounded harsh, maybe angry. He was not used to being defied—even by a foreign prince.

"I am more than just a king. I am a son of Zeus." He looked up at the sky. "A favorite son of Zeus."

His words got progressively louder, and on the second repetition of *Zeus*, thunder punctuated his words, even though the sky was clear.

The Athenians on deck all cowered at the sound, and even Minos's own guards looked uneasy. I knew I should have backed down, but the idea of Minos taking Chloe against her will was too horrible to contemplate. Not even the son of a god should do such things.

"Son of Zeus, I am…favored by Poseidon."

Minos laughed again, a joyless sound. "Anyone may claim such an honor, but how favored could you possibly be?"

"Favored enough to teach a king that he should rule justly—or not at all."

Hands went to sword hilts again, and again Minos signaled for the guards to stand down. He pulled a gold ring from his finger and tossed it into the sea as if it were some worthless rock.

"Prove how favored you are then," said Minos, flashing me his executioner's smile again. "Let your patron return that ring to me, and I will be convinced."

"Will you swear to leave the women untouched if I bring it back?" I asked. "Swear to your father, the protector of the sanctity of oaths."

"I so swear," said Minos, smiling triumphantly at me, sure of my failure.

I walked to the side of the ship and looked over. I don't know what I was expecting to see. Poseidon's trident with the ring on its middle spike? I don't know, but I was hoping for more than the calm waters of the sea, glittering in the sunlight and mocking me.

Minos had called my bluff. I would look like an idle boaster—and he would rape an innocent girl with impunity.

But Athena had said Poseidon would come to my aid. I had no choice but to believe she meant now.

Without looking back to Minos, I climbed up on the side of the ship and jumped off. In seconds I plunged downward through cold, salty water, sure that my impulsiveness would cost me my life.

So rash was I that I had forgotten even to take a full breath before diving in. Holding my breath should have become difficult, even painful, almost immediately. Yet I felt no pressure, no urge to breathe.

Equally strange, my body kept descending. Under normal conditions, I should have started to float upward once the momentum from my dive was exhausted. Instead, I continued downward as if I were being pulled down by invisible hands.

The sunlight from above diminished as I descended, yet I could still see. Where was the soft light coming from?

"Follow us," said a gentle, female voice, quiet as the sea washing across a sandy beach, yet perfectly audible. Trying to look past the multicolored schools of fish that swam all around me, I saw not one but several women, their long, dark hair floating behind them like cloaks lifted upward by a gentle breeze. Their eyes flashed like sparkles of sunset reflecting on seawater. Their skin was smooth and bright as pearls. Their pearlescent bodies were partially concealed by garments of something that looked like luminous seaweed. All of them were completely at home in the depths of the sea. Nereids! It was they who had drawn me down, they who enabled me to survive in this watery kingdom.

Smiling, they turned and swam away from me, and I followed effortlessly, the sea itself pushing me to match their pace. The fish seemed oblivious to me, except that they swam around me when they needed to. However, the Nereids were not the only ones who noticed me. Dolphins, far more intelligent than most sea creatures, swam with me on both sides, as well as above me and below me. In the bubble they created, I felt protected. Stories spoke of great monsters beneath the sea, but I was not afraid. My Nereid and dolphin escorts would not allow harm to befall me.

My father would not allow harm to befall me.

Up ahead, I could see a palace made of white gold, glowing as if light were radiating outward from it. The entry gate, several times the height of the one at Athens, swung open, and, led by the Nereids, I swam through. My dolphin escort stayed behind.

Now I swam through corridors of glittering white gold decorated by mosaics made from polished stones of various colors. I was still moving fast, but I did pick up some details. The ones nearest the entrance portrayed Poseidon's role in battles against the titans and other menaces. As I drew closer to what had to be the center of the palace, the mosaics represented mortal men and women instead. No, not quite mortal. They were all exceptionally good-looking, and each one had some touch connecting him or her with the sea—bits of seaweed, waves rising behind them, dolphins paying homage to them, a distant trident flashing in the background. Some of them were pictured doing heroic, even impossible feats.

These could only be my brothers and sisters, the many mortal children of Poseidon. My eyes widened when I saw Bellerophon, my mother's lost love, riding Pegasus over a turbulent sea.

Near the end of this gallery, I managed to slow my Nereid-inspired pace just a little. Could it be? There I was, represented in a mosaic composed of thousands of sea stones as I fought Procrustes. Such a medium did not normally look realistic, but this one seemed as lifelike as the earlier mosaics. The gods can craft works of art in ways no mortal can.

I had always felt distant from my divine father. But now, seeing myself as part of the epic that was his life, I felt bonded with him in a way I had never anticipated. It was as if I were seeing every childhood dream gleaming in the stones so lovingly placed that I had to wonder if Poseidon himself had taken a hand in the work.

I felt myself pulled away. I caught a glimpse of Hippothous, sitting on the throne of Eleusis, then a brief view of a few others I didn't recognize. Whatever magic that had impelled me forward dissipated, and I found myself in an enormous throne room. There, sitting on two thrones of carefully carved coral, were Poseidon and Amphitrite, his queen and the eldest of the Nereids.

Poseidon looked somewhat like his nephew, Minos. Both were distinguished; both were strong. Of course, Poseidon pulsed with power that even a son of Zeus could not hope to match. His trident, which he held in his right hand, like a scepter, could create a tidal wave if he struck the sea with it or an earthquake if he struck the land. But the god himself looked as if he didn't really need such a weapon, as if he could strangle a world-encircling serpent and not be winded by the effort.

Minos's eyes and smile had both been cold as the seawater that now surrounded me, even though I didn't feel its chill. Poseidon's eyes, deep as that sea, hinted of turbulence that could sink ships. Yet he looked at me with warmth in his eyes and a genuine smile on his lips. I fell to my knees before him, but he was at my side almost immediately, lifting me up with his own hands.

"My son," he said in a voice like the roar of the sea, yet gentle at the same time. "Long have I waited to meet you."

I should have returned his greeting, but I hesitated for a moment. Much as I wished to embrace him, I could not just forget all the years of neglect.

"I would have been with you always if I could have." He spoke as if he could read my mind, though I did not think even the gods had such a power. "But the realm of the gods is as fraught with troubles as is the mortal world." His smile faded for a moment. "Zeus still blames me for spoiling Pelops and...some of your brothers and sisters as well. "His disapproval, as well as my other duties, kept me from appearing to you before. But all worked out for the best. For if I had been too constant in my attentions, you would never have become a hero in your own right."

I stepped into his open arms and felt his firm embrace. It was that of a parent to a much-loved son. But I would never have forgiven myself if I had not spoken my mind.

"My mother suffered much," I mumbled. He let me go and looked me in the eye.

"She played the role she had to play, just as Athena has told you. We regret her suffering, but far worse misery would have come into the world had she refused. Even she would agree with that, I think."

I opened my mouth, but I could say no more. He might have been deceiving me, but his every word, every look, every gesture seemed natural and sincere. Whatever had befallen my mother and me in the past, now I stood before a loving father, ready to show that love in such ways as he could. Rejecting him would not have lessened my mother's suffering—but it might have made my own mission impossible to complete, rendering that suffering pointless.

"Even before I knew you were my father, I always loved playing by the sea," I said. It sounded childish, but it was all I could think of at that moment.

He smiled, and I thought of dawn at the seashore.

"I watched you there sometimes, though you did not know it. I watched you also on your journey to Athens, and at other times besides. I saw you looking at your likeness in the hall. Realistic, was it not? Only an eyewitness could have captured so much detail."

"It was...amazing," I wasn't sure what else to say. All my training in rhetoric and in manners had not prepared me for this occasion. What could have?

"I have something for you," said, holding out the gold ring Minos had tossed into the sea. "With this, you can make Minos look like the fool he is."

I raised an eyebrow. "Will not Zeus be angry?"

Poseidon chuckled. "Perhaps, but he knows Minos has ruled too long. He was a good king once. Now he is a tyrant in all but name. Zeus daily hears the prayers of those Greeks who wish to be delivered from him, and he is not deaf to them."

"Yet he thundered to confirm the tyrant's words."

"Zeus is in a difficult position. He loves his sons, even when they end up doing evil. He still hopes, I think, for Minos to atone for his sins and return to the right path. I have been where he is. I have had sons wreak havoc—but they were still my sons. Few fathers would feel otherwise."

For a moment, the lord of the sea was not the embodiment of divine might. He seemed almost human. The storytellers were not wrong when they portrayed the gods in that way.

The moment passed, though. The hint of sorrow over things past faded from Poseidon's eyes. Once again, he was the ruler of the sea, one of the most powerful gods, second only to Zeus in raw strength.

"Ah, but I have forgotten. I have other gifts for you as well. Wife, bring forth what else we will give him."

Amphitrite stood and moved forward, bringing with her a purple cloak and a golden crown. However, my eyes were drawn to her rather than to the gifts. Her beauty was almost too much to look upon, more radiant by far than the while gold palace in which she dwelt, more even than all her Nereid sisters put together. She was like an aquatic sun, and if the real sun fell, she would fill the sea with enough light to brighten the rest of the world.

Remembering the stories of Hera's jealousies over Zeus's infidelities, I feared her wrath, but she was not the same kind of goddess. Her eyes looked upon me as I were her son as much as Poseidon's. What she really thought, I had no way to know. But she betrayed no hint of hostility toward me.

"This cloak and this crown are both wedding gifts from Aphrodite," she said in a voice like hidden music echoing up from the depths. "Minos could conceivably dismiss your finding the ring as incredible luck, but he will know these for the divinely made objects they are. Thus, he will believe you are favored by Poseidon."

"I don't suppose that will prevent him from offering me to the minotaur," I said.

"No, indeed," said Poseidon. "But if he didn't go through with your sacrifice, your plan would be ruined, would it not?

"You will, however, have him in an awkward position. He will wish you dead but know he cannot just kill you, any more than you could kill him with impunity. He will think it safe to let the minotaur kill you, though. If he does not do the deed with his own hands, he will believe himself safe from the bloodguilt."

Amphitrite shook her head. "Such a curious human notion. Anyone reading the ancient tales of wisdom should know how foolish that is. Plotting someone's death is still murder, even if one's own hands do not do the deed."

She held out the gifts, and, embarrassed by my own preoccupation, I took them. "I thank you both with all my heart. I could not have survived this time without your help."

"Yes," said Poseidon. "That is precisely why I could help you now, and Zeus could not object. While you are here, I have one more gift to give." He placed his hand on my forehead, and I stumbled backward from the disconcerting sensation. It was as if, for a moment, the sea roared within me.

"I grant you one wish," said Poseidon. "You may use it for anything that is in my power to give, but use it wisely. If you do so, it will do you great good. Otherwise, it could lead to great evil."

He spoke the last few words sternly, as if fearing my judgment would fail me. But then he smiled at me again.

"I am well-pleased with you. Thus far, you have shown yourself to be an admirable man. May it always be so!"

"But now, I fear you must leave us," said Amphitrite. "Stay too much longer, and Minos will assume you drowned and sail away. He has stayed as long as he has only to torment your fellow captives. They will despair if you do not reappear soon."

Poseidon hugged me again, longer this time. "I do not know when we will meet again, for there are many things even the gods do not know. But I will always be with you."

"And I will always endeavor to make you proud of me," I said, meaning every word.

The Nereids led me back out, and dolphins surrounded me with their protective presence. The trip back up seemed much faster than the one down. I waved goodbye to my escort, who raised me out of the sea in a spray of water that propelled me onto the deck of Minos's ship.

Despite himself, the Cretan king backed away as if I were a dead man risen from the Underworld. "What...how—?"

"Majesty, I fetched your ring, just as you requested," I said, handing it to him. "And look at what else I have brought. These are gifts from Poseidon and Amphitrite."

Since I was condemned to death, Minos would have seized these treasures from me, anyway. By giving them to him before he had the chance to, I robbed him of another opportunity to humiliate me and made myself look generous at the same time.

Minos wanted to strike me. I could see the red anger in his eyes. But common sense prevailed, and he contented himself with taking the cloak and the crown. Instead of putting either one on, he passed them to one of his guards. Nor did he thank me, but his obvious confusion was thanks enough.

My Athenian partners in sacrifice looked at me in awe. My words had been no idle boast, and now they knew it. When we returned to Athens, the tales they would tell would dispel any remaining opposition to me as a foreigner. I would be accepted as Aegeus's heir by all.

Minos looked back at me, and his eyes narrowed. "Perhaps this is a sign from Poseidon that the sacrifices to the minotaur are no longer necessary." His tone was emotionless, though I suspected he had much more intense feelings than he was letting on. What they were, I could not say for certain.

I wouldn't have trusted anything Minos said, but the Athenians looked at him as if they dared to hope they had been reprieved.

"Theseus, I will offer you first to the creature. If he does not kill you, that will be a sign. Your companions may live if that happens."

The Athenians sagged as if they all had the same thought at the same time. Minos was not sincere. He was just playing with us.

He was also playing right into my hands. I wanted to be the first one thrown into the labyrinth but hadn't been sure exactly how to arrange that. Now the Cretan king had solved that problem. He would regret that decision—and so many others—if I had anything to say about it.

THE LABYRINTH

Minos's palace at Knossos was unimpressive compared to the palace of Poseidon, but it was larger than any human palace I had ever seen. Even the fortifications of Mycenae, rebuilt by Perseus a few generations before my time, looked small in comparison. I later learned that the Cretans were experts in using beams to reinforce their construction, which, among other things, enabled them to build taller structures.

Yet what had once symbolized Crete's wealth and power was now more ironic than the Cretans would have admitted. We were brought in through the north entrance, the one closest to the harbor, and marched through a broad hallway supported by equidistant, reddish-brown pillars. Every wall had at least one fresco, but the ones I saw mostly portrayed bulls, a representation of power—until the minotaur came along to mock that power. The frescoes were still expertly painted, but they could no longer have given Minos the same pleasure they once had.

We were marched straight south and out into the central court of the palace, with bull imagery everywhere. However, there was such a large crowd that we could see only a little of it. Every notable in the city was there to bear witness to our arrival and to jeer at us. Minos stood in the very middle, right next to the altar placed there to offer various sacrifices, particularly to Zeus. Needless to say, that was not where the minotaur received *its* sacrifices.

"Today, the tribute from Athens has arrived once more," said Minos. "Our position as the mightiest kingdom in the world is once again confirmed."

I tried hard not to laugh openly. Crete *was* strong, but it was hardly the mightiest in the world, at least not if what I'd heard about Egypt and other kingdoms of the east was true at all. Even the Greek cities, if properly united, could probably overcome Crete. But let Minos boast while he could. It would do him little good in the long run.

I stopped listening to Minos and looked around. His citizens were mostly focused on him and doing a good job of pretending to listen to his babbling. Here and there, I saw hints of skepticism, slight eye rolls when the king was looking elsewhere. I also caught a few fidgets as the speech dragged on. Poseidon was right—Minos had ruled too long. I doubted he was in any immediate danger of rebellion, but if even the handpicked audience right in front of him was not entirely impressed, I could only imagine what I'd hear if I walked around among the common people.

I caught sight of a woman, crowned and richly dressed, who could only be Minos's queen, Pasiphae. I was far enough away from her that I couldn't see the golden glint in her eye, but her beauty made me believe the story that she was the daughter of Helios, the sun god, and of Perseis, the Oceanid. That made her Medea's aunt, but, given her divine parentage, she looked no older than her niece. At first glance, she didn't look like a schemer, much less the depraved bed partner of a bull—but she did look bored. Rumor had it she had resisted marrying Minos, son of a god though he was. She had wanted to marry a god, or so the story went. As she stood there, studying the audience as I was, I wondered why she hadn't. Perfect as a sculpture, she looked as if Eros had fashioned her to be irresistible. The sunlight caught her hair and made it glisten as if Aphrodite herself had been the queen's hairdresser. What god would have turned her down?

Yet Minos, with only a slightly more prestigious lineage than my own, had married Pasiphae. Someday, I would have to take a wife, and my mother had always urged me to find a woman worthy of me.

I had to close my eyes for a moment. Perhaps gazing on such divine loveliness was a mistake. I could not afford to lose focus, and it was unlikely my wife would be a goddess. I mustn't long for what I could never have. Besides, given how Pasiphae's life had turned out, did I really want a woman like her, so easily gripped by unnatural lust? Certainly not!

When I opened my eyes again, I noticed a man who looked oddly familiar standing near Minos. While the king gloated, the other stared out into empty space, a look of intense sorrow in his eyes, as if the sacrifices to the minotaur were his own children, not strangers.

It was hard to tell if he was old or just worn out by life. His face was pale, his hair gray, his back bent. But, even though clouded by sorrow, his eyes looked alert, and his hands were almost delicate, despite their calluses. They were the hands of a craftsman, not a menial laborer.

Then I realized why he looked familiar, and the reason for his sorrow became immediately apparent. I knew his look because he resembled other sons of Metion, the usurper who overthrew my grandfather, his own brother, and seized the throne of Athens. I had heard Daedalus, a son of Metion, was in Crete, but I had not expected to see him, for rumor had it that Minos held him prisoner.

When Aegeus and his brothers had overthrown Metion, many of his family members fled, including Daedalus, even though he had played no part in his father's evil. A clever man, Daedalus was said to have been trained in various crafts by Athena herself. When he sought sanctuary in Crete, Minos welcomed him, eager to have the services of such a famous inventor.

If the tales were true, their relationship soured after the wrath of Poseidon fell upon Minos. Pasiphae tricked the inventor into swearing an oath to give her what she most desired. Then she forced him to craft the cow in which she hid to have unnatural relations with the bull Minos had so foolishly failed to sacrifice.

Minos offered to forgive Daedalus for his part in that disaster if he built the labyrinth in which to hide the minotaur. Once the inventor had complied, though, he and his young son, Icarus, were held prisoner in a tower.

But if those stories were true, what was Daedalus doing here now? I looked again at Minos, and I saw the little glances he gave to the inventor. Every time the king looked in his direction, he gave Daedalus a faint but mocking smile.

Daedalus was here to see the captives who would die. They were all young, just like his son. Was this Minos's way of reminding the inventor of his own son's mortality? My fists clenched. I longed to kill Minos, even though I knew I could not. I closed my eyes again, hoping to forget that cruel smile.

When I opened them, I noticed the two young women behind Pasiphae. How could I have missed them before? She must have been standing right in front of them at first. Now, she had shifted position, giving me a glimpse of them.

I knew Minos and Pasiphae had two daughters, both mostly of divine blood, both beautiful. I glanced at Phaedra, the younger of the two, but she was looking at the ground beneath her feet, perhaps not wishing to look into the eyes of the condemned. She looked so sad that I almost wished I had some way to comfort her, but even had we been closer, even if I could have spoken to her, what words of comfort could I possibly have offered?

When I looked away from her, my eyes fell upon Ariadne, her taller sister, and my heart started beating faster.

Truly, the stories had not done her justice. She was as beautiful as her mother. No, even more beautiful, for her expression wasn't marred by the obvious disdain her mother showed for all those around her. Not so long ago, I had beheld the peerless beauty of the queen of the sea, and I could not honestly say that Ariadne was more beautiful. It would have been nearer the truth to say she was differently beautiful. If Amphitrite was an aquatic sun, Ariadne was like the silver moon, shining all the brighter for being surrounded by darkness. Compared to her, everyone else in the courtyard, even her divine mother, was no more than a shadow, at least for that one moment when I first beheld her.

Unlike Phaedra, who feared to look upon me and my fellow captives, Ariadne looked at us without a hint of reluctance or fear. If her face showed her true feelings, she wished with all her heart to free us, as if she would run from her father's side and stand between the sacrifices and the guards, shielding us against her father's evil like a guardian goddess.

Then her eyes met mine, and I felt as if I should look away to keep from being blinded by the brightness of her gaze. Did I see an arrow flying in that bright light? Had Eros struck me through the heart with one of his irresistible shots? My heart beat faster, but not from fear or stress this time. My palms started sweating as if I were a young boy who had just discovered girls for the first time.

It was ridiculous to think that there could be any future with Ariadne. Even if she had somehow fallen in love with me, as her rapt expression suggested she had, she knew I was condemned to death. The only way I could save myself would be to defy her own father. Relationships could not be built upon such rocky soil as that.

Yet Perigune had cared for me, perhaps even loved me, despite seeing me kill her father, despite beholding me drenched in his blood.

I tried to shove these thoughts aside. Athena had warned me of the need for balance in my life, the importance of not making love my only priority. But the thoughts clung to me like gentle spider webs, seemingly weak but surprisingly difficult to be free of. What did it really matter? I was just daydreaming. Even if Ariadne and I shared the greatest love that ever man and woman shared, we would never have the chance to be together.

Minos, still wrapped up in promoting his own glory, didn't notice the looks exchanged between Ariadne and me. But Pasiphae did. She took a couple of steps toward Minos, cutting off my view of her daughters, and glared at me. But I was not afraid of her. She could not use her magic to kill me, for then I could not serve my purpose as an offering to her bloodthirsty monster of a son. She didn't know what might happen if the sacrifice was not fulfilled any more than Minos did.

At last, Minos's speech came to an end, and he ordered the guards to take us to our cells. Pasiphae made sure to position herself in such a way that Ariadne and I could not exchange glances again.

Minos's palace had no real cells in it, but he apparently didn't trust the prison of Knossos to keep us secure. Instead, we were lodged in the storage rooms just inside the palace's western wall. Each had no window and only one door. The doors all opened on a long corridor that guards could easily patrol. Even one guard would probably have been enough to prevent escape. There was no hidden way to flee, even if someone could pick the door lock.

I knew I was to be the first one sent to the minotaur, so I was not surprised when I heard the sound of a key in the lock. However, I was shocked when the door swung open, and Ariadne was standing there like a dream made flesh. Or was I dreaming? No. I could feel my rapid pulse, and my breath caught in my throat. This was no dream.

"Princess, what brings you here?" I tried to sound calm, but my voice betrayed my excitement.

She put a finger to her lips and pulled the door almost closed behind her. "We must speak quietly," she whispered. "I persuaded a guard to let me see you, but he remains nearby."

"I am impressed by your...persuasive abilities," I said, though, in truth, that was not what most impressed me.

She smiled. "We do not normally have princes offered as tribute. It was not hard to convince the guards I had been sent by my father to see if I could extract some valuable information from you.

"You do not really intend to let the minotaur kill you," she said as if she knew what was in my heart.

I hesitated. She seemed as enthralled by Eros as I was, but what if she were just pretending? What if she really were sent here by her father to find out what I was up to?

It mattered not. If Minos suspected me, I probably couldn't carry out my plan, anyway. Besides, I wanted to trust her—to do far more than trust her.

"I intend to kill it."

"And so perhaps you could, by the look of you. But what then? How would you escape from the labyrinth once you had done the deed? None but Daedalus knows how to navigate the place."

I was embarrassed to say I had no idea. I had assumed that the labyrinth's reputation was exaggerated, that it might fool some dumb beast but not someone like me.

"Athena has told me that I will be able to prevail."

Ariadne laughed. I wanted nothing more at that moment than to hear that laugh all the rest of my life.

"Athena told Daedalus a lot of things, too—or so he says. Look at how well that worked out for him.

"Don't worry, though. As you may have seen, my father parades him around on public occasions. I was able to speak with him before he was locked up again. As you can imagine, his loyalty to my father is...not what it used to be."

She held up a ball of yarn I hadn't noticed when she had first come in. "Conceal this in your clothing. Once you are inside, attached one end to something. Daedalus says there are lots of sharp edges that will serve. Then unwind the ball as you go. Once you have killed the minotaur, just follow the string back out."

I took the yarn and looked at it skeptically. "What if it comes loose? What if the minotaur tears while we battle, or worse, finds it and breaks it before encountering me?"

"By all accounts, the beast is too stupid to even notice the yarn. But just in case, Daedalus tells me this yarn is blessed by Athena. You can rely on it."

I raised an eyebrow. "Weren't you just talking about how little Daedalus could rely on her?"

"The ways of the gods are unknowable by mortals," she said, her smile undercutting the mock-solemnity of her words. "Athena will perhaps rescue Daedalus at some future point. But is not this yarn something like the aid she promised you? And is it not better than the nothing you had before I came?"

"I cannot argue with that, Princess."

"There is one more matter we must discuss," said Ariadne. "My father must never learn of the yarn. Gather it up as you return to the entrance. I assured Daedalus that Minos would never find out what he has done."

"I will do as you ask," I replied. "Daedalus deserves better than death."

"But I must ask more of you than just that," she said slowly. "I can distract the guards when you return to rescue your fellow Athenians. I can also find all of you a safe way to get back to your ship. However, my father will learn what I have done. I will no longer be safe here. I need to ask you to take me with you when you depart."

"Do you not…know how I feel? Can you not see it in my eyes?"

"I dared to hope, Theseus, but hope can be such a fragile thing."

I took her in my arms. "Silly as it sounds, I loved you from the moment I saw you. I promise to take you to safety."

"To Athens?" she asked, pressing closer to me.

"Yes, to Athens—to be my queen if that is what you want."

"I thought you would never ask. Of course, that is what I want."

I longed to make love to her that instant, but there was a noise in the hall, and she slipped away from my arms. "Do not forget what I have said." Then she was gone like a ray of moon6light vanishing when a cloud passes over.

I barely managed to get the yarn beneath my tunic before I heard the sound of a key in the lock again. Four guards entered and gestured for me to follow them. Putting on an expression that was both calm and grim, I did what they wanted. The last thing I wanted was to attract attention.

I had half-expected Minos to watch me being put in the labyrinth, but I was relieved that he hadn't shown up. Perhaps he didn't want another interaction with one of Poseidon's favorites.

I should have asked Ariadne where the entrance to the labyrinth was. I would have been less surprised when I was led back to the same central courtyard where the crowd had gathered to gawk at us earlier. Right next to the altar, the guards rolled back a stone I hadn't noticed earlier. Beneath the stone was a grate, which they raised.

"In here," said one of the guards, gesturing to me. I had never imagined finding the labyrinth in such a place, but it made sense that it would be here. Inside the palace, the entrance would always be guarded. Its placement right next to the altar suggested Minos was trying to pretend what he was doing was some kind of religious rite, even though the gods abhorred human sacrifices.

The entrance was wide enough for me to slide right in, but Daedalus had also designed it to minimize the fall. I dropped just far enough to be completely in. From there, I had to crouch, but only for a moment, and then I was in a corridor I could comfortably walk down.

I heard the guards slamming the metal grate shut and rolling the stone over it, cutting off the light from outside. However, Daedalus had positioned lamps every so often down the length of the corridor.

As I tied the yarn around the first one, I noticed it was attached to the wall. Were slaves sent down here to refill it? That seemed dangerous, to say the least, and the last thing Minos would have wanted would be to draw the minotaur closer to the entrance. But no, Daedalus had seen to that as well. There was just enough separation between the body of the lamp and the labyrinth wall for me to see a little bit of the pipe that projected out from the wall and attached to the lamp. Oil was pumped from somewhere else to feed the flame. Ingenious!

As much as I admired Daedalus's handiwork, it didn't distract me from where I was. Even this close to the entrance, the place smelled of death—rotting flesh, dry blood. Worse, I could feel the presence of the men and women who had died here. Their spirits, unblessed by the proper funeral rites, would never be able to find even the shadowy peace the Underworld offered. I had heard their families performed rites and offered prayers for them, not just once but regularly. But without a body —without a way to get an obol to Charon for safe passage across the river that bordered the land of the dead—were such rites effective? The caress of cold fingers in the breezeless hallway told me they were not.

"I will avenge you," I whispered. "I do not know if that will bring you peace or not. But when I return to Athens, I will add my prayers to those of your families. Surely, the gods will have mercy at some point."

If the ghosts heard me, they didn't respond. But I had not expected thanks from them. Knowing I was doing all I could for them was enough.

Aside from being haunted and smelling foul, the labyrinth was huge. As I walked, untwining my thread as I went, I wondered if it filled the space beneath the palace. Perhaps it was even bigger than that. I walked for a long time but had no way to measure exactly how long. All I knew was that, though I wasn't able to move in a straight line, I never crossed my thread.

I heard the minotaur before I saw it. Its roar echoed through the dismal halls, making it impossible for me to tell from which direction it was coming.

Though I was being as quiet as I could, it either smelled me or sensed me, for its roar grew louder. I still couldn't judge its direction, but I knew that louder meant closer.

The corridors of the labyrinth were all bordered by unbroken walls— no doors to hide behind, no alcoves to lurk in. There was no way to take the beast by surprise. My only hope was to avoid being surprised myself.

As soon as I reached a relatively long stretch of corridor, I stopped midway down it. That way, I had a clear view in either direction. When the minotaur struck, I would be ready.

Or so I thought. I did see the monster when it turned the corner, but the sight of it froze me for a second. The tales had given me a rough idea of its appearance, but nothing could have prepared me for coming face to face with it.

It was taller than the average man and far more muscular. Had it not been filthy, its body could have been mistaken for that of an athlete. From the neck up, though, it was all bull. No, worse. No natural bull would have eyes so filled with hatred. Dirty as it was, its horns gleamed in the faint lamplight as if they had been polished like fine swords.

It charged with a deafening roar. I waited as long as I dared, then dodged. It proved itself just as stupid as I had hoped. Instead of anticipating that I might move, it seemed surprised. Its momentum carried it straight into the wall with an enormous thud.

However, the impact, which would have stunned an ordinary man, did not even slow the minotaur. The creature spun to face me and roared again. At such close quarters, I realized how the sound was unlike what a bull would make.

Overcoming the beast barehanded seemed impossible. As I dodged again, I thought about what I could use. Now would have been a good time for Athena to offer a specific suggestion, but she didn't.

The minotaur struck the wall again. I wondered for a second how it ever managed to kill anyone, but the answer was obvious. Most people were not as fast as I. They couldn't keep dodging. But even I couldn't do it indefinitely —and even cracking its skull against the wall didn't seem to slow the minotaur. Another crash. Then another. Eventually, it would wear me down.

The bull of Marathon had calmed for me. Could the minotaur be made to do the same?

"Nephew!" I called as I kept running. "Is this any way to greet your kinsman?"

Much to my surprise, the creature hesitated. Perhaps it had never heard human speech. Screams of terror could be all that had ever greeted it in the labyrinth.

"The bull who was your father was my brother," I said. "That makes you my nephew. Can you not sense it?"

I could. It might have been my imagination, but, despite all the filth and odors of rot, I caught a whiff of sea air, much as I had smelled around other descendants of Poseidon.

The minotaur tilted its head slightly. Was it trying to understand me, or did it understand, and was it trying to tell whether I spoke the truth or not?

While it spent a few seconds pondering, so did I. One of its wall strikes had damaged one of the lamps. I could see a tiny stream of olive oil trickling down the wall.

Long ago, when Athena competed with Poseidon to be the patron god of Athens, he made a spring bubble up on the Acropolis, and she made an olive tree sprout from the stony ground. Was olive oil a hint? It was flammable.

I ripped off a piece of my tunic. The minotaur, its concentration broken, snarled and charged again. I feinted in one direction, then ran in the other, toward the tiny stream of oil. As before, the minotaur didn't adjust fast enough and missed me completely.

With my left hand, I rubbed the tunic strip in oil. With the other, I pulled the broken lamp away from the wall. Oil now gushed rather than trickled.

As the minotaur charged again, I flung a handful of oil at it. The fluid struck it in the face, and some of it got in its eyes, enraging it but causing its charge to falter. Not knowing exactly what to do, it rubbed its eyes.

I splashed it with fluid three more times, and it kept fussing with its eyes. Never before had it been attacked in this way, and it didn't know enough to understand the real danger.

Running to the nearest connected lamp, I invoked Athena as I set my tunic strip on fire, then threw it at the beast. Its bull hair, soaked with olive oil, caught fire.

It had the animal fear of fire but not the human understanding of how to put it out. Its roar became a scream as it beat ineffectually at the flames with its hands.

Taking advantage of its distraction, I wiped my hands on my tunic, drying them enough to be able to charge the beast and get a good grip on its neck. Under normal conditions, it should have been able to tear my hands away, but it continued to beat at the fire, which, luckily for me, burned in the hair on its head but hadn't yet spread to its neck. Its distraction gave me time to get a good grip.

The beast's neck was thicker than a man's, but my strength was sufficient to squeeze hard enough to cut off the blood supply to its head. The burning pain kept the beast flailing around for a while, but its struggles weakened as its brain felt the effects of being deprived of blood.

Just before it lost consciousness, though, it managed to wheeze one word out.

Kinsman.

ESCAPE

SQUEEZING the remaining life out of him was easy enough. Then I fled without stopping to put out the flames. Let them be his pyre if the gods wished it so.

I ran fast, not because I was afraid of the fire, not even because I could no longer stand the stench of the place.

I fled because its word, perhaps the first it had ever spoken, haunted me more than I had expected.

Despite his seeming lack of wit, he had the power of speech. Not only that, but he knew me from the bond of Poseidon's blood between us.

Was there human emotion behind that word? Was it a plea—or an expression of disbelief that one kinsman could inflict such pain on another?

I'd been assuming that killing him was the only way to save my fellow Athenians. But what if I was wrong? What if I could have communicated with him, persuaded him to abstain from human flesh?

Of course, that notion was ridiculous. There was too much beast in him, too much divine malice, for him to ever become tame.

Yet he had called me kinsman. And in my fevered imaginings, I thought his tone suggested that he truly understood the word. Some of the killers I had slain on the way to Athens were kinsmen as well. But they had chosen evil over good. Had the minotaur ever been offered a choice? If not, how could I be sure what he would have chosen had I given him the chance?

Rattled as I was, I remembered my promise to Ariadne. Despite the smell of burned flesh that now permeated that part of the labyrinth, I had to go back, pick up the ball of yarn, and use it to rewind the string that was my guide. There would be no clue left behind to betray Daedalus.

I reached the entrance, unhooked the yarn from the first lamp, and shoved the ball into what was left of my tunic. As I did so, I pondered how to get out.

The shaft I had come down was rough enough to provide handholds. Daedalus must have made it so to allow someone to enter and then climb back out if need be. So far, so good. But what was I to do about the grate that sealed the exit? It had taken four men to lift the stone off the top of it.

I remembered the task Aegeus had left me to prove my manhood—lifting the stone off the gifts he had left me. It was a smaller stone, though, not as heavy as this one. But surely, if I had not been able to push hard enough to raise the grate, even with the stone on top of it, Athena would have realized the problem.

With some difficulty, I got to the top of the shaft and managed to brace myself with my legs and press both hands against the grate.

I pushed as hard as I could. My muscles strained, but the stone didn't shift.

I was the son of Poseidon, the cousin of Heracles. I would not be defeated by such a small obstacle!

I pushed even harder, praying to Poseidon and Athena as I did so. I pushed with both my arms and my legs. Sweat dripped down my brow. My arms felt as if they would break.

I felt the stone shift a little. That gave me the willpower to continue, even though my arms were screaming in protest. It shifted a few finger widths more.

I could raise the grate a little, but not nearly far enough to crawl out.

The pain in my arms had spread to my shoulders and neck. But I kept going. I had no other choice.

The only thing working in my favor was that Minos had posted no guards to watch the exit to the labyrinth. He had not foreseen the possibility that someone might survive the minotaur, let alone find his way back to the grate.

I had to choke back a cry of victory when at last, the stone shifted enough to allow me to raise the grate and crawl out. It was late at night, and no one was around, but if I made too much noise, I still might draw unwanted attention.

I crept back to the long corridor to which the storage rooms connected. No one was standing guard. Ariadne was there alone, just as she had promised. She held out a hand to me, and I could see keys glittering in her palm.

"You did it!" I whispered.

"Did you doubt I could?" she asked, her tone playful. "I didn't doubt that you would best the minotaur. By comparison, manipulating the guards was child's play."

Beautiful and intelligent! What a fine queen she would make—if I could get us out of here. We unlocked the makeshift cells, liberating all the Athenians, who could scarcely believe what was happening.

"My prince, you have worked a miracle!" whispered one of them.

"With much help from the gods—and Princess Ariadne," I said.

"Come," she said once all of them were free. "Even I can't get us out of one of the main entrances, but I know a secret way." At her direction, we moved quietly to the northernmost storage room, which hadn't been used to house prisoners. The other men and I moved crates in the northwest corner of the room. Barely visible in the dust beneath them was a trapdoor, bolted from the inside.

"Another hint from Daedalus," said Ariadne. "No one knows the architecture of this palace better than he. In case the palace was about to fall to attackers, the royal family could escape via this tunnel. It was dug so long ago that I doubt even my father remembers it is here. It goes clear out almost to the harbor. When we emerge, we will be just a short distance from your ship."

Unlike the labyrinth, this forgotten tunnel wasn't lit, but Ariadne had brought a lamp with her. She and I led the way, she with confident step and I somewhat more tentatively. The joy of freeing the other captives had made me forget the minotaur for a moment, but being underground again brought those memories back vividly. I could not show how shaken I was, though. It would be all too easy for my companions to panic, and then all might be lost. We needed to keep our heads.

The tunnel was very narrow, barely wide enough for two to walk abreast, but at least there was no danger of anyone getting lost, even in the semi-darkness.

"It's well-maintained for a tunnel no one knows about," I said, not wanting to continue in silence now that we were well away from the palace. I needed something to think about besides the minotaur's last word.

"It should have collapsed long ago," said Ariadne. "Not that there is any danger," she added when the Athenians started fidgeting. "See how smooth the walls are—no cracks, no holes. Not a dirt clod out of place. Remember that the island is sacred to Zeus. It is his birthplace if one believes the old tales. In any case, Daedalus thinks the tunnel was blessed by him. Seeing it, I have little doubt that the inventor is right to think Zeus has laid his hand upon it."

Touched by a god? It could have been. I knew all too well how much of a role gods played in the world.

By the time we emerged, it was nearly dawn.

"We have to hurry," said Ariadne. "The slaves will be at work soon, and someone is bound to notice that the entrance to the labyrinth has been disturbed. It will not take my father long to realize what has happened.

Ariadne had to extinguish the lamp, but our modest Athenian ship was still easy to distinguish from the bigger, more impressive Cretan vessels that dominated the harbor. Normally, the ship from Athens left after the tribute was delivered, but this time I had told the captain to wait. I could see questions in his eyes that I could not answer, but fortunately, he did as he was told.

When we arrived, the eyes so troubled by questions were now filled with joy. The crew had restocked the provisions they needed, and so we were able to leave immediately.

"What of King Minos?" asked the captain as the harbor disappeared into the pre-dawn grayness behind us. "He can pursue us with much faster ships." His words chilled the party. The Athenians had not thought to question how we would get away. However, I had already pondered that question.

"Minos will expect us to head back to Athens by the quickest route —west along the coast, then north to Athens," I said. "Let us head straight north from here instead. We have a head start, and by the time they realize we didn't sail directly back to Athens, we will have had time to conceal ourselves among the islands north of here."

The captain frowned. "Minos's influence is strong among the islanders. Many of those islands trade heavily with Crete. Some even have Cretan colonies. An Athenian ship would be noticed. It would not be so easy to hide then."

"On the other hand, the wind is northerly now," I said. "Without oars, our travel west will be slow—and we can easily be spotted from the coast. Minos will be able to snatch us up at his leisure before we can reach the point at which we can sail straight north to Athens.

"Minos can sound the alarm through Crete much more rapidly than he can get the word out to the islands north of here. And if he is not expecting us to go that way, perhaps he will not do so immediately. If we make good enough time, the islanders will have no particular reason to notice us, much less attack us."

The captain nodded. "There is wisdom in what you say. But what will happen when we reach Athens? Will Minos make war upon the city to have us back?"

"You have nothing to fear in that regard, Captain," said Ariadne. He had been too busy to pay much attention to her before, but now he looked at her closely.

"I recognize you," he said, turning pale. "You are Princess Ariadne." He turned to me. "My prince, you...you have stolen the princess of Crete. Minos will make war on us for sure!"

"He will not," said Ariadne. "At least, he will not if he takes the suggestion in a letter I left for him in my room."

"What?" I was confused. What letter could possibly keep Minos's wrath from descending on us?

"There was not time to tell you everything before. I anticipated the possibility that Minos would try to recapture you and take me back for punishment. But he will see the wisdom in my words and choose a different course.

"You would not have heard much about this in Athens, but my father's popularity has been waning lately. Don't be fooled by that public display he put on when he was parading you captives around. There are Cretans who know him for the tyrant he is becoming. There are those who question his savage vengeance against Athens as well. And many wonder why he did not just kill the minotaur instead of feeding it innocent people. Killing someone in war is one thing. But shedding blood in such a way? It is like human sacrifice, which all the gods abhor.

"Minos has faced no revolt so far in part because Zeus so obviously favors him. But when you surprised him with your display of Poseidon's favor, that story was carried back by the sailors on his ship. It spread like wildfire throughout Knossos. Many people took it as a sign.

"If Minos had been able to announce your death by minotaur, he could have put an end to any talk of signs—but instead, you killed the creature. That he could conceal, but there is no way to conceal the fact that you freed the prisoners and fled with them. Taking me with you makes the situation even worse."

"Pardon me for interrupting," said the captain. "But is not what you have just said the exact reason Minos must pursue us? How else is he to silence those who believe he has lost Zeus's favor?"

"A reasonable question," said Ariadne. "But consider the circumstances. My father knows that Theseus has the favor of Poseidon. Is it at all likely that a pursuing navy would be allowed to reach us? Even if it did, would Poseidon watch his favorite carried away in chains and do nothing?"

Despite my recent meeting with Poseidon, I could easily imagine him doing just that, for the ways of the gods still puzzled me. But now was not the time to say so.

"At the very least, even if Poseidon allowed such things to happen, they would anger him. Minos has tasted the wrath of the sea god already

—over a bull the king should have sacrificed but didn't. Will he be eager for another taste of that wrath if anything happens to Theseus? Certainly not!

"But I have suggested to him a way to save face without risking the anger of Poseidon. Minos will say he saw in you a chance to be rid of the minotaur. He did not have permission to slay Poseidon's beast, but he knew you could obtain such permission."

"You expect him to say that killing the minotaur was his idea?" I asked.

"I do indeed. He agreed to free you and the other captives in exchange, but because of excessive modesty, you left instead of staying to receive his public thanks."

"And how do we explain why you came with me?"

"He will say I am his ambassador, gone to Athens to negotiate a more sensible and humane tribute. Or I am more...depending upon your will, Prince Theseus."

"My will?" She was several steps ahead of me. I couldn't even pretend otherwise.

"I would not presume to rely solely on our hasty conversation before, but in my letter to my father, I left open the possibility that, if you chose, I might become your wife. Settling a dispute with a marriage alliance is a common enough practice. It is also a way for Minos to show the people of Crete that he is willing to give up his excessive vengeance.

"Of course, if I have misunderstood your intent—"

I took her in my arms. "Nothing would please me more than for you to be my wife." I kissed her more passionately than would normally have been proper for such an occasion, but I didn't care. Neither did the Athenians, both tribute and crew, who had taken a liking to her. The ones she had helped save looked at her as if she were a gift sent from the gods. They cheered us on. Even the captain, so worried a few minutes before, smiled.

"A granddaughter of Zeus indeed!" he said. "And, judging by her masterful plan, blessed by Athena as well."

Her plan *was* excellent. Of that, I had no doubt. But I could not help but wonder whether Minos would react as Ariadne expected. She knew him well, but perhaps her love for her father influenced her judgment. Just to be on the safe side, we continued our indirect route back to Athens. The captain, calmed by her words, did not object.

The wind, blowing strongly north, favored such a plan. We passed the small island of Anaphe sooner than I expected. I took both the wind and the island as favorable signs, for Apollo had revealed Anaphe to the Argonauts as a place of refuge just a few years ago. As we passed by, I said a silent prayer to the radiant god, and I was careful also to thank Poseidon for the calm sea and wind, and Athena for her guidance. We had come too far for me to risk losing all we had accomplished by inadvertently slighting some god.

As soon as I was done praying, the captain, anxious once again, caught my attention. "We should have passed by Thera, not Anaphe, my prince. The wind is blowing more to the northeast than I realized."

"What do you recommend we do about that?" I asked.

"If we continue to just follow the wind, we will pass close by Amorgos. One of its principal cities is Minoa—a rather frightening name, don't you think?"

"It suggests Cretan settlement," I replied. "Perhaps a Cretan naval presence. Even if Minos reacts differently than Ariadne anticipated, though, could a message reach Amorgos before we do?"

"I would rather not take the chance, my prince. If I make our course slightly more northwest, we can keep our distance from Amorgos and reach Naxos quickly. That's where I thought we would arrive, and there is a secluded cove on the southeast side of the island where we are unlikely to be spotted. The men need rest, I think, for this has been a more...stressful return trip than they are used to."

I nodded. "It is a small crew, and they can only rest in shifts while we are at sea. Even if Minos is pursuing us, we cannot outrun him by exhausting your faithful men."

The captain wasted no time in steering us toward Naxos. He had considerable help, for the wind changed direction just enough to speed us on toward the sacred island of Dionysus. Another sign? We must still have been following the best course—or so I told myself.

The cove where we dropped anchor did seem secluded. Indeed, had I not known of the flourishing settlements in the northwestern part of the island, I would have thought the island completely uninhabited.

This respite gave Ariadne and me a chance to be alone—there was no such thing as privacy on such a small, cramped ship. The captain, crew, and the rescued Athenians all stayed on board. Particularly in the case of the Athenians, I think they feared to leave the ship before it reached Athens.

I worried a little myself about being too far separated from the ship, but Ariadne encouraged me. She was even more eager for privacy than I was.

"My father is not pursuing us. Hard he may be—cruel even, sometimes. And definitely self-centered. But he is not stupid."

We lay together on the beach, just out of sight of the ship. I longed for Ariadne but did not wish her to yield to me simply because I was her rescuer. I did not have to wait long, for she was at least as avid for me as I was for her. In no time, we were making love.

This was not the fumbling of two innocents that I had shared with Perigune. Nor, thank the gods, did I have the guilt of having shed the blood of my partner's father to distract me. Ariadne and I loved each other as if we were destined to be together, as if Aphrodite had finally given up her feud with the family of Aegeus and blessed our union.

If only that had been the case!

LOSS

ONCE WE WERE BOTH SATISFIED, we slept. I found myself in a vivid dream and shuddered. Vivid dreams before had always signaled the visit from some god or goddess. Was it Athena coming to warn me that Ariadne was wrong, that Minos's flagship was only minutes away from the cove?

I sensed the setting of the dream was Naxos, but I was far away from the beach and Ariadne. I was in a grove of lemon trees. The random way in which they grew suggested this was a natural grove, not a man-made orchard. The grove was given variety by olive trees that grew here and there among the lemons, but what struck me most was the wild profusion of grapevines. Like the orchard, the vineyard was not manmade. Its growth was not entirely natural, though. It did not take me long to spot the god whose very presence threw the vines into such frenzied growth.

Dionysus looked younger than I. His features were soft, almost feminine, but there was power in his eyes. Just looking into them for a second made me feel as if I had downed a goblet of wine uncut by water. Those eyes called me to celebration—or to madness. I did my best to try to focus on something else.

On the god's head rested a crown crafted from ivy vines and leaves. In his right hand, he held a thyrsus, a long staff with a pinecone at its tip. In his left hand, he held a goblet. Its silver sparkled in the moonlight, and the wine within it gleamed.

Not being sure how to behave with this particular god, I fell to my knees. One thought filled my head.

What could he possibly want with me?

"Fear not," said Dionysus, his voice soft but deep. "I wish you no harm, Theseus. Rise and face me, cousin, for we have much to discuss."

I got slowly to my feet. "Oh, Great One, what do you have to discuss with one such as I?"

"Matters of great joy—and great sorrow. You have misinterpreted your fate, but I can help you correct the mistake before it is too late."

"Should I not have killed the minotaur?" I asked, confused. "Athena and Poseidon both assured me—"

"I do not come about the minotaur," said Dionysus. "Everyone is well rid of that beast. No, I come about Ariadne."

The rest of my body remained still as death, but my heart shuddered in my chest. "What...what do you mean?"

"She is not meant for you. You were supposed to bring her here for me."

"But...but I love her, and she loves me."

Now there was sympathy in his enthralling eyes—but there was also a hint of wrath. "She believes herself in love with you because you rescued her. You believe you love her because she is beautiful and perhaps because your lust has not been sated since you and Perigune parted ways. A man should not so long deny his urges, Theseus. It always leads to trouble."

I knew without having to ask that I was at one of those forks in the road Athena had spoken of. The darkness around me was alive with fate, patiently waiting for me to save myself—or doom myself.

My love for Ariadne was no mere infatuation over her beauty, even less animal lust. It was a true love, forged by our souls rather than our bodies. Of that, I was certain. But even if I could somehow set that love aside, how could I break the promise I had made to Ariadne? I had pledged to marry her. Did my word count for nothing now?

On the other hand, a mortal defying a god had never won, not even

175

once. I might refuse him now, in this dream, but in the end, he would have what he wanted.

Nor was that the only problem. Athena had warned me of Aphrodite's wiles and the possibility that she was still hostile to my family. Could my love for Ariadne be the work of the wrathful goddess?

There was no question—I should yield to the will of Dionysus. But in my heart, I felt a deep sense of wrongness. What if the wine god was wrong, and it was I, not he, who was destined to be with Ariadne?

"I am pledged to her, and she to me. Great as you are, Dionysus, I must respectfully decline your request."

I heard something from the surrounding darkness. I wasn't sure whether it was a laugh or a shout. Either way, I had given fate its answer. I had set my foot upon a path and could not now retrace my steps.

"Think of Ariadne," said Dionysus. Just like his eyes, his voice had the ability to convey contradictory emotions at once. His tone was calm and reasonable, almost like Athena's. Yet beneath that veneer of reason, I heard frenzy as well. I could not help but think of the Maenads, the mad women of Dionysus, who had torn to bits more than one man for defying their god.

"I have Zeus's permission to make her a god. She will become immortal. Would you deny her such a gift?"

"I...no, I would not. If she prefers to go with you and become a goddess, I will not stand in her way. That's how much I love her. But the choice must be hers, not yours. If she chooses you and immortality, you can have her with my blessing. If she chooses me and mortality, I trust you will give her to me with your blessing."

Dionysus shook his head sadly. "I will not force myself upon her. I will not have to. You see, she has chosen me already."

"She is an honorable woman. She would have told me—"

"She would have told you if she remembered. Her story is somewhat...unusual."

"Tell me," I said. My tone was more abrupt than a mortal should have used with a god. The nearby vines twitched as if they wanted to grab me and strangle me, but Dionysus only looked at me with eyes that hinted at ecstasy or madness.

"You know that Minos has sat several generations upon the throne of

Crete. Some of his children are long dead. One of them was a daughter named Ariadne."

"He gave two children the same name?"

"The second Ariadne was not born until the first was dead. But let us not get lost in the details. The important part is that the first Ariadne was born to be my bride. Do not cast such a judgmental look at me. I mean *bride*, not bed partner. I know that most gods do not take formal wives, and those that do are often disloyal to them. But I am not as other gods are, for I was born twice."

"How can anyone, even a god, be born twice?" I asked.

"So full of questions!" said Dionysus. He chuckled, and the vines swayed gently at the sound. "No wonder Athena likes you so well. My first birth came about not by accident, but by the will of Zeus himself. It was the key part of a plan by the king of the gods to avert the dire prophecy that he would one day be overthrown by one of his own sons.

"He wanted to prevent not only his own downfall, but also the dire consequences that a war among gods would have in the mortal world. He reasoned that, if he abdicated voluntarily, he could not be overthrown, and the prophecy would be nullified."

"Can even the king of the gods avoid his fate?" I asked. I shouldn't have kept interrupting, but I was having trouble making sense of what he was saying.

Dionysus smiled, but it was not the approving smile of Athena. It was more like the smile of one whom the gods have struck mad. His eyes looked less conflicted, more manic, than they had just a second before.

"Probably not—but that has never stopped anyone from trying, has it? In any case, he reasoned that selecting one of his sons to be his heir would create conflicts of its own. Instead, he wanted to create a new son, one so obviously worthy that the other gods would accept the heir as king when the time came.

"For the mother of this new child, Zeus chose Persephone, a goddess who embodies both spring and fall, life and death. He came to her in the form of a dragon and put more power into the lovemaking than he had ever done before.

"Thus, I was born—the first time. I am told horns sprouted from my head to emphasize my special nature and that, even as an infant, I could touch the thunderbolts of Zeus, a sure sign that I was chosen one day to wield them.

"Yet fate is not so easily thwarted. Some of the titans, the earlier powers who rules before the Olympians, escaped their confinement in Tartarus. Some say Hera helped them, but if so, she was a tool of fate."

"In a surprise attack, they killed me—"

"But I thought gods could not die."

"We can't—not completely, anyway. But they tore my young body to shreds and then ate me. Zeus, who had come belatedly to my rescue, incinerated them with his thunderbolts, leaving only ashes behind.

"Not much could have been done with the ashes. Luckily for me, Athena found my heart, the one piece the titans had not yet devoured. She carried it to Zeus, who made it into a potion for Princess Semele of Thebes to drink. Hence it was that she became pregnant. The body in her womb was different from my own, but it was still my soul within it. Zeus had contrived a way for me to be born again.

"But fate was not done with him—or me—yet. Zeus was living with Semele as if she were his wife. Hera, seeing this as an affront to her marriage with Zeus, disguised herself as a mortal and visited Semele.

"She worked hard to plant doubts in Semele's heart. 'Your husband says he is Zeus, does he? Well, all men say such things. It is but bragging.' When Semele protested, Hera suggested putting him to the test. 'Get him to swear an oath on the River Styx, a pledge so powerful that even the gods may not break it, to grant you a wish. After he swears the oath, ask him to show himself to you in his full glory. Only then will you know for sure.'

"Semele faced a choice then. She could have trusted her husband and forgotten Hera's words. Had she done so, then all would have been well. But instead, she chose the path of mistrust, tricking the unsuspecting Zeus into the oath that would destroy her.

"When she made her wish, Zeus begged her to relent. He told her that no mortal could endure seeing him in his full glory. But she would not yield, even though she knew in her heart that he spoke the truth. She made him reveal himself to banish any possible doubt—and banished herself instead.

"But Zeus, distraught though he was, was ready when Semele burst into flames. He could not save her, but he rescued me from her blazing womb, and, reshaping the natural order of things by sheer force of will, he implanted me in his own body, where I could safely grow until it was time to be born."

Some of the story I had heard before, but the frenetic way Dionysus told it made even the familiar parts sound like total madness.

"After I was born, I grew quickly to manhood, as gods do. Short as that time was, it gave Zeus time to reconsider. Having seen the catastrophes that his plan to abdicate had led to, Zeus decided that he would remain as king, at least for a while. I happily accepted his decision. I had no desire to rule the gods. No, I preferred to play a different role. Having come as close to death as a god can and having both life and death within my nature, I sought to change the way death operated in the mortal world. I wanted mortals to have the opportunity to be reborn, just as I was."

Now I had no doubt—Dionysus was insane. Death was death. There was no changing it.

"My biggest obstacle was Hades, of course. He rules the Underworld with an iron hand, and he will not willingly let go of any mortal soul once its body has died. Zeus could order him to make exceptions in particular cases, but even he would not go so far as to compel Hades to change the entire process. That would have broken the agreement by which Zeus and his brothers divided the government of the world and drew lots to see which of them would govern each portion. As a result of that drawing, Zeus rules the sky, Poseidon the sea, and Hades the Underworld. Zeus is the ultimate authority, but he is constrained to allow Poseidon and Hades some freedom in the way they rule their own domains.

"No, if I wanted to change the nature of death, I would need to win the approval of Hades to do it. That would be like a mortal trying to persuade a mountain to move itself. Still, I had to try."

Crazy Dionysus might be, but it was hard to listen to him without finding his story compelling. Despite myself, I wanted to believe what he was saying. I wanted to believe that people could return from death.

"I met Hades, but not under the best circumstances. Zeus had sent me to the Underworld to liberate Semele so that she could return to the living and then become a goddess. Hades acknowledged Zeus's authority but dragged out the fulfillment of the order as long as he possibly could.

"It would have been easy to show my irritation, but instead, I pretended not to notice. I engaged Hades in conversation, asking questions about everything I saw. That was a risk because I might have annoyed him that way—but I didn't.

"As lord of the Underworld, Hades receives few willing visitors. Even the gods have little desire to enter that gloomy place, and Hades, infected over the centuries by that gloom, has little desire to leave it. He did not even bother to keep a residence on Olympus, as all the gods of high enough stature do.

"But the social part of him was not as dead as the mortals he governed. His answers to my questions were brief and grudging at first, but as time passed, they became slightly less so. By the time I departed with my mother, Hades was, if not my friend, at least not my enemy.

"His stony expression changed little when I visited him again, though I think he was surprised. I brought wine and managed to get myself an invitation to dine with him and Persephone.

"I could not very well flaunt the fact that she was my first mother, but she knew, and she quickly became my ally. Of all the immortals, she is the one with the best chance of persuading Hades of anything. He loves her as much as he is capable of loving anyone—not much, but perhaps enough for my purposes.

"I also had an ally in my half-brother, Hermes, who, as you know, guides the souls of the dead to the Underworld. As a result, Hermes sees more of Hades than most of the gods do. Hades isn't his friend, either, but the king of the dead appreciates Hermes's efficiency in performing his tasks.

"Hermes had long considered the Underworld too static a place. He loves both magic and movement, and the dreariness of the place to which he brought mortal souls concerned him.

"When the Underworld first came into existence, all souls were left to float aimlessly, unable to talk, unable even to think, except in the most instinctive ways. At the request of the other gods, Hades added to the original Underworld a place of eternal punishment for those mortals who had most grievously offended the gods. Hades endowed these mortals with enough sense to realize their tortured condition.

"But if it made sense to punish the sinners, it also made sense to reward the virtuous. Hermes was one of many gods who urged Hades to create the Elysian Fields for those mortals who were worthy. Logical as the suggestion was, it took a great deal of effort to get Hades to accept it. He did, though. In the process, he removed the immutability of the Underworld that had already been weakened by the creation of the Place of Punishment. Where one change could be made, another might be made as well. Where two changes have been made? There anything might happen.

"It was not hard to get Hermes invited to dinner along with me, and together we worked with Persephone to move Hades subtly in the direction of allowing at least some mortals to be reborn.

"Hades was cold to the idea at first—colder than the most frigid place on Earth. But icicle by icicle, we worked him toward allowing at least some few mortals the opportunity. Persephone pointed out that they would all return to him ultimately, which seemed to help."

"Pardon me for interrupting, Great One, but, interesting as this tale is, I am having a hard time discerning how it relates to Ariadne."

Dionysus smiled at me as if we were good friends, as if he had forgotten the potential conflict between us. "Ah, yes, a perceptive point. The connection is one forged by fate itself. As you recall, I mentioned an earlier Ariadne, another daughter of Minos. I took her to be my bride during the time when I was introducing my worship throughout Greece."

For a moment, the manic happiness in his eyes faded, to be replaced by sorrow sharp as daggers. "I should not have wed her during those turbulent times. I faced much opposition, and, though I tried to protect her from the violence with which I was threatened, she insisted on being close by. An ill-omened arrow struck her through the heart, killing her before I could save her.

"Fortunately, my allies and I had already persuaded Hades to try the idea of having mortals be reborn. Ariadne was one of the first fruits of that decision."

I must have looked as confused as I felt.

"Do you not see it?" asked Dionysus. "The obvious truth? Ariadne does not remember it, for she drank the water of Lethe while in the Underworld and forgot her first life, but that does not change the reality. The Ariadne I married was reborn as the Ariadne who slumbers even now at your side.

"My claim to her is prior to yours. Fate's claim on her is prior to yours. Do you not understand? This is no selfish and arbitrary request on my part. She was reborn to be mine again, reborn to become a goddess and to be at my side forever.

"I thank you much for bringing her to me. I regret that you fell in love with her in the process, and I will find some way to compensate you for your sorrow, but you must relinquish her to me."

I should have done as he said. He was a god, after all, and he could have just killed me and taken her if he had wanted. His story must be true, for he had no reason to lie to me.

Yet I could not accept that Ariadne was fated to be his. He admitted himself that she remembered nothing of her first life. And in this life, she loved me—and I loved her.

I don't know if I was drunk on the constant scent of wine or on the presence of Dionysus, but in that moment, I threw rational thought out the window. I had one desperate hope—the wish that Poseidon had given me. I would use it to ensure Dionysus never got his hands on her. Let Fate be damned!

Dionysus must have read my intent in my eyes. Or perhaps he felt the power of Poseidon stirring as I readied myself to invoke it. Either way, moving faster than any mortal could, he struck me on the forehead with his thyrsus. Physically, the blow was just a light tap, but it scattered my thoughts like dry leaves in a storm. I fell to the ground, almost unconscious, too weak even to use my wish.

"I could kill you for such hubris," said Dionysus. "Even Poseidon and Athena could not blame me. But *she* might. For her sake, you will live—but for the moment, you will forget."

HOMECOMING

I AWOKE AT DAWN. My head throbbed as if I had drunk too much. Odd, because I hadn't touched a drop of wine last night. I didn't think there was wine or liquor of any kind in the ship's supplies.

I got up and brushed the sand off me. Without looking around, I staggered back to the ship. When I reached it, I was surprised to see the crew and even the captain looking as if they had all gotten drunk the night before.

"I don't know what happened," he said to me, bowing his head. "I swear I had nothing to drink last night. I should not feel this way."

I smiled. "Nor should I, but perhaps it is the stress of our recent adventures. Let's get underway as soon as we can. We will feel better once we are back in Athens."

Despite the impaired condition of the crew, it was not long before we were underway. Traveling northwest, we came to Delos, where we made offerings at the shrine of Apollo and Artemis.

I don't know if it was the place—the power of Apollo, who supports order, is sometimes said to be hostile to that of Dionysus, who brings chaos—but as our sacrifices concluded, the veil the wine god had cast over all of us shredded like cobwebs in the wind. We no longer felt hung over. More importantly, we remembered Ariadne—and I remembered the plan Dionysus had for her.

"What has become of the princess?" asked the captain, looking around as if he expected her to appear from nowhere. "Surely, we didn't really—"

"We must set sail at once," I said. "We must return to Naxos."

It was madness to go back the way we had come, especially since we couldn't be absolutely sure Minos wasn't pursuing us. Yet no one questioned my order.

With the wind against us and no oars, getting back would have taken far too long, if we could have managed it at all. We had to spend time cutting down some nearby trees from which to carve crude oars. I did what I could, though I had never performed such a task before. The bulk of the work fell to the captain and the sailors, who were fortunately very good at it.

Better equipped, we struggled back against a wind that still blew in the opposite direction. I myself became one of the oarsmen and focused what strength I had on pushing the boat through the sea.

Of course, by the time we reached Naxos again, Ariadne was gone. Where she and I had lain together on the beach, a cluster of grapevines grew. They had not been there when I first awakened.

"This is some trick of Dionysus," said the captain.

He was right, but I hadn't the heart to tell him so. And my thoughts flowed as slowly as a silt-choked river.

The wish. I still had the wish. With it, I could get Ariadne back.

I felt a gentle touch on my shoulder, but when I looked in that direction, no one was there.

"Do not attempt to bring two gods into conflict," whispered the wind. "You will destroy the one you think to save."

Athena.

"Whatever may have happened here...there is nothing to be done now," I said slowly, dragging each word from my mouth. "We must sail back to Athens as fast as we can."

I was positive Athena walked by my side invisibly as we returned to the ship. I had encountered her enough to sense her strong presence. But she didn't speak again.

Once back on the ship, it was hard to find privacy. I wanted to weep but knew that I should not in front of the men. Holding back my emotions was one of the hardest things I have ever had to do, but I managed it.

As with so much else, I had no choice.

With the wind finally on our side again, we returned to Delos before an impending storm forced us to drop anchor and wait it out. Just like Naxians, most of the Delians lived on the north side of their island, and the captain was able to find us a somewhat protected little cove on the south side where we were unlikely to be spotted.

That the wind, which had cooperated with us at every stage of our journey except on the return to Naxos, now suddenly turned hostile, I took to be a bad sign. Had Zeus changed his mind and decided to help Minos recapture us? Even this far north, the Cretan navy had been active driving away Carian pirates. A Cretan ship might very well be in the area.

I could not share this fear with the crew. It would panic them for no purpose. Once again, I had to keep my feelings bottled up inside me.

I did what little I could. I went below deck and prayed to Apollo and Artemis, to whom the island was sacred. I prayed to Zeus, Poseidon, and Athena as well. But none of them saw fit to answer me. Once I became accustomed to the howling of the wind and incessant beating of the rain upon the deck, sleep overtook me despite my anxiety—and very suddenly. One moment, I was awake. The next, I was in a sleep so deep I doubt a trumpet blast in my ear could have awakened me.

In my dream, which at first I thought might be a nightmare, I was back on the beach at Naxos. I half expected a group of Maenads, the mad women of Dionysus, to rush out from the nearby woods and tear me to pieces—my punishment for not immediately yielding to the will of Dionysus. But instead, I saw Ariadne, walking toward me on the beach.

Ariadne—but not quite the same Ariadne. She was radiant in a way that went beyond even her considerable physical beauty. The simple gown she had fled in had been replaced by a wine-dark one that made her skin look like ivory. Despite the darkness of the fabric, I could make out a pattern formed by the images of grapevines. Even more of a change was a crown more magnificent than any she could have worn as a Cretan princess. It sparkled as if someone had drawn down stars from the sky to adorn it.

Dionysus had kept his word. Ariadne was already his bride—and a goddess.

"Do not look at me as if I have three heads," said Ariadne, smiling at me as she used to when she was mortal. "I am still the Ariadne you knew just a short time ago."

"Not quite," I said. I should have said more, much more, but I did not know what else to say. Nor did I know what it was safe to say. Dionysus might be listening.

"I wanted you to know that I am happy," she said. "I did not want you to fear what might have become of me."

"I am glad to hear it," I said, though my voice betrayed my bitterness. Happy so short a time after being parted from me without even being given a choice! How little she must have cared for me!

"Don't say it like that." Ariadne's smile disappeared. Even in sorrow, she was almost too beautiful to look at. "It wasn't easy for me, you know, waking up on the beach and finding you gone. I thought you had abandoned me. I was so tormented by grief that I looked about for a quick way to kill myself.

"I didn't mean...I would never want—"

"I know," she said, trying to look happy again and not quite succeeding. "But before I could do anything desperate, Dionysus appeared and asked me to marry him.

"He told me the same story I imagine he told you—that I was my dead sister, born again for the very purpose of becoming his bride. That is why you left, isn't it?"

"He told me the story. I left because he struck me with his thyrsus and made me forget all about you. Everyone else on board forgot as well. As soon as I remembered, I made the captain turn the ship around—but we were too late."

Ariadne's smile was genuine again. "I suspected something like that, but I couldn't very well ask Dionysus. Growing up so near the gods, I knew well how...unpredictable they can be."

"But you are happy?" I asked, my suspicion renewed. For one wild moment, I thought of hunting him down and making him pay if he had hurt her.

"Do not worry. Dionysus is a god of many moods, but he has pledged to show only love to me, and I believe him."

"Did he swear on the Styx?"

She laughed. "If I had to make him do that, I would have turned him down. I almost did, anyway. My mind accepted what he told me of my destiny—but my heart dissented with such violence that I thought it might burst. I did love you, Theseus, more than I thought it was possible to love a man. And when I knew you were out there...but it was the hope that you still loved me that convinced me to accept his proposal."

"I don't understand," I said. "Not that I would have had you risk the wrath of a god for my sake, but—"

"I was afraid that wrath might fall on you. Dionysus might have cursed you, and even your father, Poseidon, could do nothing to save you, then."

"Did he threaten to curse me?"

"He spoke nothing but words of love, and he meant them—at least enough that I did not fear what he might do to me. But I wasn't sure what he might have done to you if I had not chosen him over you."

"Then you do not truly love him?" It was rash of me to ask. Dionysus might be listening, but Ariadne wasn't speaking as if she thought he was lurking nearby. She was a goddess now and ought to be able to tell such things.

"That is the oddest part," said Ariadne. "I didn't, but I do now."

"He has made you love him?"

"No, that's not what happened. At least, I don't think so. It was... sudden. From the moment I agreed, it was as if I had never loved any man before. Nor could I ever love any other man ever again. Don't look at me like that. It could have been Aphrodite working her will upon me, I suppose. Or it could be that she worked her will upon me when I loved you, and I have been her puppet all along. But I refuse to believe that. I did love you. I still remember how that felt. But now, I love him. Perhaps he was able to grant me the memory of how I felt in my previous life."

I couldn't help myself. My frustration showed on my face. Athena had forced my mother to have sex, first with Aegeus, then with Poseidon, through guilt. Dionysus had forced Ariadne to marry him through guilt, too, though more subtly. In the god's mind, she was born for that purpose, after all. How can a mortal refuse her destiny?

"I should not have come," said Ariadne, looking at me with pity instead of love. "I cannot properly explain what has happened to me. I made my choice, and I am happy with what I have done. Theseus, if you were aware of the way love works among the gods, you would be happy for me...happy for the world, too. I may do much more good as the wife of Dionysus than I ever could have as the queen of Athens."

I did a poor job of hiding my skepticism. "What will you do? Make wine with him?"

Ariadne looked hurt, but only for a moment. "Dionysus is far more than the god of wine. He is a god who intends to promise new life to mortals, to make what comes after one life—or many—far better than it has been. And I can help.

"You must have noticed that Dionysus is the bringer of great joy. But that joy, experienced in excess, can lead to madness—or worse. As his wife, I can help to temper him, much as water is used to reduce the potency of wine.

"Persephone has helped to temper the severity of Hades with mercy, and that gives her comfort in what would otherwise be a loveless marriage. Amphitrite has helped to moderate the storminess of your divine father as well.

"It is this way in good mortal marriages. Husband and wife help to balance each other. It should not surprise us that the same pattern exists among the gods."

"So this marriage is...like a task to you? Something you must do?"

"Something I wish to do with all my heart," said Ariadne. "One day, you will understand that. Meanwhile, do not grieve for me overly long. Instead, find a woman who will be a good balance for you. And do not worry about me, not even for a second, for I will always be happy now. I could never have achieved such a state as a mortal—though I might have come close as your wife."

The dream ended as abruptly as it had begun. I awoke to find the captain hovering over me.

"My prince, the storm has subsided. Shall we continue our voyage?"

I nodded, though for me, the storm was far from over. I wondered if it ever would be.

The wind was once again our ally, and we raced across the sea, almost as if we were flying. Near the southern tip of Andros, we needed to shift to a westward course, and the wind obliged.

It was not long before we passed near Cape Sounion, the southernmost point in Attica. Looking in its direction, I realized how close we were to home. Yet instead of feeling joy, I shuddered. I thought I saw someone fall from the cliff. But it must have been my imagination. We were too far distant for me to have seen anything of the kind.

That did not keep a feeling of dread from descending upon me as we sailed along the coast toward Piraeus, the port of Athens. Something was wrong. That much I was sure of.

My mood did not improve when we docked. My father's counselors, who must have been monitoring all reports of incoming ships, appeared almost at once, looking as grave as if they had come for funeral rites rather than for what should have been a joyous homecoming.

They all bowed to me.

"There is no need for such ceremony now," I said. "Get up, get up. Send word to the worried families that their sons and daughters have been returned to them. See, there they are, coming up on deck even now. And send word to my father."

The eldest counselor, who looked as if he would rather be anywhere but here, took a step forward. "My prince...there has been an accident."

"What are you talking about?" I asked, my heart racing. "Speak plainly, man."

"You father...your father...he would go down to Cape Sounion and watch for your ship for several hours each day. He...we think he slipped and fell. We have not yet recovered his body, but..." The counselor looked down, unable to finish. But I knew then the figure I saw falling had not been my imagination.

No one could have survived such a fall.

I looked back at the crew and upon the liberated captives. Every one of them had drawn the same conclusion, and they looked as if they wished to comfort me but did not know how.

Behind them, the black sails caught my eye.

Distracted by all that had happened—or maybe it was the result of the magic of Dionysus—I had forgotten the one thing my father had asked of me before I left. I had not taken down the black sails and put up the white ones.

When Aegeus had seen the ship from a distance, he had seen those black sails. He thought I had died, another victim of the minotaur.

He had not fallen. I knew that now. He had jumped.

And it was all my fault.

GRIEF AND CROWN

How much my mother had sacrificed to keep Aegeus alive—and how little good it had done her. He was dead anyway. And I, meant to be his deliverer, was the instrument of his death.

I wanted to denounce myself to the assembled crowd. Then I wanted to ride the fastest horse in Athens full speed to Cape Sounion, from which I would fling myself in partial expiation of the evil I had wrought.

I wanted to, but I didn't. My grief and guilt surrounded me like a black cloud, nearly suffocating me, but I could see one thing through that cloud. If I died now, with no heir left to succeed me, Athens would fall into chaos. Rival factions would each put forward their own candidate and try to enforce the allegiance of the people at sword point. By the time one king had finally emerged victorious, the city, choked with corpses, would lie in ruins. Nor would that be the end of it. Minos could not resist such a tempting target. He would crawl over those corpses and through those ruins to proclaim himself king of Athens. I could not allow such horrors to come to pass.

I could barely think, but in the face of such a shock, my subjects would understand if I seemed stunned. I let myself be escorted back to the palace by the quickest way, barely aware of what was around me. I know that some in the crowd cried out in sympathy. And at least some of the families of those I'd rescued cried out their thanks. I managed to spare each of them a look and a nod of acknowledgment. There would be time to properly receive their thanks later.

Bereft of both my love and my father within such a short period of time, I wished nothing more than to be left alone with my thoughts. But I was king now. I could have ordered everyone away, but there was business to be done first. My father's advisers—no, my advisers now—buzzed around me like angry bees.

In the short time between Aegeus's plunge from Cape Sounion and my arrival at Piraeus, the sons of Pallas and the kin of Metion had both stirred. Rumors of revolt whispered through the marketplace.

"Double the guard for the moment," I said. "And send forth heralds to proclaim my return."

"Wise steps, majesty," said the eldest of the counselors. I had been so focused on Aegeus since coming to Athens that I didn't even know the counselor's name. Having known him for months, I was too embarrassed to ask.

"Wise steps," he repeated, "but perhaps not by themselves sufficient to calm the city."

"What would you recommend?" I asked.

"Legally, you were king the moment your father...perished. But many of the people will not see you as king until you are duly crowned, in the sight of gods and men. Usually, such things require long preparation, but I believe it would be prudent if the ceremony could be completed before sunset."

"What?" I wondered if the man had been struck mad by Dionysus, but I knew better than to ask that. Anyway, that was one god's name I didn't want on my lips, at least for now.

"I know it seems hasty," said the counselor. He kept his eyes on mine, for he wanted to seem as confident as possible. "But there are... rumors, Majesty. Your father's death is called suspicious. It is even hinted that you may have played some part in it, that you hired someone to push him from the cliff."

I jumped up so fast that I knocked over my chair. "Who dares spread such lies?" I shouted. "Bring the culprits to me now!"

To his credit, the counselor did not back away from me, and his eyes

192

stayed focused on mine. "I'm sure the guards will make every effort to do that, and your father's attendants have already done what they could to put any such suspicions to rest. But nothing will kill those rumors faster than your being crowned before Athena and the other gods. If you are accepted by the goddess, no one can question your right to rule—or accuse you of patricide."

Other counselors had already repositioned my chair. I made myself sit in it, though I would rather have used it to bash out the brains of anyone who would dare tell such a lie.

It did not help that my rage burned mostly against myself. I did not hire someone to assassinate my father, as the potential rebels wanted people to believe. But I had killed him just as surely, though not deliberately, as if I had pushed him off the cliff with my own hands.

"I am worn out by my journey…and much more so by my grief. Is it not proper that funeral rites be performed for my father before I am crowned?"

The counselor looked back at the guard captain. "Report to your king. Has his father's body been found?"

The man stepped forward and bowed to me. "Majesty, I regret that we have not yet secured your father's remains, but our search continues. We have consulted the captain of the ship that brought you back, hoping to learn what we could of tides from him. He says the waters directly below Sounion are shallow, and the current there is not strong. If we keep searching, we are likely to find something."

"In which case, it would be better to wait until we can find your father's body before performing the rites," said the counselor. "Yet we cannot put off your formal recognition as king."

My head pounded. I wondered if this was what Zeus felt like right before Hephaestus had to split his skull to release the full-grown Athena.

"Have I not cleared the isthmian road of bandits? Did I not tame the bull of Marathon? Did I not drive away the witch, Medea? Have I not slain the minotaur and liberated those upon whom it would have dined? What more proof do Athenians need that I am favored by the gods?"

"The people have no doubt of you—in general. But there are some men who would not believe you worthy even if you stood in the market-place holding up the minotaur's head for all to see. There are few such people right now, but the longer we delay, the more numerous they will become. I wish it were not so, Majesty, but it is."

I looked at the other counselors, who avoided meeting my eyes. Most of them looked as if they wished for the invisibility helm of Hades so that they could just disappear.

"Forgive my sudden anger," I said, trying to keep my voice as calm and even as possible. "A king who fails to consider the wisdom of others is nothing but a fool. What say the rest of you, then? Must I be crowned before sunset?"

"It would…be better," said one of them, his voice quavering.

"Never fear to be honest with me in council. Do the rest of you agree?"

Heads nodded, some more reluctantly than others.

"It appears you all agree. So be it, then. Send messengers to the priests to request their cooperation. If they are able to prepare for the ceremony in time, I shall be crowned today.

"Oh, and while I doubt a messenger can travel to and from Eleusis in the time available, send one to King Hippothous. Tell him I send not an order but a request for him to come and see me crowned."

I wanted the chance to see Hippothous again, both because I reckoned him a friend—one of the few I had—and because I thought he might be a reasonable choice to become my heir so that I could abdicate with a clear conscience. After all, he was generally considered a fine ruler in Eleusis. There was no reason he couldn't be an equally fine king of Athens.

Of course, I couldn't very well reveal my plans to the council, and some of the counselors were looking at me strangely. They didn't understand why I would single out one particular local ruler.

"Actually, it would be proper form to send to the leaders of all the demes, would it not?" I asked. "Hippothous is one of the few that I know personally, but it is right that all of them be invited. I know," I added, forestalling the obvious objection, "that some will be too far away for the invitation to reach them and for them to reach Athens before the ceremony is over. Let the invitations acknowledge that, but say that I wish to meet with them, even if the suddenness of the invitation means they cannot be here for the ceremony. What say you? Is that the proper etiquette for such an occasion?"

The counselor who had first spoken up for a rapid coronation smiled. "Under the circumstances, you could not possibly do any better, Majesty. And bringing the leaders of the demes here at the start of your reign will make your right to rule even more unquestionable. But we need not send for Hippothous."

"Why not?" I tried to stay calm, but fear gripped my heart. Was he dead as well?

"Because he is already here, Majesty. He came when he heard your return was expected."

"Excellent," I said, suppressing a sigh of relief. "If our business here is for the moment complete, I would meet with him."

The counselor nodded. "We will make the necessary arrangements. You should have at least a little time to spare for…the Eleusinian ruler."

It did not take the buzzing bees long to get to the business of making honey. Nor did it take long for Hippothous to be brought to me.

He knelt, but I pulled him to his feet. "Such formality is not necessary. I fear I will have far too much of it before the day is done."

Hippothous looked older than I had remembered him, but given his divine blood, he probably wasn't aging any faster than I. Perhaps governing Eleusis was more tiring than he expected.

"I have heard the council is determined to crown you by day's end," he said. "I am so sorry that you have to take the kingship so suddenly."

"As I recall, you had to assume command at Eleusis pretty suddenly, too."

"The situations are not the same. I didn't grieve for Cercyon, who was trying to kill me, after all. With you and your father, it was different. I am so sorry for your loss."

"I knew him so briefly," I said. "I wish I could have been by his side for decades more."

Again, I wanted to weep for Aegeus, but I restrained myself. Even with Hippothous, I didn't want to reveal how much pain my father's death had inflicted on me. Nor could I reveal my plans to renounce the throne—not yet, anyway. Even he would not have understood.

As the ceremony neared, I excused myself to prepare, but I was not to have even a few minutes alone. As soon as I entered my chamber and closed the door, Athena appeared before me. I started to fall to my knees, but she gestured for me to remain standing.

"Is this…is this a dream?" I asked.

"No, I thought it best to appear in person, for the advice I bring is of grave importance. You must not renounce the throne."

"Goddess, I would never have considered such an idea if there were any other choice. But I am…unfit for the office. And Hippothous has already proved himself to be a good king. He will serve Athens—"

"Should he take the throne, he will bring nothing but death," said Athena, staring at me so sternly that I feared to argue the point. "He is a good king in Eleusis, but he was the legitimate heir to the throne there. He has no claim on the throne of Athens."

"But if I name him my heir—"

"Name him whatever you want," the goddess replied, her gray eyes cold as a stormy sky. "That will not matter to potential rebels. You will bring about the very disaster that your birth was meant to prevent."

"I thought my birth was meant to save Aegeus," I said. My voice betrayed my bitterness more than was proper. "Yet instead of saving him, I killed him."

Athena waved her spear as if she wanted to skewer me with it. "Never speak such words again—not to me, not to anyone. You are not to blame for Aegeus's death."

"Then who is? Dionysus? Perhaps his scrambling of my brains is what made me negligent enough to forget to trade the black sails for the white ones? And what about Aphrodite? Perhaps it was her filling my heart with love for a woman I was not meant to have that made me so forgetful."

I had expected Athena to cut me off, but she let me speak. However, she stood as stiff as a statue, her face carved with lines of mute disapproval. I looked into her eyes and felt ashamed.

"But all of that is wrong, and I know it. It is wrong of us mortals to blame the gods when we are the ones at fault."

Athena nodded, and her posture became less rigid. "I am glad to see that wisdom has not altogether abandoned you. As far as I know, no god contrived Aegeus's death, but you would gain nothing by such an accusation even if one of them were guilty. Right or wrong, there is no way the gods can be judged by men."

Her expression softened. "But it is equally fruitless to blame yourself in a case like this. There were strange magics upon you. Of that, there is no doubt. Those, and the distraction of losing Ariadne, interacted in ways no one intended. You bear no responsibility for what you cannot control.

"I will speak the words that you may not. If fault there is, it does indeed lie with the gods. Dionysus should have appeared to you before you left for Crete to tell you of Ariadne's destiny and to instruct you to bring her to Naxos. He should then have appeared to her so that she would have known that destiny as well. She was a tender-hearted girl who could scarcely have avoided feeling sympathy for the victims of the minotaur. And for a man as handsome as yourself? One doesn't need to be Aphrodite to figure out that she would fall in love with one such as you. Nor does it take the insight of Eros to see that you would be drawn to a woman brave enough to risk everything to save you.

"But Dionysus wasn't paying attention. He was too busy dreaming his dreams of how to make this world and the next better places for mortals—all the while ignoring the individual mortals who stumble into his way."

I almost wanted to hug Athena but knew I dared not. "You see him...much as I do."

"Be sure you do not speak of that again," said Athena, her voice mock stern. "But the god of wine, reckless as he is, did not intend your father's death or even your heartbreak. I spoke of him only to make you realize that you were caught up in forces larger than yourself. You are not to blame in such a case. If Aegeus were here, he would say the same."

"Goddess, forgive me if this is presumptuous, but can even you know what he would say?"

"Under the circumstances, yes. By the way, your searchers will not find the body. Poseidon has it. And while it is fitting that you perform funeral rites for him, Poseidon has already done so to ensure that Aegeus would find peace.

"But he and I have done more than that. We have secured Aegeus's entry into the Elysian Fields, where one day you and he will be reunited. He will not know a moment of sorrow there, Theseus."

"I...I thank you. But it is so hard to imagine such a thing."

Athena smiled. "Mortals fear death. It is a natural response. But those who are favored by the gods need have no fear. Unlike those who are tormented for their sins, the blessed dead will know only peace and happiness. Unlike ordinary souls, who float mindlessly about in the shadows of the Underworld, the blessed dead will retain their memories and intellect. Aegeus remembers you, Theseus—and he is proud of you."

Conflicting emotions warred within me. I wanted to believe Athena, to embrace the vision of Aegeus leading an ideal life. But I kept imagining him plunging from the cliff. The thought made me shudder.

"Now that you know the truth, you will give up the idea of abdicating, will you not?"

Was Athena telling me the truth or just telling me what I wanted to hear so that I would do her bidding? I had no way to know.

"As long as I am worthy, there is no reason for me to renounce the crown."

Athena raised an eyebrow. "That is more like a platitude than a promise—but I will settle for it right now. I must leave you, but I will be with you again for the ceremony. Until then, farewell."

"Farewell," I replied, even though the goddess was already gone.

I should have felt warmed by her personal attention and reassurance, but there was a cold spot in my heart that would not have thawed even if I had been able to throw it into the fire.

Of course, even if Athena were deceiving me, she was right—I could not abdicate right away. The only way to make Athens accept an heir was to father one and see him grown to manhood. Only then would I be free to walk away.

I put on the white robe in which I would be made king. Then, like a condemned man being led to the place of execution, I was led by a party of royal officials out of the palace and over to the temples. As we neared them, my mood shifted a little. It was hard to see them without being reminded of the long history of Athens and the even longer history of the gods who watched over it.

The Erechtheum, which unites the temples of Athena and Poseidon, did not exist then. Instead, there were two separate structures. The temple of Athena stood to the east. Within it was said to lurk her sacred serpent, fed on honey cakes by the priestesses. Even better hidden than the serpent was the palladion, a statue of Athena said to have fallen from the sky in a time so long ago that no one was sure how many years had passed since then. Visible to all was the olive tree Athena planted when she was competing with Poseidon for the right to be the patron of Athens. Oil made from its olives was highly prized throughout Greece.

To the west stood the temple of Poseidon, built around the saltwater spring that bubbled up where Poseidon's trident had struck the rock. A large group of priests met my party at a carefully calculated point between the two temples. Athena had won the contest to be the patron of Athens, but it was always prudent for a coastal city like Athens to pay equal tribute to Poseidon.

Kept at a distance by the guards was a large group of Athenian citizens, come to see their king be proclaimed officially. They could not be the whole population of the city, but they were rapidly filling all the available space on the acropolis as far as I could see. It was like the crowd that had watched the sacrifice of the bull of Marathon—only this time, I was the sacrifice.

A large number of priests stood before me, some looking as nervous as I felt. They were usually in charge when rituals were concerned and probably were unsettled by the request to crown a king with little of the normal preparation.

However, the one who was in charge of the ceremony had been away from the city for some time but looked as if he had been planning for this moment for months. He was Butes, fourth of that name, for his office, priest of both Athena and Poseidon, was more or less hereditary. Considering the first Butes had been the brother of King Erectheus, it was not surprising that subsequent kings might have preferred his family to be priests rather than contenders for the throne.

Butes's gray hair suggested he was elderly, but he stood tall, and his expression left no doubt who was in charge. Had he ever decided he wanted to be king, he would not have been without supporters.

"Prince Theseus, come forward," he said in a voice that immediately silenced the crowd. He beckoned me to approach just as I had led the bull to the sacrificial altar. I positioned myself as I had been told earlier, facing him rather than standing at his side.

"Theseus, son of Aegeus, son of Pandion the Second, son of Cecrops, son of Erectheus, son of Pandion the First, son of Erichthonius, son of Hephaestus, son of Zeus, today you stand before the people of Athens, rightful heir to the throne, to be elevated to the kingship in the sight of all the gods. Are you prepared to receive this office?"

"I am." Part of me wanted to flee, to be far away from this place, but I knew I could not. The city depended on me—whether I liked it or not.

"Then you will be anointed this day with saltwater and with olive oil so that our two patron deities will bless your assumption of the kingship." From behind him, one priest stepped forward with the water, another with the oil. Butes sprinkled me with the saltwater from Poseidon's own spring, then poured on my head a little bit of the olive oil made from olives grown on Athena's own tree.

I hadn't expected to feel anything, but at that moment, I felt the two deities touch my forehead. My earlier glumness faded for a moment. I was not a sacrifice. I was part of an institution that stretched back generations, to the gods themselves. And they had chosen me, perhaps more than most kings. I had been born to sit on the throne. How could I ever have thought of saying no?

Shouts of alarm came from the direction of Athena's temple. Butes looked in that direction, first annoyed, then surprised.

"Fear not!" he bellowed so loudly that he could be heard across the whole length of the acropolis. "This is a sign from the goddess herself."

The shouting stopped, but people scrambled out of the way, clearing the path for...what exactly? I couldn't see yet.

Only gradually did the crowd part enough for me to get a decent view. Across the stone of the acropolis slithered the biggest serpent I had ever seen. It could only be the sacred snake from Athena's temple, though it was never supposed to leave that sanctuary. Yet here it was, with the priestesses of Athena trailing nervously behind it. Nothing like this had ever happened in their lifetime, nor at any time since the temple had been built.

I felt a tightness in my chest, but I didn't show fear. The gods might be unpredictable, but it was inconceivable that Athena had gone to so much trouble just to have me bitten by her snake and killed on the very day I had been proclaimed king.

"Majesty, stay still," said Butes. "The snake comes to bless you, not to bite you. Let it proceed as it will."

The crowd was silent as death as the citizens watched the serpent crawl toward me. The creature was moving much faster than others of its kind. It covered the distance between Athena's temple and me as fast as I could have. But it did not seem so at the time. The few moments it took felt like an eternity.

When it reached me, it coiled gently around me. I heard a few gasps from the audience, though they were quickly silenced by a glare from Butes.

Up it stretched, coiling higher and higher, until my eyes looked into its cold, reptilian ones. No, not cold. Somehow, they were Athena's eyes. Nor did the snake's body feel as cold as it should have, though perhaps the crawl across stone heated in the afternoon sun had made a difference.

We were twined together in a way that made us seem more like two lovers than like man and snake. It even leaned closer and ran its narrow and rapid tongue across my cheek—the closest it could come to a kiss. Then it slowly unwound, sliding gently back to the ground. Once it had separated from me, it slithered back the way it had come, with the priestesses sighing with relief as they trailed it back to the temple.

The silence was broken by one of my counselors, who I think did not intend the sound of his voice to carry so far.

"Who could now question that he is Athena's chosen one?"

With a wave of his hand, Butes restarted the interrupted ritual. Another priest came forward with a gold crown. Even from a distance, I could see the delicacy of its shaping, as if the smith that had created it had been taught by Hephaestus himself. Perhaps he had been.

The crown was light, but it felt cold upon my brow. The moment Butes had it properly settled, the crowd burst into wild applause.

There would be no rebellion now. Athena could not have made her support plainer if she had appeared by my side in person.

But she and Poseidon were not the only gods present. As I looked out at the crowd, I caught a momentary glimpse of Ariadne and her bright smile before she vanished, back to Naxos or Olympus. It mattered not which it was—she would be equally unreachable in both places.

She had not appeared to me to be cruel. She just wanted to affirm once again that she did not hold my leaving her on the island against me, that she was happy—and wanted me to be happy as well.

Yet her appearance reminded me of everything I wanted and could not have. I wanted to feel her in my arms, not a scaled thing. I wanted to feel her lips on mine, not a serpentine tongue thrust from between its fangs.

Despite the heat of the afternoon sun, the crown still felt cold on my brow, but I could not take it off. I had to be displayed to all the people before being led away.

I was king now—yet no one in Athens was less free than I.

NEW FRIENDS

I DID NOT WEAR the crown after that day, except on ceremonial occasions when there was no choice. But I did throw myself into the job of being king, and in time, I was less haunted by the memory of Ariadne.

It is said that kings grow wiser and rule better through experience, but for me, my earliest years were my best. I brought peace to Athens and the surrounding territories. Farming, the various crafts, and trade all flourished. I reformed the currency, making it more stable and thus more trustworthy. I drew the demes into a tighter union with Athens, reducing the possibility of revolt—not that there was much talk of revolt in those days.

I did not forget the teachings of my mother. But it would not be easy to change the status of women in Athens. The horrified looks on the faces of my counselors when I brought up the idea of citizenship for women reminded me of just how difficult it would be to get men to accept such a notion.

I decided I could not move as rapidly in that area as I had wanted. Perhaps what I needed to do was lead by example. I needed a wife who would not be just an ornament for social functions but an influential force in government as well. That way, I could encourage other men to think of their wives in a different way.

Of course, to do that, I needed to be married. Even if I had not been thinking about social reform, I would still have needed to father an heir, or else I would end up in the same mess Aegeus had been in.

But it was not enough to just be married. The Greek cities had many beautiful princesses trained to be obedient to their future husbands. But I didn't want a wife who would merely obey me. I wanted a true partner, a woman who was intelligent and independent as well as beautiful.

I wanted a wife like Ariadne, though I dared not speak those words aloud.

"My king," said Alexius, my chief counselor—whose name I had eventually learned. I didn't like having my contemplation of my future wife being interrupted, but I knew he would not have disturbed me if he didn't have an important matter to discuss.

"Someone is attempting to steal your herd of cattle from Marathon,"

I rose from my chair so fast that I knocked it over. "Who would dare do such a thing?"

"Based on the message we just received, it is Pirithous, king of the Lapiths."

"The king is a cattle rustler?" I asked. I had heard the Lapiths were less civilized than the Athenians, but I still could not imagine a ruler behaving in such a way.

Alexius shook his head. "Not generally, my king, but nor is he a ruler such as yourself. He is…unpredictable."

"How many men are with him?"

"If the message is to be believed, he is alone."

"How could a single man move a herd of cattle rapidly enough to have any hope of getting away with them?"

Alexius surprised me by shrugging. "Logically, he could not expect to succeed."

"Do not the Lapiths live in Thessaly, near Mount Pelion?"

"Indeed, they do."

"Then…what he does is insane. Getting as far as Ramnous might be possible, maybe even Oropos. But Pelion? That must be at least fifteen hundred stadia from Marathon."

"More, Majesty. I think it is closer to seventeen hundred."

"That would take a man many days to travel. But with a herd of cattle? Months, at the very least—if he could even keep the herd together that long. Other thieves will see it as a tempting target."

"If I had to guess, my king, I would say he may not really intend to steal the cattle. He is known for having an…odd sense of humor."

"This is a prank of some kind? What sort of king is this, who commits an act of war as a joke?"

"One who is a menace to peace," said Alexius. "I have already given orders for troops to march out and intercept him."

"No, if it is a king stealing the cattle, it falls to a king to stop him," I said.

"If you wish to lead the expedition—"

"If Pirithous has come alone, it should hardly be necessary for me to take an armed escort. I will meet him alone."

"Majesty, such a course would be ill-advised. What if he has men lurking somewhere nearby? You could end up his prisoner."

I sighed. "Fine, I will take some soldiers with me. But they will remain at a distance unless more Lapiths appear. I intend to take this Pirithous prisoner myself."

Alexius scowled but did not argue. In less than half an hour, I was riding toward Marathon at the head of twenty or so men who rode a discreet distance behind me.

The plain of Marathon lay about one hundred and fifty-seven stadia to the northeast of Athens. Even walking, a horse could cover almost twice that distance in eight hours, and we trotted as often as we could. I wanted to arrive before dark to prevent Pirithous from being able to disappear into the shadows, but I also wanted the horses to have a little energy left in case he attempted to ride away. Pirithous was presumably trying to herd cattle on horseback, in which case his horse would be tired by the time we reached him, anyway. But who knew whether Pirithous was trying to do any herding at all? For all I knew, he was just sitting and waiting for someone to arrive. The farther we traveled, the more convinced I became that the man had to be insane.

By the time we caught up with him, it was midafternoon, and, instead of trying to get away as fast as possible, the thief king was sitting under a tree not more than a handful of stadia away from Marathon. The cattle grazed peacefully nearby, oblivious to their abduction.

Motioning for the soldiers to stay back, I galloped to where Pirithous watched me from the shade of his tree.

"It took you long enough to get here," said Pirithous, looking me up and down but making no move to get up. "I was expecting you at least an hour earlier—but then, I suppose your nursemaids must have slowed you down a little."

"I am not here to banter with you but to call you to account for your crimes," I said, dismounting and drawing my sword. "Come forth and face me."

Pirithous got up slowly, stretched as if he had all the time in the world, and then ambled slowly out into the sunlight. His smile was as insolent as his voice. Angry as I was with him, I had to admit he was handsome and well-muscled. Though I doubted anyone would think us brothers, we were alike in the color of our hair, eyes, and skin. We were also nearly the same height and looked to be about the same age. But what I really noticed was the spark I felt when he got close enough. It was not as strong as the one I felt when Heracles, but it was strong enough for me to tell that he, like the cousin I so admired, was a son of Zeus. Though I did not wish to acknowledge it, the thief king and I were family.

Pirithous nodded, and his smile broadened as if he had felt something himself. "Son of a god, too, are you? Which one?"

"I am the son of Aegeus," I said stiffly.

Pirithous glanced over my shoulder. "Don't worry. They are too far away to hear us. You can tell me the truth."

"I have told you the truth," I said, my voice cold as steel. "Not that I owe you any truth. You, however, owe me restitution for stealing my cattle. Will you come along peacefully, or will you fight me?"

The Lapith king rolled his eyes. "All right, have it your way—fight, of course. I didn't come here for cattle, you know. I came to see if the stories about you were true."

"Then draw," I said. "I would have taken you peacefully, as befits your rank, but I will take you like the thief you are if you insist."

Having already drawn my sword, I took from my back the shield that I often strapped there from old habit. Pirithous picked up his shield from the ground where he had carelessly laid it and drew his sword.

"Stay back!" I shouted to the soldiers, who had started to ride in our direction when they saw Pirithous's sword flash. Alexius would not have approved, but I didn't care. It was I whom this insolent thief had wronged, and I who would administer his punishment.

As soon as he was ready, I swung at him with all the speed I could muster. He blocked my stroke with his sword and countered with a slice of his, which I blocked—but barely. He was at least as fast as I. From a son of Zeus, I should have expected no less.

On and on it went, minute after minute. Thrust, block, counterthrust, block, repeat. If I varied my pattern, he compensated.

Aside from Heracles, I had never met a man who was my equal in skill. I had met a few who were stronger, but they always erred in some way, and I defeated them.

With Pirithous, it was different. We were equally matched, even in wit. Crazy as his early actions had seemed, careless as the way he placed his shield had been, while we fought, he watched, eagle-eyed, every move I made and responded in the most effective way possible. He did not make even the tiniest mistake.

After a while, my muscles ached, and I had to vary my pattern enough to keep the sweat from running into my eyes. Pirithous, however, had to do the same, so we remained even.

"Do you yield?" I asked, my voice sounding as dry as my throat felt.

"And why should I yield, kinsman?" His voice also came from a dry throat, but it still sounded insolent. "This battle has been at most a draw. I might just as well ask you if you will yield to me."

"Never!" I shouted. I made my strokes even harder. He compensated. Our strength was as even as our speed. If our endurance was the same, we would both drop from exhaustion at the same time, with nothing resolved between us.

I thought about using the wish Poseidon had granted me to defeat him, but such an act would have been dishonorable in these circumstances. Pirithous was a scoundrel—but he was no real threat to Athens, no monster in human form such as the men I had killed on the road to Athens years ago. Even as we fought, he smiled. Despite his criminal behavior, I found my hatred toward him cooling.

Just when I despaired of bringing the battle to an end, he said, "I yield," and lowered his sword.

I stood there, my mouth hanging open, uncertain how to react. He had no more reason to yield now than he had a few minutes before. Was this some kind of trick?

"Don't look so surprised. I told you that I came to see if the stories about you were true. Apparently, they are. I have no further need to fight you."

"I...do you acknowledge your guilt, then?"

"Yes, I stole your cattle, though I never intended to keep them. But, see here," he added, taking a purse from his belt. "I brought ample gold along to compensate you for...the inconvenience."

I took the purse. It felt heavier in my hand than I had expected. I could not deny that it was reasonable recompense.

I still wasn't sure he was sane—but he wasn't really an enemy. That much was clear. And if he truly came just to see if I lived up to my legend, well, I'd met people who'd done crazier things than that.

"I accept this gold and the return of the cattle as just recompense," I said. "Let there be no further conflict between us."

We were now both standing in the shadow of the tree under which I had first seen Pirithous. We had been fighting longer than I thought. It was only an hour or so until sunset.

"It is too late for you to begin your journey back to your kingdom today," I said. "If you wish, you may join me as my guest in the city of Marathon. I can offer you less hospitality there than I could in Athens, but it is much closer."

"I will happily be your guest," said Pirithous. "I know that the stories about you are true, but I would know more about you."

"And I about you," I said. I gave instructions to the soldiers to bring the herdsmen and help them return the cattle to their rightful place. I also told them to send word to Alexius and the other counselors that I would spend the night in Marathon.

It took Pirithous and me only a few minutes to reach the city. Once word that I was in the city got out—which was about three minutes after Pirithous and I rode through the gate—it took a few more minutes for us to make our way through the crowd that came out to greet me. I was

208

glad we had not tried to ride back to Athens, where it would have taken far longer.

That said, it saddened me to see the demarchos of Marathon so flustered by my unexpected appearance.

"Architeles, forgive me for my unannounced arrival," I said. "I was engaged in…negotiations with Pirithous, the king of the Lapiths, and they took longer than I anticipated."

"It is I who apologize," replied Architeles. "I should always be ready to entertain distinguished guests. The deme of Marathon is famous for its hospitality, after all."

I had never heard the hospitality of Marathon praised above that of any other place, but I said nothing. Architeles claimed descent from his namesake, the son of Achaeus and thus a member of one of the most distinguished families in all of Greece, but he was a fairly ordinary man himself. He stood before me, his head tilted down, slightly shaking as he waited for what he must have expected to be my wrath. It would have been cruel to have done anything to make him more uncomfortable.

"It would be too much for me to expect even such a hospitable place as Marathon to be constantly ready for a royal visit. King Pirithous and I will be content with whatever you have to offer."

"Speak for yourself," muttered Pirithous, but his smile remained undiminished.

"My own home is far less splendid than your palace in Athens," said Architeles. "But I am sure my wife will welcome such distinguished guests for dinner. And if you wish to spend the night, as it seems you do, there is a small guest house reserved for just such a purpose right across the street from mine. While we eat, I shall see to it that it is prepared."

The demarchos ushered us into his house, seated us comfortably in the courtyard, and excused himself to announce our presence to his wife. The sound of raised voices told me that she was not as enthusiastic about our visit as her husband. But what woman would be happy about having to serve dinner to a king without any time to prepare?

Pirithous raised an eyebrow. "The lady of the house is less than pleased. Never fear, for I will soothe her."

Many words had occurred to me to describe Pirithous during our short acquaintance. *Soothing* was not among them.

"Just be sure to treat everyone here with respect," I said, remembering how he had dealt with me during our first meeting.

"Always," he said, but a smirk ran crookedly across his face.

"Honored guests, may I present my wife, Ligeia?" Despite the volume of the earlier argument, his wife looked very timid. I think she would have hidden behind him like a shy little girl if she could have.

"Of course," I said, rising from my seat.

"This could not possibly be your wife," said Pirithous, rising as I had but then bowing. "Surely, she is a goddess in disguise."

Such exaggerated compliments were not unheard of, but they sounded strange on Pirithous's lips. Despite that, they were also strangely persuasive. Ligeia blushed and giggled like a young girl being courted for the first time.

"Oh, Great One, you are too kind," she said in a voice little above a whisper.

"I fear not kind enough. Please, goddess, forgive me my lack of enthusiasm, and let not your wrath fall upon me."

Ligeia giggled again. "I am no goddess—and you are a king. It is I who should be begging forgiveness from you, for I have no suitable feast ready."

Pirithous at last rose from his bow. "I am a king, but I am a warrior before that, as are all rulers among the Lapiths. We are used to meager fare in times of war. Banquets and battlefields do not mix, you know. Anything you offer me will be a feast in comparison to most of the meals I have had. I'm sure your own king would agree."

"To being a warrior before a king? No, I am king first, warrior only when I must be. As for the quality of the food, I agree completely. I have not experienced the battlefield as much as Pirithous, but I have found that the quality of the food owes much to the spirit in which it was offered. The most opulent feast, offered without true feeling, is inferior to the simplest meal, offered in the true spirit of hospitality."

Ligeia, much relieved, bowed her way out of the room and hustled back to the kitchen. I could hear her footsteps echoing in the hallway as she almost ran—but not from fear. Pirithous had filled her with enthusiasm for what she had dreaded only moments before.

"Majesty, pardon me if I sound abrupt," said Architeles nervously. "But is it wise to compare mortals to the gods in that way?"

"She is clearly a woman of modesty and virtue," said Pirithous. "If she had compared herself to a goddess, that might be considered *hubris*, and some goddess might indeed have taken offense. But if I compare her —particularly if she humbly declines my praise—then she has committed no sin, has she? And as for me, I am a son of Zeus. I have a little latitude if perhaps my compliments seem excessive."

Even though Architeles reckoned Prometheus, the titan, among his ancestors, Pirithous's claim seemed to unnerve him. "I…I did not realize. I had heard that your father was—"

"I prefer not to speak of him," said Pirithous. He was still smiling, but there was steel in his tone.

"I meant no offense," said Architeles. "If you will excuse me, I should go and see how the dinner preparations are going." He scurried out of the room without actually waiting to be excused.

"You did not need to be so harsh with him," I said. "I, too, had heard that your father was…someone else."

"But you sense the truth, don't you?" he asked me, leaning closer. "I can certainly tell that you have divine blood."

"Yes, but I don't speak of mine. My claim to the throne rests on my being the son of Aegeus, after all."

"But does it?" he asked, looking genuinely puzzled. "Among the Lapiths, it is deeds, not bloodline, that make a true king. Truth to tell, my people would far rather be ruled by a son of Zeus than by a son of their prior, disgraced king. And have I not heard that the goddess Athena herself, through her snake, blessed your accession? If the gods crown a man, who among men would dare to object?"

"I suppose so," I said. "I had not thought of it in quite that way."

"Well, you can be sure the gods do," said Pirithous, as if he had received this truth from their lips. For all I knew, perhaps he had.

The Lapith king glanced at the door through which our host had disappeared. "Aside from your ancestry, I also sense a bond between us. We were meant to meet. We were meant to become friends. The gods have some purpose for us. Do you not feel that as well?"

"Not like other divine messages I've received," I said. "But I do feel as if I've known you longer than I really have—much longer."

Pirithous nodded. "As if we were friends, kinsmen, brothers even—and had been so since birth. Tell me, Theseus, did you have many friends growing up?"

I shook my head. "It is hard to make friends when one is as different from everyone else as I was."

"Just so. People may admire someone like us. They may fear us. They almost certainly will envy us. But they will never want to befriend us."

"Before today, I would have said that my only real friend was Hippothous. You know, the king of Eleusis. He is a son of Poseidon just like me."

Pirithous frowned slightly. "I've heard of him. Wears his crown as if it's too heavy for his head, though, doesn't he?"

"He is…conscious of the enormous responsibility he has to his people. I feel the same way. Don't you?"

Pirithous snorted as if I had just told a hilarious joke. "You need to loosen up, my friend. Yes, the kingship comes with some tasks, but people like you and me, children of the gods that we are, were born to enjoy life. We are special, the best of the best among mortals. We should be able to enjoy that status, should we not?"

"It seems to me that Heracles spends most of his time suffering. Most heroes do, at least if all the stories about them are true. Look at Bellerophon. Look at Jason."

"Look at you, minotaur slayer, savior of Athens. Look at me, king of the Lapiths. Do we not have more than most men can even dream of? It's true that some heroes are unlucky, but even the most long-suffering have pleasures beyond the wildest imaginings of ordinary men. Have you not heard the story of the daughters of Thespius? When Heracles was young, he came to help Thespius deal with a lion that was ravaging the countryside. Old Thespius knew that Heracles was the son of Zeus and longed for the hero to be the father of his grandchildren. But he sensed Heracles was too young and innocent then to want to sleep with all fifty daughters, so Thespius tricked him. The king told the hero that his eldest daughter wished to spend the nights with him while he was their guest. Heracles was embarrassed but feared it might be a breach of the host-guest relationship to refuse. He bedded the eldest daughter each night—or so he thought. With the aid of darkness, Thespius smuggled in a different daughter each night. Heracles impregnated every single one of them. And, hero though he was, it took him fifty days to catch and kill the lion—no wonder, if you think about it. Anyway, Thespius got his wish, and Heracles got every man's fantasy—sex with numerous women, without any lasting commitment to any of them."

"But wasn't Heracles horrified when he learned the truth?"

Pirithous snorted again. "Hardly! He went on to father enough sons with other women to form a small army. And why shouldn't he? Why shouldn't you and I? Our sons will be heroes, too, after all. Is it not our duty to father as many heroes as possible?"

"But can we be good fathers to all of those sons?" I asked. The memory of my childhood without a father still stung.

Pirithous glanced again at the door. It was clear he didn't want our host or his wife to overhear our conversation.

"Sometimes, men are better off without fathers," he said. His tone was bitter, and his smile was gone. "Consider my supposed father, Ixion. He was a son of Ares. Much as I revere the god of war, his savage nature does not always suit a mortal, and it certainly didn't suit Ixion. He successfully wooed my mother, Dia, a true beauty among women. But then, unwilling to pay the bride price he had promised, he killed his father-in-law by burning him alive."

"That's...horrible," I said, not knowing what else to say.

"That was exactly what everyone except Ixion himself thought. His fellow kings were so horrified that none of them would absolve him of his bloodguilt. He would have lost his throne and possibly his life, but my true father, Zeus, took pity on him, for reasons I will never understand.

"Think of it—not only did Zeus pardon Ixion, but he brought him for a while to live on Olympus, a favor bestowed on very few mortals."

"Poseidon invited my ancestor, Pelops, to be his guest on Olympus," I said. "That experience did not work out so well for Pelops."

"It worked out even less well for Ixion. Instead of being grateful for the favor Zeus had bestowed upon him, he sought to find a way to seduce Hera herself.

"When Zeus first heard of this plan, he refused to believe it. To test Ixion, Zeus fashioned a cloud into a woman, whom he made to look exactly like Hera. Given the chance, Ixion slept with Hera's double. Zeus, enraged, cast Ixion out of Olympus and blasted him to ashes with a thunderbolt. Not content with that, he ordered Hermes to bind the soul of Ixion to a fiery wheel that spun perpetually. For a short time, the wheel spun through the sky, that all men might learn the cost of sin. Later, Zeus had him taken to the place of punishment in the Underworld, where he spins to this day.

"That fiery wheel haunts my nightmares. Nor is that the only way in which Ixion's past reaches out for me. By Hera's cloudy double, Ixion fathered a deformed son, Centaurus, who mated with the mares near Mount Pelion and fathered the Thessalian race of Centaurs. They live in an uneasy peace with the Lapiths. It is believed among my people that they will one day try to wipe us out. As much as I love a good battle, though, I cannot find it in my heart to try to wipe them out peremptorily. I look into their eyes, and I see the fires of my father's sins reflected there. Those sins are not mine—but I sometimes feel as if they are. When that feeling comes over me, I also sense that the centaurs are my brothers in misery, both tortured by the memory of the same man, neither quite able to break away from our father's legacy.

"So don't tell me that a boy needs a father. Though Ixion was already dead, I grew up as his son, and believe me, I would have been better off as a fatherless boy."

"Did…Zeus ever visit you?"

"The king of the gods has no time to visit all his mortal children," said Pirithous, his tone suddenly defensive. "I know he watches over me —and I know he is proud of me. What more do I need?"

As far as I was concerned, Pirithous's story cut against his own argument that a boy doesn't need a father. Pirithous certainly wouldn't have benefitted from having the murderous, adulterous Ixion there to rock his cradle—but he should have had Zeus there, at least from time to time.

I would have given anything to see Poseidon when I first learned I was his son.

At the sound of approaching footsteps, Pirithous changed his expression as fast as an actor putting on a mask. His mouth stretched into a broad smile. His eyes hid away the memories that would have tarnished them with sadness. In an instant, he was again shining with charisma, the favorite of the gods who could charm men but still retain the inner feeling of superiority.

A feeling I suspected was more self-deception than reality.

I was tired enough by that time that I remember little of dinner—except that Pirithous was a master of small talk. Architeles, so unnerved by our visit at first, was thoroughly charmed by his manner. I was not the only one who felt I had known the Lapith king longer than I really had. By the end of the meal, Architeles was talking to him in the easy way one speaks to old friends. And Pirithous, despite the pain he still felt over his father, chatted on as if he had not a care in the world.

It was with regret that I finally excused myself. "Your hospitality indeed lives up to Marathon's reputation, but my earlier exertions have made me weary."

"Are you tiring so soon?" asked Pirithous, his voice full of gentle mockery, his smile crooked. "I could go on like this all night."

He looked bleary-eyed, so I knew he was lying. "Do not stop on my account. I'm sure I can find my way across the street without your help."

"No, I'm sure our host will want to show you the way, and I don't want to make him do that twice," said Pirithous, rising unsteadily.

Just as he had predicted, Architeles would not allow us to walk over to the guest house on our own. "Marathon is a quiet town, but still, one can never be too careful."

"Unless there is an army lying in wait for us, I'm sure we will be fine," said Pirithous, but Architeles looked so downcast at the idea of us leaving alone that the Lapith king relented and allowed him to escort us the few steps it took to reach our night's lodgings. Then he insisted on checking to make sure that the house had been properly prepared. Only when he was satisfied did he finally bid us good night."

"Persistent fellow," said Pirithous. "I'm surprised he didn't try to tuck us in. Speaking of which, Cousin, there is a matter we should discuss before we sleep. I fear if we wait until morning, our host will be a distraction."

"If it is a serious matter, I would be able to handle it better after rest-ing," I said. "This day has been…more eventful than I anticipated."

Pirithous grinned. "That worn out? One would think you never fought before. I'll be brief then. I am soon to wed a woman named Hippodamia, and I would be honored if you could attend."

"It is hard for me to be away from Athens for that long," I said. "But I suppose I could persuade my advisers that a state visit to Thessaly would be worth the time."

Pirithous raised an eyebrow. "Isn't it the job of advisers to try to persuade you, not be persuaded by you? I needed no one's permission to come here and raid your cattle. I simply came."

"It is not a question of permission," I replied, irritated. "But I have found it best not to unduly worry those upon whom I depend to assist me in the administration of the city."

"Tomorrow morning, you can word an appropriately diplomatic note and send it to them. I don't think we have time to go back to Athens before starting out. The wedding is in just a few days."

I had been getting drowsy, but that woke me up. "You journeyed so far from home right before your wedding? Surely, the bride's family—"

"Know that I will be back in time for the ceremony."

"Still, it seems unwise—"

"You worry too much. We are kings. We are sons of gods. It is for us to say what is right and what is wrong, not for ordinary men to do so."

Though I had known him for only a day, I realized continuing this argument was pointless. "You have given me no time to select a suitable gift."

"Gifts!" he said, waving his hand dismissively. "We are friends. Your presence is enough. If you desire to give more, invite me to your own wedding. Surely, that cannot be far in the future. No doubt, your advisers are pestering you about it already."

I sighed. "They have, but I have not yet found a suitable bride."

He looked at me more closely. "Are you still pining for Ariadne? I've heard about her. But she is with Dionysus, is she not? It is long past time to forget her."

"That is easier said than done. But in any case, I find the eligible princesses near Athens too…oh, it is hard to explain. Too…tame, I suppose you would say."

"A woman, like a horse, should be tame," said Pirithous, winking at me.

"And is Hippodamia tame?" I asked, smiling.

"Indeed not! She would give me a good slap for saying what I just said—and then we would both laugh about it."

My eyes widened. "Then you know what I mean? It is better for a woman to have some independence, some spirit, is it not?"

Pirithous clapped me on the back. "Just so! It is a good thing you are coming to Larissa with me, for I can find you any number of spirited women among the Lapiths. But wait—perhaps your ambition is even greater than that. If you really want a spirited wife, you must woo an Amazon."

"But Amazons do not marry," I said, looking at him as if he really were insane. "They have sex with men from nearby towns to produce children. The boys they leave with their fathers. The girls they keep themselves and raise them as Amazons. It has always been that way."

Pirithous grinned broadly. "I didn't say it would be easy to win an Amazon for your bride. But for men like us, nothing is impossible."

The idea was crazy. Of course, it was. And I wanted to dismiss it from my mind. But the seed Pirithous had planted had already taken root. The more I thought about it, the more the idea made sense. After all, who would be a more fit partner for me than a woman raised to be independent?

If I had only known what bitter fruit that plant would eventually bear!

SPECIES FUSIONS AND GENDER CONFUSIONS

I'D HEARD many tales about what a savage land Thessaly was, but almost none of them were true. The Lapiths didn't maraud across the land in uncivilized warbands. They lived in towns and cities just as the Athenians did. Larissa, the largest city in the area and Pirithous's capital, wasn't as large as Athens, but it was no less civilized—unless one considered the centaurs.

Of course, I knew there were centaurs in Thessaly. Pirithous had told me that himself. I expected that I might see a few of them from a distance. What I didn't expect was to see large numbers of them roaming the city streets.

"You didn't tell me Lapiths and centaurs lived together like this."

Pirithous chuckled. "We don't live with them. They have no use for cities. The ones you see around us are only here for the wedding."

Maybe Pirithous was crazy after all.

"You invited them to the wedding?" I tried to keep my tone as neutral as possible, but some of my skepticism crept in, anyway.

"I didn't intend to frighten you, Cousin," said the Lapith king. He winked at me as if we shared some elaborate joke that would be lost on anybody else. "Many of them live in this area, and they might have taken exclusion as an insult. Much as I like a good battle, I'd rather have the centaurs on my side or at least keep them neutral."

"They are good fighters, then?" The fact that the Lapiths tended to avoid eye contact and walk as far away from them as possible made it clear what ordinary citizens thought of the centaurs, but I wanted to hear Pirithous's assessment.

"Centaurus's mother Nephele, though created by Zeus rather than being born, was still divine, you know. That means the centaurs are all grandsons of a goddess. Even were they not, they can run faster than a man on horseback can ride, I suppose because they are less heavy than a horse and a rider together. They have excellent aim, despite being handicapped by having to throw spears rather than shoot arrows, which reduces their range. If they must fight at close quarters, they are strong enough to wield small trees like clubs. It might take five or more ordinary men to defeat a centaur in combat. Even someone like you or me would find defeating one a challenge."

Pirithous was smiling as broadly as always. I couldn't help wondering if this smile was just another one of his masks. I still remembered the pain in his eyes when he had first told me of the way the centaurs reminded him of his father's sins.

"So you wish to avoid offending them?"

"I wish to make them allies if I can. Think what formidable friends they would be on a battlefield? No one in Thessaly could defeat us if they fought by our side."

His eyes were distant, as if he were looking right through me and seeing all the future triumphs the Lapith-centaur alliance would win.

"Your people would certainly be safe and prosperous if you could negotiate such an alliance," I said.

The centaurs were not afraid to make eye contact with the Lapiths, but they eyed Pirithous's people warily. It was hard to see either group being willing to fight side by side with the other. The centaurs were sufficiently preoccupied by their study of the Lapith passersby that they seemed oblivious to the presence of the man who had invited them.

Pirithous looked at me and snorted. "Safe and prosperous? My plans are not so limited. For years, the Lapiths have been looked down on by the other societies in Thessaly. With the centaurs' help, I will teach respect to our uppity neighbors. From Olympus to Pelion, all men shall say the Lapiths are the greatest among them. Perhaps even further than that."

I couldn't stop myself from frowning. "But are these other people any kind of real threat to you? If not, why go to war with them?"

"For honor, of course," said Pirithous. He looked as if he didn't understand my question at all.

"Pirithous!" Someone was shouting so loudly that the word echoed in the streets. Lapiths and centaurs both looked in our direction, aware for the first time that a king walked among them.

The man who had shouted was rushing toward us. He was covering the ground between us in great strides, and his face was twisted by anger.

Though Larissa was far inland, I smelled salt air for a moment. Was this stranger another son of Poseidon? No, I didn't get the same feeling from him I had gotten from Hippothous and the other sons I'd met. Yet there was some connection between him and my father. What could it be?

That was not the only thing that confused me about him. Though his body looked manly enough, even from a distance, his face, reddened by rage as it was, looked far more pretty than handsome—almost a woman's face. And despite his outrage, he ran with feminine grace. I did not know what to make of him.

Pirithous's smile drooped at the sight of him, but only for a second. "Caeneus, it is good to see you again. I'd like to introduce you to—"

"Where have you been?" Caeneus almost snarled his words. If he was a Lapith, it was not the tone he should have been using with his king.

"To Athens, as you know full well," replied Pirithous, still smiling, but more stiffly.

"A trip which could have waited. You have caused my sister needless anxiety. This is supposed to be the day of the wedding feast, and you have only just returned."

"Your sister is not some child but a full-grown woman. If she is so anxious, why is it you who are here complaining and not her?"

Neither of them was speaking very loudly, but almost all movement on the street had ceased. Everyone, Lapith and centaur alike, listening to every word.

"Perhaps it would be better to take this conversation elsewhere," I suggested. Such a confrontation was not for public ears.

"Among the Lapiths, kings deal openly with their citizens—and their family members," said Pirithous. He was speaking to me, but his eyes never left Caeneus. "Even if we did not, my future brother here has chosen the place of our encounter. He has challenged me, and I will not skulk away like some coward."

"Challenge?" asked Caeneus, looking a little less angry and a lot more worried. "I came only to ensure that you do not further disrespect my sister. I made no formal challenge—nor do I intend to, as long as you respond as you should."

"I am glad to hear it," said Pirithous in what I recognized as his mock-serious tone. "After all, should you defeat me, Hippodamia could no longer become queen. Being a sister to the king is not quite as glorious. Would you not agree?"

Caeneus's anger flared redly in his eyes. "You dishonor me to suggest that I would ever do anything to harm my sister."

"Then what exactly did you intend to do?" asked Pirithous. "I am about to marry into your family—but I am your king before I am your brother. How then, can you question what I do? Particularly when I have done nothing to harm your sister. I promised to be back in time for the wedding, and so I am.

"I have nothing to apologize for, and therefore, I will offer none. Nor could you have expected any. So how else could this conversation have ended but in a challenge?"

I didn't understand Lapith ways well enough to interfere, but I longed to advise Pirithous to be more conciliatory. What was there to gain by alienating his bride's brother—who, at least from the standpoint of Athenian etiquette, had a legitimate point? And why insist on making the confrontation public?

Much to my surprise, Caeneus deflated like a pierced wineskin. "Of course, you are correct, my king," he said, his eyes drifting away from Pirithous and down toward the ground. "I should have considered my words and actions more carefully. It was wrong of me to assume that you would ever do anything to harm my sister."

Wide-eyed, I looked back and forth between them. Something was definitely not right here. Relieved as I was that Caeneus had backed down, I could not understand how anyone could so easily dismiss his own rage. Were it not for the fact that I had sensed witchcraft when I met Medea, I might have assumed that Caeneus was under some kind of Thessalian spell. After all, the region had spawned more tales about witches than it had about centaurs.

"I accept your apology," said Pirithous, his smile back to normal. "Let us go to the palace and prepare for what is to come."

By then, I was numb enough to surprise that the three of us traveling together did not unnerve me too much, but a greater surprise awaiting me at the palace.

"I do not like this playacting," said Caeneus as soon as we were behind the palace walls and alone.

"If it raises my stature among the centaurs, is it not worth it?" asked Pirithous.

"You mean...you mean you only pretended to argue?" I asked. "What was the point of that?"

"Caeneus here is a well-known hero in these parts," said Pirithous. "That I could make him back down so easily will make the centaurs have more respect for me—which will make them more prone to be my allies rather than my enemies."

"Hero I'm sure he is," I said. "But even so, he is one man, standing against his king—and a son of Zeus besides. What man with even reasonable prudence wouldn't back down in such a situation?"

Pirithous smirked. "I see you have not heard the stories. Well then, a demonstration is in order."

The Lapith king drew his sword and swung it as if he intended to behead Caeneus on the spot. I should have intervened, but Pirithous was too fast for me.

The blade did indeed strike Caeneus's neck—and bounced away without even scratching him.

Perhaps there was witchcraft I couldn't sense.

"How...how is it that your blade didn't wound him?"

"A gift from Poseidon," said Pirithous, winking at me. "His skin cannot be penetrated by any weapon. Nor is that the only gift the king of the sea has bestowed upon him. Poseidon also made him a man."

Forgetting my manners, I stared openly at Caeneus. "You mean…he was a boy, and Poseidon aged him overnight into a man?"

Pirithous laughed. "No, Poseidon worked even a greater miracle than that. You see, Caeneus was once Caenis—and a woman."

Again, I found myself staring at Caeneus, remembering my earlier thoughts about his prettiness and grace. It didn't take too much effort to imagine him as a woman.

"I have never heard of such a miracle before," I said. "If I may ask, how did it come about?"

"He's curious because Poseidon is his father," said Pirithous.

As much as I liked Pirithous, his casual betrayal of my secret brought my blood to a sudden boil. "I told you that in confidence!"

Pirithous shrugged as if I spoke of trifles. "Caeneus can probably tell who your father is. Anyway, I told you, among the Lapiths being the son of a god is no cause for shame. I suspect the Athenians would feel the same way—if you gave them the chance."

"He is right," said Caeneus slowly. "There is something about you. I can sense we were both touched by Poseidon in some way. Since I've never heard of him changing another woman into a man, I would have assumed he had to be your father."

"And you don't mind Pirithous talking about your secrets?"

Caeneus laughed, though less joyfully than Pirithous had. "Around here, everyone knows. It's hard to be a woman one day and a man the next and not have people notice. But no one looks down on me because I was once a woman. If anything, they are impressed that Poseidon would favor me so much."

I felt a momentary twinge of jealousy. "And why did he?"

"When I was a woman, he looked at me lustfully. Some women would have come to him willingly enough, but I was hesitant. I knew how being with a god could complicate my life."

I nodded my head slowly. "My mother would agree with that. Athena persuaded her to let the sea god bed her so that she could give birth to someone who would be a worthy king of Athens."

"Leave it to Athena to find a seemingly rational justification for Poseidon to lust after mortal women!" said Caeneus. "She did not come to me to whisper such excuses on his behalf. Anyway, he didn't impregnate me."

I tried not to show how deeply the idea that Athena might just have been making up excuses in my case cut into me. "Then why did you let him bed you?"

"I almost didn't. But there was one thing I wanted, something only a god could give me. You see, I never felt quite right in a woman's body. It was as if I had the soul of a man from the very beginning. So I told Poseidon I would sleep with him—but only if he made me a man afterward.

"I could tell he was astounded by my request, but he agreed. They say Poseidon is rough in bed, but with me, he was very gentle. I flattered myself later that he felt something beyond mere lust for me. Anyway, when his urges were satisfied, he not only fulfilled the agreement, but he gave him impenetrable skin as well."

Jealousy gnawed at me again, though I knew it wasn't a rational response. Poseidon had intervened for me against Minos in a spectacular enough fashion to have satisfied me about how he felt. And Athena and Poseidon had both indicated he was often with me, even though he didn't show himself. He had also given me a wish, though it was hard to use it. The feeling that I would use to avert one crisis only to face a worse one the next day haunted me. Despite that, my memories of Poseidon had kept me more or less satisfied for years. Then again, I was his son. To me, he had given much. There was no denying that. But he had given a woman he hardly knew everything she wanted—and more. I struggled to see justice in the way he doled out favors.

"Don't look so glum," Caeneus said, misinterpreting my expression. "I know the tales say I was raped by the sea god. But do not think your father took me by force. Men always like a salacious tale best, whether it is true or not. I yielded to Poseidon willingly enough. I have never once regretted that choice. I am a man, just as I wanted. And I am a great warrior, greater even than Pirithous."

"We have never put that to the test," said Pirithous. I glanced over at him and caught him frowning.

Caeneus met his frown with a grin that mimicked Pirithous's usual expression. "We can if you wish, but we both know what would happen.

If you cannot wound me, how can you hope to defeat me? And if I defeated you, the Lapiths would want me to be king. Where would you be then?"

Caeneus was still smiling, but like Pirithous, he hid other emotions behind that smile. Their earlier argument might have been pretense, but there was real tension between them. I could feel it almost as much as I could feel the touch of the gods upon them.

Yet when I looked back at Pirithous, he too was smiling. Masks upon masks!

"I suppose out looking for another bride. Hippodamia would marry a king, not a former king. After all, she is, as you constantly remind me, granddaughter of a river god and great-granddaughter of Ion, the first ruler of the Ionians. Surely, such a woman would never be content with any man who did not wear a crown—not even a son of Zeus."

"Zeus has many sons," said Caeneus, waving his hand dismissively. "If they were slaves, they could be had for a drachma a dozen."

Pirithous's smile looked more and more like a grimace, and above that smile, his eyes glittered like sunlight striking steel.

"How go the wedding preparations?" I asked. In truth, I could have cared less. But I feared Pirithous and Caeneus might fight for real if the conversation continued the way it was going. Though I still felt the sting of Pirithous revealing my true parentage, I didn't want to see him get into a fight he couldn't win.

"While Hippodamia's future husband was roaming the land, she was doing what was necessary," said Caeneus. "She offered her childhood girdle to Athena and a lock of hair to Artemis, signifying her transition into womanhood, though in truth, she has been a woman for quite some time. She has also sacrificed to the gods in general to bless the wedding—though that ritual is supposed to involve both the bride and groom."

"So long as the gods get their sacrifice, I don't suppose they care," said Pirithous.

"Uh, that is about the way we handle the premarital rituals in Athens," I said quickly. "The final sacrifice is usually handled by the couple together, but it is still considered legal even if only one of them can be present."

"We are not so backward as you supposed, then?" asked Pirithous. His eyes looked less like steel, so I could tell he was joking.

"In fact, I find your people quite civilized," I replied. "The stories about them do not do them justice." Seeing that Caeneus was about to speak and fearing what he might say, I added, "My feeling that we should be allies is even stronger than before. Though I do not think the Cretans will necessarily pose a threat, uniting the cities of the mainland against them could eliminate even the possibility of such a threat."

"Exactly!" said Pirithous, giving me a discreet wink. Caeneus closed his mouth and looked back and forth between us. He didn't know me well enough to tell whether I was lying or not. He knew Pirithous better, but the Lapith king was apparently well-practiced in lying. Caeneus looked suspicious, but he did not question us further.

Not long after, Caeneus had to return to his father's house to help with the preparations for tomorrow's wedding feast. I breathed a sigh of relief. Keeping the peace between him and Pirithous was exhausting.

"You worry too much," said Pirithous. "Caeneus doesn't like me, but his dislike for me is outweighed by his love for his sister. As long as I make her happy, he will restrain himself."

"But sometimes, you goad him," I said. "Is that really necessary?"

"Sometimes I goad you, but you aren't so easily offended as he is."

"It's not the same. There are hard feelings between you that it would be best to work out—for your sister's sake, and the kingdom's."

Pirithous sighed. "If I say I will treat him better, will you stop nagging me about it? I brought you here as a friend, not as a second mother to constantly correct me."

"I'm sorry. It seems to be my nature to worry. And I did come for a wedding, not a civil war."

Pirithous laughed. It was hard not to like him when he laughed that way. "Your apology drifted so quickly into another criticism that I almost missed it. Come, critic, for there is much more of the city to see —unless you'd prefer to cower here, safe behind the walls?"

"As long as we keep clear of Caeneus, I'd love to see the rest of your city."

This time, Pirithous kept mostly to little trafficked streets—though whether to avoid Caeneus or the centaurs, I wasn't sure. Without the centaurs around as a distraction, his people noticed him much more readily and greeted him more warmly. Me they looked at like some exotic beast in a menagerie. Evidently, they didn't see too many strangers, particularly not in the company of the king.

For all his earlier dismissiveness, Pirithous didn't once introduce me as a son of Poseidon. In fact, he called me "son of Aegeus" more than once. That seemed as close to an apology as he was capable of giving, and I accepted it as such.

Yes, I could forgive him easily. But I still found myself jealous of Caeneus, showered with favors as he was by a god who seemed hardly to have noticed his own son in a long time.

But what did it matter? I could put up with Caeneus during the wedding, and before long, I would be back in Athens. Soon enough, I would forget about him—or so I thought at the time.

We were still out roaming the streets when the sun began to disappear below the western horizon, and the shadows lengthened. I was just about to suggest returning to the palace, for surely, by now, Pirithous's counselors would be fretting about where he was. But a woman stepped out of the shadows so abruptly that I jumped. She was dark-haired and beautiful as far as I could tell in the failing light, but that was not what caught my attention.

I drew my blade without hesitation. "Pirithous, a witch!"

He looked at me as if I had suddenly been struck insane. "Did you think I couldn't recognize witches just as readily as you can? Put your sword away. You won't need it right now."

I was shocked by his casual manner, and I hesitated.

The woman's eyes narrowed. "Keep your sword drawn on me, and you will surely anger my mistress, the Three-Formed, who does not tolerate such insults to her devoted followers."

Pirithous raised a hand. "He is a visitor who has not yet learned our ways. He meant no offense to you or your goddess. Theseus, sheathe your weapon *now*."

Pirithous was acting nothing like Aegeus when he had been under a spell. Reluctantly, I did as he asked—no, as he ordered. His tone left little doubt that he was speaking as a king, not as my friend.

"The king speaks the truth. I am...ignorant of your customs. I intended no insult."

The witch smiled, but it was cold as winter. "Then none will be taken. However, after you return home to Athens, just to be on the safe side, you should travel to the island of Aegina and offer there an appropriate sacrifice in the temple of my goddess."

My blood ran as cold as her smile. She knew, if not who I was, at least where I lived. Nonetheless, I nodded in agreement. "I will take your wise advice."

She nodded in return, then turned her attention back to Pirithous. "I just came to tell you that all is in readiness for the wedding, Majesty."

"I am grateful to you, your sisters, and Soteira. I will offer appropriate sacrifices when the marriage rituals have been concluded."

The witch bowed, though not quite as low as was customary, and then vanished into the shadows without asking permission to depart.

I opened my mouth to speak, but Pirithous raised a finger to his and motioned for me to follow him. Unlike our earlier, leisurely pace, we rushed back to the palace without speaking a word. Until that moment, I would never have believed that Pirithous could stay so solemn—or so focused—for that long.

Only when we were back in the palace and near enough to the hearth fire to banish all shadows, did Pirithous relax and speak to me again.

"Why would you go out of your way to anger a witch?" he asked me.

"Because...because they are evil," I said slowly, not sure how to explain this obvious fact to him if he didn't already know it. "I feared she meant to harm us."

"I did not take you for one who could be frightened so easily," said Pirithous, but he was the one who looked frightened. His skin was pale in the firelight.

"Have you not heard of Medea?" I asked. "She burned down the palace in Corinth—with the royal family inside. She killed all but one of her own sons. She put Aegeus and all of Athens under spells. She tried to trick Aegeus into poisoning me."

"I've heard the tale and know that it is true," said Pirithous. "But

Medea is not a typical witch. She is close to being a goddess and thus quite a bit more powerful than most."

"But couldn't a large number of witches acting together work significant mischief? I hear that they are numerous in this area."

"They are numerous—but they are not necessarily intent on working evil. That is slander devised by their enemies."

"Then why do you seem so…cautious about them?"

Pirithous managed to smile. "They may not be evil, but they will definitely respond if provoked—as will their goddess. For that reason, it is far better to keep them as allies rather than enemies."

"By their goddess, you mean…Hecate?"

"Well, at least you know that much. Yes, Hecate, called the triple one because Zeus himself is said to have rewarded her siding with him in the great war against her titan kin by giving her power over sky, sea, and earth. Not absolute power in any of those places, of course—but no other goddess is so versatile in her range of power as is Hecate. To all those strengths, she added power in the Underworld after she accompanied Persephone to that dark realm. Given the kind of power she already had, it did not take her long to learn the secrets of death and night as well. No wonder the witches refer to her as Soteira—savior—for she has the power to save anyone she pleases. She also has the power to destroy anyone she pleases. Now, do you see why I deal cautiously with her followers?"

In a conspiratorial whisper, he added, "Besides, they can be useful."

"But are you using them—or are they using you?"

Pirithous chuckled. It was a relief to hear the sound. "We are like man and horse. The man rides the horse, but the horse is fed and cared for by the man. Each benefits the other."

"So, are you the one riding or the one being ridden?"

Pirithous's loud laugh echoed off the walls. "Were you not my friend, I would have to challenge you to battle for such a question. I am king here, and they are my subjects. But just as I do not go out of my way to alienate the officers of my army, I do not go out of my way to alienate the witches, either. For that reason, I have made a pact with them not to outlaw their practice of magic. If they break a more general law—by murdering someone, for example—they receive the same punishment as anyone else. Otherwise, I leave them alone to serve their goddess as they will. In exchange, they do me favors from time to time. For instance, they make sure that no renegade witch operates anywhere in Lapith territory, and particularly that none seek to work against me with witchcraft. They are especially vigilant at times such as the wedding. That is why one came to speak to me tonight."

"And how do your people see this arrangement?"

"As a practical necessity. It's safe to say they fear the centaurs far more than they do the witches."

I had a hard time understanding any of this, for I had been raised to view witches with deep suspicion. Of course, I knew of places, like the temple at Aegina, where Hecate was worshiped, but those temples were manned by priests, not witches, and many came to worship there who had no skill with magic.

But I was in Pirithous's kingdom. If I didn't want to create tension between the Lapiths and the Athenians, my only choice was to follow his lead. Or so I told myself at the time. But the truth was that I already valued his friendship too much to risk losing it. Like him, as long as the witches stayed out of my way, I would stay out of theirs.

We dined late but were up early. Pirithous made sure that the palace was properly prepared to receive the bride. Even Caeneus would have been pleased by his future brother's rare conscientiousness. Alas, the woman turned man was not there to see it. He was no doubt in the house of Atrax, his father, helping to prepare the bridal feast. Nor was there any sign of Hippodamia, who, just as we still do in Athens, was having a ritual bath to purify herself for the ceremony, after which she would spend her last hours as a single woman in the company of her female relatives.

The house of Atrax, though not as magnificent as the palace, was appropriate to his position and thus large enough for a royal wedding feast. When Pirithous and I arrived, he greeted us at the door. Though much older and mostly gray-haired, he stood straight, and his handshake was firm. When close to him, I thought I could hear the distant rushing of a river—not unexpected, since he was the son of a river god.

He adhered to custom by being duly deferential to his king, but he was no idle flatterer seeking favors he had not earned. I thought he would make a good father-in-law for Pirithous.

To my surprise, some of Atrax's servants led us out of his house, down one of the main streets of Larissa, and toward a nearby forest.

"What are we doing?" I asked Pirithous. "Is there to be no bridal feast?"

"There is, but, large as Atrax's house is, he feared there might not be enough room—because of the centaurs, you know. Hence, we will dine outdoors, among the trees."

Sure enough, we walked a short distance into the forest and found ourselves in a large clearing in which two massive, oak tables sat, one for the men and the other for the women. The wood of the tables was freshly hewn and smelled of sap. Only a day or two earlier, these tables had been trees.

Seeing me studying them, Pirithous said, "They had to be built especially for this occasion. It would have been too cumbersome to put them together somewhere else and carry them here."

Indeed, each table stretched out almost as far as the length of a large ship. All this to accommodate the centaurs! Pirithous really wanted that alliance to work.

Not all the Lapiths shared his enthusiasm, however. As the Centaurs trotted in to take their places for the feast, the men of Larissa tensed. Even Atrax, sitting at the head of the table as the host, looked warily at his four-legged guests.

Most of the human guests were armed. Bringing weapons to a wedding feast would have been a grave breach of etiquette in Athens, but Pirithous had told me that in Thessaly, the guests always armed themselves as a way of honoring the warrior groom. He insisted I wear my sword and carry my shield and club on my back, as I was in the habit of doing. They had felt like excess weight as we walked to the grove, but now, seeing the centaurs standing across the table from us, I was glad to be armed.

CENTAURS AT A WEDDING

THE CENTAURS LOOKED JUST as suspicious of the humans as most of the humans were of them. And, like their human counterparts, they were armed. Some carried tree branches more than heavy enough to be used as clubs. Others carried crude spears tipped with sharpened stones.

"Where are your guards?" I muttered to Pirithous. Even at a wedding, a king should have some men nearby.

"I couldn't very well surround myself with armed men," said Pirithous, unconscious of the irony. "The centaurs would take it as a sign of weakness." Under other circumstances, I might have laughed.

"I have men nearby," he continued quietly. "They will move at the first sign of trouble and can be here in a couple of minutes. They won't be needed, though."

Pirithous left my side to join Atrax in greeting the guests. Not wanting to risk offending the centaurs by appearing to stare at them, I turned to see how the women were faring at their table. It had never occurred to me to ask about female centaurs, and I saw none, making me wonder if all centaurs were male. What I did see was an uneasy gathering of human women, stealing glances at the centaurs whenever they could.

The exception had to be the bride, Hippodamia. She never looked in our direction. If the Lapiths followed the same customs as the Athenians, she was veiled and deliberately positioned so that she faced away from the men's table. That way, there was no chance the groom would see her face when she raised her veil to eat. Later, when the time came for her to leave the feast with Pirithous, he would remove her veil, symbolizing the fact that they were now husband and wife. Technically, though, the marriage would not be legal until he had taken her into his home.

"I do not recognize you. What is your name?"

The voice was deep but hoarse. When I turned to respond, I saw that it belonged to the centaur standing directly across from where I was sitting.

"I am Theseus, son of Aegeus."

"You humans are curiously attached to your fathers. I am Eurytion, son of Centaurus, the son of Ixion, the son of Ares. But I am neither more nor less than I would be if I had other forebears." He did his best to lean a little closer to me, a movement made difficult by the width of the table. "My great-grandfather was a god I have never met. My grandfather was a notorious sinner, and my father was intended to be a curse upon him. This is no lineage to boast of. Yet if I were human, it would give me a fair claim upon the Lapith throne. I ask you, where is the sense in that?"

Though uneasy with his line of conversation, I tried to smile. "I agree with you, Eurytion. Men and other thinking beings, such as you centaurs, should be judged by what they do, not from whom they descend. I use my father's name only to distinguish me from other men called Theseus."

Eurytion nodded vigorously. "Well spoken. How do you come to be here, Theseus? Your accent tells me you are no Lapith. You come from the south?"

"Yes, from Athens," I said, marveling at the centaur's civilized demeanor. I had always heard the Thessalian centaurs were savages, but this one certainly wasn't. He seemed more like Chiron, the ancient centaur son of Cronus who lived on Mount Pelion and had been a teacher of many great heroes.

"And you are here because…" prompted Eurytion.

"I am the king of Athens, come here in hopes of negotiating a treaty with your king."

"You mean Pirithous? He is not *my* king. Centaurs acknowledge no man as their ruler. We have chiefs, of whom I am one."

"I meant no offense," I said. "I have never visited this land before, and in Athens, I heard only rumors about centaurs. To be honest, I doubted you really existed."

Eurytion laughed heartily at that. "In Thessaly, we only hear rumors about Athenians. I never doubted they existed, though. In any case, I also am here to negotiate—or so Pirithous claims. I begin to wonder if my brothers and I are not just exotic decorations for his feast."

I wondered if Eurytion was joking, but his expression was serious as death.

"I haven't known Pirithous that long, but he has always been honest with me. I'm sure he intends to negotiate with you in good faith."

"Don't let this one get on your nerves," said Pirithous, sitting down beside me. "He is notorious for being a straight-faced kidder."

The centaur smiled, and the ones on either side of him chuckled.

I glanced at Pirithous. "You didn't tell me the centaurs had such a sense of humor."

"I wasn't sure I needed to. They only share it with humans they like."

The centaurs chuckled again. I had seen them as almost intruders here, but for a moment, the relationships among us shifted. It was they who could share an inside joke with Pirithous, while I, whom he had called friend, was suddenly the outsider.

Before I could respond, slaves began heaping food upon the table. I knew that the cooked meats from which steam rose couldn't have been carried all the way from the palace or even from Atrax's home, so I looked around. Sure enough, there were fire pits at the far end of the grove that I hadn't noticed before.

I wasn't sure what centaurs ate, but it quickly became clear that their diet was more like that of humans than like that of horses. Their table manners were less formal than what I was accustomed to in Athens, but the Lapith men ate in much the same way—as if the meal set before them might be their last. It was not long before crumbs and bits of meat were scattered all over the table, but no one seemed to mind.

I was beginning to reconsider the idea that centaurs were less civilized than men—and then the wine was served.

Since I couldn't bring myself to trust Dionysus, ever since my ill-fated landing on Naxos, I drank as little wine as possible. Usually, I had a sip or two—a few at most—so as not to seem antisocial. Of course, I drank in the Greek manner, diluting the wine with water. One sip of the Lapith wine told me there was almost no water in it. No one else seemed to notice, which meant the Lapith men were accustomed to drinking in this way.

Pirithous sipped little more than I did. Despite the festive occasion, he was in an unusually serious mood, mostly ignoring his cup as he chatted with the centaurs across the table about his idea for an alliance between centaurs and Lapiths.

"You could hunt your food much more easily with bows and arrows than with spears and clubs," said the Lapith king, leaning over the table. "The bowyers of Larissa could provide you with the finest in the land; the fletchers could keep you supplied with arrows. All you would need to do in return is serve as cavalry for the Lapith army in time of war."

"My people are…accustomed to their ways," said Eurytion, slurring his words a little. It occurred to me that centaurs might not be used to wine. "They may not wish to change their method of hunting. And… and fighting in human wars may not appeal to them."

"They seem eager enough to fight," said Pirithous.

"If they have a personal grievance, yes. They may not muster that kind of enthusiasm for someone else's grievance."

"But will not a threat to the Lapiths be a threat to you as well? If we are conquered—"

"It matters little to us which group of humans…sits behind city walls," interrupted the centaur to the left of Eurytion. He was weaving back and forth slightly, as if unsteady on his legs. "They will not trouble us in the forest."

"Unless they wish to cut part of it down and build another city," said Pirithous. "If you are allies of ours, we will respect the boundaries of the woods you claim. Other men might not be so respectful."

"Enough talk!" bellowed the centaur to the right of Eurytion as he pounded his goblet on the table. "This is a celebration, not a negotiation. What we need is more wine, not more words."

I glanced over at Pirithous. His smile was fading as he realized, perhaps for the first time, that it would not be as easy to win over the centaurs as he thought.

"I will have more wine brought—"

"Is that wise?" I asked before he could finish. "It is nearly time for you to remove your bride's veil and take her back to the palace with you."

What I was really thinking was that the last thing the centaurs needed was more wine, but I didn't want to start an argument.

"More wine!" bellowed the centaur, smashing his empty cup repeatedly on the table. Some of the others joined in.

I looked at Eurytion, hoping he would do something to restrain his people, but he seemed more amused than worried. "Yes, more wine! Should not a host attend to the wishes of his guests?"

Pirithous turned and signaled to the slaves, but Caeneus waved them off, then walked over to Pirithous.

"My king, it is time—"

"Yes, he is your king," said one of the centaurs. "So why are you giving him orders? More wine!"

The centaurs, drunk enough that they could hardly stay on their feet, quickly discarded the human manners they had so carefully tried to maintain earlier in the evening. Flush-faced and bleary-eyed, they shouted, pounded on the table, or both. The human guests, just drunk enough to be quick to anger, started to rise from their chairs, their hands resting upon their sword hilts.

"Friends!" yelled Caeneus, looking more at the humans than the centaurs. "This is a wedding feast, not a tavern brawl."

He intended to say more, but a goblet struck him in the forehead with considerable force. It could not break his skin, but surprise closed his mouth.

I turned my attention back to the centaurs, who were perhaps only seconds away from rioting. In their eyes, I saw the glint of something more than ordinary drunkenness—something dark and powerful. Was this some trickery of Dionysus, or had Pirithous's witches betrayed him?

236

"If we cannot have the wine, we will have the women!" yelled Eurytion, his face twisted in irrational rage. Despite the earlier indications that the centaurs were losing control, most of the Lapiths were caught by surprise when the centaurs, with unexpected coordination, lifted the massive table and threw it at us.

I dropped to the floor and rolled away from the centaurs to avoid being smashed against the tabletop. I was only barely able to get to my feet before the charging centaurs would have trampled me with their hooves. The screams echoing in my ears told me that not everyone had been so lucky.

Even so, the centaurs could have overwhelmed me if I had been a target. But instead of finishing me off, they headed straight for the women's table.

Pirithous, who had also escaped being bashed or trampled, leaped into the air and landed on one of the centaur's backs. The centaur reared and tried to throw the Lapith king, who hung on, then surprised the centaur by leaping again, this time onto the women's table. He drew his sword, which glittered in the moonlight.

"Stop!" he yelled. But the centaurs might as well have been deaf. They surged forward. Some of them threw their spears at him, though he managed to dodge. He could not fight such a large number of the beasts on his own, though, nor with my aid.

I spared a second to see how many more men we had to join us. To my horror, I realized that only a small number of them had evaded the first attack. A few twisted arms and legs projected out from beneath the toppled table, and blood was oozing out in all directions. Atrax, who had been at the head of the table, had not been crushed by it, but he lay groaning nearby, perhaps shoved aside by the centaurs as he tried to interfere.

The situation looked hopeless—until a muffled battle cry sounded beneath the table. It was loud enough to distract the centaurs, who were just about to topple the women's table and Pirithous with it. The table shuddered up from the ground enough to allow Caeneus, uncrushed and untrampled, to dart out, grab a fallen spear, and fling it with enough force and accuracy to pierce the heart of one of the centaurs, who gave a cry that sounded like a horse's neigh and collapsed. The centaurs froze for a moment. They must have heard tales of Caeneus's impenetrable skin, but they had never before seen him in combat.

Where were the guards Pirithous had stationed nearby? There was no sign of them, but surely, they had heard the crashes, screams, and shouts from the grove.

I could hear the distant sounds of combat, and I realized the truth.

Just as not every citizen of Larissa had been invited to the wedding, every centaur had not been, either. Some of the centaur commoners must have engaged the guards intended to come to our relief.

Had the other centaurs been drinking, too? Or was something more sinister and coordinated going on? At that moment, it didn't matter. Pirithous, Caeneus, and I would have to fight off the centaurs on our own.

Choosing the Hephaestus-made club over the Athenian-forged sword, I raced at the nearest centaur, knocking his own tree branch club away with one blow. Next to me, Caeneus was swinging his sword in wild fury, tearing into the flesh of any beast who dared to get too close. He might have started life as a woman, but he had clearly spent long hours mastering weapons once he became a man.

Caeneus and I proved to be enough of a threat to keep the centaurs from advancing on the women. But as they turned to face us, Pirithous struck from behind, slicing with his sword, occasionally pausing to pick up a dropped spear and plunge it into a centaur too far away for the sword to reach. Addled as they were by drink, though, it didn't take the centaurs long to realize that their best strategy would be to divide their forces, with one-third of them focused on Pirithous and two-thirds focused on Caeneus and me.

Nor did it take the centaurs too long to realize how to fight Caeneus. Spears and other pointed weapons were useless against him, but his impenetrable skin didn't prevent him from being stunned momentarily, so the centaurs began striking him with the tree branch clubs repeatedly. They didn't do much damage that way, but they kept him out of action, allowing the rest of the centaurs to focus on me.

It was then that I noticed another anomaly—the centaurs, who should have been made slow and clumsy by drink and had seemed so earlier, performed now with almost as much speed and skill as if they had not drunk a drop. They even adapted to my fighting style, dodging my club swings but staying close enough to poke at me with their spears. The ones focused on me formed a ring around me that rapidly shifted as I moved. If I charged one of the encircling beasts, the one I was charging pulled back, while the ones to my left, right, and rear struck with their spears. By now, I had my shield on my left arm, but they struck it with enough force to nearly knock me off my feet. They also managed to scratch my right arm a couple of times. The wounds were minor, but if they kept bleeding, I would wear down much faster.

Initially, I managed to take a couple of them down with my club, but once they got themselves organized, I couldn't get close enough to one to strike without leaving myself open to the others. Caeneus, befuddled by the constant barrage of club blows, had fallen to his knees. Pirithous had taken a defensive position, his back to a tree whose thick trunk partially protected him against attacks from the rear. His tree was also near the fire pit, and the women had put themselves between it and another large tree. Some of them had also taken burning bits of wood from the fire and had raised them to threaten any centaur who might try to reach them. Hippodamia, veil thrown up over the top of her head, had picked up a spear and was also using it to threaten any centaur who might try to bypass Pirithous and head straight for the women. From a distance, she looked like Athena, beautiful and serene, surprisingly unrattled by finding herself in the middle of combat.

These deployments were clever, but neither Pirithous nor the women could hold out long if Caeneus and I remained stalemated by the centaurs. The bride's brother was already effectively out of the fight, and I could feel myself tiring. Eventually, I would fall, and the centaurs would unite against Pirithous.

I had met powerful opponents before, but always one at a time. Each centaur was stronger and faster than a normal man—and several of them were keeping me hemmed in. Heracles could have defeated them, but I wasn't sure I could.

I heard a cracking sound and glanced in that direction. My eyes widened when I saw that a centaur had managed to uproot a whole tree. He moved toward Caeneus with it, slowly but steadily.

Realizing what he was going to attempt, I knew I had to reach

Caeneus somehow. I drew my sword and flung it at the nearest centaur as if the weapon were a throwing dagger. It was too heavy for such a maneuver, but the centaur was close, and the blade pierced his chest. He dropped to the ground, creating a hole in the circle around me. The centaurs, surprised, didn't immediately move to close the gap. I ran through it, dodging spear tips as best I could.

I thought I could reach Caeneus's side, but I had underestimated the centaurs who had encircled him. Reacting far more alertly than drunkards should have been able to, they turned, spears extended, and did their best to block my path. The ones that had been surrounding me closed in from behind. Concentrated this way, they had the numbers to overwhelm me.

I prayed silently to Athena, to Poseidon, and to Zeus. All three had a stake in the outcome of this battle—if gods cared about humans at all. If they heard me, they gave no sign. I would have to save Caeneus myself.

The centaur with the tree brought it down in a stroke hard enough to shake the ground and shatter the skull of any ordinary man. It could not crack Caeneus's tougher bone nor even scratch his skin—but it could and did drive him partially into the ground. If the centaur could get the hero buried completely, he would be unable to breathe.

The centaurs attacking me had made one mistake. To block my charge toward Caeneus, they had surrounded me closely enough that they were no longer out of reach of my club. I struck again and again, breaking spears and bones indiscriminately, heedless of my blood falling, drop by drop, to the ground below.

I managed to wound or kill several before they pulled back from my fury, but those still standing reformed well enough to keep me from Caeneus, who had been struck twice more by the tree trunk. Only the top of his head was still visible.

"Poseidon!" I yelled as if my voice could carry across the world to wherever he was. The remaining spears poked at me from all sides, and I could only fend off the ones more or less in front of me. I just barely avoided being impaled through the back.

An earthquake shook the ground hard enough to knock me off my feet. I would have been a dead man then, except that the centaurs couldn't keep their footing, either. It was a miracle that none fell upon me and crushed me.

Finally, their hybrid forms put them at a disadvantage. Horses, who had the gift of being able to sleep standing up, were not able to get up quickly from the ground. Neither were the fallen centaurs. While they clumsily pulled themselves to their feet, I leaped over them to reach the place where Caeneus had been trapped. There was no sign of him. Instead, the ground that had entrapped him had collapsed, leaving a large, dark hole. In the gathering darkness of night, I couldn't see how deep it was or what had become of Caeneus.

Was this the best Poseidon could have done for someone he cared about as much as he supposedly cared about Caeneus? I wish I had been surprised, but I wasn't.

A couple of quick sword strokes killed two of the nearby centaurs, but by then, the others had gotten to their feet, and I was still hopelessly outnumbered.

Pirithous was only a little better off. He'd killed four centaurs while they'd been down, and Hippodamia had wounded a fifth with her spear, but he was still facing too many to defeat without a miracle. To be more precise, another miracle. We'd already had one—and it hadn't saved us.

I thought about jumping down the hole, but I had no idea what I'd find. Worse, I'd be abandoning Pirithous and the women to their fate. No, I had to stand and fight.

The centaurs had me encircled again. I deflected their club strikes and spear pokes as best I could, but I would have needed eyes in the back of my head and four arms to keep up with them indefinitely.

A golden arrow struck one of the centaurs from behind, and he fell to the ground, lifeless. Another fell, then another. No human archer could have made such short work of them.

The others looked back in the direction the arrows came from. I should have taken advantage of their confusion, but first, I had to see for myself what mighty archer had come to my rescue.

In the growing darkness, the stranger glowed. His blond hair was bright as the sun, his eyes blue as the sky. His face and body would have inspired sculptors. His bow, bright as his hair, was the same unearthly gold color as his arrows.

That he was a god was certain, but he was neither Pirithous's father nor mine. Instead, he was my cousin—Apollo. I had never met him before, but he was exactly like some of his images in art and descriptions in literature. Only an ignorant man could have had any doubt.

"Centaurs, cease this senseless violence," said Apollo. His voice was quiet, but there was no mistaking his commanding tone. Instead of obeying, the centaurs turned and fled into the woods. He watched them go but made no move to stop them.

"They're...they're getting away," said Pirithous. He looked pale, as if he had never seen a god before.

"There has been enough killing here today," said Apollo. "Did you see the fear in their eyes? They will not attack you again. In the morning, you can gather troops and check the area to be sure, but I think you will find them gone. Nor will they return to trouble you."

"But—" began Pirithous.

"Apollo knows the future," I said. Shaken as Pirithous seemed to be, he looked as if he might try to argue, and Apollo could have taken offense. The last thing my friend needed right now was to get on a god's bad side.

The god nodded. "Even I cannot see all, but I see more than most. The centaur leaders are either dead or frightened out of their wits. They will flee from the area around Mount Pelion and never return to it." He looked over at the fallen table. "Some of the men beneath that are still alive. We must attend to them."

I helped Apollo lift the table, though he probably didn't need my help. Though his muscles were not overly big, they were powered by divinity.

Apollo examined the men, then glanced over his shoulder. "Lapith king, ladies, I need bandages. Healing herbs might also be helpful if someone can fetch some from the city."

Apollo had been right—several of the men, presumably the ones who had been bashed by the table but not directly trampled by the centaurs, still lived, though some had lost much blood, and nearly all had broken bones.

Apollo was the god of healing, among other things, and his hands flew over the wounded, stopping bleeding here, setting a bone there. We mortals helped as we could, mostly sustaining the injured as well as we were able until the god had time to attend to them.

Atrax, barely able to walk, nonetheless tried to help as well until Apollo had time for him. The father of Caeneus spared a glance or two for the hole into which his once-daughter, now-son, had fallen, but these glances barely interrupted the flow of his bandaging and comforting. He was no stranger to the battlefield or to the wounded left to die there.

When Apollo was nearly done, Hippodamia, her veil back in place, approached him.

"Great One, can you save my...brother. He has fallen down that hole over there."

Apollo hesitated a moment before answering. "He lives but is beyond my power to help."

"This is no time for riddles," said Pirithous. I put a restraining hand on his shoulder, but he shook it off.

"And I gave none," said Apollo, his face unreadable. "*He lives* is plain enough, is it not? As for the second part, he is beyond my power to help him because he has fallen clear into the Underworld. Most gods cannot enter there without the permission of Hades, which I do not have. But fear not, for he will before long be in the Elysian Fields. He will know paradise without having to go through actual death to get there. Poseidon will be able to arrange for that."

Jealousy slipped through my heart like a dark, slimy dagger. Would Poseidon have done the same for me? I wasn't so sure anymore.

"Then...then we will never see him again?" asked Hippodamia.

"When you die, you will be reunited with him, but not before."

Hippodamia's disappointment was hidden by her veil. Atrax's was camouflaged by his stoic exterior. But Pirithous was neither veiled nor stoic.

"If he is still alive, how can he belong to Hades? Why can he not be returned to us?"

"That question I cannot answer," said Apollo. I wasn't surprised, for the gods were often sparing with the information they gave to mortals. But I longed for a way to change the subject that would keep Pirithous from badgering Apollo. He had already done more than most gods would have. To push for even more ran the risk of angering him.

The god looked at me as if he could read my mind. But I didn't think even the gods could do that.

"You are wondering about why I came, Theseus?"

I hadn't been, but I nodded.

"It was your father who sent the earthquake, for he heard your cry. He is far away, in the land of the Ethiopians, and could not have traveled back fast enough to be here in person. Athena could have, but she sent me instead, for she knew my healing skills would be needed. But there is another reason as well.

"By the nymph, Stilbe, I was the father of Lapithus, the ancestor of the Lapith royal line. I also helped Zeus create Nephele, the cloud woman, mother of Centaurus, so in a sense, I am also related to the Centaurs. Doubly so, in fact, since Ixion, legally the heir to the throne of Lapithus, was the father of Centaurus. As kin to both sides in this conflict, I wanted to prevent as much bloodshed as I could. If only Pirithous's plan for an alliance had succeeded! Ah, but that was not to be. The best I could do was to prevent the extermination of all the Lapith leaders."

"What has any of this to do with the fate of Caeneus?" asked Pirithous, the anger in his tone unmistakable.

I half expected Apollo to put one of his golden arrows through Pirithous's heart, but instead, the god put his hand on his shoulder in a big brotherly way. "I was answering a question Theseus was about to ask. For your question, I have no answer—or at least, not a complete one. But I can tell you Hades is unbending. Even Zeus avoids interfering with him except in the most dire cases."

"But, surely, the loss of a hero such as Caeneus is dire enough," said Pirithous, sounding less angry but more desperate. "And I am a son of Zeus. If I ask—"

"By all means, pray to Zeus," said Apollo. "But be not surprised if you do not get the answer you crave. The world is not as simple as you think it should be, and the gods have many concerns of which you are unaware."

Pirithous pulled away from Apollo, but before he could do something really stupid, Hippodamia put her arms around him.

"Husband—if such I may call you with the rituals incomplete—be content. We may never see my brother again, yet we know he is alive, and we know he will be happy. How much more than that can we ask?"

I don't know if even she could have persuaded Pirithous not to keep arguing with Apollo, but the god took the opportunity to vanish, leaving the grove in almost total darkness. Fortunately, torches had been brought during the preparations, and the women got as many of these as they could lit.

Pirithous had the expression of a little boy who had been long lost in the woods, but he had the presence of mind to ask the men Apollo had saved how they were faring and to express his sorrow over those who had died. However, even Hippodamia was unable to keep his attention from wandering back to the pit into which Caeneus had vanished. Had Pirithous been alone, I was sure he would have thrown himself down it and tried to bring back Caeneus, pulling him from Hades's very grasp if necessary.

The one person who did get his attention was the witch he had met on the street earlier. He saw her torchlight approaching and ran to meet her.

"You promised me protection, and look what has happened!"

"There is no need to shout," she said. "And protection you had. Did you not hear the battle nearby? My sisters and I helped your guards with magic, or they would have been overwhelmed by the centaurs, who would then have reinforced those in the grove. Instead, your men defeated them, and the survivors fled."

"But what about the centaurs in the grove?" asked Pirithous. "Had Apollo not intervened, they would have killed all the men and carried away all the women. What of that?"

The witch, so steady up until then, flinched a little at his words. "Our power has its limits, Majesty. We were able to protect the grove from attack, and we also kept certain rogue witches away. We had not the strength left to also deal with a threat from within the grove."

Was Pirithous, so recently saved from a conflict with Apollo, now determined to bring Hecate's wrath down upon him? The anger on his face made me fear what he might do. I had to make sure he didn't do something to bring a curse down upon himself—or even worse, upon his kingdom.

"You say no rogue witches got through, yet I think there was hostile magic here. I felt it. Did you not feel the same, Pirithous?"

He looked at me as if he had forgotten I was there. "Something did seem…strange to me."

The witch looked for a moment as if she were sniffing the air. "There is…unfamiliar magic here. I must seek it out."

She moved forward slowly, one step at a time, trying to discern the source of the magic. We followed her and were in turn followed by a fresh group of guards, who arrived from the palace and stood as close to their king as they could manage.

Having heard of the disaster or witnessed the battle between centaurs and guards outside the grove, family members of the wedding guests poured in to take their healing kin home or claim their bodies. The women were taken away by their kin, all except Hippodamia, still stubbornly veiled and waiting to complete the required rituals. Atrax stood with her. Everyone else had done what they needed to do and left the grove as quickly as possible.

Perhaps they, too, sensed something amiss.

"The wine," I said. "The wine wasn't watered, which could just have been a mistake, but its effects were also odd. The centaurs became drunk, yet they were as fit for battle as if they had been sober."

The witch glanced at me, eyes narrowed. "Is any of this wine left?"

"There should be some over next to the fire pit where the meat was prepared, Aikaterine," said Pirithous. The name sounded strange on his tongue, but it fit the witch well, for it was a variation on the name of her goddess.

Aikaterine moved swiftly now, almost running, until she reached the wineskins. Sure enough, one of them was still full. Instead of pulling out the stopper immediately, which I expected her to do, she stroked the wineskin.

"Goatskin, yes? Made from the skin of a goat sacrificed to Dionysus?"

"As is the custom," said Pirithous.

"Did Dionysus cause this?" I asked.

"Be patient, king of Athens. All will be revealed in good time.

The moon was already high in the sky, making her eyes look silver in its reflected light. I had no idea what her definition of *good time* was, but I found myself growing impatient as she felt all the empty wineskins.

At last, she looked up at us again. "It may be the custom to use goatskin from animals sacrificed to the god, but it was not done with these wineskins. The skin is not goat, and the animal from which it came was never offered to Dionysus. Someone must have been afraid that the usual wineskin might disturb the magic."

"So there was something wrong with the wine?" I asked.

She nodded, pulled the stopper on the full skin, and sniffed. She sniffed a second time and then stood, still as a statue, for a long time.

"And what was wrong with it?" asked Pirithous when he could no longer contain himself.

"It has been tainted with herbs and magic," said Aikaterine. "Clever magic, designed to affect humans and centaurs differently. Never have I seen a spell quite like it. The humans would feel the power of the sleep god, Hypnos, and become drowsy."

"Which explains why most of the human guests were too slow to respond," said Pirithous.

"Yes, exactly. The centaurs, on the other hand, would feel the savagery of Ares coursing through their veins. The emotions would be heightened and darkened, and their judgment would wither away.

"The effects of both kinds of magic would be amplified by twisting the power of Dionysus inherent in the wine. The spell was designed to be subtle, working gradually enough that, at first, it would have looked much like the normal effects of the beverage. Masterful!"

"And you allowed this to happen?" asked Pirithous. "How could such magic have been smuggled past you?"

"We checked the grove beforehand," said Aikaterine. "We did not think to check the food and drink being brought from the palace. We assumed you had control over your own people, and you did not ask us to check their work."

"You're saying this was my fault? Choose your words carefully, witch!"

"I am stating facts, not assigning fault. If you wish, I can check all those who are employed at the palace for magical ability."

"Do so as soon as you can," said Pirithous. He was a little calmer but still looked as if he could lash out at any moment. Aikaterine bowed to him—very slightly—and got away only a little more slowly than Apollo.

"Can I trust the witches?" Pirithous asked me. "I know you don't in Athens."

"You cannot trust all witches," I said carefully. "Someone has used magic against you. On that, we all agree. Whether it was one of the witches who are your allies, I cannot say."

"Either it was one of them or someone in the palace—perhaps even someone in a position of trust."

"All of which you will work out—tomorrow," said Hippodamia. "The hour is late, and you have yet to remove my veil or take me to my home. Without taking those steps, we will not be married."

Pirithous gave her a sad smile. "Beloved, this was not the wedding day I hoped for you to have."

"I know, but it was not your fault. You wanted to bring peace between men and centaurs. Even Apollo himself thought that was a worthy idea. Someone deliberately ruined that plan."

Pirithous reached up, gently lifted her veil, and kissed her. "I must speak to the guards for a moment. Then, we will return to the palace and be husband and wife beyond any doubt."

As he stepped away, she looked at me. "Can you stay for a while? A day or so, at least?"

"If you wish it—but I think you will have little time to notice whether I am here or not." I tried to smile, but her expression froze on my lips.

"There were many Lapiths who resisted the idea of an alliance with the centaurs. They will use the night's events as proof that they were right. Someone may challenge Pirithous to combat for the crown. Or worse—they will dishonor themselves by open revolt against their king."

"But after what Apollo said—"

"Aye, that was well-spoken, and praise the god for saying so—but there were not many people near to hear him say it. And even if Pirithous's plan for the centaurs was a good one, what of his alliance with the witches? The centaurs were driven mad by magic. Will not people suspect Pirithous's own witches of betraying him? You are suspicious of them yourself. I see it in your eyes."

"I would watch them carefully if I were Pirithous," I said. "But there is no proof that they betrayed him."

"And how would one obtain such proof when the only ones who can sense the true nature of magic are the very ones we suspect?"

"One can always consult an oracle. Is not the famous oracle of Zeus at Dodona not far from here?"

Hippodamia nodded very reluctantly. "And so it is, but...I do not trust Zeus."

She said the last words in a whisper, though I doubted that would prevent Zeus from hearing if he were paying attention.

"I believe that Pirithous is Zeus's son—but people have long whispered that there is little evidence of that."

"He is a great fighter," I protested. "A great hero."

"He is formidable in combat," she agreed. "But if he is Ixion's son, he would be the grandson of Ares. That could be enough to explain his abilities."

"I feel his kinship to Zeus. It is the same feeling I had when I met Heracles, and no one doubts that he is the son of Zeus."

"But ordinary mortals cannot feel such things. They look at Pirithous and see a man, no more. He is not as mighty as Heracles, nor as favored as Zeus's other sons. Everyone here has heard the story of you and Minos—how Zeus thundered to confirm that Minos was his son, and how Poseidon brought you to his palace deep beneath the sea and gave you treasures to confirm that he favored you—or more, if the recent rumors I have heard are true. Well, Zeus has never so much as let a single drop of rain fall to confirm that Pirithous is his son.

"And consider how the gods intervened tonight. *Your*...father, or so I have heard, sent an earthquake. Athena, your patron, sent Apollo himself. And Zeus? Even though his own son was here and at just as much risk as you or Caeneus, he did nothing."

"Perhaps he knew he didn't need to."

"Or perhaps he doesn't care what happens to Pirithous. Or, as some gossips will say, perhaps Pirithous is no kin to him at all."

She shocked me by grabbing my arm. "Listen to me. Despite their frequent quarrels, Caeneus would have supported Pirithous, no matter what. Now he is gone. My father would support Pirithous, but he is old and now recovering from grave injuries. Theseus, there is no one else, no one I can trust with certainty. The night's catastrophe has made Pirithous vulnerable in a way he has not been since taking the throne. Please, please stay until he is secure on that throne once again. You are the only one I can turn to now."

For a moment, I felt the breath of destiny in the wind. Was this another one of those moments of the type Athena had told me about? A moment when I would choose a path, and with it a particular fate?

Perhaps. Perhaps not. I could not know the future, but I could know one thing: Pirithous was my friend. I could not abandon him now.

"I cannot stay forever," I said. "For I have a kingdom of my own to rule. But I can stay for a while."

That *while* turned out to be longer than I thought.

AMAZONS

JUST AS APOLLO HAD PREDICTED, the surviving centaurs fled the area. But Larissa and other Lapith settlements remained uneasy.

From my experience with Athens, I knew all too well how the slightest discontent could stir thoughts of rebellion in men's secret hearts. Larissa felt the same way to me now. Every shadow could be a cloak for a potential rebel. Every private conversation could be the beginning of a conspiracy.

Once Pirithous recovered from the initial shock of the centaur battle, he seemed happy enough—but I had seen him change masks too often to be fooled, and I could read the signs. His smile was just a little too broad, too strained, and sometimes he kept smiling a second or so too long. And when he thought no one was watching, I saw him brush away a tear more than once. The failure of his alliance plan had hit him hard. Every slight tremor in his hand, every unexpected hesitation, told me that he was far from completely recovered.

Hippodamia did what she could to support him. The first time I saw her without a veil and in full sunlight, I realized how beautiful she was, but beauty was hardly her most important quality. Her ever-moving eyes showed her watchfulness. Her wise suggestions showed her intelligence.

Her strength I already knew from the way she helped Pirithous protect the other women, spear in hand, unshakable.

But my mother would have gnashed her teeth over the way the other men treated Hippodamia. They did not fail to give her the respect owed a queen—but they did not want Pirithous to include her in the council, and they resolutely ignored any advice she gave, no matter how well-thought-out it was.

Pirithous's advice to me, on the other hand, was sometimes downright strange.

"It is time we found you a bride," he said one day in the middle of a discussion about needed repairs on the western wall. "That trip to see the Amazons is long overdue."

I always tried to avoid arguing with him in front of his counselors, but only Hippodamia and Atrax were present for this particular conversation, so I felt free to speak my mind.

"I have been away from Athens for weeks as it is. More important, the Amazons don't marry. Seeking a bride among them would be a waste of time. You and I both have more important things to do."

Pirithous managed a smile that almost looked genuine. "The western wall can wait."

"Well, if there is nothing pressing here, I should go back to—"

"Athens can wait as well," he said. "You spend half the day reading letters from and writing letters to Alexius. The city has not been without your guidance. But its king has been without an heir—and you know how dangerous that can be."

"Why make such a long journey?" said Hippodamia. "Even if a willing Amazon could be found, are there not women enough to choose from nearby? After all, Husband, you didn't need to go so far to find a wife that suited you."

Pirithous took her hand. "You suit me well. But I cannot think of another woman like you. Perhaps if you had a sister—"

He stopped abruptly, remembering Caeneus, who had once been Hippodamia's sister, Caenis. His eyes had that haunted look he seldom allowed others to see.

"You have always said you wanted a strong woman," said Atrax, looking nervously at Pirithous. "Lapith women may not all be like my daughter, but they *are* all strong. I can find you a woman of good family—"

"Uh, Theseus is the son of Poseidon," said Pirithous, his eyes focusing on me. "Only a woman of divine descent would be strong enough for him. Aside from Hippodamia, I can think of none in Larissa."

"On the contrary, there are many—" began Hippodamia.

"Who are four or more generations separated from a god," said Pirithous. "I'm not talking about a great, great-granddaughter of some minor deity."

I caught Hippodamia, granddaughter of a river god, flinching slightly, but that was the only sign she gave of how much Pirithous's careless words had hurt her. Her husband, who should have chosen his words more carefully, just kept on talking.

"It is said that Antiope, queen of the Amazons, is a daughter of Ares."

Despite myself, I laughed. "So you want me to win, not just any Amazon, but their queen? You might as well have me woo Aphrodite herself."

Pirithous waved his hand dismissively. "She would not be the type to settle down with a mortal." He spoke as if I had been serious. "That's why I wasn't suggesting a goddess, merely the daughter of a god."

"This conversation is pointless," said Hippodamia. "I will concede that if the Amazon queen would have any man, it might well be one such as Theseus—but she will not. What is the point of arguing about it further?"

"Don't you see?" asked Pirithous, looking first at Hippodamia and then at me. "The Amazon queen commands a great army, rules the strategically placed city of Themiscyra, on the northern coast of Asia Minor, and has spread Amazon settlement throughout the region. She would be the most formidable ally imaginable. Just think of it—Athens, Larissa, the Amazons, together forming the mightiest force Greece has ever seen."

His eyes lit up as he talked of the future glories our cities could win if only the Amazons fought by our side. It was at that moment I realized why he kept coming back to the idea. It was a replacement for his dream of supremacy aided by centaur allies. For the first time since his wedding night, he seemed happy, even excited.

"Making a marriage proposal might be foolish," I said. "But the idea of an alliance may have…possibilities."

Hippodamia looked at me as if I had gone insane. "Did not you, yourself, tell us of your cousin's Heracles's disastrous visit to the Amazons. Hippolyte, sister of the very Antiope who now rules, was killed in that battle, was she not?"

"I've heard the story as often as you have—and you are leaving out some of the key details," said Pirithous. "Hippolyte fell in love with Heracles. It was only because her fellow Amazon misunderstood and thought that Heracles was trying to abduct her that she died—killed in a fight to rescue her when she needed no rescuing."

"Which suggests that a visit from Theseus could get another Amazon queen killed," said Hippodamia.

"Which proves that even an Amazon queen can be wooed by a man if he is a great enough hero," replied Pirithous. "The battle that followed was a misunderstanding, one that could be easily avoided this time."

Atrax shrugged. "In that case, what's the worst that could happen? Antiope refuses both marriage and an alliance—in which case you are no worse off than when you started. But if she accepts either, the results could be beneficial. And if she accepts both, Theseus becomes the most powerful man in all of Greece."

"Pirithous and I become the most powerful men," I said. "I will not accept any alliance that does not include Larissa on an equal basis."

Hippodamia threw up her hands in frustration. "Men!" she shouted as she stormed out of the room.

"I will calm her," said Pirithous, rising from his chair. "Then we will begin to make preparations for our journey."

Calming Hippodamia took almost as long as the preparations. Eventually, I regretted not listening to her warnings—the very mistake for which I was so critical of Pirithous's counselors—but at the time, I was thinking mostly of Pirithous. Perhaps what he needed was an adventure. Perhaps he also needed to have a triumph that would rival or even exceed what he could have gained through a centaur alliance. I remained skeptical of the outcome, but if we were cautious, we should be able to avoid any major harm.

While his men gathered supplies, I composed a letter to Alexius, who I knew would be choked by frustration when he learned that my return to Athens would be delayed again. I had promised him that I would be returning soon, and I tried to be diplomatic in the way I described the trip. He had been interested in a Lapith alliance and suspicious of a centaur one. I doubted his reaction to an Amazon alliance would be any better than Hippodamia's. Nor would he be pleased by the several weeks that the trip would require or how far away from Athens it would take me.

To be honest, neither was I, but I couldn't just abandon Pirithous. I would make a good show of honoring his suggestions, and then I would return to Athens as quickly as I could.

I will not trouble you with all the details of our trip, which was uneventful. Pirithous would have made the trip in disguise, but I insisted we travel openly, with an armed escort, as befit the dignity of two kings.

The problem with traveling openly was that diplomacy required we visit every single king through whose domain we passed. Given the number of small cities ruled by a king, that was a lot of visits, each more tedious than the last.

When we passed near Mount Olympus, I couldn't help staring up toward its summit and wondering if my father was staring down at me. Pirithous did the same—but with a stolen glance, rather than with a long stare. He must not have wanted me to catch him looking.

Did he think that if he united Lapiths, Athenians, and Amazons in one huge army, Zeus would pay more attention to him? He was wearing his happy mask, and I could not see behind it.

Custom dictated that we also stop and offer sacrifices at each major shrine we passed. We did our duty, but Pirithous's heart didn't seem to be in it. His body stood next to me as I performed the rites, but his mind was somewhere far to the east, imagining Amazon hordes and queens who looked like Aphrodite but could fight like Ares. For the most part, I left him alone unless he wanted to talk.

By the time our group bought passage across the Hellespont, I found myself growing impatient. I longed to pray to Athena to give me the bridle of Pegasus, that Pirithous and I might fly the rest of the way, but I didn't. I couldn't help remembering how riding Pegasus had gone to Bellerophon's head and ruined his life. Besides, if the stories were true, he had once attacked the Amazons while flying on Pegasus. The last thing I wanted to do was remind them of the aggressions of earlier heroes against them.

Themiscyra was far enough east that we had to travel many stadia along the northern coast of Asia Minor to reach it. Though there were a few cities, the area was not as populated as it is now, and we traveled long stretches of beach without seeing a single person. That part of the trip gave me too much time to look out to sea. I tried not to wonder if my father would appear to me or at least whisper to me through the relentless tides.

Pirithous was now happy to the point of being almost manic, but his face looked more strained than ever. I wasn't sure what would happen if our mission proved fruitless. That was something else I tried not to wonder about.

When at last we were near enough to Themiscyra to see the city's highest buildings in the distance, I found myself becoming a little excited. Perhaps it was just because the tedium of the journey was nearly over, but I began to feel hope. If we were careful, we might get something out of this mission, after all.

We were met by an Amazon patrol before we could draw much nearer. The Amazons were all mounted, but they would have looked formidable even on foot.

They were not the savages some men thought them to be. Their well-made armor gleamed in the sunlight, and their spears were well-fashioned also, not like the primitive, stone-tipped poles wielded by the centaurs. They looked as if they were ready to skewer every last one of us if the need arose.

"What is your business here?" asked the tallest among them, her voice calm but firm.

"I am Theseus, king of Athens, and this is Pirithous, king of the Lapiths. We have come in peace to request an audience with Queen Antiope. It is our hope to negotiate to our mutual benefit."

The Amazon's eyes narrowed. "Men always say they come in peace, but that is very seldom true. Nonetheless, the queen herself has the prerogative to decide whether she will see you or not. Ride with us to the city wall, and I will go within and speak to her."

The Amazon had a good understanding of strategy. Our group was too small to pose much of a threat to the city in any case, but she positioned us near enough to the wall that the archers posted at the top could shoot all of us down if we tried anything.

"Not exactly friendly," muttered Pirithous as soon as the leader had gone through the city gates. The other guards remained mounted nearby, their spears deliberately kept visible, though not pointed directly at us.

"Would you receive strangers that much differently?" I asked. "The Amazons have had to fight off a number of attackers over the years. I would not have expected them to open their gates to us without at least some consideration."

Pirithous looked down for just a second, and I realized I had said the wrong thing. Without meaning to, I had reminded him of the way he had opened his gates to the centaurs.

It did not take long for the patrol leader to return. "Queen Antiope has agreed to see the two kings. Your men will have to camp out here. If they are in need of any supplies, we will provide them.

This wasn't exactly a warm welcome, but it was probably the best we could expect.

Themiscyra was an odd city then, much different from what it is today. Even then, it was a port city with an impressive dock. Unlike many cities, in which the homes of the wealthier merchants and the marketplace are both near the center of town, here they were clustered near the docks. The rest of the city more resembled an army camp, with the palace looking much more like a fortress than the less martial palaces of the kings in most Greek cities.

The palace was surrounded by its own wall that looked taller than the city wall. I suspected it had been built as a fort, then adapted as the royal headquarters after the founding of the city. Whatever its origin might have been, it would have been difficult to break into it—or out of it.

The guards opened the gate for us, and then we passed through an inner gate that led to the palace itself. In the courtyard, we dismounted and surrendered our weapons. Neither of us was happy about that, but we couldn't complain—few rulers allowed armed strangers into their presence.

The patrol leader led us silently to the great hall, at the far end of which sat a throne that looked as if it had been crafted from weapon-quality bronze. On the throne sat Queen Antiope, fully armed and wearing a crown that looked more like a helmet than a ceremonial piece, though little sword points projected up from the top in a way that superficially resembled other crowns I'd seen.

From a distance, she could almost have been Ares, but as we approached, I felt my heart pounding, for she had a face more like Aphrodite's. Her arms and legs were muscled like those of a warrior. The rest of her body was hidden beneath her armor. That might have been off-putting, but it wasn't. It made me all the more eager to explore what lay beneath. Despite her stern expression, I could not help imagining my lips upon hers, my arms around her, our clothing lying in two heaps on the floor.

Not sure of Amazon protocol, Pirithous and I both bowed. Antiope motioned us to rise.

"It is not often I have royal visitors," she said, her voice carefully neutral. "And less often that I agree to see them."

"We are grateful for your willingness to meet," I said. "Having heard much of the martial prowess of the Amazons, we can understand why you would seldom need to negotiate."

She frowned slightly. "A good ruler knows when to fight and when to parley. Surely, you did not take me for some savage who knows only war."

"Of course, I did not," I said quickly. I hadn't noticed much except Antiope when I first entered the room, but now I was acutely aware of the two rows of Amazon warriors, one row standing against each of the side walls. "Such military discipline as I see displayed all around me could hardly be maintained by savages. Nor is your record one of savagery."

"You speak well," she said, looking at me as she might a horse she was considering buying. "But is there substance behind those words? Why did you come so far to seek me out?"

"My fellow monarch and I wish to negotiate treaties of alliance among our peoples."

Antiope smiled, but her expression seemed more mocking than warm. "Were you under the impression I was in need of allies, or that, if I were, I would prefer ones too far away to do me any good? Athens is far, far away, and Larissa is not much nearer. In the unlikely event that I require aid, my cause would be lost before a message could even reach you."

I don't know why such a simple truth had escaped me when Pirithous had first proposed the idea. Moving an army of any size to the aid of the Amazons would take months. The same would be true if the Amazons attempted to come to our aid. Our alleged reason for being here looked hollow to her.

"Ah, but allies do not wait for their friends to be in trouble," said Pirithous. "They anticipate hostilities and start moving troops long before they are needed. They also share valuable secrets with each other. Our troops would have much to learn from the Amazons—but you might have a thing or two to learn from us as well."

Antiope laughed—and not in a friendly way. "My sisters and I are daughters of Ares, and our mother, Otrera, was a favorite of Artemis, who taught us both archery and self-discipline. Can either of you offer anything that matches that?"

"The support of even more powerful gods," said Pirithous. "Great as the Amazons are—and all the world acknowledges that greatness—they have not always been victorious."

"And can you offer us a guarantee that we will win every battle—because, if not, I will have to assume you are an idle braggart and send you from my sight."

"King Pirithous is no braggart," I said. "We are both sons of gods—though, to speak the whole truth, we cannot make promises that bind them."

Pirithous scowled and would have interrupted, but I glared at him, and he thought better of it.

"Then what good are you to me?" asked Antiope, her tone harsher.

"The gods do as they will. Does your father, Ares, fight by your side in every battle? No. Your trainer, Artemis? No. Yet both have come to your aid from time to time. It is the same for us. I am a son of Poseidon, who once brought me to his palace under the sea and another time sent an earthquake to confound my enemies. Pirithous's father, Zeus—"

Too late, I realized my mistake. As far as I knew, Zeus had never done anything for Pirithous, at least not that either of us knew of.

"The Amazon queen does not believe us," said Pirithous. "It may be that, unlike us, she cannot sense divinity in another. We must show her." Turning to Antiope, he said, "Put us to the test. Have the two of us fight two of your best warriors, and you will see whose gods will provide the most aid."

For a moment, Antiope hesitated. "As Theseus has said, the gods do as they will. We look for their aid in challenging times but do not try to manipulate them into giving it."

"Well, if you are afraid—" began Pirithous.

"The queen speaks with wisdom, not with fear," I said quickly. "None of us can be sure when—or if—the gods will choose to intervene. It is a mystery beyond mortal understanding. Yet it is also wise to think that an alliance with those favored by the gods will sooner or later prove to be an advantage, is it not? Meanwhile, put us—not our fathers—to the test. We will fight your two best warriors, and if we prevail, we will have proven that Amazons may have something to learn from us."

"A fight to the death?" asked Antiope as if she were asking us if we would stay for dinner.

"Neither one of us gains by sending good people to the Underworld," I replied. "We will fight only until we or our opponents yield."

"Wise answer," said Antiope slowly. "The blood of Ares within me always demands blood, but the voice of Artemis whispers to me that restraint is many times a better course. Your challenge is accepted. I and my sister, Penthesilea, will fight you and Pirithous."

Antiope pointed toward one of the women standing guard. She must have been Penthesilea, though I couldn't tell much about her from a distance.

"I...I did not think we would have the honor of fighting the queen herself," I said. In truth, I would rather have faced her in the bedroom than on the battlefield.

"You asked to meet my best warriors," said Antiope. "In Amazon society, the best warriors are also the rulers."

"It is so with the Lapiths as well," said Pirithous. "We are ready whenever you are."

"Let us proceed, then," said Antiope. "Follow me to the arena in the center of town. There you will prove your worth—or fail, as the case may be."

Antiope was off her throne and marching toward the door before I had the chance to say anything. Penthesilea followed her at the same pace, and the other guards flowed after them as if they been drilled on this exact situation hundreds of times.

Pirithous and I followed them, trying to synchronize with their perfect military rhythm. It was a good thing that we did, for word had somehow gotten out that the queen and her sister were to fight two visiting heroes. The streets were lined with spectators, mostly Amazons, as we moved down one of the main avenues toward an arena massive enough to be clearly visible over the tallest buildings. Even today, Athens has nothing like it.

Antiope led us to a small entrance in what must have been the back of the arena. A few guards stayed with us. The rest split off, presumably to do crowd control.

"Choose your weapons," said Antiope, pointing to racks on which a wide variety of weapons were displayed.

"The ones we came with would probably suit us best," I said.

"A good warrior can make do with what is at hand," said Antiope, giving me a slight smile. "Or is your prowess dependent on that Hephaestus-forged club you carry?"

"Of course, it is not. I choose hand-to-hand. My fists will serve me well enough."

Antiope raised an eyebrow. "Normally in our arena fights, each side makes its own choice, but yours effectively dictates ours. It would be unseemly to fight you with weapons when you have only bare flesh. I do not like to have my choice taken from me."

"If it is against your rules—" I began.

She raised a hand to silence me. "No, there is no rule forbidding

261

bare-handed fighting." Her tone and her frown both suggested disapproval.

"Then I'm sure you can make do with what is…at hand," I said.

She smiled despite herself. "Then it shall be as you have requested. Hand to hand. But I am curious and would know the reason for your choice."

"Fighting with weapons is more likely to lead to injury," I replied. "There is little point in seeking allies only to maim them."

"If, in fact, you end up with allies—but you must defeat us first, and that I think will be more challenging than you imagine."

As Antiope led us toward the arena entrance, Pirithous put his hand on my shoulder. "Do you know what you're doing?" he whispered.

"Their combat training is probably impeccable, but we have the advantage in weight and muscle," I whispered back.

The cheering was as loud as a thousand lions roaring when the queen and her sister entered the arena. It took the heralds a couple of minutes to silence the audience enough for Antiope to announce the match.

"The king of Athens and the king of the Lapiths have come to prove their worth against Amazon warriors," said the queen. "Penthesilea and I have accepted their challenge. We fight hand-to-hand until one side yields."

"To the death!" yelled someone in the audience. Others took up the demand until it became a chant.

"Silence!" yelled the queen. Her heralds did what they could to enforce her command.

"We fight until one side yields," she repeated as soon as the audience had returned to a reasonably calm state. "We do this because the challenge was made in a friendly spirit, not a threatening one."

The earlier lion roars were replaced by a beelike buzzing. The Amazons would not openly defy their queen, but they clearly didn't like either me or Pirithous. Probably, Heracles's disastrous visit, which had resulted in the death of Hippolyte, Antiope's sister, was still fresh in their memory. Why should they trust male heroes when one had brought such tragedy to their city?

An official joined us to ask what the rules were. I explained how boxing was done in Athens, and Antiope nodded her agreement. I wasn't sure about Pirithous, but I had been fighting in that style for as long as I could remember.

Antiope laid aside her crown and other armor, as did her sister. In lighter garb, the shape of Antiope's body was easier to determine and just as alluring as I had imagined it. Penthesilea looked much like her sister, though she was younger—so much so, she would have been thought of as a girl in many Greek cities. But her muscles were looked nearly as formidable as her sister's. As with all Amazons, she would have started arms training and physical conditioning the day she first walked.

When the official declared the match begun, Penthesilea charged Pirithous, and Antiope charged me. Somehow, I had known that was the way we would pair up.

I struck as soon as Antiope got within range, but she dodged my blow effortlessly and then countered with a flying kick. Having never seen a move quite like that, I reacted too slowly. She had been trying to make a head shot and missed, but her foot hit my shoulder hard enough to throw me off balance. She hit the ground and threw a punch of her own. My stumbling dodge was just good enough, but I would have to do better to beat her.

When she threw another punch, I dropped low, then charged her in an effort to get under her guard and hit her with my full body weight. She recovered faster than I anticipated, though. She rolled out of my way and struck me on the back as I shot past, knocking me to the ground.

She tried to pounce on me then, but I rolled out the way just in time. She kicked again as I tried to get to my feet. This time, she struck me in the center of my chest, propelling me backward. Unable to get my balance, I fell on the ground with bruising force.

She landed on me before I could even start to rise and tried to pin my arms to the ground. If she succeeded, I would have little choice but to yield.

Despite her muscle tone, I had assumed she was weaker than I was physically, but her strength as she sought to push my arms down was at least as great as the force I was using to fight her.

Like Pirithous, she was a match for me, maybe even superior to me. It would be no disgrace to lose to such an opponent. But if I did so, I would lose my chance to make her people my allies.

Worse, I would lose the chance to make her my wife. Even as my arm muscles felt as if they were tearing in half, thoughts of marriage ran through my mind.

Pirithous, crazy as some of his ideas had seemed, had been right all along. If I wanted to find a true partner, the best place to look was among the Amazons.

With that thought in my mind, I pushed back with all my might. My muscles, which had felt only a moment before like shredding cloth, were now as strong as steel. I used enough force to surprise Antiope. She was off-balance, and I managed to push her off me.

Before she could recover, I was on top of her, but my sudden advantage did me little good. She managed to knee me in the groin and push back with every ounce of strength she possessed. She pushed me off and threw herself on top of me again.

I prayed silently to Athena and Poseidon, but if they heard, they gave no sign.

Being close to Antiope, I sensed the blood of Ares burning within her, its savage force controlled only by the icy self-discipline Artemis had taught her. But I had divine blood, too. If Poseidon wouldn't come to my aid in person, I still had his blood. I would invoke my inner Poseidon.

I felt my blood surging like the restless sea. It rose higher and higher, pushing back against Antiope's determined arms, dampening the fire of her blood. I threw her arms backward, then rose like a tidal wave, throwing her off me and toward the ground.

As I pounced on her, I saw a new expression in her eyes—respect. She still struggled against me, her blood a raging conflagration, mine a swelling flood. But she was losing ground, bit by bit. Victory would be mine!

I spared a moment to glance toward Pirithous. Despite her youth and lesser experience, Penthesilea remained unconquered. Still on their feet, they circled each other, jabbing when the opportunity presented itself. He had a black eye and some other facial bruising.

To win completely, we theoretically had to win both matches, but I could not spare his part of the battle any more thought. I was still on top of Antiope, and her arms were nearly to the ground. All it would take was—

An arrow dug into the ground right next to us. A confused rumble came from the stands.

Someone was firing on us? Surely, the guards would take care of that.

Another arrow hit, this one even closer to us.

Antiope's eyes betrayed her fury, but it was not directed at me. "I yield!" she yelled. "Penthesilea, do the same! Theseus, release me!"

"But I can—" began Penthesilea.

"Yield! We are under attack."

I rose as fast as I could, and Antiope was on her feet immediately after.

"Guards! Put a stop to this! And seal the arena. This vile assassin must not escape."

Another arrow was speeding down toward us. Standing where she was, it would hit her in the back. I tried to push her down, but she, not seeing the arrow and misunderstanding my intent, pushed me away.

I did the only thing I was sure would save her. I lunged between her and the arrow, trying to position myself so that I would block the arrow's path to her without getting myself killed.

I felt the arrow pierce my shoulder, and blood reddened my tunic.

"Sister, he was trying to save you," yelled Penthesilea. Antiope looked at me, surprised, then turned her attention back to the immediate threat.

"Guards! Find me that archer. Sister, Pirithous, help me get Theseus out of here."

"I can walk," I protested, but I was beginning to feel lightheaded. Tired as she was, the queen lifted me into her arms and ran for the exit without waiting for Penthesilea and Pirithous to catch up. Another arrow whizzed past us, but we made it back through the doorway.

"Sister, if a doctor is not already on the way, fetch one at once. This wound is serious!"

She lay me down upon a nearby bench and tore away part of my tunic to get a better look at the wound.

"Pirithous, assist me," she yelled, but he was already rushing to her side.

"The arrowhead went clear through. Cut it away, that I may extract the rest and stop the bleeding."

Pirithous, no stranger to such wounds, did as he was told. Antiope pulled out the arrow shaft and pressed down on the wound with a piece of cloth, doing what she could to slow the bleeding. I would have protested again, but even in my steadily groggier state, I could tell the wound really was serious.

Penthesilea, who must have been moving as fast as Hermes, had already returned with the doctor—unless I had lost time. My thoughts were becoming confused, blurring together.

From what random bits of conversation I picked up around me, the doctor was the only woman known to have been trained in medicine by Apollo himself. I would have liked to see her work, but I was too dizzy to do much more than keep my eyes closed and pray.

I don't know how much time passed while the doctor strove to halt the bleeding and prepare the wound to heal properly, but I must have lost consciousness at some point.

When I opened my eyes again, the first face I saw was Antiope's. She was bending over me and looking concerned, but she smiled when I opened my eyes.

"Theseus, how do you feel?"

"Tired—but better. I take it...I take it the doctor stopped the bleeding."

"And more," said Antiope. "She anointed the wound with salve given her by Apollo himself at the request of his sister, Artemis. The wound will heal completely. Otherwise, your arm would have been permanently weakened, so great was the damage to the blood vessels and muscle."

"I did not realize the Amazons had such a fine healer among them," I said.

"There are many things about us that the stories your people tell do not reveal. Just as there are many things you have not revealed to me."

I tried to sit up, but she held me back. "Rest now."

"How can I rest when you have just accused me of dishonesty?"

"Not dishonesty...exactly. But your mission is about more than just an alliance, is it not?"

"The alliance would be valuable to both of our peoples."

"Perhaps, but that is not what I asked you. I'm sure you do want an alliance—but you also want something else, do you not?"

"This is not…this is not at all how I imagined our first real conversation would go. But yes, there is something else in my heart."

Antiope nodded. "I knew it. There was something about the way you threw yourself in the path of an arrow meant for me."

"Was it meant for you, or did you just get in the way? The first arrows would have been most likely to hit me. I was on top of you at the time. I thought perhaps a renegade Amazon—"

"As a rule, my people do not go rogue. And, while it is true that we are not very trusting of strangers, particularly male ones, none of them would dare shoot at you while you were my guest. However, the port brings in a certain number of people who are not Amazons. One of them could easily have been in the arena. Your arrival was known for some time before we fought. Someone could have prepared. Tell me, Theseus, have you enemies in this part of the world?"

I was going to say no, but then I thought of Medea. Rumor had it she was on the other side of the Black Sea, in Colchis. Ships doubtless sailed from there to Themiscyra.

"Did you catch the assassin?"

"That is the strangest part. The guards searched for him or her, but the person somehow vanished into the crowd. With so many Amazons among them, I would have thought that someone would have seen something to give us a clue, but not one person, Amazon or otherwise, did."

"Witchcraft," I said. "The witch Medea bears a grudge against me."

"She is not the only witch in the world. Does not your friend come from the witch-haunted region of Thessaly? And is there not a great temple of Hecate on an island only a little way south of Athens? Of course, you could be right, but if a witch is involved, there are many other candidates besides Medea. Doubtless, I have some enemies among them, for they are not permitted to reside in Themiscyra—too dangerous, if you ask me."

"But perhaps not as dangerous as excluding them," I said, thinking about Pirithous's decision to allow them in Larissa.

"Either way, that is a subject we will not resolve tonight. And now, oh changer of subjects, what was your other reason for coming?"

I wanted to work my way to the subject more gradually, but there was an impatience in her expression that forbade any further delay. "I seek a wife...among the Amazons."

Antiope looked more sad than surprised. "And that you might have had—if Amazons were like other women. We do not marry, as well you know. The most we can offer you is a brief union. That is how we maintain our population. We mate with the men in this area from time to time. Any male children we give to them to raise as they will. The female children we take to raise as Amazons. But marriage? You might as well ask me to give you the moon as to give you the hand of any Amazon woman."

"I don't want just any Amazon woman—I want you." Weak as I was, the words came out forcefully enough that Antiope took a step back.

"But marriage to me would not be the same as marriage to any other man," I continued before she could interrupt. "I do not seek a subservient woman. I seek a wife who will be my true partner, who will help me teach Athenian men the value of women."

"A worthy goal, but one I cannot help you achieve."

"Did you take a vow to Artemis or something like that?"

She shook her head. "I am not bound by a vow but by the custom of my people."

"But you are the queen. Can you not just change the custom?"

"You almost make me wish I could. But could you return to Athens and immediately make women equal to men?"

"Of course not, but—"

"But nothing. King you may be, but some changes people will not quickly accept. Your city has decreed that women are inferior to men. My people have decreed that Amazons must preserve our independence by not marrying. Neither one of us can change such deep-seated patterns.

"But your trip will not have been in vain. After your show of prowess in the arena, not to mention your brave rescue of me, my people will accept the alliance you want. That is the best...the only offer I can make."

"There is one other offer you can make," I said, looking into her eyes. "You said Amazon custom permitted brief unions. Stay with me tonight. In the morning, if you still feel an alliance is all you can offer me, I will happily accept it."

Antiope laughed, but not as mockingly as before. "You think you are so magnificent in bed that I will be unable to resist you?"

I smiled my most winning smile. "There is only one way to find out."

FLIGHT

I AWOKE in the morning with Antiope in my arms. She was already awake and watching me when I looked at her.

I hadn't really thought about it before, but she didn't have the same kind of ethereal beauty Ariadne had possessed even before she was a goddess. I didn't care one bit. Antiope's beauty was more like the glow of sunlight upon a sword blade—sharp and dependable, a lifesaver for desperate situations. Beneath that martial façade was a tenderness I didn't think she showed to most people, perhaps not to anyone but me. I could see that part of her in her eyes and in the gentle curve of her mouth. Another man might look at her expression and not see the beauty in it, but to me, it made her face the most beautiful one I had ever seen. Perhaps I was being influenced by what I knew of her mind and heart, but they were far more important than raw physical beauty, anyway.

She was still looking at me, still letting the tender side of her peer out, but she didn't speak a word. She was waiting for me to say something.

"Well, was I persuasive enough?"

"You were...not like any man who has ever slept with me. They

270

either showed fear of me or determination to assert dominance over me, at least in bed. You did neither.

"If I were to marry any man, it would be you—but the problem I mentioned last night remains. Amazons do not marry. Their queen certainly does not."

I don't know what I had expected. Perhaps my hope for more had been irrational. But her words cut me as much as her sword would have.

"I cannot believe a woman as resourceful as yourself couldn't find some way."

Antiope pulled away from me, got out of bed, and began to dress. "Much as I wish it were otherwise, there is no way. However, just to be sure, I will pay a quick visit to the temples of Artemis and Ares. I do not expect that either of them will support your desire. *If* they do, though, it *might* be possible to persuade the Amazons to go along."

"That is all I can ask," I told her, though the idea didn't much raise my spirits. If the principal gods of the Amazons had been Athena and Poseidon, I might have been more optimistic. But Artemis, patron of hunting bands of unmarried women? Ares, who cared only for war? Neither one had any personal connection to me or any logical reason to support my marriage to Antiope.

"Since you are recovering from a wound, no one will be surprised if you stay here, and that is exactly what you should do. Both temples are near enough that I should be able to visit them and return in under an hour. In the unlikely event that I receive the blessing of the gods, we must quickly plan what we will do."

She was out the door before I had a chance to respond. I rolled out of bed, dressed—being careful of my injured shoulder—and stared out the window. There wasn't much else I could do.

The view would have been more interesting in the commercial section. So near the palace, I saw Amazon patrols and very little else. Counting them made me nervous. The forces at the disposal of the Amazons were more numerous than I had thought. That would make them a formidable ally. But it would also make them a formidable enemy.

It was not long before Antiope returned. Her expression was frustratingly neutral.

"Well," I prompted after about a minute, during which she stared at me but said nothing.

"The reaction of the gods was…mixed," she said, looking out the window as if hoping for a different divine answer somewhere in the clouds. "Artemis sent me a vision in which you made me the mother of a great son. As you know, Artemis normally encourages strong, independent women to stay unmarried. For her to send me such a vision suggests that she is in favor of our marriage."

"Then why do you look so grim."

"Because Ares is decidedly not in favor. From him, I felt…anger hot as the desert. Anger, surrounded by hints of darkness. I could not help thinking of death."

"The god would kill you?"

"Or perhaps he would simply let me die. From him, I received no vision, only feelings."

There was only one thing I could do in such a situation. "You are like no woman I have ever met before. And, though I have reason to distrust Aphrodite, I do not distrust the love I feel for you. But if loving you could lead to your death, I will go back to Athens and never lay eyes on you again."

I expected her to nod her head sadly and wish me well. Instead, she ran to me and threw her strong arms around me, clinging to me as if I were a piece of wood in a stormy sea in which she was drowning.

"There is…something about you, Theseus," she whispered to me as if she dared not speak aloud. "You accept me for who I am in a way no man ever has—or ever will, likely. I never desired a man's approval, but now that I have experienced yours, I do not want to let you go so easily."

One of the hardest things I had ever done was pull away from her at that moment. Taking my sword and hacking off my own arm would have been easier.

"I do not want to let you go at all—but I will not let you die, either."

"But if you accept me as an equal, then you must accept that it is not your place to make that choice for me. If I risk death by staying at your side, is that not my right? Or did you mean nothing you said?"

"I meant every word." I pulled her back into my arms. I held her so close that our tears mingled.

"Then I shall marry you—if you, too, are willing to take a risk."

"Anything," I murmured.

Now it was her turn to pull away. "No, listen to me. I must be sure you understand fully. You came here looking for a marriage *and* an alliance. I can offer you one or the other, but not both."

"But did not Artemis bless our union?" I asked. "Wouldn't that convince your fellow Amazons—"

"I cannot prove she did," said Antiope. "Nor can I offer Ares's endorsement as confirmation. My people will never be convinced by my word alone.

"Had you come before Heracles, it might have been different, but his disastrous visit has hardened the hearts of Amazons against heroes from the outside. Most of them believe he came to abduct my sister, Hippolyte, though, in truth, she fell in love with him and would have gone with him willingly. She was killed in the ensuing fight, never having had the chance to make clear what really happened.

"Under such circumstances, no matter what I say, most Amazons will believe that you have somehow coerced me—or perhaps bewitched me. Your friend is said to traffic with witches, after all. Once I announce my desire to forsake the Amazon way, they will attempt to take me prisoner —for my own good, or so they will think—and they will attack you and Pirithous. Even fighters as great as you are cannot withstand any assault by the entire Amazon nation.

"No, the only way for me to stay at your side is to leave with you secretly. And once my departure has been discovered, Amazons will forever after hate you—and Athens. Any hope of an alliance will be dead."

"I meant what I said about wanting an alliance with your people— but I want you more."

Antiope wiped away her tears and forced her face into a more neutral expression. "So be it, then. Here is what you must do. Leave the city with your friend, Pirithous, and rejoin the rest of your men. Prepare them to depart on short notice. When night falls, I will slip away through a secret passage that leads from my quarters to a hidden spot outside the walls. From there, I shall rejoin you. If we ride all night, we will be far enough by the time my absence is discovered in the morning to have a decent chance of escape."

"Your people will pursue us?"

"Absolutely. I will write a letter explaining what I have decided to do, but they will believe it was written under duress. However, they will not find us where they will first look, for we will not follow the same path you took to reach here. Instead, we will move southwest across Asia Minor, then west until we reach the coast. We should be able to book passage on a ship sailing from any one of several places, but I would suggest Knidos, for Poseidon is much worshiped there, and it is said the people are friendly to Athenians."

"You would have us take a longer way—and through more Amazon territory?" I asked, raising an eyebrow.

"If we move fast enough, that will be an advantage. I am known in the territories where Amazon tribes roam. They consider themselves as separate from the city Amazons, but they will acknowledge my authority enough to let me pass through their territories as rapidly as we wish. If all goes well, we will be far from those lands before word of my supposed abduction arrives."

The plan sounded crazy, but I couldn't see any better way to extract us from the city, so I went along with it. We embraced once more, and then I rushed off to find Pirithous, who I found sharing combat strategies with Penthesilea. I noticed again how girlish she looked by comparison with Antiope, but she had the poise of someone twice her age.

I bowed to her. "Princess, please pardon the interruption, but I have received urgent news from home. I must speak with Pirithous about it at once."

"Of course," she said, looking concerned. "I hope it is nothing serious."

"Nothing Pirithous and I cannot fix if we attend to it," I replied. "Come, my friend, I will explain on the way back to camp."

"We are leaving?" asked Pirithous, shocked. Had he not been married, I would have wondered if he, too, was contemplating an Amazon bride.

"Not right away," I said. More quietly, I added, "But we must speak where no one can overhear."

We walked through and out of the city gate in silence. In the short time it took us to walk back to camp, I could see that Pirithous was ready to explode from his impatience.

"Just a little longer," I muttered. He looked as if he wanted to punch me in the face, but he contained himself as I strolled around the camp, checking to make sure we had no Amazon visitors. Then, as if we were just taking a stroll, I led him out of the camp a short distance, so even his own men couldn't overhear us. We would have to tell them what was happening, but that could wait until I'd informed Pirithous.

"For the love of the gods, what is it?" Pirithous demanded when I finally turned to face him. "Something you were afraid an amazon might overhear, I take it."

"Indeed," I replied. "Antiope has agreed to marry me—but to do that, she must leave her people."

"And the alliance?" he asked.

I didn't know how to respond. He knew as well as I did that the alliance story was a pretext for the trip, not our actual goal.

"I could not have both Antiope and the alliance," I said. "I had to choose. But this is what you wanted me to do, right?"

He nodded, but with such reluctance that I realized I should have consulted with him first. He looked right through me, as if he were looking at his own future rather than me. For a moment, something that looked oddly like despair flashed across his face. Then it was gone, concealed once again behind his happy mask.

"Of course, this is what I wanted. The alliance proposal was just to get us in the door."

I thought back on our earlier conversations and realized that he had expected to get me married *and* to get the Amazons as allies. He wanted to make up for the collapse of his centaur alliance plan. For all his talk about kings being able to ignore what their people thought, in that cold moment, I realized he was worried. The Lapiths were skeptical of his leadership. And now, instead of bringing back an alliance that would make his people much stronger, he would come back with a wife for me —and nothing at all for them.

Part of me wanted to call off the marriage and take the alliance instead. But even if I could have made myself do that, it was too late.

There was no safe way to get word to Antiope that I had changed my mind. And even if I could, how would she react? Would she view my change of heart as a rejection? And, if she did, might that not end the prospect of an alliance just as swiftly as her running off to marry me? My conversation with Antiope had been another one of those moments Athena had told me of. I had stepped onto a path I could not now leave.

Pirithous and I shuffled back to camp, neither of us happy, and Pirithous told the men what was up.

I could see disappointment on some of their faces, too, but at least they were loyal enough to their king not to question him. And they were Lapiths, after all. The idea of having to move stealthily but swiftly across the countryside, possibly with Amazons in pursuit, appealed to their sense of adventure.

The men packed as much as they could. They kept the tents up and worked behind them, so that anyone watching from the city walls would be unable to see what they did. There was always the possibility of an Amazon patrol appearing from the other side, but the Amazons were accustomed to the presence of the camp by now and paid little attention to it—at least as far as I could tell. Anyway, there would be nothing suspicious about packing to leave. It wasn't as if anyone thought we intended to settle here.

At dusk, we ate dinner as quickly as we could. However, it was not until later at night that Antiope appeared. I mean *appeared* literally. One minute, she wasn't there. The next she was, as if Artemis had brought her to us invisibly. Covered by a dark, hooded cloak, she would not have been easy to spot at night. Even so, I was impressed by her stealth. Our own lookouts were as surprised as I to find her in camp.

"How did you get here?" asked Pirithous in a low voice.

Antiope smiled. "There is a passageway from my room in the palace that leads out beyond the city walls. No one living knows about it except Penthesilea and me. I left that way, then circled around as far from the city as I could to reach your camp.

"Likely, no one has noticed me. Barring an emergency, no one will realize I'm gone until morning, but it is imperative that we leave at once. The success of this plan rests on putting enough distance between my people and us that it will be impossible for them to catch us."

"Take down and fold the tents," said Pirithous to his men quietly but firmly. "Load the remaining gear onto the horses."

"Someone watching from the walls will see some activity in this direction and wonder what we're doing," I said. "No one would travel at night unless they were fleeing. We are bound to arouse suspicion."

"I thought of that and prayed to the goddess about it," said Antiope. "She hunts at night, remember? She will ask Selene, the moon goddess, to shield us from the eyes of the guards. Look at the moon! Artemis's request is answered already."

The crescent moon above us looked brighter than it should have, but it no longer seemed to illuminate our immediate area. Looking toward the city, I saw what appeared to be a curtain of silvery light. I could almost miss that there was a city there.

"They will not be able to see us any better than we can see them," said Antiope. "From their perspective, it will look as if a mist has rolled in. By the time it lifts, there will be nothing here to see."

Some of them stopped to gape at the strange light. "Keep moving," said Pirithous.

His men worked so efficiently that we were ready to go in five minutes.

"We must move slowly at first, yes?" asked Pirithous, looking at Antiope. "If the horses run too fast, the watchers might pick up the sound of hooves hitting the ground."

"Exactly," said Antiope. "But once we are out of earshot, we can move faster."

"The horses may stumble in the dark," said one of the men. "We should have torches."

"Artemis will provide," said Antiope. Sure enough, once we got out of sight of the city, the unnatural moonlight lit our way. It was not as good as daylight, but if we were cautious in the way we handled the horses, they should be able to see well enough to avoid what obstacles the terrain presented.

We didn't make good time that way, but with eight hours or so before dawn, we should be more than far enough away to evade capture, especially if the Amazons assumed we had left along the northern coastal route and started after us that way.

We rode all night, but by dawn, we needed to rest the horses, not to mention ourselves. Antiope, who knew the land well, led us to a ravine we could nap and have breakfast before we continued our journey.

"No one will see us from a distance," she explained. "The tribal Amazons don't ride through this area very often, anyway."

Reassured, we lay down and closed our eyes. Despite how tense I felt, I dozed off almost immediately, but I did not sleep well.

I dreamed hordes of Amazons descended upon us, having somehow caught up with us. Outnumbered a thousand to one, we fought under a sky red as blood. Soon enough, the ground was equally red.

I awakened suddenly just before an Amazon sword could chop my head from my neck. Around me, everyone else was jerking awake as if we had all experienced the same nightmare.

I could hear the pounding of distant hooves—many of them. We were in an isolated area, with no city nearby and no reason for a large number of horsemen to be approaching.

I risked a quick glance over the edge of the ravine. A horde of men on horseback was riding in our general direction.

No, women on horseback. Amazons! But how?

"Arm yourselves," I said, trying to keep my voice low enough that the approaching Amazons wouldn't be able to hear it over the hoofbeats of their own horses.

"Who approaches?" asked Antiope.

"Your people. Probably too many for us to fight, but by the time we get saddled up, it will be too late to run."

"How could this have happened?" asked Pirithous, drawing his sword.

"Ares!" Antiope snarled his name. "He must have sounded the alarm right after we left and steered the pursuers in our direction. It's the only way they could have reached us so fast."

I said a silent prayer to Athena, but even if she could reach us fast enough, unless she took the battlefield herself, it seemed unlikely she could help enough.

The hoofbeats were very close now. They slowed a bit as they approached the ravine. We were all poised to attack. If we managed to surprise them, we might have a chance.

Before the Amazons could get close enough to have a chance of spotting us, I heard frightened neighs from the horses, uneven hoofbeats, and even a few frantic hoofbeats that sounded as if they were running in the other direction.

It was risky to peak over the edge of the ravine again, but I had to know if something had happened that we could exploit. What I saw made my eyes widen in amazement.

The horses were wild-eyed with panic. Some of them reared as their riders tried to control them. A few of the riders had already been thrown and lay on the ground, stunned and bruised. Others were still riding their contrary mounts, who were galloping away as fast as they could. What could have caused so many horses to take fright so quickly?

At first, I saw no answer. Then I felt a slight chill in the air, a sign that a restless spirit might be nearby.

I only caught a glimpse of him for a second, so insubstantial was he to human eyes, but when he looked at me over his shoulder, I realized I'd seen his likeness many times. He was Sphaerus, charioteer of Pelops, for whom my family had built so many monuments and made so many offerings. Apparently, placating the notorious horse scarer had not been as pointless as I had thought.

"Mount up and ride as fast as you can," I said quietly but emphatically. There was no way of knowing how long Sphaerus could keep our pursuers at bay, and once they realized how close we were, they could charge us on foot.

The Lapith men looked at their king, who nodded his assent. Antiope was already on her horse. It didn't take the rest of our party long to follow her example.

Naturally, the Amazons heard us as we galloped out of the ravine and away from them. But none of them were able to immediately pursue us on horseback, and not even an Amazon could run fast enough to catch us.

After an hour, we had to slow our frantic pace a little for the sake of the horses. That made it easier for me to talk to Antiope and Pirithous so that we could plan our next move.

"Will they be able to catch us?" asked Pirithous.

"Normally, I would say no, for by the time they could have gotten their horses back under control, they will be at least half an hour behind us. Some of their mounts will have been injured, as well. Nonetheless, if Ares is determined to stop me, he may find a way to help them close that gap."

"Can we still reach Knidos?" I asked.

"Perhaps, but from where we are now, it would be a shorter journey to Ephesus. It is almost as close to the coast as Knidos, and there is a temple of Artemis there. If our pursuers get too close, we can seek sanctuary in the temple. Even Ares at his most battle-crazed would be reluctant to violate the land hallowed by another god. And the Amazons do not have anything like the equipment needed to besiege a city."

"Are there not cities closer than Ephesus?" asked Pirithous.

"Indeed—but what few there are nearby are not closely allied with any Greek state. They might as soon give us up to the Amazons to avoid trouble as fight for us. And some of them still worship the old Hittite gods. What we need is a Greek city, and, since all of those are near the coast, we may as well seek Ephesus, where the goddess can best protect us."

Ephesus may have been closer than Knidos, but it wasn't close. We had to cover as much ground as we could each day without injuring the horses. Each night, we posted sentries to make sure the Amazons didn't surprise us, but the men who watched during the night never saw a sign of them. Even so, worry constantly gnawed at my heart.

Ephesus was not anywhere nearly as large as it is today, and the temple of Artemis is not the magnificent one you are thinking of. Still, the city had a decent wall, and the temple would make adequate sanctuary if need be.

We were sufficiently travel-worn and dust-covered that the gatekeepers at first were skeptical of admitting us. Pirithous and I looked little like the kings we claimed to be, and his claim to be the son of Zeus drew only eye-rolls from the guards.

It was our purses that saved us. We had enough gold on us to refute the idea that we were nomads with no business in the city. The giving of generous gifts helped oil the gate hinges, and in no time, we were inside the walls.

"That was humiliating!" said Pirithous, anger making his face twitch.

"For kings to have to bribe our way in! When I get back to Larissa, I will—"

"Do nothing," I said quickly. "Would the guards of Larissa have let in a party like ours? We do look more like refugees than royalty at this point. And it appears we have enough enemies without adding a Greek city to the list."

It was not hard to find Artemis's temple, and there the priestesses helped us clean up and then admitted us to the temple's main room, where a statue of the goddess twice as large as life stared down at us with total detachment.

We all knelt, and Antiope prayed on our behalf.

"Goddess, you who have brought us this far, we pray that you will favor us with your continued blessing and help to complete our escape."

"If you would escape, leave an offering with the priestesses and head at once to the docks."

I gasped at the sound. I had not expected anyone's prayer to get quite that immediate and concrete a response. Certainly, mine seldom did. But the voice was more commanding than any mortal voice I had ever heard.

We remained silent, not knowing what to do.

"You may stand and face me," said the goddess, this time with a hint of impatience in her voice.

As quickly as we could, we rose and turned. Sure enough, behind us stood Artemis herself. Her hair was dark as midnight, her face pale as moonlight and far beyond beautiful, her body slender and lithe but also shapely enough to make it easy to understand why men had destroyed themselves by striving for a glimpse of her naked body. She carried a large bow, and on her back was a quiver filled with silver arrows.

"Ares has been hastening your pursuers as much as he could. They will arrive at the gate within the hour and demand that you be turned over to them."

"We thought that we could seek sanctuary here," said Antiope.

"And so you could—but your pursuers are tenacious. They will try to outwait you if they must. I do not think that you want to live the rest of your life within these walls."

"Goddess, why not appear to them as you have just appeared to us?" If you tell them to, they will give up the pursuit."

Artemis sighed. "Their minds are so filled with Ares now that I am not sure I could. It is better for you to do as I say—and quickly. You have enough coin to get you back to Greece. The Amazon party that has been following you is too small to be a threat to you once you have the resources of your own kingdoms to draw upon."

Artemis faded away in a flicker of moonlight, leaving us alone.

"We must do what she says," Antiope told us—as if even Pirithous would have been impulsive enough to disregard such an obvious divine command. We hastened to make appropriate offerings and then rushed off to the nearby port.

There we hit one final snag.

"What do you mean we can't take the horses?" asked Pirithous, shocked to his core.

"I mean what I said," replied the captain, too far away from the Lapith realm to care whether Pirithous was its king or not.

"But we brought them when we crossed the straights!"

"A much shorter journey," said the captain. "And you weren't in a hurry, then, right? Even if I had a big enough cargo hold, it would take time to make proper accommodations. Anything less would be cruel to the animals. They might not even survive it."

Pirithous, who had been with his horse since the creature was a colt, looking as if he was holding back tears. "But if we paid more—"

"Even if you could afford to buy my ship, it would make no difference. You said you had to leave within the hour. It just couldn't be done. And my ship is the only one in port at the moment. It will be a squeeze just to get your whole party safely onboard."

Pirithous looked at me. "What about Poseidon?"

Despite myself, I almost laughed when I imagined what Pirithous was thinking—a magic wave that would gently lift the horses and carry them all the way to Greece across a sea otherwise smooth as glass.

"My friend, Poseidon has intervened to save my life. Anything much less than that isn't going to get his attention."

"Make them a donation to the priestesses of Artemis," said Antiope. "We never would have made it this far without her. They will see that the horses are well-cared for and sold to people who treat them well. That is the most you can do for them now."

"All right, do it!" snapped Pirithous, as if he were addressing one of his slaves rather than an Amazon queen. However, she ignored his tone, and, with the help of a few of the Lapiths, took the horses to the harbormaster, who, for a fee, was more than happy to ensure they got to the temple of Artemis.

By the time Antiope and the others returned, Pirithous had finished paying for our passage. We boarded as fast as we could, and the captain, good as his word, got us out to sea before there was any sign of the other Amazons.

"You're sure they will not follow us?" I asked Antiope.

"The Amazons are not yet a seafaring people. They might have tried to follow in any case, but without ships in port, how would they do that? By the time another ship arrived in Ephesus or the Amazons rode to another port, we would be too far ahead for them to catch up before we landed in Athens. Amazons are brave always, but foolish seldom. Such a small party would never take on the army of a major city. For the moment, we are quite safe."

I didn't like the *for the moment* part, but I didn't ask any more questions. It would take the Amazons time to raise a big enough army to take on Athens and its allies, even longer to assemble a navy big enough to transport such an army. Surely, even they would not hold a grudge for so long.

While we talked, Pirithous stared back toward the coast as if he could reunite with his horse by sheer force of will. The Lapiths were such great horse breeders and trainers in part because of how much they cared for their animals. He would have no difficulty finding a horse of equal speed and endurance—but it would never be the same for him.

Poseidon granted us a fair wind and calm seas all the way, so it was only a few days before we arrived in Athens. I invited Pirithous to stay for a while, but I was just being polite. He should be getting back to Larissa, and he knew that as well as I did, so he declined my invitation. He accepted the loan of some horses for him and his men to ride back to his kingdom. Then he was gone—leaving me to face the ill-concealed anger of Alexius. I wasn't quite alone, though. Antiope was with me, though I advised her to let me handle whatever complaints he had.

"You were gone much longer than you should have been," he said.

"And yet the city still stands," I replied. I hadn't meant to be that flippant. I spoke before I thought, and he looked a little shocked. Nonetheless, he stood his ground.

"The systems you have developed made it easier for us to make do in your absence, but a kingdom is not meant to be so long without its king. The people became anxious. And had there been an emergency—"

"You would have handled it with your usual skill."

"And what if you had been killed? You told me yourself that you were in danger more than once. You still have no heir—"

"A lack that will soon be remedied," said Antiope. "I carry his child—his firstborn son."

My heart pounded, and my eyes lost focus for a moment. I wasn't sure who was more surprised—Alexius or me. Antiope and I had only been together once.

"Yes," she said in answer to my unspoken question. "The child was conceived the very first time I lay in your arms."

My mind wrestled with that detail as I tried to keep my facial expression impassive for the benefit of Alexius.

Artemis must have known Antiope was already pregnant when she helped us run away together. But if the goddess's only interest had been in the child, since he was male, Antiope could have sent him to me after he was born, just as the Amazons always did with male children. Why encourage us to break Amazon tradition? I wasn't at all unhappy with what Artemis had done—but I was puzzled by it.

The only thing I could think of was that Artemis must have foreseen the child's need to be raised by both of us to reach his full potential. Yes, that was it! It would take Antiope and me to raise him.

Alexius cleared his throat to get back my attention.

"Though this is joyous news, there will be...complications. You are not married—"

"Which can easily be remedied."

"And your prospective wife is...is..."

"An Amazon," Antiope finished for him. What of it? Amazons do not normally marry, but that is a breach of the tradition of my people, not yours."

Alexius looked her straight in the eye. "You are not Athenian-born, nor even Greek-born. Such a foreign marriage—"

"Foreign, am I?" she asked with steel in her voice. "My mother was a Greek colonist in Asia Minor. My father was a Greek god. How much more Greek could I be?"

"Have the council draft any necessary legal changes, and I will sign them," I said in my calmest voice. "Antiope will be my queen, and her son will be my heir. Do whatever is needed to make that so."

Alexius did nothing to conceal his dislike for the situation, but he didn't try to argue any further. Instead, he asked leave to go and bowed his way out of the room, though much more stiffly than usual.

"That man is stubborn," said Antiope. "But he is also brave."

I nodded. "I can always depend on honesty from him."

"I like him," she said, giving me a smile more untroubled than I had seen since with left her kingdom.

There was some grumbling in the streets, but I was still popular enough to smooth over the original reaction to Antiope. Similarly, when I added her to the council, the counselors swallowed her new role, some more gracefully than others. Alexius, who had already gotten used to Antiope, did not object.

He did object to my proposal to make her co-ruler of Athens, but she advised me not to press that point right away.

"Even if Amazons married, they would never accept a male co-ruler, so I understand why your people would not accept a female one. Let it be for now. Perhaps when I have proved my worth, the question can be raised again."

She was right, as was often the case, so I backed down on that particular idea, but my imagination was filled with bright visions of the future. Antiope would lead the way to a society in which women played roles suited to their abilities, just as men did. I would fulfill the hopes of my mother. I would change society more than any king had in a thousand years.

As my ambitions to change society became more concrete, my love for Antiope became deeper. She was as perfectly matched for me as if the gods had fashioned her to be my wife and my partner in all things. She remained always in my mind. The flame of our love became the light that guided me, that heat that warmed me when cold crisis threatened.

As Antiope's pregnancy became more obvious, she agreed, somewhat grudgingly, to more limited activities. But she still attended council meetings, and I noticed that, as the weeks passed, the counselors paid more and more attention to her ideas. She was as great a thinker as she was a warrior, and even their strong biases could not entirely blind them to her worth.

Then came the message that shattered my peace.

FATHERHOOD AND PARLEY

It was a letter from Penthesilea, now styling herself, "acting queen of the Amazons." She demanded the return of Antiope, the "kidnapped Amazon queen," promising to go to war if that demand was not met. She also insisted on the payment of considerable reparations.

I would have paid a large sum to keep the peace, but Penthesilea scornfully rejected that idea. "My sister—our queen—is not for sale. Whatever else happens, she must be returned."

Antiope tried writing to her sister but received no answer.

"How can she still believe you were abducted?" I asked. "She must have seen your earlier letter as well."

Antiope shrugged. "Witchcraft? Things like the strange moonlight that covered our escape and the panic of the horses could easily be ascribed to dark spells. Penthesilea has no way to know that we were receiving divine aid, not magic aid."

"Why doesn't Artemis just appear to her and explain it?"

"Who can understand the ways of the gods? I do not. Perhaps the goddess has tried, and Penthesilea simply refused to believe. Could not a powerful witch send a false vision of a deity to a receptive mind? I think I have heard tales of such."

"But if she refuses to believe, what else can we do?"

Antiope cast a sad glance in my direction. "Prepare for war."

I shuddered. By now, Antiope was eight months pregnant, and I had visions of her trying to rush onto the battlefield in such a condition, but she assured me even Amazons would abstain from combat in such a case.

As it turned out, I need not have worried, for it took the Amazons long enough to assemble a suitable fleet that my son—named Hippolytus after Antiope's sister—had already been born by the time the greatest Amazon army yet assembled set sail.

The event was unprecedented. The Amazons and their allies had always confined themselves to a part of northern and central Asia Minor. Never before had they attacked a target so far away. Even though they knew full well that the girdle of Hippolyte, symbol of the Amazon monarchy, had been taken by Heracles as part of one of his labors and was in the treasury of Mycenae, they made no attempt to attack that city. Of course, such an attack would have forced the Amazons to march many miles through Greek territory, and Mycenae was at that time the strongest Greek city, with cyclopean walls that put the walls of Athens to shame.

It will seem strange to you now, but Athens was low-hanging fruit by comparison. Prosperous as it was, its army was far smaller than the Mycenean one. Its navy could probably have defeated the Amazons, who were not used to naval battles, easily enough. However, the warrior women had been wise enough to hire large mercenary crews who knew the sea and naval combat far better than they. I could no longer have been sure of victory in a sea battle. Anyway, the Amazons would never have been stupid enough to try to force a landing close to Athens. Without knowing what route they were taking or where they planned to land, I could not deploy the navy to stop them.

I prayed to Poseidon, but as was usual with him, I got no immediate answer. From what I had seen and from what I could gather from the tales, gods did not go out of their way to fight each other directly. There was no question Ares was backing the Amazon invasion. Poseidon could easily have stopped a fleet, no matter how large, but that would have brought him into direct conflict with the god of war. Perhaps once the Amazons had landed and threatened Athens, Athena and Poseidon would feel freer to respond.

The one sign of divine presence in those days was an ambiguous one. On more than one occasion, when I went to the nursery to hold my son, I found Artemis already there. Most of the time, she wasn't fully visible. Rather, there was a flicker like moonlight surrounding the child, even in the middle of the day. Once, though, I came upon her holding him in her arms. As a virgin goddess, Artemis could never be a mother, yet she held Hippolytus as if she were his mother. She was the guardian of newborns and other young creatures, but knowing that did not prepare me for the sight of her staring down at the child with something very like love in her eyes.

I fell to my knees, fearful that disturbing her would have consequences.

"Protect him well," she said, her voice more like a plea than a command. Then she was gone, and the child lay in his cradle, sleeping peacefully, too little to realize that he was the favorite of a goddess.

"I will," I said, hoping she would hear me, but dark dread crawled up my spine with its chilly fingers. Artemis would not be worried about Hippolytus unless she thought the Amazons might breach the walls and get into the city. But they had no siege engines, at least not that I knew of. How could they stand a chance, even against our relatively unimpressive walls? And fighting clear through the city. up the Acropolis, and into the palace itself? It seemed impossible.

Yet Artemis was worried.

I did my best to put her out of my mind, which wasn't too hard, considering how many other things there were to worry about. I walked straight from the nursery into a heated council meeting in which every Athenian strategos protested the queen's plan to join us on the battlefield.

"She will distract your majesty," said the most senior of them, trying hard not to look in Antiope's direction. "And the need to protect her will distort our deployments."

Antiope chuckled. "Protect me? It's more likely I'll be protecting some of you. Aside from our king, there is no greater warrior than I in all of Athens. If anyone challenges that assumption, I will happily meet him in single combat."

"But have you not just given birth?" asked one of the counselors.

Antiope shrugged. "That was a few days ago, and the birthing went well. I am fit enough now for anything—battle included. The doctors have said as much."

I chuckled inwardly. The doctors had probably been afraid not to.

I didn't want to override the military leadership of Athens so close to a major battle, mostly for reasons of morale. And I confess that the idea of Antiope on the battlefield didn't please me. On the other hand, she was the best warrior we had, and I could hardly be true to my own principles—to say nothing of my promises to her—if I treated her as if she were made out of glass.

"The queen has led armies before. It's not reasonable to argue that she is incapable of joining the battle."

"But does not your infant son require care?" asked another one of the counselors.

"I have spent much time with my son," said Antiope. "More than most women of your upper class. Do they not often turn the nursing and even the raising of their sons over to others? By comparison, all I propose to do is fight a battle and return to him."

"There is also another point to consider," said Alexius slowly. "As I understand it, the Amazons believe that Theseus has kidnapped their queen. If she herself is on the battlefield, fighting by your side, does that not undermine such a claim?

"They seem to believe she is bewitched, or at least could be," I said. "I'm not sure even seeing her up-close will refute that theory. Still, if they don't see her at all, they can easily think she is imprisoned somewhere. They know she would fight if she could."

"Then it seems there is an advantage to her presence on the field," said Alexius, eying the strategoi. "When one adds her military prowess to that, I do not see what kind of argument could outweigh it. For all we've heard of the size of the force we face, we will need every able-bodied man we can get—and at least this able-bodied woman."

The strategoi and the more skeptical counselors might have dismissed what I had to say as the result of being blinded by love. But they couldn't ignore what Alexius had to say so easily. Most of them nodded, albeit grudgingly in some cases. Antiope would be permitted to join the battle without my having to force the issue.

The following day, I greeted a large cavalry contingent from Pirithous. He sent word he could not come himself—Hippodamia was near to giving birth to his first son. I felt the regret in his words but knew he was making the right choice.

I wasn't as convinced some of his other choices were right.

Along with the cavalry had come a witch—a strong one, to judge by the power pulsing from her.

"The Amazons are already suspicious we have bewitched their queen," I said. "It may be the using witchcraft against them will only reinforce that feeling."

"I can be subtle. They will never know," said the witch. She was a striking woman, hair and eyes both dark as the deepest shadow, skin pale as starlight, and beguiling features—though far less so than those of Artemis. She was also tall for a woman and dressed entirely in black. She looked about as subtle as a colony of bats. But refusing her help carried risks of its own, and Pirithous wouldn't have sent her if he hadn't trusted her.

"Very well, but I expect you to stay out of sight."

She raised an eyebrow. "I have no intention of standing in the middle of the battlefield, but some castings require that I be able to see my target. Fear not, though, for I will not be visible. I may not conceal myself as much as the gods, but certainly well enough to escape notice by the average person."

"Keep in mind that the new Amazon queen is a daughter of Ares, and thus more prone to sense otherworldly power."

"I shall not forget it, majesty. Now, with your permission, I have preparations to make."

I dismissed her, and she departed with only the slightest of bows.

"I do not trust her," said Antiope. "Pirithous did an ill thing when he sent her to us."

"He meant well," I said. "And she may prove useful. In any case, she is only one against a multitude of us. If she somehow works against us, it will not be hard to put an end to that."

Or so I hoped. The story of Medea riding away in a chariot pulled by dragons popped into my mind.

The next day, a scout reported that the Amazon fleet had landed just northwest of Cape Sounion.

"What of the villagers in that area? What of Lavrion and Thorikos?"

"As you instructed, the troops we had in that area helped the citizens to evacuate, taking what supplies they could carry. The Amazons may—probably will—burn the villages, but the villagers themselves are safe."

I nodded, satisfied that at least that part of our plans had gone well. I had small numbers of troops stationed near every one of the coastal areas under Athenian control to help prevent a massacre of civilians near whichever landing point the Amazons might pick. They were not an especially brutal people, but war is a brutal business in general, and they were being goaded by Ares.

"Then we will prepare the city's defenses, and we will meet the Amazons before the city walls," I said.

"I doubt the Amazons will just march up to Athens, where your advantage is at its greatest," said Antiope.

"But part of the reason for the invasion is to 'rescue' you," said Alexius. "They have to come to Athens to do that."

"Ah, but they do not have to come right away. They could, for example, march straight north, toward Marathon, forcing you to decide between abandoning the city, splitting your forces, or meeting them in battle along the way."

"Abandoning Marathon would cost many lives, and, if the inhabitants don't succeed in burning the city, would hand the Amazons a decent base," said Alexius. "From there, they could ravage the lands to the north, possibly sweep past Athens to strike someplace like Eleusis."

"On the other hand, if we move toward Marathon, and that's not where they're going, we run the risk of being attacked by surprise at a moment when we may not be ready," said one of the strategoi.

"We can't just allow the outlying demes to be plundered," I said. "The people would begin to wonder why they submit to Athenian rule if Athens cannot protect them."

"But we cannot leave Athens ungarrisoned, just in case the Amazons slip troops by us," said Alexius. "And splitting our forces may be equally dangerous. If our scouts speak the truth, their army could be larger than ours in the first place."

"So you need to know what the Amazons are planning," said the witch, who had appeared abruptly in the doorway, having somehow passed through without being noticed by the guards. She smiled, much pleased with herself.

I, however, was not pleased. "You have not been invited here."

"The servants of Hecate require no invitation—or at least, no wise ruler would enforce such a requirement."

In one sentence, the witch had managed to declare herself independent of royal authority and to imply that I was not a worthy ruler. Her expression remained unchanged, but her smile now looked insolent to me.

Antiope, taking note of the insult, tensed visibly, and her hand wandered toward the hilt of her sword. Alexius looked ready to call the guards, though he seemed to be waiting for a signal from me. The strategos seemed as if he wished he had the witch's invisibility trick.

Much as I hated to admit it, though, we did need to know which way the Amazons were headed. None of the official oracles were close enough to visit in the time we had. I could always pray, but that seemed to produce mixed results, at best.

"We are listening," I said slowly. "But be warned—do not waste our time, for every moment is precious."

"Which is exactly why I am here," she replied. "Within minutes, I can give you the information you need—if you are willing to listen."

"We are. Just be sure that what you tell us is the whole truth."

The witch gave a tiny bow and pulled back into the shadows. I heard nothing suggesting the guards outside had seen her leave.

"Was that wise?" asked Alexius.

"A better question is, do we have a choice?" I replied.

"If the only choice is a bad one, that it is singular doesn't make it good," said Butes. Since he was the highest-ranking priest in Athens and was associated with both Athena and Poseidon, I had taken to inviting him to council meetings, though he seldom spoke. On this particular day, I had almost forgotten he was there.

"Well said, Butes, but is not the only choice still the only choice, good or bad?" I asked. Now was not the time for a philosophical discussion, but I knew Butes never spoke without reason.

"There is seldom only one choice," he replied. "It is just that we are not always wise enough to perceive the others."

"And do you have a suggestion?" I asked, wondering if I was going to have to pry his point out of him, bit by bit.

"What course might you pursue if Pirithous hadn't sent you a witch?" I noticed he slightly grimaced when he said my friend's name. "Because that course is still an option."

"I don't feel any more comfortable with witches than you do," I said. "But is it fair of us to assume that all of them are evil? They derive their power from Hecate, do they not? Would it make any difference if they derived their power from Poseidon and Athena?"

Butes sat back in his chair and suddenly looked smaller and more tired, not at all the commanding figure he usually was. "Hecate is a strange case—a paradox, if you will. On one hand, she is part of the divine order. A titan who sided with Zeus and his siblings in the great war, she was rewarded by Zeus with authority in the sky, in the sea, and on land. How could anyone be more part of the Olympian order than that?

"But, in giving her authority that overlapped with his own in the sky, with Poseidon's in the sea, and with a number of goddesses on Earth, Zeus left room for ambiguity. If she and Poseidon disagree over a sea-related matter, whose word is final? Poseidon's, presumably, but Zeus did not make that clear. In any case, no other god, besides Zeus himself, has authority covering as wide a range of subjects as Hecate's does. The other gods came to resent her—and she them."

"What has any of this to do with us?" asked Alexius.

"Old I may be, but I do not ramble without purpose," said Butes. "Despite the friction between Hecate and other gods, she was at one time a benevolent goddess. She tried to help Demeter find Persephone, and when Persephone was bound to spend half the year in the Under-world with Hades, it was Hecate who accompanied her into that dark realm.

"The only difference is, Hecate stayed there year-round, becoming suffused, as Hades is, with the gloom of the place. And somehow, though no tale preserves exactly what happened, she gained a measure of power in the Underworld as well. There are elder powers there, forces that existed before Hades. It may be that she made an alliance with them. It may be that she somehow tricked Hades himself. Either way, she gained some control in the one area where Zeus had given her none.

"Hecate does not risk open war with Zeus or any other god—yet, at any rate. But she *is* a paradox, a part of the divine order that seems to try to subvert that very order. Mortals should not have too much power, for power corrupts. Gods do grant them some, but sparingly. Through witchcraft, Hecate gives them more. But should they be trusted with more? And why does Hecate give it?

"I cannot answer those questions, but they should be pondered before we ally ourselves with witches. Perhaps they are not always evil, but have you ever met one that you could call good? And what of Pirithous? He has allied the Lapiths with them, but how has that gone for him?"

My muscles tensed, and my mouth felt dry. Pirithous had received aid from witches more than once, but somehow, his plans never came to fruition. Were they really trying to help, or were they just tricking him? And was the witch supposedly finding out what the Amazons were up to tricking me in the same way?

I would have gone forth and told her not to use her witchcraft to seek out the Amazon secrets, but there she was, back already.

"The Amazons march toward Athens by the most direct route. You may meet them here, before the city walls."

"That is both good and bad," I said slowly. "We don't have to risk something like splitting our forces—but if we lose this battle, the Amazons will be right at the gates of Athens. They may lack the equipment to force the walls, but starving the city into submission is still a possibility."

"Prepare for war just as you normally would," said the witch. "Leave the rest to me." Then she was gone again. She had not asked for leave to depart nor bowed as she left. Butes looked at me as if to say, "I told you so."

"See that she is watched," I said to the strategos.

"How are my men to watch someone who can appear and disappear at will?" he asked. I had no idea what to tell him.

"My king, it is you who must keep an eye on her," said Butes. "You have some feeling for divine and magical things, do you not? You may see what others will miss."

I nodded. "There is wisdom in that. Now, is there anything else we need to discuss?"

"I agree we must prepare for war," said Antiope. "But I would like one last chance to try to make peace."

"I thought the Amazons believed you bewitched."

She nodded. "They do, but perhaps if they can see me, talk to me, I can overcome that notion. They may still feel that I have betrayed them, but at least they will know that I do not need rescuing. The rationale for the war will be undermined."

"It seems worth a try," said Alexius.

"I will send a herald with a request to parley before the battle," I said. "I cannot guarantee that they will accept."

Either way, the Amazons would reach Athens by the next day if they made good time on their march. I ended the meeting and sent each man —and woman—off to perform their assigned tasks. Mindful of Artemis's warning, I also posted extra guards on the nursery.

The Amazons arrived the following day, but relatively late, meaning they probably would set up camp and wait for the following day to fight. I was not surprised that my herald returned with a letter accepting our request to parley.

Antiope and I walked out under white flags to await Penthesilea. To the southeast, I could see the Amazon tents, thousands of them, covering the plain. It was clear they outnumbered us, but at least we could fall back behind the city walls if need be.

Behind me, much of the Athenian army, together with the Lapith cavalry, was assembled just in case. Antiope assured me that the Amazons would honor a truce, and my troops were back just far enough not to seem menacing.

When Penthesilea came toward us carrying her own flag of truce, Amazon warriors spread out behind her. The Amazons were taking no chances, either, except that Penthesilea came completely alone. That was perhaps an encouraging sign.

"Greetings, Amazon Queen," I said to her as I gestured toward a chair. Once she sat, Antiope and I took our seats on the other side of the table.

"Why did you call me here?" she asked, looking at me suspiciously. "Do you intend to acknowledge the justice of our claim and return my sister to her people?"

"As I wrote to you twice, I was not abducted, Sister," said Antiope. "I am here of my own free will."

"So you have said, but how can that be? You are not the type to betray your people."

"Is it betrayal to follow the words of the goddess herself? Artemis told me of my destiny to bear Theseus a son, and so I have. You have a nephew, sister, a fine boy who will one day become a great man."

"I am sure you believe that," said Penthesilea. "But why would Artemis, of all goddesses, want to see an Amazon married to a man? It goes against everything we know of her. She could have had all the Amazons married off in the beginning, yet she did not."

"Most men would not have treated us as equals," replied Antiope. "Theseus does. Perhaps that is why Artemis was so willing to make an exception for him. I am married—and yet I did not have to give up my Amazon ways. I am still a warrior."

"You wear the armor," Penthesilea conceded. "But you cannot still be an Amazon in your heart. If you were, how could you have abandoned your throne?"

"Because I knew you would be there to fill it."

"And yet your departure leaves me the last of the daughters of Ortrera by Ares. Should something happen to me, the Amazons would have no queen."

I looked around. I couldn't explain why, but I felt suddenly uneasy. Superficially, all seemed well. The Amazons had moved no nearer nor braced themselves to charge. My men seemed equally obedient to the requirements of the truce. I could feel Ares somewhere, perhaps near the outskirts of the Amazon camp, but even he didn't seem inclined to intervene at the moment. So what was it that made me feel so unsettled? While my wife and her sister talked, I continued to examine the surroundings. I had to figure out what was wrong—and fast!

DEATH AND LIFE

I saw her weaving back and forth among the men—the witch. The sun was setting, and in the dusky light, she was barely visible, but I could feel her power. In her hand, she carried a small glass bottle with a clear fluid inside it. Water? It might have been, were it not for the energy within it. It was something far more powerful. But why bring such a thing with her to watch us negotiate?

"Sister, I would not have thousands of Amazons and Athenians slaughter each other over a misunderstanding. Let us fight in single combat and let the gods decide what is right. If you win, I will return with you to meet whatever fate our people decide. If I win, you and the army will return home and leave us in peace. Either way, the honor of the Amazons will be preserved."

Penthesilea's face still made her look younger than Antiope, yet the Amazon ways and the responsibilities of the queenship had hardened her, matured her faster than normal, even for an Amazon. She didn't look as if she would be easily persuaded. However, her pensive expression and the fact that she didn't immediately respond made it look as if she was considering Antiope's proposal.

Having seen them both fight, I had little doubt Antiope would win.

I don't think Penthesilea doubted it, either. So why was she even considering such an arrangement?

She didn't really want a war any more than we did. That had to be it. Antiope had been right. Giving Penthesilea a chance to talk to her had been the right move to convince the Amazon queen that her sister was not bewitched. And the single combat would give Penthesilea a way to satisfy any Amazon hotheads without having to fight an actual war.

At the edge of my vision, I saw motion. I only had to turn my head a little to see that the witch, covered by the growing darkness, had moved closer and was raising her arm to throw the bottle. It must be some kind of contact poison—and she seemed to be aiming it right at Penthesilea.

My heart pounding in my chest, I jumped up and started to run in her direction.

"Antiope! Penthesilea! Run!" I could manage no more words than that as I raced toward the witch. Could they move fast enough to save themselves if I could not reach her in time?

I was almost upon the witch when she threw the bottle. The moment it left her hand, she vanished, leaving me to plunge right through the spot where she had been standing and strike the ground with stunning force.

I manage to flip over and sit up enough to see what had happened. Antiope and Penthesilea must both have moved fast enough to avoid being splattered with whatever was in the bottle. At least, I hoped so, for I saw no sign of either of them.

What I did see was fluid that glowed with its own light in the gathering darkness. And yet it didn't really illuminate anything except itself. Beneath it, the grass had died. Above it, a cloud of luminous poison was rising into the sky.

Neither the Amazons nor my own army could clearly see what was happening, and judging by the shouts, both sides feared the worst. "Betrayal!" I heard shouted often, together with many other angry words. I had no doubt that, unable to see very well, each side thought that the other had broken the truce to attack.

Penthesilea might know the truth—but I had no idea where she was. I could hear the Amazons charging, and my own men were already countering.

BILL HIATT

"I brought your weapons," said Butes, panting. How the old man had reached me so quickly, I had no idea, but he carried my sword, club, and shield. Armor I already had. Reluctantly, I took the weapons.

"It was the witch, Butes. She has betrayed us. We must—"

"Prepare for the attack, Majesty. There is no way to prevent a battle now."

I knew he was right, but as you know, there are good reasons not for fighting at night. It becomes hard to tell friend from foe. Archers are mostly useless until the enemy is on top of them. So too are cavalry, for there is too great a risk of horses breaking legs as they stumble through the darkness. Nearby, I could see the shadowy forms of the Lapiths dismounting.

"Antiope!" I yelled, but my words were lost in the turmoil around me. I motioned to Butes to fall back. The old man had come in armor and with a sword of his own. That was how brave he was, for he must have known he was no match for the Amazons. I could not prevent the battle, but there was no need for him to die in it.

I looked up at the sky. There should be a visible moon, nearly full, but there was nothing. Clouds must have rolled in and obscured it. More witchcraft—of that, I had no doubt. Some of the Amazons and some of my men carried torches, but very few. They made one a target for archers and left only one arm usable for weapon or shield. Yet without them, a man couldn't see at all.

The only other light came from whatever vile potion the witch had flung at Penthesilea. I moved in that direction, hoping to find Antiope. The Amazon charge reached me before I could get very far, and instead of using my shield, I found myself fighting two-handed, sword in my right and club in my left. That wouldn't have been as easy with ordinary weapons, but the sword was exceptionally well balanced, and the Hephaestus-made club, heavy when it struck, felt light in my hands. Bashing with one and stabbing with the other, I managed to keep my opponents, nearly blind, just as I was, at bay. I tried to wound rather than kill, but I knew I couldn't keep that up for long.

Of course, I should have fallen back toward the bulk of my own army instead of plunging into an area in which I was fighting practically alone against the Amazons. But had I done that, I would have taken myself farther away from Antiope. I had to find her. Even if the Amazons spared her, they would take her prisoner, and they could get away with her even if they lost the battle.

I wasn't about to let that happen.

As I swung my weapons, I prayed to Athena, Poseidon, Artemis—really, to anyone who would listen. In the chaos surrounding me, anything could happen.

The smell of blood filled the air as more and more warriors on both sides were wounded. The occasional cry chilled my heart with the certainty that at least some were dead already. And all for nothing. When I found that witch, I would wring her neck and let Hecate make of that what she would.

By now, my men, who had been searching for me from the beginning, had found me. Enough were carrying torches for me to make out a little of my surroundings.

Together, we fought against the seemingly endless stream of Amazons. Not that I had at least a little light, I made good use of it. When I could, I struck death blows, not because I wanted to, but because I had to. The Amazons were fighting to kill now. And within them, I could feel the power of Ares driving them to more and more frenetic action. They were all swords and spears and would skewer me a dozen times over if I gave them the chance.

I still couldn't see Antiope, but at least I was no longer alone. I had my soldiers, yes, but within me, I could also feel Athena and Poseidon, amplifying my skill, guiding my arms, keeping my muscles from wearying too much, countering the Ares power in my opponents.

I could have been wrong, but from time to time, I also thought I spotted silver arrows glimmering past, aimed by the eyes of Artemis and thus, unlimited by darkness. I wondered why she hadn't simply appeared to the Amazons and put a stop to the battle, but her arrows, aimed as I had been at the beginning, to wound rather than kill, were throwing confusion into the Amazon ranks.

Outnumbered as we were, we might have a chance.

At last, I spotted Antiope, locked in desperate combat with some of her former Amazon sisters. As my men and I moved to support her, I spotted Penthesilea coming from the other side, spear ready to strike.

"Get back!" yelled Penthesilea to her troops. "Break off the attack! Our differences with Antiope will be settled by single combat!"

"But the treachery—" began one of them.

"I don't believe it was either my sister or Theseus who broke the truce. Spread the word! Stop the battle! Theseus, give the same order to your men. We have each lost much, but there is still something left that can be saved."

"Stop the fighting!" I bellowed at my men. "And run and spread the word. This battle is needless. Our differences will be resolved by single combat."

However, words, even when spoken by kings and queens, are only words if their subjects do not hear them. The Amazons, warped by the wrath of Ares, stopped fighting only in the area immediately around Penthesilea, and it was much the same with the Greeks. In the darkness and confusion, some of them had heard my order, but, faced with opponents who kept on fighting, they could not lay down their weapons.

Working together, Antiope and I ran with Penthesilea along the shifting boundaries between Amazon and Greek forces, shouting all the while, she at the Amazons, and Antiope and I at the Greeks. At times, I wondered if we could be seen clearly enough in the darkness, if our words could be heard clearly enough over the clang of sword against sword. We pressed on because we had no other choice.

With agonizing slowness, we made headway. But no matter what we did, we kept hearing the clash of weapons in the distance. Nor could we rely on the warriors to whom we had already spoken to keep the peace very long after we left them. It was as if they were holding onto their reason with weak and shaking hands. Any moment, they would lose it again and plunge back into senseless slaughter.

"It is not enough to stop them in place," said Penthesilea, hoarse from shouting. "We must order them back, yours to the city, mine to the tents. This mob is too large to manage in the darkness."

I did as she advised, and that helped. But it was still almost dawn before the field was cleared completely of combatants. By then, the ground was covered with blood and corpses, and the air was filled with the cries of the wounded.

I had the cold comfort of knowing that even more might have died.

But as it was, the Athenians and Amazons had both lost the better part of their forces in a battle that neither of them needed to fight. Many of the Lapiths had fallen as well. Only their horses had been spared, as had those of the Amazons.

Penthesilea, Antiope, and I stood almost alone in the middle of the desolation, though messengers ran back and forth from us to our respective armies. I could not see them clearly, but I was sure Amazons peered at us from their tents, and Athenians did the same from the top of the city wall.

"Can we bring this war to an end?" I asked. "Further violence would serve no purpose."

Penthesilea nodded, but her face was grim. "It will take time for me to convince my people of the truth of that. Many of them still believe that you tried to use witchcraft to kill me while we were meeting under a flag of truce." There was no question in her voice, but I could see it in her eyes.

"The witch acted without my approval," I said. "I hope you know that."

"I might have been unsure if you hadn't tried to stop her," said the Amazon queen. "But why was she here? Is it possible that some other Athenian told her to attack?"

"Pirithous sent her along with the cavalry. She used magic to find out what route your army would follow. I gave her no other orders—and no other Athenian would dare. I also asked one of my strategoi to make sure she was being watched."

"I will take your word, and I think I can convince my people to accept the outcome of single combat. But I am filled with sorrow. Once Amazon honor was satisfied, I had hoped the day would come when our two peoples might have been allies. Now, I will never live to see such a day. If it happens at all, it will be many generations hence."

I had to take a moment to receive news from a messenger. Penthesilea had to deal with two approaching. No, when I looked more closely, I saw that one was a messenger, and the other was Molpadia, one of her aides.

"What news?" I asked my messenger.

Before he could respond, someone shouted, "Die, traitor!" almost right behind me. I spun around just in time to see Molpadia slice her sword across Antiope's neck, just above the armor line.

Though the clouds had dispersed, and it was a sunny morning, I could see only darkness. As if my body was possessed by the spirit of Ares, I reflexively drew my own sword and took Molpadia's head in a single stroke. I could hear cries from the Amazon camp, but I paid no attention to them.

"Fetch a healer!" I yelled to the messenger. He ran as fast as he could back toward the wall. I looked down at my poor, fallen Antiope. The amount of blood on the ground told me a healer could never return in time.

I bent down to do what I could, but Penthesilea was already kneeling and trying to stop the bleeding. The blood kept flowing, despite her best efforts. The wound had been even more serious than I thought. For a second, despair hit me in cold, overwhelming waves, but I pushed it back as if I were my father calming the sea. I would not give in to hopelessness. There had to be something I could do.

The wish! It lay within my grasp, still unused after all these years. There would never be a better moment than now.

I invoked the wish's power. A second later, I heard the sea roar in my ears, felt Poseidon's might splash around me, through me. I was ready.

Antiope's eyes met mine as I started to make my wish. But before I could finish it, those eyes began to dull. I spoke the final words anyway, and Poseidon's power rushed toward her—only to be deflected by shadows only I could see. From their depths, the grim, cloaked figure of Thanatos raised his hand, palm outward, in a forbidding gesture.

The wish could only grant what was in Poseidon's power to give. Antiope, dead only for a second, slipped through its grasp, already tied to Hades in a way only he—or maybe Zeus—could change.

I struggled to silence the racket from my soul as it screamed within me. My life with Antiope couldn't end like this. The wish had failed, but there had to be a way to save her.

Sisyphus had tricked his way out of Thanatos's grasp, if only for a short while, by appealing to Persephone. That strategy would not work for me now, for I was not the dead one. What else, what else could I try?

Heracles had wrestled Thanatos for the life of Alcestis and won, at least if the tales spoke the truth. I was not as strong, but the wish, thwarted, had returned to me unspent. I could wish for the strength of Heracles, challenge Thanatos, beat him—

But no, it was already too late. Perhaps sensing my intent, the darkness of Thanatos grabbed up a light I only briefly glimpsed—Antiope's soul it must have been—and disappeared with it as quickly as he had appeared. The early morning sun shone mockingly on me, as if true light had not just been take away from me forever.

"I love you," I whispered, but Antiope. She was gone. I kissed her lips, still warm, and my body became taut as a bow.

Thank the gods I did not turn my wrath upon Penthesilea, who in Antiope's last moments had done everything she could. But I did rise as Amazons rushed from their tents. Nothing but murder was in my heart. Without speaking, I raised my bloody sword into the air.

"Murderers!" I yelled. "Would you kill me as well? Come and try! I will kill so many of you that there will not be room enough for all of you in the Underworld!"

I felt arms around me and thought for a moment that some kind god had sent Antiope back to me. But no, the gods are never that kind. It was her sister, not she, and she held me in a gesture of restraint, not love.

"Theseus, listen to me. If anyone plotted with Molpadia to kill Antiope, they will receive harsh justice at my hand. But they are not all guilty! Please! They advance against only because they just saw you strike down Molpadia and are still under the influence of Ares. Please! Enough have died already!"

I stood like a statue, sword still upraised, unable to respond to her. I felt as if the energy Ares had spread among all the Amazons last night was now focused on me alone. I could kill armies all by myself. Even someone like Heracles could not stop me.

Without waiting to see what effect her words had, Penthesilea let me go of me and positioned herself between the charging Amazons and me.

"Stop! I command you!"

Her voice carried in the early morning air, and the Amazon mob hesitated. But some were close enough for me to see their facial expressions. I wasn't sure how long she could hold them back. I wasn't sure I wanted her to. Let them come. I would cut their throats with my sword. I would bash out their brains with my club. And if I fell, what of it? I would be reunited with Antiope all the sooner.

I heard the sound of the city gate swinging open and running footsteps—many of them. I glanced in that direction and saw the Athenian army surging toward me. The watchmen on the walls had seen the Amazon movement and were ready to counter it. Looking back at the Amazons, I saw them starting to move in response to the Athenians. In a minute or two, the battle would restart, and this time, there would be no stopping it. The two forces would fight until not a man or woman was left standing.

I bared my teeth in a savage smile and prepared to charge myself.

"Theseus!" The voice was faint but emphatic.

I jumped when I saw Antiope standing right beside me.

She wasn't Antiope exactly. She was paler, harder to see in the early morning sun. My outstretched hand passed right through her and felt slightly chilled.

I was face to face with her ghost, not yet on its long trek to the Underworld. No, Thanatos had already started her along that road. Yet here she was again.

"Antiope?" I asked, barely able to speak her name for fear she would disappear.

I must not have been the only one who could see her. Athenians and Amazons both stumbled to a halt. They remained tense, though, ready to spring forward. Even the appearance of a ghost would not hold them long.

"Theseus!" she said again. Her face was sad, but there were no tears. Perhaps ghosts couldn't cry.

But why was she so sad? Now that she was within reach, I might yet have her back.

"The...the wish Poseidon gave me. Now that you are here again—"

"Do not waste your life resisting what you cannot change. The wish still has no power to make Hades relinquish me. That Hermes granted me a moment to return to you is as much a miracle as either one of us can hope for now.

My momentary hope died like a dove caught in the mouth of a wolf.

What kind of miracle was it to taunt me with sight of the woman who could no longer be mine? I felt as cold as if I myself were dead. But Ares, belatedly my friend, would warm me up.

"Then I am ready to avenge you!"

"Do not!" she said. Her hand reached out and touched my cheek. I felt a chill, and the Ares-bred madness fled from it. I was myself again—cold and wretched, but sane.

"Do not, for Molpadia alone was responsible. Not my blood sister. Not my Amazon sisters. If you love me…loved me, you will not shed more blood on my account. Think of our son."

She frostbit my lips with her kiss, and she was gone. At that moment, I would willingly have turned the sword against myself to follow her, but her last words stopped me. My son had already lost a mother. I could not take his father from him, too.

With shouts on both sides, the armies were in motion again, flowing at each other like two flood-swelled rivers.

Without hesitation, I stood facing my troops, back to back with Penthesilea, who faced hers.

"Halt!" I yelled. "Any man who keeps moving toward the Amazons shall face my wrath!" Heartened by my sudden transformation, Penthesilea said much the same.

Even the gods have limits. Perhaps Ares had exhausted himself trying to enflame the violent passions of such large masses over such a long period. Perhaps Antiope's ghost had tipped the scales. Or perhaps it was the sight of Penthesilea and me, belatedly united to keep the peace. Whatever the cause, our armies withdrew—slowly they moved, and with much grumbling, but move they did. Soon the field was cleared of all living beings except the Amazon queen and me.

"I still don't approve of what Antiope did," Penthesilea told me. "But, seeing you in action, I can understand why she made such a choice."

I tried to smile, but my lips refused. A half-hearted grimace was all I could manage.

"I will take my people back over the sea as soon as we have collected our dead. But you should keep Antiope's body."

Even if Penthesilea had wanted it, I would never have given it to her.

Despite the rawness of my feelings, I managed to restrain myself from saying that.

"She chose to be your wife. She belongs to you now."

"She belongs to no one but herself," I said quietly.

Penthesilea nodded slowly. "I see that now. Farewell, Theseus."

She moved quickly to begin the collection of the bodies. I did the same. They needed proper burial preparation in order for their spirits to be at rest.

As I had suspected, it took hours to clear the field. I personally oversaw the arrangements for Antiope. Then I went as fast as my exhausted legs could carry me back to the palace.

I needed to see my son. I needed to hold him in my arms.

As I approached the nursery, my heart convulsed within my chest. Two guards lay unconscious, one on either side of the door.

Charging forward, I threw open the doors. The first thing I saw was Hippolytus—in the witch's arms. Again I felt the chill of death. Was it an omen?

"Put him down!" I said, drawing my sword.

"Would you risk your baby's life? You are tired, Theseus. What if you were to stab at me and miss?"

She had a point, but I couldn't risk her escaping with the child, and she might disappear at any moment.

"You cannot hold him forever—and if you harm him in any way or try to take him, I will hunt you to the end of the earth."

"And leave Athens for how long? Do that if you wish. You will only serve my purpose."

"And what is your purpose?"

I didn't really expect an answer, but keeping her talking seemed better than the alternative.

"You thwarted my plan to have my son sit on the throne of Athens. He will have one among the Medes, but soon, he will have Athens as well."

At first, I thought I had misheard her. How could a Thessalian witch have a son with the most remote claim to the Athenian throne? But then, she dropped the illusion with which she had cloaked herself, and I saw her as she truly was. I shuddered from an even more intense chill, not that of one death only, but of a second, ghastly as the first, enough to rend the heart from my chest.

"Medea!"

"You did not think I could be stopped so easily, surely. I have been watching all you have done, waiting for just the right moment. It was easy to take the place of the witch Pirithous had sent to you. That way, I was positioned to ensure hostilities when you and Penthesilea seemed close to a solution.

"I had hoped you'd die on the battlefield, but I can make this work. Going on a prolonged quest to find your son will give me plenty of time to circle back around and undermine you here. Or perhaps I should just make a trade—the child for your throne. Abdicate in favor of Medus, and I will give you Hippolytus back unharmed. Cling stubbornly to your crown, and Hippolytus will suffer for it!

"I killed most of my sons. Do not think I would hesitate for a second when it comes to killing yours."

"The child is under the protection of Artemis. If you harm him, I will not need to hunt you down. Artemis will do that in my stead."

The room echoed with Medea's laughter. "And where is that protective goddess now? Why did she not stop me when I entered this chamber? Because that isn't the way gods work. You, of all people, should know that by now. They may favor this or that mortal, but they are erratic in their help and fickle in their loyalty."

I silently prayed to Artemis, but Medea had shaken my faith. After all, Artemis could have intervened without my prompting if she truly cared. And she had encouraged Antiope to leave the Amazons but done nothing to protect her from Molpadia.

I could not let my son die. But I could not give Athens to Medea, either. I had seen the misery she brought by ruling from the shadows. Medus would be king, but she would hold the real power.

I recalled how she had fled the club of Hephaestus. But how could I wield it against her fast enough to keep her from harming Hippolytus?

The easiest way for her to take power now would be for me to accept her demand and abdicate in her son's favor. But to accept her demand and sign an abdication, I'd need to be alive. Perhaps I could turn her need for me to my advantage.

I took one step toward her, staggered, and dropped my sword. I probably looked worn out enough to make it seem plausible that I was near to fainting.

"Theseus?" Her tone was neutral.

I put my hands over my face. "My head! It feels as if it's splitting open."

From what I'd heard, Medea had powerful healing magic. If only I could convince her I needed it!

I had a rustling that could have been Medea putting Hippolytus back in his cradle. Then she made a step or two in my direction.

"What is happening?" I muttered, sinking to my knees.

"The potion I threw at Penthesilea contained just a little water from the River Styx—instant poison to any mortal thing. Perhaps when you were close, you breathed just enough of the vapor to put yourself in jeopardy. If so, my magic can—"

She was probably too far away, but I couldn't take the chance that she would use her magic to confirm I wasn't ill. I was on my feet in a second and ready to fling Hephaestus's club at her with all the force I could manage.

Medea saw what I was doing and turned back toward the cradle, intending either to use Hippolytus as a shield or to harm him before I could stop her.

But standing right in front of the cradle, her usually impassive face twisted in wrath, was Artemis, who had one of her silver arrows aimed right at Medea's heart.

The witch, almost a goddess herself, nonetheless lacked the art to deflect such an arrow. She vanished, leaving me alone with Artemis, who lowered her arrow and looked at me.

"That was well done, Theseus. You almost had her."

"*Almost* would not have been good enough," I said, letting a little of my bitterness leak into my tone. The words could be taken as self-criticism, but in truth, I intended them as a mild reproof of Artemis, who cut her rescue far too close.

"That is why I came. It is also why I will give you another warning. Hippolytus is not safe here. Take him to Troezen to have him fostered by your grandfather and mother. I have made arrangements to protect him there."

"Why not just protect him here?" I asked.

"Because the danger is greater. I can conceal him there in a way that Medea will not be able to find him. Remnants of her power still linger in Athens. I would not be able to do the same here, at least until the residual magic fades. Nor can I be always at his side."

"Pardon me if I am presuming too much in asking this question, but why not just kill her?"

Artemis laughed, though not mockingly. "She lives as a mortal, but she may not be one, at least not in the usual sense. Her parents are both divine, and her power is great. It is possible that, like gods, she may be injured but not killed.

"And then there is her alliance with Hecate, who would be likely to come to her defense if she faced a threat serious enough. Medea might step beyond what even that protection would provide if she did something truly foolish, such as openly defying Zeus. Aside from that, few gods would want to battle Hecate unless they had absolutely no choice. I would certainly be reluctant to take her on.

"To make matters even more complicated, Medea is a favorite of her grandfather, Helios, the sun god, though no one knows quite why. Helios is normally not that hot-tempered, but he is, like Hecate, of an older generation than the Olympians and has ties to other elder powers. No one fears him as much as Hecate—but neither is anyone eager to pick a quarrel with him."

"So Medea is just left to do as she will?"

Artemis raised an eyebrow. "It is not seemly for a mortal to keep questioning a goddess, but because you are grieving, and because you are Hippolytus's father, I will answer this one last question. All creatures, even the most powerful of gods, are part of the pattern woven by fate. And, like ordinary mortals, Medea's evil will influence her fate for the worse. That may not fit your mortal idea of justice, but it is justice as the universe understands it.

"One warning before I go. My brother, Apollo, has given me a prophecy concerning Hippolytus. Should he ever encounter the sister of your beloved, he will inevitably die."

"Penthesilea?" I asked. "She has no further quarrel with me. Why would she be a threat to my son?"

Artemis frowned. "Apollo did not give me a name. Likely, he has not been able to discern it himself. But if she is the only sister of your beloved, then it must be she to whom the prophecy refers. As to why she might act against him, that I do not know, either. But Apollo's words do not necessarily mean that she will harm Hippolytus. Perhaps it will be something she does by accident or something brought about by their meeting that will spell his doom."

"Thank you, goddess. Her path shall never cross my son's."

Artemis smiled and vanished in a sparkle of silver. I walked over to the cradle and picked up Hippolytus, who looked up at me tranquilly. He knew neither that his mother was dead nor that his life had nearly been lost.

"I have lost Antiope, my son, but I shall never lose you. I swear that I will never allow harm to come to you, whatever I must do to prevent it."

CALM AND STORM

FEW THINGS HAVE EVER BEEN SO HARD for me as taking Hippolytus to be fostered at Troezen. In Athens, no one questioned my choice. After all, had not Aegeus left me in Troezen to put distance between his political enemies and me? But Hippolytus's childhood would not be the same as mine, I told myself. He would know his father, and I would visit as often as I could.

My grandfather was pleased to have another youngster to whom he could impart wisdom, and my mother was nearly ecstatic. The years had been kind to her. She still looked almost as she had when she caught Poseidon's eye, and certainly, she was vigorous enough to be a mother to her grandson. Though fate had robbed her of marriage, it had at least given her another opportunity to be a mother, a role for which she was admirably suited.

After reluctantly leaving Hippolytus in their hands, I returned to Athens and carefully studied every scrap of information I could find about Antiope's family. Every source agreed that there were only four sisters. Hippolyte and Melanippe had both died in the fight caused by the mistaken belief that Heracles was kidnapping Hippolyte. With Antiope gone, Penthesilea was the only sister remaining alive. As long as she didn't return to this area, Hippolytus had nothing to fear.

I kept careful track of all news coming from Asia Minor, and the years passed without even a hint that Penthesilea ever left Themiscyra. Indeed, she would have been foolish to go, for her grip on her throne was tenuous at best. Some Amazons murmured against her for not continuing the war. Others whispered that perhaps she, like her sister, was not truly loyal to the Amazon way of life.

But such mutterings were not her only problem. The Attic War, as it came to be called, had cost her practically every drachma she had in her treasury, not to mention some of her best fighters. She returned to Themiscyra much weaker than she had left it. As time went on, she was unable to rebuild her army to its former size. Meanwhile, the wandering Amazon tribes asserted their independence more and more.

I did not know it at the time, but her weakened condition was the beginning of a decline that would eventually cause Amazon civilization to disappear completely. All I knew was the one person who could threaten my son was unlikely to ever lay eyes on him.

That was enough to make me contented. Not happy, mind you. I seldom managed happiness after I lost Antiope, but I became used to my current lot. I was still a good king, and unlike Penthesilea, I was able to rebuild. Under my leadership, Athens was soon as rich and powerful as it had been before. The spot where the Styx bomb had fallen remained bare earth, a grim reminder of what had happened there. But as time passed, I dwelt on those events less and less, even though the pain remained.

To Alexius's infinite relief, I saw little of Pirithous during that time. I was sure to thank him for the cavalry he sent me in my time of need—but I could never quite get the witch out of my mind. If he had not sent her to me, Medea would not have been able to infiltrate my city, cause my wife's death, threaten my son. I never expressed my anger to him, but I'm sure he knew of it. He was a reckless man, but not a stupid one, and upon their return, his men had told him all that had happened. When he uncharacteristically asked to visit instead of just showing up, I turned him down. From then on, he took the hint and stayed away. At times, I wished we could still be friends, but I could not think of him without remembering Antiope as well. So I stayed in Athens, and he stayed in Larissa with his witches.

Years passed, and time treated me as well as it had my mother. No one could mistake me for the young man, almost a boy, who first arrived in Athens, but no one who didn't know how long I had reigned would ever have guessed how many years that I, still ungrayed and unwrinkled, had sat upon the throne.

One day, I received an unexpected visitor—the newly crowned King Deucalion of Crete, Minos's son. He came, not with an army, but only with a small escort. He said he came in the cause of peace, and I eagerly welcomed him into my palace.

Deucalion conveyed much of the authority of his father, but without his father's harsh edge. The new king was already graying, for Minos had governed Crete for three generations. But Deucalion was far from being an old man. I could imagine him leading troops into battle.

"We've never really made peace with Athens, though we should have, long ago," said Deucalion. "Some reparations were due for the murder of my brother, Androgeus, but Athens has paid that debt a thousand times over. If anything, after that business with the Minotaur, Crete owes reparations to Athens."

I shifted uneasily in my chair. Deucalion's attitude was almost too good to be true. "The sacrifices to the Minotaur were your father's idea, not yours. Athens nor I will blame you for those."

Deucalion's eyes looked unfocused, as if he were staring right through me. "My father was a wise king...once. So good was the legal code he gave to the Cretans that some believed Zeus himself had written it. But no man should rule as long as he. At some point, he lost his way. He lost even the favor of Zeus. You've heard how he died?"

I shook my head, not sure where the conversation was going. Was Deucalion trying to trick me somehow?

"But you know he kept Daedalus prisoner?"

"Yes, I saw him when I was on Crete."

"Well, Daedalus had a son, Icarus, who was also a prisoner. The great inventor might have remained a captive, but he wanted a better life for his son. Over time, he fashioned wings for them."

"Wings? You mean, to fly with?"

"That was his plan, and it almost worked. He told young Icarus not to fly too close to the sun or too close to the sea, fearing what would happen if the wax that held the feathers in place became overheated or wet. At first, Icarus followed his father's lead. They flew out the window of their tower's prison, caught a good wind, and flew out over the sea.

"But Icarus was a headstrong boy. Thrilled by the feeling of flying, he soared higher and higher. His father, realizing the danger, shouted for him to descend, but it was too late. The boy had drawn too close to the sun, you see. The wax melted, causing the feathers to drop away. Icarus fell like a stone. Daedalus tried to catch him, but he couldn't move fast enough. With horror, he watched his son plunge into the ocean and drown.

"Even if Minos was right to think that Daedalus deserved to be in prison—which I doubt—the loss of his son should have been punishment enough for any man. My father didn't think so, though. Instead, he pursued Daedalus, obsessed with the idea that someone had been able to escape him. Perhaps part of his rage came from the fact that you had slipped through his fingers earlier. But for whatever reason, Minos pursued Daedalus as if nothing else in the world was important.

"My father tracked the inventor down in Sicily, but Daedalus had won the favor of King Cocalus. With his approval, Daedalus and the Sicilian princesses trapped Minos in the bath and scalded him to death with boiling water."

"That's horrible," I said.

"You don't really think so, though, do you?" Deucalion asked, leaning forward. He was trying to trap me!

"No man deserves to die such a death." It was the most neutral thing I could think to say.

Deucalion smiled. "You are reluctant to condemn my own father before me, but he did far worse to other people. He was a good man once. A great one, even. But not by the end. You know how I avenged my father? I signed an alliance with Cocalus and gave Daedalus a full pardon for all crimes, past and present. It was my father's own fault—and the will of the gods—that he died. The king and the inventor were both merely the instruments of divine justice."

"I do not think I could have been so generous in your place," I said. In truth, I was a little shocked by Deucalion's willingness to condemn his own father.

Of course, his father really was monstrous by the end, and his long life had kept Deucalion waiting for the throne for fifty years or so longer than he would have ordinarily. And, if I was being honest, there were times I had cursed Poseidon. Never Aegeus, though. I could not imagine a sin so great that it would have made me curse him.

"I see I have made you uncomfortable," said Deucalion. "That was not my intent. Let us go back to business, then. I propose a remission to Athens of the last twenty years of tribute and an end to all future requirement for tribute. In exchange, I ask that you renew your confirmation of our rights in Megara and all other territories we currently hold outside of Crete. I also ask that you agree not to make war on Crete as long as Crete does not make war on you."

"Those are most generous terms. But what if Crete were to attack an Athenian ally?"

"As long as Athens does not deliberately ally itself with a kingdom that is already an enemy of Crete, I am willing to include in the treaty a provision that you may respond if Crete attacks one of your allies. Either way, I do not intend to pursue wars of aggression, so those provisions will never need to be invoked. Is all of this now agreeable?"

I felt more relaxed and smiled. "I would have to be a fool to reject such reasonable terms."

"And all the world knows that Theseus is no fool," said Deucalion, nodding. "I shall have my scribes put our agreement in writing, that we may both sign before I depart. However, I have one other offer to make you before we finalize the agreement."

"What more could you possibly wish to offer?" I asked, tensing up a bit. This was still too good to be true.

"I remember the tale of how you lost Ariadne."

I wondered how much he knew and didn't know what to say.

"Don't worry," he said. My anxiety must have been plain on my face. "Yes, the moment I heard the public story, I knew Ariadne had made the whole thing up. At that point, my father was no longer wise enough for such cleverness—or such reasonableness. But I also knew that, if she was making up a story to keep our father away, it meant that she had aided your escape and gone with you willingly. It made my heart glad to think that she, at least, was free.

"I have heard the story that Dionysus took her from you. Is that true?"

I nodded, once again at a loss for words.

"Then you married an Amazon who was killed in a war with her people. That I know is true."

I nodded again.

"Theseus, you have suffered more loss than most men could survive. As a gesture of good faith, I would like to bring some joy into your life." He gestured to one of his men who was standing in the doorway. The men darted out, then returned with a veiled woman.

"Since you are once again in need of a wife, I offer my daughter, Phaedra, to you."

I looked at the veiled woman, puzzled. "I don't understand. Phaedra is your sister…and Ariadne's, is she not?"

Deucalion glanced over at the veiled woman, then back at me. "I should have named her something different, I suppose. My daughter is often confused with her aunt, who has the same name. It is common in our family for names to be reused more often than is customary. I think you are aware that my father had two daughters named Ariadne, though the second wasn't born until the first one was dead. Phaedra, please show yourself to King Theseus."

As soon as Deucalion had spoken, Phaedra lifted her veil. She reminded me so much of the girl I had seen by Ariadne's side all those years ago that it was hard for me to believe she was that girl's niece. She also reminded me of Ariadne. Though Phaedra was darker—just like her namesake—, and, from the way she lowered her eyes, shyer, she was just as beautiful. When I looked at her, I couldn't help being reminded of stars twinkling in the night sky.

"It has been many years since I glimpsed the Phaedra who is your sister, and that glimpse was brief," I said slowly. "Still, your niece bears a remarkable resemblance to her."

Deucalion shifted position as if his chair had suddenly become uncomfortable. "They are closely related, after all. May I be completely open with you?"

"Of course," I replied, though he was starting to worry me.

"I…I considered offering you my sister, Phaedra, as a bride, for she is still unmarried. But I have heard of your moral strictness in matters of sexuality, and I was not sure of the laws here in Athens regarding...uh, incest."

"Unless I am unaware of something, I don't see how incest could be involved were I to marry either Phaedra. She would have to be my mother or my sister—and I am reasonably sure she is neither."

Deucalion laughed, but it sounded forced. "No, of course not. But I have heard that in some places, the prohibition extends to relatives by marriage. And since...and since—"

"In truth, I've never thought about the question of whether the sister of a man's wife, though she is called the man's sister as well, should be barred from marrying him in the event his first marriage dissolved. But since Ariadne was not my wife, there would have been no barrier to a marriage between her sister and me."

Deucalion's eyes widened, and then he looked away from me. "Would you...would you have preferred the sister of Ariadne, then?"

"Friend, be at ease," I said, a little disconcerted by how much the mighty king of Crete seemed eager to please me. "Such a match would not have been incestuous, but it might have been...complicated emotionally. I cannot think it would be easy for a woman to be happily married to a man who had first chosen her sister. Marriage to a man who had once chosen her aunt when she was probably too young to marry seems less difficult."

"I am glad to hear it," said Deucalion, wiping sweat from his brow. "I know that marrying Phaedra is not the same as having Ariadne back. But you will find her sis—uh, her niece—you see how easy it is to confuse them? Now I'm mixing them up. Anyway, her niece is also quick of wit and loyal. She will make you a good wife."

While Deucalion was fumbling through a simple statement in a nervous way so unlike his earlier confident discussion, I became uncomfortably aware of Phaedra, eyes still focused on the ground, looking as uncomfortable as a hen in a fox's lair. Her awkwardness reminded me that I hadn't dealt with the issue most important to me.

"Pardon me for what is a breach of normal tradition," I said. "But it is my desire to marry only a woman who is willing to be my bride. May I question her on this subject?"

Deucalion shrugged. "I have no need to force my daughter into a marriage with you, but by all means, verify the truth of my words." He looked relieved to not be the focus of attention for a few minutes. Was it because he was still adjusting to being king? Being under the thumb of an increasingly tyrannical father couldn't have been easy.

"Phaedra, do you want to be my wife?"

"Very much," she said quietly, still not looking me in the eye.

"Is it awkward that I once loved your aunt?"

That question caused her to look at me. Her eyes reminded me of Ariadne's.

"It is neither awkward nor not. It just is. Is it awkward for you?"

"It is not your place to—" began Deucalion.

I raised a hand. "Let her speak as she will. Let her question whatever she wants to question. I want to make sure she is comfortable. Be assured, my friend, that whatever she says will not offend me. Nor will it make me any less likely to sign the treaty you propose.

"Phaedra, I admit that it will seem strange at first to be married to Ariadne's niece. But I know you are not she. Nor do you have to try to be. If I marry you, I will expect you to be yourself."

She smiled, though her eyes dropped again. "That is most kind of you, my lord."

"In the beginning, we will not love each other. After all, we have just met. Will that make you uncomfortable?"

"A princess does not always have the luxury of marrying for love. Hardly ever, in fact," said Deucalion.

"I know that," I said. "But ideally, that would not be the case. Phaedra?"

"My lord, may I speak freely?"

"You must always speak freely with me."

"I saw you when you came to Crete...though I doubt you noticed me. Your gaze fell upon Ariadne...and Aunt Phaedra. I knew Ariadne was drawn to you, so I kept my feelings to myself—but I was drawn to you, too. After she became the bride of Dionysus, I would have asked my grandfather to try to arrange a marriage between us...but...but—"

"Your grandfather would sooner have drunk snake venom," I finished for her.

She laughed, and that too reminded me of Ariadne. "Yes, my lord, probably so. I knew he would never approve. I did not even dare ask my father to suggest the idea. I didn't want him to have to take such a risk on my behalf. But thank the gods, he never got around to finding me another match. When Deucalion told me of his plan to offer me to you, I had not felt so happy in my entire life. Nothing would fill me with joy as much as to be wedded to you."

Deucalion was smiling as he would if a trained animal had performed a trick correctly, but I felt her words were sincere. I could feel my heart warming to her already.

"Deucalion, it would be my pleasure to wed your daughter."

Deucalion smiled broadly. Phaedra looked as if she wanted to jump up and down but knew that it would not be proper decorum to do so.

The actual drafting of the treaty took little time. Even Alexius, getting older but still a stickler for detail, could find nothing to object to. We had not discussed the bride price, but it was reasonable.

Deucalion stayed for the wedding festivities, which I perhaps over-did. Some might have mistaken the feast for Eastern excess. But if so, no one complained of it, and from the way Deucalion reacted, I think cele-brations at the Cretan court were probably at least as elaborate.

When at last it was time, I took the shy virgin to my bed. I was careful to be especially gentle with her. It was not long before she was neither shy nor a virgin.

Of course, Antiope remained in my heart, but it didn't take long for me to love Phaedra, just as I had hoped. I could have wished for a some-what more assertive woman. She declined a place on my council. However, it did not take her long to become open with me when we were in private, and her advice was almost invariably good. Her enthu-siasm for being married to me, though, was what bound me to her. She had not been lying or exaggerating when she spoke of how she had been longing for me for years.

She gave me two fine sons, Demophon and Acamas. But their births introduced the first hint of trouble ahead, though it was not Phaedra who brought it. Many of my advisers wanted one of them to be my heir rather than Hippolytus, who by now was a young man. Some quibbled about his conception, which had happened before I married Antiope, though, because we had married before his birth, he was no bastard. Others worried about his Amazon lineage, though few spoke in such direct terms.

Since my other boys were mere infants, Hippolytus's age would have been an advantage. He was nearly ready to take over if need be. It would be several years before his half-brothers could make that claim. I was positive that all I would need to quiet the mutterings against him would be to bring him back to Athens. By then, it ought to have been safe to do so, just as it had been safe for me to come when I had grown to manhood.

But returning him to Athens was not as easy as you might think. My grandfather and mother both attested to the quality of his training, but there were two obstacles that stood in the way.

The first was his complete and utter disinterest in sex, which might have led to unpleasant rumors had it been noticed in Athens. Thanks to my mother's advice, I had abstained from the usual sexual outlets, such as slave girls, when I was young, but it had been a constant struggle. My mind understood the need for discipline, but my body rebelled against those restraints. It still did. To be honest, being away from Phaedra for very long was painful.

Yet my son, more than old enough to be sexually aware, behaved as if he had no sexual desire at all. During my increasingly frequent visits to Troezen, I discreetly watched him when he went swimming. His physical development was what I would have expected of a young man his age. That was a relief. But if he were capable of sex, what could explain his lack of interest?

My next thought was that he might be drawn to boys rather than girls. Such a thing was not unheard of. The only reason that would concern me was that he would need to produce an heir. But arrangements could be made. Some women, eager to be queen, would accept the crown in exchange for a certain amount of discreet sharing of their husband with a male companion. It was important that the male companion also be willing, but Hippolytus was handsome enough that I doubted that would be a problem.

However, from what I could tell, Hippolytus had no sexual interest in boys, either. I had to proceed very, very cautiously, so as not to embarrass him or anyone else. But I could see nothing suggesting he was anything but friends with any male with whom he could possibly have contact.

Physically male, but mentally asexual? Was that even possible? I finally asked Hippolytus directly, which perhaps is what I should have done in the first place.

"No, I don't feel urges that often, but what of it?" he asked me. "Did you expect me to be fathering bastards all over the place? I am trying to follow your example and grandmother's teachings. Am I wrong to do that?"

"Of course not. But there is a difference between self-control and lack of desire."

"When it comes time to marry, my wife will find me able enough to do my duty. If you must know, I have self-pleasured from time to time. My body works, if that's what you've been leading up to. Will that be enough?"

I nodded. "But you are old enough to marry now, my son."

"I hope you do not mean right away. The goddess would not be pleased."

And that, of course, was the second problem, perhaps related to the first.

Artemis, who aside from her brother, Apollo, seemed to have little use for men in general, had a great deal of affection for Hippolytus. It was she who predicted his birth and future greatness. She helped rescue him from Medea as well, and she advised me to send him to Troezen, promising to watch over him.

As a virgin goddess, Artemis had never been a mother, but, from what Aethra told me, she often behaved as if she were Hippolytus's mother. Given the way Artemis used to look at Hippolytus as an infant, Aethra's words didn't surprise me. What did surprise me was the amount of time Artemis spent with Hippolytus. Never in my experience nor in Aethra's had any god or goddess ever been around a mortal so much. As he grew older, she trained him in bowmanship, just as she had the Amazons. Pittheus had made sure he was trained in all weapons, and he was capable with all of them, but his arrows flew like the wind and never missed.

I saw the goddess at least once every time I visited, sometimes as a momentary silver light, sometimes in human form. She went on long walks with Hippolytus from the time he was old enough to walk a distance.

Then, just when he was reaching the age of sexual awareness, Artemis recruited him into her hunting band—one of the few males to ever receive such an honor.

I cannot tell you how horrified—and how helpless—I felt when I heard. I could not very well forbid him to join, but by becoming part of that band, he was putting himself in dire peril, though he didn't see it.

Artemis, kind to him though she had been, was famous for her temper. She had been known to kill men for accidentally seeing her naked. Unfortunately, she was also very beautiful. Why was that so often true of virgin goddesses? Athena was a beauty as well. But at least Athena was more thoroughly clothed, more often than not in armor. Artemis preferred more lightweight garb for hunting. Among other things, she was bare-armed and bare-legged. At least she wasn't bare-breasted, but her pale breasts bulged all too clearly beneath the fabric.

What if my asexual son was merely a late bloomer? What if he turned a lustful eye in her direction? Even worse, what if he tried to take her in his arms? Would she forgive a momentary impulse—or would she kill him on the spot?

That was the worst danger, but it was not the only problem. What if it was Artemis who was restraining his sexual desire? What if she intended to keep him as a hunting companion for the rest of his life?

I tried to tell myself that was an illogical fear. The women who joined her hunting parties were free to leave whenever they wished. Some even left to get married, and the goddess wished them well. But men she trusted were in much shorter supply. What if she had decided to keep him for that reason? Maybe in her heart, she still lusted after men, and, though she would remain a virgin, she enjoyed the company of a chaste male over whom it was safe to fantasize?

I hardly dared to think such thoughts. And being rash enough to ask the goddess such questions would certainly have been fatal. Even a much more general question, such as what her intentions toward him were, might be fraught with peril.

Perhaps my overheated imagination was inventing problems. Artemis might just have been protecting Hippolytus. No one would be foolish enough to try to harm someone who was so obviously a divine favorite.

But the situation was unnatural. The pairing of a man with virtually no sexual desire and a virgin goddess seemed too odd to be a coincidence. What if this were the result of some artifice of Medea? Or Pirithous's witches? Or maybe Hecate herself? I couldn't even rule out Pasiphae, who could conceivably be trying to eliminate the competition in order to ensure that one of her great-grandchildren inherited the Athenian throne. Her magic was said to be formidable, after all.

There might be a safe way out. I was also heir to the throne of Troezen. It would be easy enough to make Hippolytus my heir for Troezen only. Then Demophon or Acamas could follow me on the Athenian throne.

That solution would have pleased practically everybody. Hippolytus could hunt with Artemis all his life and still govern Troezen effectively. I imagined Artemis would be pleased. Anyone trying to block Hippolytus from the Athenian throne would be pleased. The inhabitants of Troezen, with whom he was popular, would doubtless be pleased as well.

But I wouldn't be. I loved my sons by Phaedra, but Hippolytus was my firstborn. The Athenian throne was his by right. He might not care about it now, but that could change at any time.

While I worried over this dilemma, I decided to take Phaedra on one of my visits to Troezen. She had met Aethra briefly when my mother came to Athens to help her after the birth of Demophon and Acamas, but she had never met either Pittheus, who might not live much longer, or Hippolytus.

However, the visit was not to be just a social one. Though Phaedra had never shown a hint of disloyalty to me, I sometimes wondered if she wanted her own sons to displace Hippolytus as my heirs. The best way to keep her unentangled from the scheming in the Athenian court was to get her to care for Hippolytus as if he were her own. She couldn't be expected to do that without even knowing him. I would bring them together, and if that meeting bore fruit, I would bring Hippolytus to Athens to meet his half-brothers and hopefully befriend them. Then and only then would his position be truly safe.

We sailed across the Saronic Gulf, arriving at Troezen in time for dinner. Pittheus, though he could barely walk, did his best to play the gracious host. Aethra, who was for all practical purposes the ruler of Troezen, handled the details. We dined together, as was now the custom in Troezen. That unsettled Phaedra a little, for she was used to men and women dining separately, a tradition I had not yet convinced the Athenians to abandon.

"It is a wise custom," I assured her. "I would rather spend more time with the woman I love whenever possible. Don't you agree? Or are you getting tired of me?"

"Never!" she said, but she wasn't looking at me when she said it. Her eyes had wandered to Hippolytus, who was sitting across the table from us. He was eating silently, which was unlike him. Phaedra would never get to know him in this way.

"Hippolytus, how is the hunting going?" I asked.

He looked up. "Pretty much as usual."

"He is too modest," said Pittheus, his voice scratchier than I remembered. "He brings home more game than the kitchen can handle. I can't remember the last time we had to buy meat."

"Father, may I hunt tonight?"

I thought about forbidding him so that he would spend more time with Phaedra, but then he might sulk and make a bad impression.

"After we are all done with dinner."

"Is it true you hunt with Artemis?" asked Phaedra.

"It is," he replied, eyes focused on his food.

"And she taught you to hunt?"

"She did."

I gnashed my teeth silently. Phaedra seemed to be trying. Hippolytus was not.

"That is impressive," said Phaedra. "I am the granddaughter of Zeus, uh, I meant great-granddaughter, but I have never met him. That you have spent so much time with Artemis must mean she sees great talent in you. And to be allowed to hunt with her? She hardly ever trusts men enough to allow that."

"I've never really thought about it," said Hippolytus, still looking down. His cheeks reddened. Perhaps Phaedra had overdone the praise.

"Hippolytus has never discussed his time with Artemis very much," said Aethra. "To him, it is a private thing. Isn't that right, Grandson?"

"Yes," said Hippolytus.

"Do you fear that if you speak of Artemis too much, she will vanish from your life?" asked Phaedra. "I don't think that is what would happen."

Hippolytus glanced in her direction. "How would you know?" Then his eyes returned to contemplating the tabletop. I was tempted to reprimand him for being rude, but I wasn't sure whether that would work.

That was the problem of having had to foster him. Pittheus and Aethra had handled his discipline all these years. I had brought Phaedra here to meet him, but I suddenly realized that I knew him only superficially myself, despite my visits. He looked a great deal like me—but in some important ways, he was a stranger.

"Hippolytus, no one can truly know what someone else is thinking or feeling," I said. "But family members share feelings with each other. Phaedra is a member of your family."

"If I offended you—" Phaedra began.

"He is not offended." I cut in before he could. My tone sounded nervous, even to me. "But...but he has had a hard life. His mother died in battle shortly after he was born. Artemis sometimes came and held him in her arms, almost as if he were her own son."

Hippolytus looked at me, eyes wide with shock, as if I betrayed a secret of his, but his mouth remained a thin, narrow line.

"Perhaps it would be best to move on to another subject," said Aethra. "Hippolytus will tell us more when *he* is ready." She gave me a glance that said, "Follow my lead."

"I have finished," said Hippolytus. "May I join the goddess now? It is later than usual."

"Go," I said. "But do not forget—the goddess may not need sleep, but you do."

With only the barest nod to me or anyone else, he jumped out of his chair and practically ran from the room.

"Husband, I too need sleep, and I am tired from the voyage," said Phaedra. "Will you join me?"

"Very soon," I said. "I must discuss a matter of state with Pittheus first."

"Of course—but I will hold you to that *very soon*." She rose, bid goodnight to Pittheus and Aethra, and left the hall.

"Why is Hippolytus being like that?" I asked as soon as I thought Phaedra was out of earshot. "He was rude. I know you taught him better than that."

Pittheus shook his head. "The boy has not been the same almost since Phaedra landed on the island. Children and stepmothers do not always get along, but I thought Hippolytus to have passed that difficult age."

"Perhaps it would be better if you cut this visit short," said Aethra. "I think Hippolytus is...uncomfortable with Phaedra—and not just because she is his stepmother."

"She has been here less than a day, and the only time she has spent with him was at dinner. What could she possibly have done to make him uncomfortable?"

"He said something to me earlier about not liking the way she looks at him. But when I asked what he meant, he didn't really give me an answer."

"Apparently, he doesn't like it when women look at him," said Pittheus, sounding annoyed.

"She's just curious about him," I said. "She'd heard much but knows little. It's natural for her to want to find out what she can. He should understand that."

An ugly thought crossed my mind like a dark cloud shrouding the face of the moon.

What if Hippolytus was not as asexual as he appeared? What if he had feelings for Phaedra? That would certainly explain why he was so awkward around her.

I shuddered and pushed the idea into the shadows at the back of my mind. Someone with self-discipline enough not to look at a beautiful goddess lustfully would certainly not look at his own stepmother in such an unchaste way.

"I don't want to cut this visit short," said Theseus. "The whole point is for Phaedra to get to know Hippolytus. This is the first step in avoiding tensions between him and her sons."

"That is wise," said Pittheus.

"But do not push too hard," said Aethra. "Hippolytus is very much his own person, perhaps eccentric as the world reckons such things. But remember the great destiny Artemis predicted for him."

I thanked them for their advice and joined Phaedra in bed. To my surprise, she was already asleep. I did not try to wake her.

The next day, Hippolytus, who had come home very late from his hunt, was off again before breakfast was even served.

"I believe he's gone for a swim," said Pittheus. "I expected him back by breakfast, though."

My eyes narrowed. "Send someone out to find him. He knew he was to eat with us this morning. He is being rude again."

"Does it matter this time?" asked Aethra, looking around. "Phaedra has not joined us, either."

I had been so upset with Hippolytus that I hadn't even noticed my wife's absence. She was still sleeping when I'd gotten up, but that was at least an hour ago. She should have appeared by now.

"I'll go tell her breakfast is ready," I said.

"Leave well enough alone," said Aethra. "She looked a little pale last night. Perhaps she has not been sleeping well."

Pittheus managed a crooked smile. "Perhaps my grandson does not let her sleep. I'm surprised you only have two sons."

I ignored his joke and her advice. Instead, I stalked off to find Phaedra, even though, with Hippolytus gone, I might as well have let her sleep. My plan was coming unraveled, thread by thread, and I was out of sorts.

To my surprise, she wasn't in our room. I hadn't passed her on the way. Where could she be?

I walked to the window and looked down, hoping to catch a glimpse of her outside. I saw no one. Looking out to sea, I caught sight of a solitary form knifing through the surf, swift as a dolphin. Though I could not be sure, I imagined it was Hippolytus, out visiting his grandfather at dawn—or so I liked to think. If it was him, watching his rhythmic passage through the waves gave me a kind of peace. Everything would work out.

By the time I returned to the great hall, I was surprised again to find no sign of Phaedra.

"Perhaps she's out walking," said Aethra. "Take advantage of the opportunity to have a talk with Hippolytus. Your grandfather took it into his head to go out in person to solve some kind of dispute between two farmers. These days, I have to help him around, and at the speed he moves, it will be a miracle if we're back by lunch."

After I said goodbye to Aethra, I went out to talk to Hippolytus, but if that had been him in the sea, he was gone now. He might have gone into the nearby woods, but he and Artemis always hunted at night, so I didn't see why he would have.

Nor could I figure out what had become of Phaedra. I left her a note and took a slow walk around the city, relishing memories from my childhood. I took no guards with me, but Troezen was a small town by comparison with Athens, and I was never more than a few blocks from the palace. Besides, everyone here knew me. It was like strolling through a large compound belonging to my extended family.

When I returned, the palace was quiet as a tomb. Pittheus and Aethra had not yet returned. Neither, as far as I could tell, had Hippolytus. But surely, Phaedra should have returned by now. In Athens, she hardly ever left the palace, except for state functions. It was difficult to imagine her roaming the streets of a strange city alone.

There were still a few guards around, following their daily routines, as were the slaves. But even their footsteps seemed strangely hushed, as if silence had descended on the whole city.

Feeling nervous, I went back to the room Phaedra and I shared and opened the door.

I froze as if I had gazed into the eyes of Medusa and was now stone.

PROPHECY AND TRAGEDY

I HAD SEEN many horrible things in my life, but none as horrible as what I then beheld. Phaedra was hanging by a thick rope from one of the ceiling beams. Her eyes, dull and lifeless, were still open and stared at nothing. Her skin was pale as death. Beneath her, a chair had been kicked over.

I cut her down at once and checked for any sign of life, though I knew I would find none. Not one single heartbeat, not one solitary breath.

She had taken her own life—but why? It made no sense.

That was when I noticed the crumpled note on the floor. I picked it up and recognized her handwriting at once. My blood ran cold as I read her words.

Husband,

I never thought I would leave you, but I am too ashamed to go on living.

Your son has had impure thoughts, both adulterous and incestuous, toward me. He wanted to take me to his bed. When I refused, he raped me. I cannot go on after betraying you, involuntarily though it was. Please help our boys understand.

THE NOTE WAS SIGNED with her name and stained by her tears.

People talk about seeing red when they are angry, but I never had until that moment known what they meant. My vision was reddened so much that the walls looked as if they had been painted with blood.

Clutching Phaedra's cold flesh to my chest, I ran down the hall, screaming like a man bereft of all reason, shattering the unnatural quiet of the place. Slaves fled from my approach. Even the best trained of the guards quivered.

I stopped when I had reached the great hall did I finally stop. My vision was little more than a red mist by then.

"Guards!" I screamed. "Guards!" I kept screaming until I thought my throat would burst.

"What...what is it, my prince?" It was the captain of the guard, walking shakily toward me.

"Unspeakable crimes have been done here," I said, trying to sound calm. I failed, and my voice was hoarse from all the shouting. I held out Phaedra's body as if he could somehow read Hippolytus's guilt upon it.

"Find my son and bring him here to me," I said. "Do not let him escape."

Technically, the guards here were under Pittheus's command, not mine, but the captain saw I was in no mood to quibble about legalities. It only took him and his men a few minutes to find Hippolytus, who was brazenly loitering near the palace as if he had not just committed a vile crime.

The guards did not even have to drag him to me. He came of his own free will and looked me in the eye, appearing to be the incarnation of innocence itself. Even when his eyes fell on Phaedra's body, he looked horrified but not guilty.

"You tried to seduce her," I said slowly. Angry as I was, it was hard to make the words come out. "Your own stepmother. And when she refused your immoral advances, you raped her."

"Father, no! It was *she* who tried to seduce *me*. When I told her I would never lie with her, she left without saying another word. I yelled after her that I would tell you what she had done when you returned. Then I went outside to clear my head. Question the guards at the entrance. They saw me leave."

"That could have been after you raped her," I said, gently putting the body down and waving her letter in his face. "Before she hanged herself, she wrote down what really happened."

"Lies!" said Hippolytus, still shameless enough to look me in the eye. "Do you not remember the story of Bellerophon? He, too, was falsely accused of rape, and he nearly died as a result."

"You're nothing like Bellerophon. I know Phaedra. She was so reserved, so proper. The very idea that she would seduce her own stepson is ridiculous. And she loved me for years. For years!" I repeated, shouting each word so loudly that they echoed back to me. "She would never do what you accuse her of. But you will not die like Bellerophon. No, live with what you have done—but far away from here. You are banished. Only if you return will you die."

I had no more right to banish someone from Troezen than I did to command the palace guard, but, though some of the men looked uncomfortable, none moved to stop me. They probably thought that Pittheus would return and perhaps investigate to determine whether Hippolytus was really guilty. I had no doubt that my grandfather would stand with me. One glimpse of Phaedra, one reading of her letter, and he would feel the same as I did.

"I will go—but I go protesting my innocence. Someday, I pray the gods will reveal the truth."

"The gods do not hear the prayers of such as you." I snarled the words. Hippolytus turned and left without speaking a word.

I knelt beside Phaedra. "I don't know if you can hear me, but I pray you can," I whispered. "This was not your fault. Being raped was not your fault. Oh, how I wish you had talked to me about it!"

I knew the body should be prepared for burial, but I stayed with her for a while. Through consideration or fear, everyone left me alone.

As I looked at Phaedra's dead face, I knew that banishment was not enough punishment for what Hippolytus had done. But, even filled with rage as I was, I wasn't sure I could kill him with my own hands.

Then I remembered I didn't need to.

I had often thought of using the wish Poseidon gave me, but either the circumstances were not desperate enough, or disaster struck too fast. This situation seemed perfect for it. I had failed to bring life to Hippolytus's mother. But I would not fail to bring death to him.

I invoked the wish. Power gathered around like a tidal wave, cold and massive as my desire for revenge.

"Kill Hippolytus," I thought to myself. The accumulated power rolled away from me with a mighty rumble. I had no doubt it was heading toward Hippolytus and would not stop until it found him.

I smiled. I never thought I would do such a thing, but I smiled at the thought of my son's death. What he had done had broken the bonds of kinship between us.

Not long after, I heard a scream nearby. It was a woman's scream but amplified as no human voice could be. Even my own grieving cries had not shaken the palace as this one, mournful sound did.

My breath caught in my throat when Artemis herself appeared before me. In her arms, she carried the broken body of Hippolytus. He was entangled in horses' reins, suggesting he must have been driving away in the chariot his grandfather had given him for his birthday. The wish made him fall and become entangled in the reins, after which the horses dragged him until he was dead.

The goddess's white arms were smeared with his blood, and his skin was even paler now than hers. I could hear running footsteps as the few people lingering nearby fled. They didn't want to be caught in the goddess's wrath.

I stood and faced her.

"Goddess, I am sorry you happened upon such a dreadful scene. Hippolytus, who lies in your arms, has raped his stepmother and received just recompense for—"

"Foolish man!" she yelled, her usually serene face twisted with rage as great as mine. "He is innocent! It was Phaedra, not Hippolytus, who sinned. Her letter is a horrible lie."

"That…that cannot be!" I knew how much she favored him. She was refusing to accept the truth, that was all.

"Do you question the word of a goddess? I should strike you down where you stand!"

"Don't," whispered Hippolytus. I had been so focused on Artemis that I hadn't noticed he was not quite dead yet. He stirred in Artemis's arms and tried to raise his head. "Don't harm him. He didn't know. I for…forgive him. If…if I am still dear to you, you will…do the same."

He finally managed to get his head far enough up to look at me. "Father, I am innocent. But I forgive you. With all my heart…"

He fell backward, and with a sudden jerk, he breathed his last.

"I don't understand," I said. "I knew Phaedra. She was not the kind of woman to falsely accuse a man, let alone try to seduce him. And her own stepson? It is…it is unthinkable."

"Any more unthinkable than that your chaste son is an adulterer and a rapist?" asked Artemis. "Theseus, look upon him. Even dead, he is still beautiful. Do you think he would have had any shortage of bed partners if that is what he desired? And there was no hint in him of the violent nature, the inhumanity that makes a rapist."

"So neither one of them could have been guilty. Yet one of them has to have been. How do you explain that?"

"I know all too well who must have been at fault. Aphrodite, I sense you nearby. I know you're watching. Show yourself. Show yourself this instant, or I will go and hunt down one of your mortal favorites and drive a silver arrow right through his heart. Not one god would fault me for it…not after this!" She thrust Hippolytus's body at empty air.

I felt another presence in the room. There was a vague shimmer at the far end, then a pale and transparent image of Aphrodite. Even in that partial appearance, she was the most beautiful female I had ever beheld, beyond any woman I had known, even those I had loved, beyond even the other goddesses. Though she trembled with fear of Artemis, which diminished her appeal, had I not been mired in grief and confusion, I would have begged her to come to my bed, so great was the charisma that flowed from her.

"Hippolytus denied love, which was an affront to me," the goddess said after a long, uncomfortable silence. "To compound that insult, he refused to sacrifice to me. In fact, I think he worshiped only Artemis. Had I not acted, another god would have, sooner or later."

So Aphrodite had been responsible. And I condemned Hippolytus without even listening to him! The truth was like a knife thrusting through my heart. Would that it had been a real knife so that I could catch up with him on his way to the Underworld and tell him how sorry I was.

But I could not die just yet. The truth might cut like knives, but I must know all of it. I must understand every detail of my misdeeds. Only thus could I truly repent of them.

"It cannot be that he so neglected other gods!" said Artemis, but her face was unguarded enough for me to see uncertainty there. "But even if it were true, his punishment was too harsh."

"Really?" asked Aphrodite, suddenly more solid and more confident. "When the pious Oeneus forgot to sacrifice to you *once*, you sent the Calydonian Boar to ravage his kingdom, causing the deaths of many good men in the process. I tolerated Hippolytus's neglect of my worship for *years*.

"I also tried other measures first. I thought if I could make him fall in love, his approach to life would become more balanced. As you your-self said, it would not have been hard to find a girl to share his bed if he had been inclined to ask one. I should have been able to awaken the desire in him easily. I can induce such feelings even in gods. Yet I could not move him. Either he has a heart of stone—or you did something to him!"

"I acted only to preserve his free will," said Artemis. "I suspected you might try something, so I learned of an herb that would deaden him to your influence. He could still fall in love or even in lust if he wished. He just couldn't be forced into it by you."

My mind was moving sluggishly, but even so, what Artemis said didn't sound right. Unless the tales were all wrong, Artemis had no special skill with herbs.

"You resorted to magic to thwart me?" asked Aphrodite. "Had you not done so, Hippolytus would still be alive—and much happier than he was in the unnatural celibacy his desire to please you forced him into."

"It was…you should have come to me."

Artemis wasn't denying resorting to magic like some common witch. But no common witch could block the power of Aphrodite. Could it be? Could Artemis have trafficked with Hecate?

"Oh, should I?" asked Aphrodite mockingly. "You have never taken me seriously. If you had your way, all mortals would be celibate, and this generation would be the last."

"If you had your way, all women would be nothing more than sex slaves for their husbands," said Artemis. "I offer a different path, but only to those who wish it. You and Eros toy with their emotions whether they wish it or not."

"Goddesses—" I began.

"Silence, mortal!" said Artemis. "It is not your place to interrupt when deities are talking."

"That body in your arms is my son's," I said.

"Whom you killed," she said, looking at me as she fired each word at me like one of her arrows.

"For once, you and I agree," said Aphrodite. "I did not intend Hippolytus to die, just suffer a little. It was Theseus who sealed the lad's fate, not I."

I wanted to shout her down. I wanted to grab Artemis's bow away from her, shoot them both, and make war on Olympus itself.

But I could not, for they were both right. I could have given Hippolytus a real trial. Perhaps others in the palace had seen enough to cast doubt on Phaedra's letter. If not that, I could at least have been content with banishment, which could eventually be reversed. No, I had to have death instead.

With horror, I realized that I had failed Hippolytus long before Phaedra accused him. The prophecy of Artemis echoed in my head. *Should he ever encounter the sister of your beloved, he will inevitably die.* Consumed by grief for Antiope, I had assumed she was the beloved referred to by the prophecy. But there was a time when I would have called Ariadne beloved.

Memories of that meeting with Deucalion came back, and for the first time, I knew why the king of Crete had been so nervous when I said something about his niece looking so much like his sister. She was his sister—and therefore Ariadne's as well!

But why lie about such a thing? I tried to be angry with Deucalion, but all I could manage was a weak annoyance. My anger was still reserved for my own stupidity.

Deucalion had wanted to atone for his father's sins, and he wanted peace with Athens. Bringing me a beautiful bride would help with both. That part I understood completely. But why conceal the bride's identity?

I hadn't thought much about that conversation in years, but now I knew as clearly as if someone had scratched the answer into my brain with a nail. The only unmarried royal woman he had available at that point was his sister. Misunderstanding my morality, he had assumed I would reject her because of my former love for her sister. He introduced her as his daughter instead of his sister. When he realized the truth about my attitudes, it was too late for him to tell me who she really was without seeming foolish or dishonest—or both.

But I should have known. He almost called her sister once, and she'd had plenty slips of the tongue since our marriage. She looked like the Phaedra I remembered, and even the little spark when I was near her was as strong as Ariadne's. Someone another generation removed from Zeus would have had a weaker spark.

I saw all the obvious signs, yet I never realized the truth. Phaedra was the sister of my beloved—and I, stupid beyond belief, had brought her to Hippolytus myself!

The goddesses had played a role—but it was I who killed my son. It was I who should die for it.

I knelt before them. "I have sinned beyond all reckoning. Artemis, I ask you to execute me with your arrows."

The goddess shook her head. "Much as I would like to, I cannot. To do so would be to ignore my Hippolytus's dying wish—and that I could never do. Live, Theseus. Live and suffer. Worship me, as you must. But do not expect that I will ever answer your prayers."

In a silver flash, she was gone, taking Hippolytus with her. I was not to be permitted even to bury his body.

Aphrodite remained. I had one more mistake to make that day.

"Goddess, I understand your grievance with Hippolytus. But what had Phaedra ever done that you would drive her mad?"

"I did not drive her mad," said Aphrodite. "My touch was gentle. I worked with what she was already feeling. When she beheld Hippolytus's young and perfect form, lust awakened inside her. It grew when she saw him swimming naked in the sea. I did make those feelings harder to resist. That much I admit. But I did not take all choice from her. Had she chosen differently, I would have found a different way to repay Hippolytus for his impiety."

"You lie!"

You think I should not have said such a thing to a goddess, and you are right. But my brain was addled by a mixture of guilt and grief far more potent than any wine.

"I do not, king of Athens. But I promise you this—I will prove the truth of my words to you. I will place you in a position in which your heart will be at war with your morals. Then you will see that the choice is still yours. If you make the right one, all will be well. If you make the wrong one, just as Phaedra did, you will bring about your own ruin."

Aphrodite disappeared before I could respond. In one day, I had alienated two different goddesses.

Had I lost the favor of all the gods? What would they think of a king who killed his own son? Would Athena turn away? Would Poseidon, whose power I had used to perpetrate such injustice?

The only way to save Athens from being destroyed by the wrath of the gods as it descended on me would be to end my life now. It would be hard to bash my own brains in with my club, but easy to fall upon my own sword.

I had it in my hands, ready to plunge it through my cursed guts, when Aethra and Pittheus returned. "My son, put that down!" she yelled, running to me. Not wanting to make her watch me end my life, I complied. I could always kill myself later.

With much urging, I told them what had happened. My face was wet with tears and my voice almost inaudible by the end, but I got through it.

Pittheus sat upon his throne as if he could no longer stand. His eyes, too, were filled with tears. He had loved Hippolytus in his way.

"Listen to me," said Aethra. "Yes, you made a mistake. The results were horrendous, but the mistake itself was understandable. You know I loved Hippolytus as if he were my own, and yet I still say you are no murderer. Even he would not say that. He forgave you. Now you must forgive yourself."

"But why?" I asked. "What is there left to live for now?"

"There is Athens," said Pittheus, sitting up a little straighter. "What will happen if you die now? Demophon and Acamas are too young to rule yet. The place will dissolve into chaos—and likely, the two boys will both lose their lives. No usurper could afford to let them live. You know that as well as I."

"But what if the gods seek to destroy me? Will not they destroy Athens in the process?"

"Artemis has pledged not to harm you. And Aphrodite may forget you the next time a handsome man or god takes her to bed. She is not known to carry long grudges."

I was distraught at that moment to remember how long Aphrodite had carried a grudge against Aegeus. What would it have mattered, anyway? The damage was already done.

"Who else among the gods do you think would even care about what has happened here?" asked Pittheus.

"Do not gods punish sinners?" I asked. "Do they need a personal reason to do so?"

"Come with me," she said. "I will prove to you that the gods have not turned against you."

I wanted to refuse, but I was exhausted from the emotional turmoil within me. She led me to the beach, and I shuddered. If I looked closely, I could find the very spot where Hippolytus had lost control of his horses. Just a little searching would find the blood where he fell, became tangled in the reins, and was dragged until Artemis rescued what was left of him.

Aethra turned toward the sea. "Poseidon, come forth and speak to your son. He has blood guilt of which he needs to be cleansed."

I had not even thought of that. But Poseidon had only appeared to me once. What made Aethra think he would appear at her bidding?

"Theseus, walk into the waves," said a voice. It was far younger and higher than Poseidon's, but I did as I was told.

When I was roughly waist-deep, a dolphin jumped out of the water a little farther out. On its back was a handsome boy, younger looking than

Hippolytus, but with the glow of divinity about him. He slid off the dolphin's back and swam effortlessly toward me.

"I am Palaemon, protector of lost sailors—and now lost kings, apparently. Poseidon has sent me to absolve you of your guilt."

"He...he did not come himself?"

Palaemon laughed like the child he appeared to be. "He cannot answer every summons by mortals—even one he loves as much as you, Theseus."

I had a hard time believing he loved me. How much effort would it have taken to tell me that in person? It had been years since he had brought me down to his white-gold palace and embraced me. Was not my peril as great now as it had been when he rescued me so many years ago? Still, a thousand mortals could have come to that same beach and not been greeted by any god.

"Do you doubt me?" asked Palaemon. "I would have thought calling Aphrodite a liar would have satisfied your appetite for that sort of thing, at least for a while."

"I do...I do not doubt you," I said.

"Nor should you doubt me when I tell you that all may yet be well. I am well-versed in such things. I was a poor child, almost drowned by the madness of my mother. But Zeus took pity on us, and now she is a goddess, and I am a god. How is that for an unexpected twist?"

I'd heard his story, which was popular among the Corinthians, but I'd never believed it. "Yes, that is quite a twist."

"Well, your life has twists and turns as well. Some enemy of Aegeus might have found you when you were a child and killed you. Medea might have killed you—almost did, in fact. You could have died fighting the minotaur, or the centaurs, or any one of a dozen other times. Yet here you are, still drawing breath."

"My wife is not. My son is not."

"I cannot yet say more," said Palaemon. "Except that all may not be as it seems. Love the family you have left. Govern your city well. And do something to placate Aphrodite. These three things did Poseidon bid me tell you. And now he would want me to cleanse your blood guilt. Are you ready?"

I nodded slowly.

"Good. Then down on your knees."

When I bent down, the water covered me nearly to my chest. With his small, gentle hands, Palaemon poured seawater over my head. With his high, childlike voice, he pronounced the words that cleansed me of my blood guilt. Then he was gone. I caught one more glimpse of him, waving at me from the back of his dolphin, before he plunged into the waves.

I walked back to the shore, where Aethra was waiting for me.

"Do you feel better?" she asked.

Much to my surprise, I did.

OLD FRIENDS

THE GOOD FEELINGS Palaemon had blessed me did not last long, but at least the urge to fall upon my own sword did not return. I resolved to do as the boy-god had advised. I still had a family. I still had a kingdom. And Aphrodite might yet be placated. All could be, if not well, then at least tolerable.

That resolve was put to the test more than once in the weeks that followed. Almost immediately after returning to Athens, I had to journey back to Troezen. Pittheus, already weak, had finally died. People whispered that it was grief over his grandson's death that had killed him. I couldn't disagree.

I thought everyone else had fled when Artemis had come screaming in, but apparently, someone had been close enough to eavesdrop, and word of the goddess's condemnation of me had spread throughout the city. As I went through the funeral rites for my grandfather, I felt the piercing eyes of the citizens upon me, unblinking eyes whose mute accusation made me want to run and hide. They blamed me for Pittheus's death and even more for Hippolytus's.

Someone put up a small statue of Hippolytus in the very center of town. I couldn't imagine how someone could have carved it so fast, especially considering how remarkable the likeness was. Hippolytus turned to stone by the eyes of Medusa would have looked much as the statue did. Fashioned from white Pentelic marble of the finest quality, it must also have been expensive. Yet, despite the combination of artistry and cost, no one admitted to knowing the patron who commissioned it or the artist who crafted it.

Women came daily to put fresh garlands of flowers around the statue's neck and arms. Sometimes, they added a laurel garland upon its head. To me, that last touch was a bitter reminder of all the victories my son would never win.

Some women also anointed the statue with their own tears, and more than once, I saw a woman press her warm lips against the statue's cold marble ones. I could not help but think of the tale of Pygmalion, who, by Aphrodite's wrath, fell in love with a statue he had made. By Aphrodite's mercy, the statue became a living woman, whom Pygmalion married.

That tale I did not believe at all. If Aphrodite were so merciful, the kisses of those women would breathe Hippolytus's soul into that marble and bring him to life. He would marry one of them, but Artemis would be so overjoyed to have him back that she would let him hunt with her sometimes. He would rule both Athens and Troezen, just as I had intended, have many children, and be remembered after death as the greatest ruler any Greek city had ever had.

But Aphrodite was not so merciful, and the statue was just a statue. No matter how much I stared at it, those eyes would never look back at me.

I tried to shake off such melancholy fancies long enough to take care of business. As I walked back to the palace, I saw graffiti scrawled on several walls. The handwriting was different, but the message was always the same—*Remember Hippolytus*.

Gods! How could I possibly forget him?

The counselors said little to me when I arrived for our meeting, but their expressions were more like judges waiting to pass a sentence of execution than subjects waiting to hear the will of their king.

I loved Troezen, my birthplace, my childhood home—but it would have been apparent even to someone stupider than I that I could not possibly remain its king. Even those few who might not hate me would never trust me. The only way to retain authority would be to oppress the city with Athenian troops—and such a thing I would never do.

The council thawed slightly when I announced my intention to renounce the crown. I offered to abdicate in favor of my younger son, Acamas, whose regent would be Aethra until he came of age. The counselors' disapproving frowns made me realize what a blunder that suggestion had been. Acamas was an innocent child—but his mother was Phaedra, the one person the citizens of Troezen might have hated even more than me. The same consideration would rule out Demophon.

I could not just abdicate and leave Troezen without a king, though. The city would eventually fall prey to a larger power. It would be better if it could choose a wise ruler rather than just be conquered by someone. There was no one of royal blood left within the city, so unless the gods chose to proclaim someone, the city would have to offer itself to one of the local rulers.

The closest great city aside from Athens was Mycenae, but it was still ruled by the incompetent Eurystheus. King Adrastus of Argos was a better man. I offered the council the protection of Athens until a satisfactory arrangement with Adrastus would be negotiated.

The counselors accepted my offer somewhat grudgingly and then accepted my abdication with much greater eagerness.

My homeland was no longer mine.

Aethra met me on the way out. "I think it is time that I left Troezen. There is nothing more here for me."

"You are always welcome in Athens, but are you sure you wish to leave?"

"With the city likely to pass into the hands of another family, the only surviving daughter of the previous ruler is likely to be…an inconvenience. At the very least, I suspect I will be given little freedom. In Athens, I would be a threat to no one."

So it came to pass that we sailed away from Troezen together. I knew we would never see the place again, though neither of us spoke of that. For the sake of our own sanity, we had to leave the past in the past.

I offered Aethra rooms in the palace, but she chose instead to settle in Aphidnae, one of the outer demes of Athens. "I'll be close enough to visit, but not close enough to get in your way," she said.

"You would never be in my way," I assured her.

Aethra shook her head. "I am used to being part of the royal council in Troezen. It is one thing for the king's daughter to play such a role, or even the king's wife, as Antiope did. But for the king's mother to do the same? No, that is only done when the king is not yet of age. My presence would create the wrong impression. No, I will stay a little distance away, and I will content myself with being the mistress of my own home."

I couldn't argue with her logic, though I hated to think of how circumstance had diminished her role in government. Nor did I like to think about how little progress I could now make in giving women in general more of a role in society. I would never have another woman like Antiope to aid me in that task. Phaedra was now being used as a cautionary tale of how women were not to be trusted.

I tried to make the best of my situation. At least in Athens, I was still well-respected and might yet do some good. Athens was more in need of a strong leader than ever, for all around us, the world seemed to be falling apart.

Asclepius, son of Apollo and great healer, was blasted to ashes by a thunderbolt on the steps of Apollo's own temple in Epidaurus. Men whispered Zeus had killed him for some undisclosed sin. It was also said that Apollo had tried to kill the cyclopes in retaliation and was sentenced to live for a time as a mortal slave.

How could a god be a slave? Surely, such a story was nonsense. Yet oracles and prophets alike proclaimed that there was some imbalance in the world, as if the temporary absence of Apollo had not fully been covered by the other gods.

"The musical instruments will not tune properly," one of the musicians told me. "It is as if the strings themselves know that something is amiss."

Then came rumors that Artemis had left Greece and was somewhere in Italy, though why the goddess would go to such a savage place I couldn't imagine. Perhaps her familiar haunts reminded her too much of Hippolytus. I wondered, but there was no one I could ask.

As for Aphrodite, my least-favorite goddess, even I could not help feeling sympathy for her when news reached me that her lover, Adonis, said to be the most handsome man in the world, was mauled to death by a boar he was hunting. Aphrodite, convinced one of the gods was responsible, vowed vengeance and then retired into solitude. For a while, it was said, prayers to her went unanswered and sacrifices unaccepted. Seldom had any deity cut herself off so completely from her worshipers. She did return after a short time, but her priests remained frightened, as if she might at any moment withdraw from the world completely, taking all love with her.

With the gods in turmoil, it was no surprise that mortals were in equal chaos. Adrastus, to whom I had entrusted Troezen, embroiled Argos in a series of bloody wars with Thebes that eventually resulted in the destruction of large parts of the city and the evacuation of most of the population. Though it was rebuilt later, that did not bring back all the good men on both sides who lost their lives.

Palaemon had told me to love my family. That was easy with my two sons and Aethra, far harder with more distant relations. My grandfather's much younger brothers, Atreus and Thyestes, exiled by Pelops himself for murdering their half-brother, had suffered so many disasters that they made my life seem almost happy by comparison. But like me, they brought many catastrophes upon themselves. The rumors of adultery, incest, rape, and murder that reached my ears made my skin crawl.

The bringers of those rumors would whisper of the curse of Hermes upon my family, but I began to doubt them. How could Atreus and Thyestes blame Hermes—how could I blame Hermes—when at every turn, we, not the god, had been at fault?

A few times, I heard of Heracles, whose seemingly endless labors were still going on. He deserved better than what looked to me like a life of endless misery. If he, son of Zeus and perhaps the greatest warrior ever, was entitled to no more, then what could I look forward to? What even worse misery had fate prepared for me?

And then a messenger told me that Pirithous was at the gate, asking for an audience with me.

I had several letters from him, none of which I'd opened. But the mishap with his witch was long ago.

"See that he is let in, and tell him I will receive him in the great hall."

The messenger nodded and bowed himself out. I went to the great hall and ordered that refreshments be brought.

So many years had passed, and yet Pirithous looked to me at first like the same young, rash man who had stolen my cattle. A closer look, however, revealed that his face was lined by worry, if not age. He grinned as he had in the old days, but his eyes looked as haunted as mine must now.

"I had not heard from you in so long that I was almost afraid you would refuse to see me," said Pirithous. "You have been much missed in Larissa."

"I am sorry I did not answer your letters. As you can imagine, I have been...preoccupied."

"Though I wasn't invited to come and grieve with you, I grieved from a distance for Antiope, as well as Hippolytus...the boy whom I never met."

I raised an eyebrow. "That sounded more like reproof than condolence."

Pirithous's smile faded. "It is both. Theseus, you must have realized by now that my intentions were pure when I sent a witch to help you. I had no idea Medea would take her place and wreak such havoc. You do know that, don't you?"

I nodded as if my head were suddenly twice as heavy. "You meant no harm, but...but I worry about your reliance on witches. Everything I have seen suggests they are not to be trusted."

"Thessaly is not Athens," he said. "The place has a witch lurking behind every tree. I can try to find ways to coexist peacefully with them —or I can brace for a war in which the other side can blast me with magic. Which would you pick?"

"You have a point. Just, please, do not involve them in my business again."

"Whatever you want. Now, can we be...friends again? We've talked about this before. How many people are there that we can really call friends? Our blood and our position make it almost impossible to befriend anyone. And Theseus...I really need a friend right now."

I leaned toward him. "Why? What has happened?"

"Hippodamia has just died. She died giving birth to Polypoetes, my son. I don't think I really knew how much I loved her—until she was gone."

The pain on his face, the loneliness in his eyes, made me throw my arms around him. My anger melted away like frost in sunlight. We embraced as if no time had passed at all, as if we were still young and at the very beginning of our friendship.

We spent the next few hours together. I even waved off Alexius when he came in with important business. Whatever it was, short of outright war, could wait. I had neglected Pirithous, my ally and my friend, for too long.

We had a leisurely dinner, followed by what even Pirithous thought was too much wine. As it turned out, it was just enough to get him to reveal one of his purposes in coming to Athens.

"I think it is time we had another adventure together," he said, slurring some of the words.

The suggestion penetrated the happy fog I felt I'd been in for hours. Our previous adventures had led to war with the centaurs and war with the Amazons.

"You need time to grieve your wife, do you not? And we both have duties to perform."

"What is it with you and duties?" asked Pirithous. "You've set up Athens so well it could run without you for months, if need be. Besides, if you must know, what I am proposing fulfills one of our duties. We both need to find new wives."

I raised an eyebrow. "How is that in any way a duty? You and I have both fathered heirs. We have no need to marry again."

"You have two, and I have only one," said Pirithous. "We should each have more. Mortal life is...so fragile. And if something were to happen to our heirs, what then?"

My eyes were tired, but I blinked a couple of times and tried to see him as clearly as I could. He was wearing his familiar, smiling mask, but it was cracked and worn. His eyes betrayed as much pain as if blood were gushing out of them.

Perhaps he was in even worse shape than I was. What harm would it do to hear him out?

"What are you suggesting? Men do not normally seek out wives in pairs."

"Backup," he said, smiling more broadly. "To find women worthy of us may involve...some risk."

I sat up as straight in my chair as I could manage. "You know we cannot return to the Amazons, right? Penthesilea might not want to kill us, but I think her warriors would finish us off before we ever got to her."

Pirithous looked at me as if I were stupid. "I'm not talking about Amazons again. No, even better—only daughters of Zeus would be truly worthy of men such as us."

"You want to marry your half-sister? Is that not incest?"

"The divine part of our ancestry doesn't count when determining whether sex is incestuous or not. If it did, the gods themselves would all be guilty of incest."

In my grimmer moods, I often thought they were guilty, but I held my tongue.

"Who did you have in mind? I don't offhand recall two women around here who are daughters of Zeus."

Pirithous sighed. "Sometimes, you bury yourself in your work so far you hardly know if it is the sun or the moon that is rising. Have you not heard of Helen of Sparta?"

"I have, but her father—"

"Her *mortal* father."

"All right, her mortal father has said he will not receive suitors for her until she is old enough to be married. She is only...what is it now? Ten, I think."

"But she looks at least fourteen, and girls often marry at fourteen."

"Children of gods mature faster. But I think Tyndareus was judging by calendar age, not looks. Anyway, he has made his wishes clear. Perhaps, when he announces that he will receive suitors, I will be among them."

"Why wait to compete with every king in Greece and several outside of it? Helen is said to be the most beautiful woman in Greece even now. Besides that, she is a daughter of Zeus. And if all that were not enough, it is said she has the gift of prophecy. Think of it, Theseus—a prophet right in your own household. She would be worth marrying just for that, even if she were as ugly as a gorgon.

"No, it is not wise to wait. Go now to Tyndareus and make him an offer he cannot refuse. Half your treasury ought to be enough of a bride price."

"Indeed, it is more than I am willing to part with," I said. "What if an emergency arises, and I need the money? Half the world is mad these days."

"And the other half should seize opportunity while it can," said Pirithous. "What harm can there be in asking? The worst he can say is no."

I refused to consider the idea several times, but Pirithous was so insistent that I finally agreed just to placate him. After all, I could ask Tyndareus politely and accept his refusal graciously. Well-handled, the situation need not do any harm to the relationship between Sparta and Athens.

"One more thing," said Pirithous. "As we are like brothers in all things except blood, let us swear an oath to bind us together. Let us pledge by Zeus, upholder of oaths, that we will each do whatever we can to help the other win the wife of his choice."

Tales of how the gods themselves had suffered from hastily sworn oaths should have made me decline Pirithous's proposition. But he looked at me with desperation in his eyes, as if he were drowning, and only I could save him. Besides, I was drunk. I took his hand and swore the oath with him.

Much to Alexius's annoyance, we set out the very next day for Sparta. He insisted on a small escort, but when we reached the outer edge of Athenian territory, I sent them back at Pirithous's insistence.

"What danger between here and Sparta could possibly threaten us?" asked Pirithous. "Besides, few even know that we are going."

"Except for the various gods who hate me," I thought, but I didn't voice that concern. Athenian guards would be little use against gods, anyway. Besides, Pirithous looked genuinely happy for once. Just to see that expression, I was willing to take a little risk.

The journey to Sparta was about as long as the journey to Larissa would have been, though in nearly the opposite direction. We rode across the Isthmus of Corinth. I couldn't help but keep looking out to sea for any sign of Palaemon and his dolphin, but I saw none. From Corinth, we moved southwest, passing Nemea and Argos before veering more sharply south and finding the trail that led across a less developed area and finally to Sparta.

In those days, Sparta and Athens had not yet become the rivals they later grew into. That was not surprising, as they were far apart by the standards of the time. Also, Athens was a sea power, and Sparta was far from any coast.

The Spartan royal line boasted divine roots, just as the Athenian kings did. Tyndareus was only five generations away from Zeus, six away from the titan Atlas on his father's side. His mother was a daughter of Perseus, giving him an even closer connection to Zeus.

Though surprised by the sudden arrival of two kings, Tyndareus welcomed us at once and bestowed upon us every all the hospitality of which he was capable.

.

The Spartan king reminded me of Pittheus when I was first born. Tyndareus was no youth, but no one could have called him an old man, either. He wore a full beard, such as one sees in statues of Zeus, and his brown hair had only begun to fade to gray. His eyes were friendly but also had a piercing quality to them, as if he could see through any falsehood to the truth.

As it was nearly dinnertime, we dined with him. The Spartans followed the practice of men and women dining separately, so I had no opportunity to see the already-famous Helen. I did, however, get to meet his two promising young sons, Castor and Pollux. They were lively, intelligent—and totally confusing.

If the tales were true, Leda, Tyndareus's wife, had given birth to four children at the same time: the girls Helen and Clytemnestra, and the boys Pollux and Castor. As she had slept with Tyndareus at about the time she slept with Zeus, two of the children, Clytemnestra and Castor, were fathered by Tyndareus. The other two, Helen and Pollux, were fathered by Zeus. That was how the storytellers would have it, but instead of feeling a clear spark of Zeus in Pollux, the way I had with Heracles and Pirithous, I felt two flickering half sparks, one in each boy.

"Do you have a question?" asked Tyndareus, who had noticed me watching his sons.

I shook my head, not knowing how to ask my question politely, but Pollux looked closely and said, "Oh, I know what it is. King Theseus, you're a son of…Poseidon, I think. You thought to find a connection to Zeus in me, but instead, you see a little connection in both my brother and me. Isn't that right?"

"Uh, it is, but—"

"But you didn't want to bring up the subject of my wife sleeping with Zeus," Tyndareus finished for me. "Don't avoid the subject on my account. I don't consider Leda unfaithful for having slept with Zeus. The king of the gods knows whom he must sleep with to father great heroes, men and women who benefit the land in ways we cannot foresee. It was her duty, not an act of adultery, to sleep with him. I am honored, not bothered, by it. And I raise all the children as my own, for in my heart, that is what they are."

"Wise policy!" said Pirithous, nodding his approval.

"As for the boys—"

"Oh, can I tell it, father?" asked Castor. Tyndareus nodded indulgently. "Pollux and I have been as close as brothers could possibly be ever since we were born. But we found out about a prophecy that said that Pollux had inherited enough divinity from Zeus to eventually become a god on Olympus. That made me sad, because I knew that one day we would be separated by death. But Pollux, the best brother in the world, found a way to share his divine nature with me. When the time comes, we will both spend part of our time in the Underworld and part of it on Olympus."

Pollux hugged his brother. "Being only half a god is worth it to be able to stay with my brother forever."

I realized my mouth was hanging open and did my best to close it.

"I…I have never heard of such a noble act."

Tyndareus smiled broadly. "Yes, Zeus knew what he was doing when he fathered Pollux. It is uncommon to see such selflessness in children."

But were they really children? It was hard to judge their ages, for they blended the normal mortal growth rate with the precocity of divine children. Possibly, there was something else at work, as well. At times, they looked ten, but if I blinked and looked again, they appeared closer to sixteen—lightly bearded and almost like warriors in their bearing. Yet if he blinked again, they looked older than I was.

I wanted to say something about this strange phenomenon to Pirithous, but the Lapith king was looking down. He seemed less charmed by the boys than I was. He was a son of Zeus, just like Pollux, but no one had ever prophesized that Pirithous would eventually become a god. However, that was probably a rare thing. Few children who were half divine matured into full gods.

"Boys, I think you're confusing our guests," said Tyndareus.

"Oh, sorry," said Castor. "You mean because we didn't settle on an appearance. How's this?" No matter how I looked at the boys now, they were at least as old as I was. But if they were born with Helen, they must be only ten. Even divine precocity could hardly account for such a thing unless they were both full gods.

Tyndareus laughed in a friendly way at my obvious confusion. "The stories about them are wrong in a couple of ways. They and the girls didn't hatch from eggs. I've told the storytellers that many times, but to no avail. Also, they and the girls aren't really the same age."

"You mean—"

"Yes, you can say it. Zeus visited Leda twice, once for the boys and once for the girls. The boys aren't really boys. They were old enough to sail on the Argo and hunt the Calydonian Boar."

"I'd heard that, come to think of it," I said. "But why do they sometimes look ten?"

"Their appearances were already a little…fluid because of the different ways mortal children and half-divine children mature. When Pollux shared his divine nature with Castor, they sometimes looked their mortal age, sometimes older. But when the girls were born, Pollux and Castor, though grown up by that time, both wanted to be as close to their sisters as possible. Somehow—even they don't know how—they developed the gift of appearing the same rough age as their younger sisters. I think they may have prayed for that to Zeus without even realizing it."

I could have sworn I heard Pirithous grind his teeth at that.

"Such close brothers and sisters!" I said. "My boys always seem to be fighting."

Of course, my boys lost their mother when she committed suicide after trying to seduce their half-brother, but Tyndareus didn't need to know that.

"I think it is normal for boys to fight," said Tyndareus. "These two are just...very different that way. But don't let that fool you. They are fine hunters and fine warriors when the need arises."

Hunters. Hippolytus would probably have gotten along well with them. I found myself wanting to cry and pushed the thought as far back in my head as I could.

I felt Tyndareus's eyes on me. I looked back in his direction. He was examining me just as I had examined Castor and Pollux.

"I imagine you did not come all this way just to meet my children," said Tyndareus. "Boys, why don't you go see how your sisters are doing? They should be about done with dinner by now." The twins, looking at that moment as young as their sisters, scampered out of the room as fast as they could.

"So, what brings you here?" asked their father. His voice wasn't exactly suspicious, but at the very least, our seemingly random arrival had piqued his curiosity.

"Actually, it is in relation to one of your children that I have come. I wish to negotiate a marriage with your daughter, Helen."

Tyndareus's smile vanished as quickly as the sun when fast-moving clouds cover it. "You are not from this area, so perhaps you did not realize I have announced that I will take no suitors for Helen's hand until she comes of age."

I began to wonder why I had let Pirithous talk me into this. But I was here now. Tyndareus might think me foolish if I dropped the matter so fast that it appeared I had not thought it through.

"I mean no disrespect to your rights as Helen's father," I said. "But marriages are often negotiated years before they are consummated."

"Many are interested in Helen's hand," said Tyndareus. "I have need of all the time I can get to determine what sort of husband would be best for her."

"As you should," I said, trying to sound casual. "But I think if you consider my qualifications, you will find me a worthy match. I am the son of Poseidon, I have governed Athens well for many years now, and I could both protect and provide for your daughter."

"Theseus, no one questions your merit as a king or your divine ancestry. But…may I speak frankly? I would not wish to offend a guest, but I have an objection to you as a possible husband."

My back pressed against the back of the chair as if I were cornered. "We are in your home. You should always be able to speak frankly here."

"Here is the truth, then. You lost Ariadne. That wasn't your fault, I know—Dionysus took her. I am as aware as any man that the gods will take what they want. But then your first wife, Antiope, died fighting at your side. Why would you put your wife in so much danger?"

Did everyone in the world know every detail of my life?

"As you probably know, Antiope was an Amazon. The only way I could have kept her from the battle was to tie her up—and even then, she would probably have broken free."

"But why marry an Amazon? Since they *never* marry, I fear you courted her as some kind of challenge. And now I fear you may have come seeking Helen's hand for the same reason. First a woman from a group of women who never marry. Then a woman sought after by every unmarried king in Greece, a woman whose father has expressly denied all suitors until a later time. To me, this seems a pattern of wanting a woman not for her merits but because you cannot have her."

"You make it sound as if I look at women as trophies of some kind," I said. "What I am looking for is not a prize but a partner. I value strength, intelligence, and independence in women."

"But how do you know that Helen possesses any of these traits?" asked Tyndareus. "You have never met the girl, and the stories you have heard doubtless emphasized her beauty, not her wit."

"She is a daughter of Zeus, just like my patron, Athena. How could such a girl be witless?"

"Certainly, you are not," said Tyndareus. "Quick of wit and glib of tongue is what you are. But tell me this, then, son of Poseidon. Why did your second wife, Phaedra, kill herself?"

My mouth opened, but I could not force words out. I didn't wish to lie to him, but what would he think of the truth?

"Father?" asked a high, almost musical voice behind me. "I hear you have visitors from far away. May I meet them?"

I turned and saw a girl who could only be Helen. Like most children with divine blood, she looked older than she was, more than old enough to marry. Even I, who had seen goddesses, not only in dreams but in the flesh, had never seen her like. She glowed in a way I thought even a completely mortal eye might perceive. She was like Pandora, crafted to draw the eye of any man, but without Pandora's flaws. Her hair was golden like the sun, her eyes pure sapphire, her skin polished ivory, her figure hypnotic.

Aphrodite, get out of my head!

This was the moment of which the goddess had warned me.

"I will place you in a position in which your heart will be at war with your morals."

Here I was, bewitched by the beauty of a girl whose father seemed dead set against giving her to me in marriage. No good could come of this. I should have made whatever excuse I could, ran through the door, and never returned.

I should have…but I didn't.

"Come in, Helen," said Tyndareus. "This is King Theseus of Athens and King Pirithous of Larissa."

Helen curtseyed gracefully, her every move looking both rehearsed and natural at the same time. "I am pleased to meet such great kings. What brings you to our city?"

"They wish to discuss…an alliance," said Tyndareus.

"Could there be more?" she asked. Her eyes became unfocused, as if she were looking beyond us to something far distant. "I…do…I do not see an alliance. I see—"

"Helen!" snapped Tyndareus with surprising force. "It is not polite to probe the future of someone who has not asked you to."

Helen's eyes focused, and she looked down at the ground, embarrassed. "I meant no offense."

"And we have taken none," I said.

Tyndareus nodded, looked at Helen, and said, "Why don't you play with your brothers and sister? My guests and I still have business to discuss."

Helen sighed loudly, but instead of arguing, she turned and left the room. Tyndareus looked back at me.

"I believe we were discussing the unfortunate death of your second wife."

"Those memories are painful to me," I replied. That much, at least, was true. "But Phaedra and I were happily married for many years. She didn't kill herself because she was unhappy in our marriage. Nor did I seek to marry the sister of an earlier love on purpose, if that is what you fear. Her brother, Deucalion, came to Athens in person to propose the match, with no prodding from me. And he presented her as his daughter, not his and Ariadne's sister. More than that, I do not wish to say."

"Theseus, if you cannot be open with me, you cannot expect me to give you Helen in marriage. Phaedra didn't kill herself for no reason. And you didn't exile your son for no reason, either."

For a moment, the allure of Helen took second place in my mind. Anger toward Tyndareus had jostled it out of the way.

"There is no reason for you to demand that I dig through every shred of the past—and I will not. Since you insist, I will say is that Phaedra fell to the malice of Aphrodite, not through her own fault—or mine. If you do not trust enough to take my word on that, then we have nothing more to discuss."

"Indeed," said Tyndareus, nodding as he rose to his feet. "It is late. You may spend the night. Guards, escort them to appropriate quarters." I opened my mouth to respond, but Tyndareus, moving more rapidly than I would have expected a man of his years to be able to, was out of the room before I could frame a proper response.

There were five guards, each resting a hand on his sword. They did nothing else that could be construed as overtly rude, but it was clear that Tyndareus would from now on do for us only what hospitality demanded.

We followed the guards, who took us to a room with two beds and ample space for both of us. It wasn't exactly what I would have offered visiting royalty in Athens, but it was enough not to seem a direct insult. The fact that two of the guards remained right outside the door, ostensibly to see to any needs we might have during the night, couldn't be called a violation of hospitality, either. Tyndareus wanted nothing more to do with me, but, conscious of the sanctity of the host-guest relationship, there were some lines he wouldn't cross.

"I didn't necessarily expect success—but I didn't expect to fail this dramatically, either," I said. "I fear we may have made an enemy of Sparta."

"That's true. But since it is, why not make the best of it?"

I looked at Pirithous's smiling face as if he had gone crazy. "How could we ever make the best of this mess?"

"Do you still want to marry Helen?"

"Who wouldn't? But I think Tyndareus is dead set against that happening. Even if I came back when he is ready to receive suitors, I doubt his answer would be any different."

"Then it's a good thing you have me as a friend," he said. Reaching over, he pulled a small bottle out of his pack. Something dark churned within it, almost as if whatever was in there was alive.

"What is that?" I asked. The hair on the back of my neck was standing up, and my spine tingled.

"I swore to help you gain your bride in whatever way I could. Fortunately for you, I still have a good working relationship with the witches.

"Wait! What do you—"

Before I could finish, he uncorked the bottle, and from it poured an odorless vapor that was dark as the night sky and even seemed to be flecked with tiny stars. I pulled back against the wall, but the uncanny mist didn't approach me. Nor did it move toward Pirithous, even though he was so close to the bottle out of which it poured. Instead, it flowed swiftly and smoothly under the door. A moment later, I head two thuds that could only be the guards falling to the ground.

NEW ENEMIES

I RAN over to Pirithous and grabbed him by both shoulders. "What have you done?"

"Never fear. No one has been harmed. Nor will anyone be." His eyes gleamed in a way I didn't like. This wasn't the sad Pirithous peeking out from behind a happy mask. It was more like a mad Pirithous peeking out from behind a sane mask.

"But I heard the guards fall!"

"They are only sleeping. They will awaken just fine. Maybe an extra bruise or two, but otherwise—"

"Even if bewitching them weren't a crazy thing to do, what good does it do us?"

He smiled too broadly. "They aren't the only ones. In just a few minutes, that cloud will have spread through the whole palace, putting everyone in it to sleep."

I looked at him as if he had started speaking some different, barbarous language.

"So you can take Helen," he added as if I were an idiot.

"You want me to abduct her? That's insane."

"It's practical," said Pirithous, waving his hand as if my objections had no more weight than the strange mist. "Tyndareus knows you would make Helen a good husband. He's just nitpicking. He will come around easily enough once he has no other option."

"Have we become barbarians, then?" I asked. "Such an act is against what any civilized society would do."

"On the contrary, many Greek kings have won wives through abduction. Sparta even has a mock abduction as part of the wedding festivities. And what of Hades? Did not the lord of the Underworld seize Persephone against her will? Was he a barbarian?"

"The ways of the gods are not for us to question," I said, even though I longed to question them myself. "Besides, there are versions of that story in which Zeus actually approved of the abduction. Obviously, Tyndareus doesn't. Besides, Helen is far too young to marry."

"She doesn't look it," said Pirithous. "But do as you will. I'm not suggesting that you take her to bed the moment we get outside the walls of Sparta. Wait until she is of age. Wait until she learns to love you—as she certainly will. Wait until Tyndareus is won over if you wish. I still think he will yield if you have her already. It isn't as if he's already pledged her to someone else."

I should have rejected all these arguments. After all, Pirithous's idea violated important principles by which I tried to live. But as I heard his words, Aphrodite kept thrusting images of Helen into my mind. What if Pirithous was right, and I could win Helen's love? That meant she should be mine and not someone else's—didn't it?

Maybe that would happen. Or perhaps she would hate me for the rest of her life. I had seen her too briefly to know how she might react.

And even if she might eventually come around, what if Tyndareus made war on Athens in the meantime? If I had a daughter abducted, that is what I would do.

"No." My teeth clenched as I said the word, but I managed to get it out.

"No?" asked Pirithous, his smile looking even broader, manic. "This is your only chance, Cousin. Tyndareus is bound to know witchcraft was used against him when he awakes. We will never get within a hundred stadia of Sparta again."

I thought once more of Helen, goddess made flesh. What man

would not hesitate in such a situation? I could not help visualizing her coming willingly to my arms.

I tried to think of other women I had loved—Ariadne, Phaedra, the long-ago Perigune, Antiope—she most of all. Yet now, all of them were like dreams—insubstantial and fading before the sunlight that was Helen.

"No." The word was barely a whisper, but I got it out. I would go back to Athens and find another wife. Or perhaps I would remain alone. I had already fathered heirs. No one would blame me.

"Very well, then," said Pirithous, still smiling. "I will not force the girl upon you. But remember, you are still bound by oath to help me win the woman of my desire."

"And so I will. Tell me whom you desire, and I will do what I can in your cause."

He patted me on the shoulder. "I am glad to hear that, for the woman I desire is…Helen!"

"What? But you were just now urging me to take her."

"I was being self-sacrificing," said Pirithous. His smile looked now almost like a smirk. "From the moment I saw her, I desired Helen for myself. But I was oathbound to help you win her—and I fulfill my oaths. However, now that you have disclaimed any interest—"

"You said nothing about abducting women when we swore that oath."

"And you said nothing about it, either. You could easily have made that a limit to how far the oath extended. But you didn't."

"We are guests," I said. "You just as much as I. Zeus himself punishes violations of the host-guest relationship."

"As he does failure to fulfill an oath. Would you be foresworn?"

At that moment, it seemed the lesser of two evils, but did Pirithous even really need my help to take Helen? Anyone who would have stopped him slumbered now too deeply to be awakened. No, he could do it even if I refused to help—unless I myself shed his blood. I looked into his eyes, and, despite their strangeness, I couldn't imagine fighting him, possibly to the death, to stop this madness.

But if I let him take her, what then? He might not be reasonable any longer. Would he try to win Helen's love, or would he take her by force?

I would have known the answer to that question once, but now I was sure of nothing.

"I have changed my mind. I will take her—but only to try to convince her to love me. If she does not within a reasonable time, I will return her to her father."

For someone who had been proclaiming his love for Helen only moments before, Pirithous's renewed smile betrayed him. "Well, then, let's go find her. Everyone in the palace should sleep until morning, so no one will get in our way."

I didn't respond, but I did follow him. In the silence of the palace, the sound of our footsteps was like the thudding of my heart in my chest. The flickering light of oil lamps in the hallway created shadows that reminded me I might be plunging into darkness. Had I set foot upon one of those roads which would determine my destiny? I feared so. But my best friend, as out of place as a reveler in a crypt, walked briskly ahead as if he were on his way to a celebration.

Neither one of us knew the layout of the palace, but normally, royal bedrooms were near the center rather than against one of the outer walls. Also, aside from the entrances, there were more guards near the royal bedrooms than in any other part of the palace. To find Helen, all we had to do was head toward the center and follow the trail of unconscious guards.

We found Helen with her siblings in one of their rooms. It was hard to tell exactly whose it was. Dolls and toy swords were equally prominent. All four of them, the boys still in their youngest form, lay on the floor around the bed rather than on it.

I picked up Helen in my arms as carefully as I could. Daughter of a god though she was, she felt so fragile that I almost renounced the plan. But I knew I couldn't unless I wanted to risk her falling into Pirithous's hands instead.

And somewhere, deep in my mind, hope whispered that she would love me soon, and everything would be all right. No, not hope. Aphrodite. I was sure she was still manipulating me, but she needn't have bothered. I was already caught in her trap.

"We'll have to wrap her up in one of the carpets if we expect to get out of the city gate," said Pirithous.

"No!" I said, tightening my grip on Helen. "We'll smother her!"

"I've done this before," said Pirithous. I struggled to imagine how that could be possible. "She can be loosely wrapped, and some of these rugs are thin. She will have ample air. But it is the only way. The sleep spell covers just the palace, not the entire city. She's just too recognizable to carry out your shoulder or something. People could be told the carpet was a guest gift from Tyndareus, but nobody is going to believe he gave away his daughter to be carried off in the dead of night."

I watched him as he wrapped her in the thinnest of the carpets, making sure he was being gentle enough and leaving her room to breathe.

"This should be tighter," said Pirithous. "If it slips only a little, the top of her head will be visible."

"Then we will have to make sure it doesn't," I said, taking the bundled princess away from him.

This time, I led the way out to the stables. One of the stable hands lay on the ground, but the horses had not been touched by the spell. I mounted my horse, asked Pirithous for Helen, and put her in front of me, with my arms clasped loosely around her. That way, I could keep an eye on her but still manage to grasp the reins.

"You can't do it that way," said Pirithous. "No one would ever hold a carpet that way. Also, it makes it too conspicuous. Behind you and draped sideways over the animal's haunches makes more sense. Someone might actually do that."

"That's too risky," I said. "We'll just have to make this work."

For the first time in quite a while, Pirithous's manic smile disappeared. "All right, but we may have to fight our way out. I just don't think—"

"Look at that," I said, pointing to an enormous peacock that was staring at us.

"It's a bird. So what?" asked Pirithous.

"It's sacred to Hera, the patron goddess of Sparta."

He looked at it more closely. It spread its multicolored tail, marked with what stories said were the eyes of Argus, turned and walked off slowly in the general direction of the city gate.

"It's a sign," I said.

Pirithous laughed. "It's a bird. It probably just got loose from the temple."

"Peacocks sleep at night," I said. "Hera sent it to us, and we need to follow it."

"But why would Hera—" Pirithous began.

"Think about it. Hera is no friend to the children of Zeus or their mothers. I think she wants us to succeed in abducting Helen. Now, hold your peace, and let's follow that bird.

I trotted after the peacock. Pirithous followed, grumbling all the way.

When the bird neared the gate, it stepped to one side and cocked its head in the general direction of the gate as if beckoning us to move past it. When we approached the gate, one of the guards challenged us.

"Who goes there?" he asked, eying us suspiciously.

"King Theseus and King Pirithous, departing on urgent business," said Pirithous. "Open the gate!" he added in his most regal, commanding tone.

"What is that?" asked the guard, pointing to the carpet I had so awkwardly clutched in front of me.

"A gift from King Tyndareus," I replied. My voice might have shaken a little. I could no longer be sure.

"Usually, if the gates need to be opened after sundown, King Tyndareus notifies us," said the guard. As he did so, he leaned closer to get a better look at the carpet. Pirithous slowly moved his hand toward his sword hilt.

"He may have forgotten because of the unusual circumstances," I said quickly. "We leave to respond to a grave threat known to us from a sign of Hera herself."

As if on cue, the peacock strutted forward, stared at the guard, and cried out in a high and forlorn tone. The guard looked at it as if he had never seen a peacock before. The bird cried two more times and clawed the ground.

Faced with such a spectacle, the guards couldn't take the chance that the bird wasn't there at Hera's command. They opened the gates for us as fast as they could, and we were off. Behind us, we heard one more shrill cry, as if the peacock were wishing us luck.

BILL HIATT

As soon as we were out of sight of the city, I insisted on freeing Helen, who was still fast asleep, from the carpet.

"What about Spartan patrols?" asked Pirithous. Looking around, he added, "Or were you expecting an army of peacocks to surround and protect us?"

"The one seemed quite sufficient. If Hera wants us to succeed, I doubt a few patrols will get in the way."

"Now who's being overly optimistic?" asked Pirithous, smiling despite himself. "All right, but let us make haste, then."

We rode all night. By the time I was able to dismount and rest, I could still feel the horse beneath me and the pounding movement of its hooves.

However, the feeling of having ridden far too long wasn't the worst part. That was the moment of panic when I saw Helen's eyes open.

My panic, not hers. Much to my surprise, she looked around as if we were going out to have a picnic. I'd imagined her weeping, or cursing us in the name of her father, or maybe even taking a punch at me. Instead, she was serene as a deep lake on a windless day.

"It was unwise to use witchcraft to steal me away from the city without my father's permission," she said, glaring at Pirithous when she mentioned witchcraft. There was no denying her prophetic insight.

Then she focused her entire attention on me. "What do you hope to gain from this? Do you intend to have your way with me?" Her voice was still calm, without even a hint of fear or pleading. Women three times her age would not have been so calm.

I knelt before her because it felt like the right thing to do. "I would never force myself upon a woman, let alone one not yet of marriageable age."

She raised an eyebrow. "Yet you did take me without my father's permission. Under Spartan law, that is as grave an offense as if you had violated me. But if you do not mean to force me, why did you abduct me? What could you possibly have thought to gain?"

"Your love, if you will give me the chance to prove myself to you."

Helen laughed, a sound so beautiful I almost didn't notice that the tone was derisive. "And do you find that women often fall in love as a result of being captured?"

366

"When you say it out loud, I admit it sounds stupid. Yet have not some women actually fallen in love in even worse circumstances?"

Helen shook her head. It was hard not to notice how her hair caught the sunlight as she did so.

"Women may accept what they cannot change. But love will never grow as it might under more natural circumstances."

"But a princess does not always have the luxury of marrying for love," I said. "Your father could arrange a marriage with someone you didn't love. What then?"

"Then I would do my duty. But my father has promised to consider my opinion before making a match. And anyway, he is my father, not some ruffian who has kidnapped me in the dead of night and has no right to arrange my marriage."

She looked back in the general direction of Sparta. "Here is what you will do. Take me back to Sparta. If you wish, you may leave me near the gate and ride away. If you choose to enter with me, I will ask my father to pardon the great affront against him which you have committed. Since you have not mistreated me, he may be merciful."

"You're in no position to order us around," said Pirithous.

"Really?" asked Helen. "Harm me in any way, and there is no turning back, no easy forgiveness, no peace. My father is fair, but he is also harsh. At the least, you would face a long, bloody war against Sparta. And that doesn't even consider what my brothers would do. They will hunt you down like dogs if you harm one hair on my head."

"But they are not here now," said Pirithous. "You will do as we command or else."

"Or else nothing," I said.

"But you know who may be here now, watching you intently?" asked Helen, ignoring me. "Zeus, my true father. How eager are you to be reduced to a pile of ashes?"

"Zeus is my father, too," said Pirithous.

Helen laughed again, even more loudly than she had with me. "I doubt that. But even if it were true, Zeus has been known to punish his own sons when they did wrong. Have you not heard how he punished Apollo for trying to kill the cyclopes? Are you dearer to him than Apollo?

Perhaps he would not kill you—but there are many other things he could do, things too terrible to describe."

"We cannot yet take you home," I said, trying to recapture the conversation. "But I swear on my own soul, here in the sight of Zeus, that I will not harm you in any way—"

"Other than holding me prisoner," said Helen.

"And that I will do whatever I can to protect you from harm by others. All I ask is that you give me a chance to prove myself to you."

Helen gave me a long, intense stare. "I believe you. In exchange for your oath, I will swear not to try to escape—unless my father or one of his allies comes to rescue me.

"But do not see this as a victory, for your cause is hopeless. Theseus, you are handsome—for a man your age—and, if the tales are true, you are both heroic and kind. Had you accepted my father's refusal and come back later, when he was ready to see me married, perhaps I would even have argued for you. But I could never now. You threw away whatever chance you had.

Then, as if she had not thrust a dagger through my heart, she looked back toward Sparta again. "If you insist on continuing this madness, we should be going. My father certainly knows I am gone by now. It will take time to assemble a whole army, but he will be riding toward us, even now, accompanied by my brothers and the strongest warriors he can call up on short notice."

With that, she mounted my horse as if she had been born to ride and stared down at me. "Well, hurry then. You may be a fool, but I don't especially want to see the soil here watered by your blood."

It was then I realized just how vilely Aphrodite had treated me. She made fall in love with Helen's beauty, but the truth was that Helen was so much more than that. Brave, intelligent, independent—exactly the kind of woman I wanted for my partner. Just as Helen said, there might even have been hope of that under other circumstances. But Aphrodite had made sure those circumstances would never come to pass.

No, not Aphrodite. She pushed, but I could have resisted, just as she told me I would be able to. Even Pirithous's manipulations I could have found a way around. Helen was right—I was nothing but a fool.

"The horses must rest a little," I said. "I've never ridden a beast to death and don't intend to start now. Pirithous and I could use some rest as well. But since we've ridden all night, there's no way your father could catch up with us."

"Sleep if you must," said Helen. "I've had more sleep than I need, so I'll see the horses are fed and watered."

"She'll just run away," muttered Pirithous.

"I swore an oath," said Helen, whose hearing must have been as exceptional as everything else about her. "That means something...to some of us."

Pirithous looked as if he wanted to argue, but I put a restraining hand on his shoulder. "We can't get all the way back to Athens without sleep. And tying her up or something like that could be taken as a violation of *my* oath. Besides, her father's troops are many stadia away. She knows that running off by herself would be even more dangerous—"

"Than staying with you?" asked Helen. "That remains to be seen. But I have sworn an oath and will live by it."

She gave me an enigmatic smile. My head knew she wasn't afraid of me. My heart dared to hope that smile was a sign that she was softening toward me, that maybe in as little as a few days, she would profess her love for me.

Despite his mistrust of Helen, Pirithous was eventually overpowered by his fatigue. Soon after, I followed, but my sleep was disrupted by a series of nightmares that struck me like blows, rattling the very skull within my head. Despite the intensity of the experience, by morning, I had lost all the details. Only a lingering sense of impending disaster remained, stroking my heart with its cold, dry fingers.

Helen had not tried to escape. Instead, she had gathered fruit for breakfast. Pirithous sniffed at it as if it were poisoned, but eventually, he ate it, just as I did.

"My father has returned to Sparta," she told us as soon as we were finished.

Pirithous's eyes narrowed. "Is this some trick to cause us to move more slowly?"

Helen sneered at him. Even that expression looked beautiful on her face.

"Move as fast as you want. But I speak the truth. He has realized you can probably beat him back to Athens or Larissa. He isn't sure what your destination is, but either way, he needs his full army if he is to attack a well-fortified city."

"If you are such a great seer, how is it that you failed to foresee your own abduction?" asked Pirithous.

Helen gave him one of her mocking laughs. "The world is like a great tapestry, so vast that even the gods cannot see all of it at once. The future is especially tricky. Some parts of it cannot be changed, but others can, as if sections of the tapestry are constantly being rewoven. The gods themselves do some of this weaving, but even mortals can move a thread here and there.

"Nor can all the gods see the same things. Zeus knows a son of his will overthrow him—but not which one. It is said that only Prometheus has been able to discern that.

"If even the king of the gods is not all-seeing, who but a fool would expect a human prophet to be able to do better?"

"Still, this was right under your nose—" began Pirithous.

"The bits of information I get are only a small fraction of the whole and not necessarily the ones most relevant to me. In fact, what I see about myself is often blurry, perhaps because by knowing the future, I may have a greater chance of changing what can be changed. It helps if I focus on a specific question—but since I thought no one would be foolish enough to try to kidnap me, I was not focused on that.

"Wait! Theseus, look to the western sky," she said, pointing with one of her perfectly shaped fingers. My eyes obeyed her, and I saw an eagle, the bird sacred to Zeus, fly far above us. But then another eagle swooped past, careless of his comrade. It scraped against the first eagle's wing and sped off as if unconscious of the injury it had done. The first eagle, wounded and shaky, managed an uneven glide toward the ground, disappearing behind the trees. I had never seen eagles behave quite like that before.

"I can also read the signs of birds," said Helen. "In this case, the eagles, represent, not Zeus, but two mortal kings. Did you see? One was diverted from his natural course by the carelessness of another.

"The first eagle is you, Theseus, soaring toward greatness. The careless eagle is your friend, Pirithous, who has wounded you and doesn't even know it. Mark me—he will be your downfall!"

"More trickery!" Pirithous's words were almost a snarl. "The bitch—"

"You will not speak of her thus!" I said in as commanding a voice as I could muster. Pirithous looked at me, shocked.

"It matters not what I call her. Can't you see that she hopes to provoke a fight between us, during which she can escape?"

"If I were willing to violate my oath, I would have run away while you slept," said Helen slowly, as if explaining to a child. "As for the truth of my words, can you deny that Theseus would have been better off without you?"

"Pirithous is my friend," I said, putting up a hand to forestall his response. "More, he is like a brother to me. Together, we have shared many misfortunes. That doesn't mean that they are his fault."

"There is nothing to be gained by arguing with you," said Helen. "If you cannot see what is right in front of your nose, then you would not see even if Athena herself appeared to tell you. Let us get on with the abduction. Take me to whatever place you intend to keep me and leave me there."

That day, we rode most of the way in silence. Pirithous kept glaring at Helen as if he would cheerfully cut her throat were I not around. Helen, still riding right in front of me, was silent as a stone. I had no idea what to say to either one of them. I longed to take her in my arms and comfort her, but her stiffness suggested she would not welcome such comfort.

The trip seemed far longer than the ride to Sparta had been. I didn't go directly to Athens. The fewer people who knew about Helen's presence, the better. Instead, I went straight to Aphidnae, intending to leave Helen in the care of Aethra, whom I knew I could trust.

My mother heard the sound of hooves and came out of her house. It was a small home even by the standards of Troezen, but Aethra had asked for just such a place to spend her last years. Modest as it was, there would still be plenty of room for a guest.

Though she had never seen Helen before, Aethra must have known who she was. Her face twisted in an emotion she had seldom shown to me—anger.

"My son, what have you done?"

"He has abducted me and intends to wed me without my father's consent," said Helen in a tone such as people might use to discuss that year's crop.

Aethra looked at me, anger warring with disbelief on her face.

"Is this true?"

Suddenly, I felt small. Even as a child, I had never done anything to so displease my mother.

"It is not as you fear, Mother. I have taken her without the consent of Tyndareus, but only because he refused to negotiate a marriage contract with me. I would never force her to wed. You know that. It is my intention that she remain with you for a while, during which time I will attempt to persuade her to agree. If she does, she will help to persuade her father. If she does not, I will send her back with no harm done."

Aethra shook her head. "No harm done? You have kidnapped a woman...a girl by her calendar age. She seems to be taking it well, but you have harmed her by the mere act of separating her from her family without her consent. And you would have me...what? Be her jailer? That I will not. Not even for you!"

"Not jailer, but mother—"

"I have a mother already," said Helen. "Take me back to her, and you will have no need to trouble yours."

"That is what you must do," said Aethra. "Even now, Tyndareus will probably not forgive you, but at least you may persuade him not to make war on Athens."

"I can help with that," said Helen. "If I ask him not to retaliate, he will not."

"I...I cannot return her," said Theseus. "I love her."

Helen looked at Aethra and rolled her eyes. "As if anyone can love a stranger so soon after a first meeting. Such 'love' cannot be true."

"Do you remember nothing of my teaching?" asked Aethra. "She does not love you. And if you think she will grow to love you with time, I doubt that will happen. She seems too strong-willed for that."

"Exactly!" I replied. "She has all the characteristics I desire in a wife."

"Except for the desire to be your wife," said Aethra. "At best, you are wasting your time and risking war with Sparta. At worst, you are tempting yourself to betray all your principles."

"We will see," I said. "Once she is settled in, I will begin to court her in the proper way, and we shall see what comes of it."

"And while she is settling in, you and I can take care of obtaining my new wife," said Pirithous.

"Uh, I know I am sworn to support you in that endeavor, but I didn't realize you'd already selected a bride."

Pirithous, sullen on the trip back, was suddenly all smiles again.

"Why, of course, I have. She is none other than Persephone, queen of the Underworld."

DEATH AND LOVE DON'T MIX

"Are you insane?" Helen and Aethra asked in eerie unison. I glanced over at Pirithous, whose manic grin and wild eyes indeed made him look the part.

"He jests," I said, hoping he'd follow my lead.

"I do not jest," said Pirithous, dashing my hopes. He turned to my mother. "I would think you would applaud my desire. Persephone was forced to marry Hades, after all. I am more liberator than lunatic, am I not?"

"You would be—if your plan had even the chance of a candle flame in a snowstorm of succeeding," said Aethra. "All you'll accomplish is getting yourself killed—and my son along with you."

"Remember the eagles," said Helen.

"It is already fall," I said. "Persephone descended to the Underworld some days ago. Do you propose to abduct her from there? I fear that is beyond what we two could accomplish."

"It is beyond what all the heroes on Earth combined could accomplish," said Aethra.

"I do not propose an abduction," said Pirithous. "Instead, I will negotiate an agreement with Hades."

"What could you possibly have to offer the lord of the Underworld?" asked Helen. "He rules a realm far vaster than yours, owns all the treasure buried in the ground, and is one of the strongest of the gods. You could give him all you had, and it would still fall far short of anything that could possibly move him."

"There is one thing he doesn't have—a willing wife. Would he not rather have that than one he has to hold captive?"

"And do you have a goddess at your beck and call who will become Hades's bride because you say so?" asked Helen.

"Not a goddess, no. I admit that. But the gods can make a mortal woman, even a dead one, into a goddess. Is that not what was done with Semele, mother of Dionysus? With Ino, who became Leucothea? Theseus, you told me you'd met her son, Palaemon, also now divine, so you know what I say is possible."

I nodded slowly. "I have met Palaemon, and he did tell me he was once a mortal boy."

"Surely, you are not accepting this wild plan?" asked Aethra.

"Who is she?" I asked. "Who is this woman who will descend into the Underworld?"

"You have met her," said Pirithous. "She is Physadeia, my own sister. With Ixion dead, she is legally mine to give in marriage. But I would not compel such a match. Why would Hades trade one unwilling bride for another? No, I have discussed the matter with her, and she is eager to become a goddess—even in the Underworld. How many women would turn down a chance at divinity? At immortality?"

"In other words, she is as insane as you are," said Aethra.

I knew my mother was right—yet Pirithous's argument did make a kind of sense.

"She is beautiful," I said. "Probably not as much so as Persephone, but perhaps after becoming a goddess—"

"Had Hades wished, he could have chosen any woman from among several centuries of the dead," said Helen. "Would not a dead woman, particularly one who did not make it the Elysian Fields, be eager to live again, especially as a goddess? That he has not done so suggests he has no interest in such a thing. His heart may be as cold as people say—but however close he can come to love, surely, he has come that close with Persephone."

"All of this argument matters not at all," said Pirithous. "Theseus is oathbound to help me, and he will not betray his vow."

Aethra looked at me, eyes wide in disbelief. "Is this true?"

"It is. I swore an oath, and I do not see how I can break it."

Aethra looked at Pirithous as if he were a poisonous snake that slithered into her garden. "Leave us for a time. I must speak to my son alone."

"Very well," said Pirithous. "But we have not long. If Theseus is to fulfill his oath and then return in time to deal with the Spartans, we must leave soon." He turned and walked away. Despite his speed, he managed to stamp his feet on the ground enough to signal his displeasure.

Helen started to walk away, but Aethra reached out gently and took her arm.

"If you will, Princess, I would have you stay with us. Perhaps you can help talk sense into my son."

"I have tried already," said Helen. "But I will try again. I would not see him dead."

"And is that what will happen?" asked Aethra. "I hear you have prophetic gifts."

"I cannot be sure of his fate," said Helen. "I think there is still time to avoid the disaster into which Pirithous is leading him. But I also keep seeing an image of him falling…falling for what seems like forever."

Aethra grabbed me by both shoulders. "Did you hear that? You are risking death. You didn't swear to sacrifice yourself for him, only to help him gain a wife. Is that not right? You can still do that. All he needs to do is select someone reasonable."

I shook my head. "You don't know Pirithous. He will never agree. And if I let him march off alone to meet Hades, and he dies when I might have saved him, I could never forgive myself."

"If that's what you're worried about, there is no need," said Helen. "Without the aid of the gods, no mortal man can reach the Underworld —except by dying. Charon will not let him buy passage across the river. And if, by some miracle, the old ferryman relents, Pirithous—and you, should you be foolish enough to go—will be torn to pieces by Cerberus. The many-headed hound is immortal, and his smallest bite is poisonous. Even if there is some secret way to kill him, Hades would destroy you for slaughtering his watchdog. There is no way this can end, except in death. Go or don't go. If Pirithous is foolish enough to try, he will die whether you are at his side or not."

Even a child knew all of this. How had I so easily forgotten it? We couldn't go after all.

Except that there was now a way the old storytellers had not known of.

"When I visited Larissa for Pirithous's wedding, remember that battle with the centaurs and how the invulnerable brother of the bride was pounded down into the ground by those half-men, half-horses? Well, he sank all the way to the Underworld. And his passing left a hole big enough to climb down. Pirithous had to set guards on the area to keep people who might not realize what it was from exploring it."

"What difference does that make?" asked Aethra.

"Who is to say that the hole doesn't bypass the normal entry routine? What if we could climb down to a spot beyond Charon and Cerberus?"

"And what if pigs had wings?" asked Aethra.

"And what if Hades has now blocked the hole partway down?" asked Helen. "It seems unlike him to allow mortals to wander in as they please."

"Look, I'm sure Pirithous must be planning to use that way to enter. If I go with him, and the hole doesn't lead to the Underworld anymore, I'm positive I can persuade him to give up his plan and marry someone more in his reach."

"But isn't the very pursuit of a married goddess for a wife blasphemous?" asked Aethra. "There could be consequences."

Helen nodded. "The gods will not be pleased by such hubris, even if it is unsuccessful."

"Remember Bellerophon," said Aethra, whose face reminded me that, even after all these years, she could never forget him.

"I'm not trying to fly up to Olympus, or even go down into the Underworld, on my own account. I'm just trying to keep my word to Pirithous and keep him alive. I pray the gods will understand."

"The sooner we go, the sooner we can return!" yelled Pirithous. Even from a distance, I could see his frown.

"He has a point," I said. "I must get back before the Spartan army is at our gates. Mother, I will send orders to the city to have a decent-sized guard posted here. Keep Helen inside. I will be back in a few days at most, hopefully with a more reasonable Pirithous at my side."

Aethra's mouth hung open. She must have thought she could talk me out of helping Pirithous. Helen frowned but said nothing.

As I turned to go, mist engulfed me, and I trembled, not from cold but from fear. Only a god could make a mist appear so quickly. Had I earned divine wrath before I'd even started out with Pirithous?

"Foolish man!" The voice was female, and at first, I thought it was Aethra, but a second later, I knew better.

"Athena," I said, falling to my knees. "How may I serve you?"

The goddess appeared out of the mist, her eyes flashing like her father's thunderbolts, her spear raised. "If only you had considered how to serve me earlier, you would not have put my plans for Athens at such risk."

"I would have harkened to your voice, goddess—but it has been long since I have heard it."

"That could not be helped," said Athena with a hint of defensiveness in her voice. "I cannot be everywhere at once, and weighty issues have demanded my attention. I thought I could trust you to govern Athens without my constant aid."

"And so I have, to the best of my ability."

"If that is true, then I have much misjudged you. Was going off on wild expeditions with the undisciplined king of the Lapiths your idea of governing Athens wisely?"

I didn't answer. How could I? I had been away from the city a lot, and I had brought war to its gates—and might again if I were not careful.

"I would have come sooner," said the goddess, her tone softer. "Unfortunately, Zeus keeps having visions of future, destructive conflicts among the gods and places more limits upon how we can interact with each other and with mortals. Your Amazon adventure embroiled you with Artemis and Ares, and Zeus told me I could not intervene unless

Athens itself were in danger of falling. With Artemis unexpectedly on your side, Athens was safe."

"But Antiope wasn't," I said. I should have tried to hide my bitterness, but I didn't.

"I could not have acted in time to save her," said Athena. "She was Ares's daughter. It was for him to save her—but instead, he worked against her."

"And Hippolytus?" I shouldn't have asked the question, but it tore itself out of my lips, bringing anger and guilt with it.

"He neglected all the gods except for Artemis," said Athena. "He especially neglected Aphrodite. Zeus would not allow me to interfere in the goddess's machinations. Your son was...an affront to balance in the universe, virtuous as he was in many ways.

"But I have not come here that you may pass judgment upon me. Indeed, I have only allowed you to press as far as you have in recognition of the hard life you have led. But I cannot indulge you any longer. Hear my words, Theseus, hear and heed.

"If you go with Pirithous, you will bring ruin on yourself and great danger to Athens as well. Stay here, do your duty, and I can mend your fortunes. I will return Helen to Tyndareus myself and procure his forgiveness of your gross offenses. You will have a long and glorious career as king of Athens ahead of you."

"But what of my oath?" I asked. "Will not breaking it bring down the wrath of Zeus upon me?"

The goddess's gray eyes looked distant for a moment. "That I cannot surely know, but there is some truth in what you say. Zeus may pursue you as an oath breaker. Pirithous may curse you, and I think Ares, who already hates you, may well hear him. But I can free you of this obligation."

"How? I have never heard that the gods can absolve mortal of their oaths."

Athena raised her spear as if she would throw it, but off into the distance rather than in my direction. "Generally, we do not. But the kind of oath you swore cannot be fulfilled if the one to whom you swore it is dead. I will take Pirithous's life, sparing you the blood guilt and freeing you of the oath."

"No!" I shouted, stopping just short of trying to wrestle the spear out of her hands. "Pirithous may be undisciplined, wild even. Perhaps his ego swells beyond what a man's should. But despite his faults, he is a good man. I have let him lead me down the wrong path more than once, but from now on, I pledge to lead him up the right one, instead."

Athena shook her head, and her eyes appeared to gleam with tears, though she never shed any.

"Once, you might have been able to do that. But it is too late, now. Pirithous is doomed, and there is no way for you to redeem him. You can redeem only yourself."

"How can allowing the death of a friend be redemptive?" I was shedding enough tears for both of us. "How can—"

"Enough questions!" snapped Athena. The earlier softness had left her voice, to be replaced by thunder and steel. "It is not for you to allow or disallow what I do."

She looked me in the eye. I could hardly see her expression through my tears. "However," she said slowly, "it will avail me nothing to end the Lapith's life if it brings you only anger, sorrow, and guilt. You will find ways to sabotage your own life, and I will not be able to stop you.

"Choose then! Accept what I have offered or reject it. But know this —if you reject it, you will be beyond even my help. Never again in this mortal life will you know any more than the briefest happiness. All else will be darkness."

"I cannot accept your killing my friend...my brother," I said. "If I must suffer for that decision, then so be it."

Did Athena shed one tear at those words? Even today, I am not sure, for she was trying to conceal it, but I think she did.

"So noble—and so doomed by that very nobility. Very well, Theseus, Pirithous will live—but countless others will die. It is not you alone that will suffer for this decision. Your family, your city, your people—all these and more will face ruin to spare that one unworthy life."

These words raised questions. Who else would suffer—and how? But I had lost the chance to ask them. The goddess was gone. The mist was gone. I looked back at Aethra and Helen, now both as tearful as I.

"Did you...did you see what just happened?" I asked.

"I did," said Helen. "I did, and it made me wish that I could love you. But I cannot order myself to find pleasure in your arms."

"And I will never force you," I said. "When I return, if your mind remains unchanged, I will send you back to your father and make what amends I can."

"I will watch over her," said Aethra.

"And I will watch over her," said Helen, embracing my mother. I was pulled into that embrace, but my mother held me far more closely than Helen did. The Spartan princess did kiss me once, on the cheek. That kiss blazed like an inferno against my skin. Had she kissed me on the lips, she might have burned away even my determination to help Pirithous, accomplish with one press of the lips what even Athena had not accomplished.

But of course, Helen didn't kiss me on the lips nor ask me to betray Pirithous. I said my last goodbyes to her and to my mother, then ran to join Pirithous, who was standing next to his horse and tapping his foot impatiently.

We spoke little to each other on the trip to Larissa. The journey felt more like a march to my own execution than anything else. The words of Athena, Helen, and Aethra kept running through my mind like dogs, and each step was like their claws tearing through my brain.

I did my best to forget those words. I could have traveled a different path, but I was traveling this one, now. Even if I prayed to Athena to accept her offer, she would not answer. It was too late.

Perhaps her worst fears would not be realized, though. Pirithous verified my theory that he intended us to travel down the hole made by Caeneus. But why would Hades have left such a gap in his walls open? Surely, it no longer led all the way to the Underworld. And if it did not, I knew I could persuade Pirithous to be more reasonable.

I told myself that same sweet-sounding lie until I believed it. Not even the occasional glint of madness in Pirithous's eyes shook me. Everything was going to be all right.

Once we arrived in Larissa, we ate as fast as we could, got some sleep, and were out in the grove where we had once fought the centaurs at dawn.

The twenty guards Pirithous had stationed around the hole got out of our way as their king strode in their direction.

"It's wider than it was, isn't it?" I asked. It had been only a little larger than the size of a human body originally and would have been very hard to climb down without digging. Now, it was more like the width of three men with arms extended, at least at the top.

"The rains widened it," said Pirithous. "We should have no trouble getting down. I've had the witches check, and it still goes all the way to the Underworld."

My heart sank. "How can they be sure?"

"They see as most mortals cannot. And remember, their power comes from Hecate, who lives in the Underworld. Working out the geography of the place is child's play for them."

The pleasant lie that the path would be blocked and Pirithous would listen to reason then was as dead as we were soon likely to be. However, I took the torch he offered to me, lit it, and started to descend with him, anyway. There was no turning back now.

"Our weapons?" I asked, conscious of the weight of my sword and the gear on my back. "Is it wise to take them into Hades's kingdom?"

Pirithous shrugged. "When we see him, we will do as he bids, just as we would with a mortal king. Our weapons cannot harm him, so he may not care if we go to him armed. But if he wants us to lay them aside, we will do so. I don't think we have to worry about him stealing them. Now, come, let us make this trip as rapidly as we can."

Stones jutted from the sides of the hole in a way that made suspiciously perfect footholds and handholds. As we climbed down, they became somewhat slicker and harder to hold. Even with the flickering torchlight, I couldn't see much down below us. It was as if we were climbing down into total darkness, as if we had somehow passed right through the Underworld and were now on the way to Erebus itself, the grim realm that is pure darkness.

I don't know how long we climbed. After a while, time lost all meaning. My muscles began to protest at some point, but I ignored them. Stopping somewhere in the middle of the hole didn't seem like an option.

I didn't know whether to be relieved or horrified when my feet touched solid ground. I looked over at Pirithous, who was on the ground as well. He seemed to be deciding between joy and nervousness. His eyes looked unfocused.

A sound like throat-clearing, but loud enough to be coming from a giant, shook the chamber. We both looked over and saw a grim figure standing at the opposite end of the cavern to which we had come.

Though my eyes could scarcely perceive colors, the prevailing impression he left was gray. Both his face and the power radiating from him reminded me of Poseidon's. But the throat clearer's face betrayed no emotion. Looking into his eyes was like staring into an abyss even darker than Erebus. As for his power, it was the equal of Poseidon, but colder even than the depths of the sea. Not physically cold—the cold of fear that makes your spine tingle.

He was dressed in robes worthy of an Olympian, with elaborate patterns in what looked like silver thread, but I couldn't take my eyes off those dark, soulless eyes.

This had to be Hades—and he had apparently been waiting for us.

Pirithous knelt before the lord of the Underworld, and I followed his example. The stone on which we knelt was cold and moist, like the floor of a crypt into which water has seeped.

"Why have you intruded into the realm of the dead?" said Hades, whose voice was loud as an earthquake, though in the dead air surrounding us, it didn't echo.

"I come to make an offering I hope will please you," said Pirithous. His throat was dry, his voice scratchy.

"I have heard something of that," said Hades. "Aside from my own glimpses of the future, I have recently acquired my own seer, Amphiarus. Like your friend, Caeneus, he tumbled down here while still alive, in his case through a rift in the earth created by one of Zeus's thunderbolts.

"But this is an ill place for bargaining. Come, let us go to my palace, which is nearby. There you will be more comfortable."

Despite myself, I began to hope. Hades already knew why we had come—and yet he had not killed us. Why keep us alive? The only answer I could think of was that he wanted Physadeia as his wife. If that were true, all might yet be well.

Hades led us through a cave that connected Caeneus's hole with the rest of the Underworld. After a surprisingly short journey, we emerged near the palace.

Parts of it were obscured by the gloom and by the trees growing nearby— white poplar and cypress mostly, with a few ironic pomegranates, rosy with fruit, sprinkled among them. One wouldn't expect to find trees in the Underworld, but perhaps they had been planted to make Persephone feel more at home. If so, Hades's choices were disquieting. Swallowing six seeds from a pomegranate in the Underworld had trapped Persephone there in the first place. White poplars were created in memory of Leuce, one of Hades's few other lovers. As for cypresses, they were trees associated with death and mourning. All of them, despite their colors being like those of their earthly counterparts, were washed out by the same gray tinge that discolored Hades himself.

As we drew closer, I saw small patches of mint, born from the dead flesh of Minthe, the only other lover Hades had ever enjoyed besides Persephone. No, the groves and gardens were not to please the queen of the Underworld. In fact, they seemed disconcertingly designed to make her sorrow deeper.

Perhaps Hades was ready for a change—but how would Physadeia survive in such a place? Was even being a goddess enough recompense for the unvarying gloom?

The palace itself was black marble and fashioned with more than human skill. I tried not to look toward closely, though. The images on the pediment were like carved nightmares. I thought staring at them too long might reduce me to madness.

We passed through gates of lusterless silver and walked across a courtyard that, though carefully tended, was just as disturbing as the vegetation outside, at least to those who knew its meaning.

We entered the door on the opposite end of the courtyard. I had expected to be taken to the great hall, but instead, Hades took the first door on the left and led us through a meandering course that made Minos's labyrinth seem straightforward.

During this unexpectedly long journey, we saw no one else. I had expected servants of some kind, but there was no one but ourselves, walking down dark corridors in which our footsteps didn't echo.

Just when I began to fear that Hades would disappear at some point, leaving us to starve before we could find our way out, he opened a door and led us into a small room with three chairs. Two of them were some kind of white stone. The third, elaborately carved ebony, was obviously meant for Hades, who sat and beckoned us to take the other two.

I felt odd as soon as we were seated. There was something magical about the chairs—something sinister. I tried to rise but could not. Somehow, I had become fused to the stone. Panicked, I looked to Pirithous for help, but he was just as trapped as I.

PRISONERS

"WHAT'S WRONG?" asked Hades mockingly. "I cannot give you my wife, Pirithous, but I thought perhaps you might find this chair a suitable substitute. Aside from Theseus, it will be the only company you have for as long as you live."

Hades smiled in a way that, despite his flesh, reminded me of a skull. "I wouldn't look for your life to end very soon, either. You see, though this is the place of the dead, as its ruler, I can prevent mortals from dying. You will not leave those chairs until so much time has passed that the Underworld itself will have come to an end."

"Why have you done this?" asked Pirithous, still struggling against the implacable grip of the chair. "I came here to bargain in good faith."

Hades laughed in a tone that would have caused flowers to wither. "You came here, impelled by your own hubris, to take a goddess as your wife—and a married goddess, at that. I knew mortals were typically stupid, but this goes beyond any ordinary stupidity. That you would have thought such a plan workable is condemnation more articulate than I could speak.

"If it makes you feel any better, I did your sister a favor. Women who lie in my arms invariably die, even goddesses. Only someone like Persephone, who holds within her the secret of regeneration and renewal, can long survive my touch."

"Leave me here, then," said Pirithous. "But my friend's fault is not as great. I beg you, let him go."

"That he is your friend is fault enough," said Hades. "I must go now. Perhaps I will visit later. Perhaps not. But do not look for mercy from Persephone. Kind she is—but even she will not overlook so great a sin. You claimed that you wanted to give her freedom, but what you really wanted was to buy her for yourself. Why did you not ask for her presence in the meeting? Because you did not care what she thought. In that respect, you are no better than I."

Hades moved quickly out of the door and slammed it hard.

"I have done this to you!" yelled Pirithous, sobbing.

"You did not force me to come down here," I said quietly. But in my heart, I knew the truth. He had as good as forced me. His oath was a knife to my throat.

After a while, I wept too. It wasn't because I was trapped forever. It was because I had left Aethra and Athens itself in precarious positions. I would not be there to negotiate with the Spartans or to fight with them if necessary.

Too late, I realized what Athena meant about suffering. If only I could journey to the past and undo my mistake! But no mortal may do that. Even the gods may not.

The disorientation here was like that in Caeneus's hole, but worse. It was not long before I lost all track of time. Had we been here two days or two millenniums? I could no longer tell.

At least I had Pirithous to talk to, but there was only so much we could say to each other now. Before, we had so often spoken of future plans, lofty goals, his ambitious dreams and mine. But none of that existed anymore. For us, there was no future. There was only the walls of this one room and the chairs that bound us to it.

Eventually, the door opened to admit a visitor, but it was not Hades.

She moved in shadows as if she were one herself, and her garment was black, but she was undeniably beautiful, with ivory skin and ebony hair. She looked as young as Artemis, but she also radiated a sense of great age, as if she had been around before Zeus himself was born. Her

BILL HIATT

features reminded me of Aphrodite's, but there was a darkness to them that surpassed that of Aphrodite, even at her most vengeful.

"Hecate?" I asked. I couldn't have knelt before her if I wanted to—which I didn't. Pirithous looked at her, and his eyes flashed with anger.

"You are perceptive for a mortal," she said in a voice that managed to be seductive and frightening at the same time. "Yes, I am Hecate."

"Your witches betrayed me!" His hands twisted as if he were imagining using them to strangle her.

"Foolish man! They always did as you asked. Is it their fault that you didn't always ask for what was best?"

"You manipulated him, though," I said. "Or they did. It doesn't really matter which."

"I did what was necessary to achieve my objectives," said the witch goddess. "You may be surprised to learn that some of them are the same as yours.

"Like you, I find the subordination of women to men intolerable. But such subordination among mortals can only survive as long as a male god remains in charge."

"Goddesses seem to me to have it much better than mortal women," I said. I wanted her to leave, but I also wanted her to stay. Any break in the monotony, even listening to her scheming tongue, was a welcome diversion.

Pirithous tried to rise from his chair and failed, just as he always did. Hecate laughed at him and turned her attention back to me.

"Yes, goddesses have more freedom than mortal women, but make no mistake—they still take second place to gods. Zeus had two brothers and three sisters fighting by his side against Cronus. But once victory was achieved, did he share power with all of them? No, only with his brothers."

"You fared well, though," I said. Pirithous fought so hard to stand and face Hecate that I feared he might kill himself in his struggle to break free of the chair. I didn't try to stop him. He would have been better off dead than as he was.

"Zeus gave me what he felt he had to—and no more. Anyway, he knew the other gods would resent me and that I would gradually become an outcast as far as most of them were concerned."

388

I tried to keep my voice neutral. "You intend to rebel against him, then?"

Hecate threw back her head and laughed. "Oh, you'd like me to admit that, wouldn't you? Not that it would matter. I am good at concealing what I do and say from other gods. But no, I do not plan to overthrow him. There is no need.

"You know of the prophecy that Zeus will eventually be overthrown by one of his own sons, just as he overthrew his own father, and his father overthrew his grandfather? No one knows who or when—except only Prometheus, who isn't telling. But all the gods know Zeus's days are numbered.

"As none of his current sons are powerful enough on their own, we must assume that it is a son yet to be born. So I remain loyal to Zeus—but I watch and wait. When the time comes, I will be ready. I have remained a virgin, not as Artemis does, in perpetuity, but as a strategy. For when Zeus is overthrown, the new king of the gods will need a wife. And who could better fill that role than I, most knowledgeable and most powerful among goddesses?

"The prophecies say a son will overthrow Zeus, not necessarily that a son will rule after him. He will sit upon the throne—but I will end up with the power. And then, there will be changes made."

"None of that explains all the scheming with your witches," I said. "Is that part of your watching and waiting?"

"It's part of keeping my fellow gods focused on the mortal realm, worrying about their favorites, worrying about the areas they patronize. An assassination here. A provoked war there. If I'm subtle, no one even realizes I am involved. And if someone does notice, the blame can always be passed off to an overzealous witch."

"You mean—" began Pirithous. His lips were white and trembling.

"Yes, fool, I used you to stir up trouble. Through you, I gave Ares some wars to occupy his time. I distracted Artemis and Ares with the Amazons—"

"Somehow, I will escape," said Pirithous, his words so filled with rage that they sounded more like an animal snarl than a human voice. "I will escape and tell my father, Zeus—"

Hecate let loose with one of her joyless laughs again. "Haven't you figured out the truth? Zeus is not your father. Your mother, fearful that the son of Ixion would be despised by the other Lapiths, invented that story. But it served my purposes so well that I almost wish I'd thought of it myself. How easy it was to play on your disappointment that Zeus never seemed to favor you, on your determination to prove your worth to him. So many impossible schemes my witches could convince you would work! And how dependent on them your desperation made you."

"But I can sense his tie to Zeus," I said. "And he is equal to me as a fighter."

"Some of my best work," she replied. "Even Zeus, who certainly knows better, might be fooled by the magic for a short time. It is easier to fool a mortal, of course. You sensed a tie to Zeus manufactured by a spell."

"As for his fighting, even I must give the fool some credit. He is a grandson of Ares, which isn't nothing. But because he thought he was a son of Zeus, he somehow managed to fight like a son of Zeus."

I looked over at Pirithous to see how he was taking all this. I had seen pain all too often, but never quite like the agony that twisted his face into a mask that would have frightened Medusa. His body looked smaller somehow, as if he were collapsing into himself.

I stared back at Hecate, my heart filled to overflowing with sheer hatred. "You came here just to torture him, didn't you?"

Hecate gave me a smile as cold as a glacier. "Hades has so little appreciation for the value of pain. I actually came to torture both of you, but if I only got to him, that's good enough for right now. I will return later."

I don't remember what impotent threat I screamed at her as she vanished into the shadows. Nor do I know how long I spent trying to comfort Pirithous. It would have been easier to see him die on the battle-field than to watch him diminish right before my ears, his self-image shattered into a thousand pieces, his soul shriveling.

I lost track of time again. The next moment into which my aware-ness of its flow returned was when the door opened again. I stiffened, fearing Hecate's return, but it was Hades who entered.

"An old friend wishes to see you," said the lord of the Underworld, looking as disinterested as possible. I relaxed a bit. Surely, even he knew Hecate was not a friend.

Hades stood aside, and into the chamber strode Heracles, whom I hadn't seen since I was eight. His hair had started to gray, his face was marked with worry lines, and he moved like a tired man, but he was still my hero, even after all these years.

"Theseus." His voice was still as deep and resonant as I remembered. "I have come here on my last labor."

"You...you have been laboring all these years? You started before I was eight."

He nodded slowly. "It ended up being twelve labors rather than ten, some took years, and much happened in between. But now, at last, I am near the completion of my atonement."

"Do what you came to do," said Hades.

"Ah, yes. My last labor is to capture Cerberus, which Hades has graciously allowed me to attempt. But when I arrived, I heard of your predicament. Hades has also given permission for me to free you."

"To attempt to free you," said Hades. "It may be that even his strength is not sufficient...or that you will perish in the attempt."

"Do you want me to try?" asked Heracles. "I'm told your connection to the chair is more than just physical. I'm more confident of beating Cerberus than I am of freeing you."

"I have nothing to lose. Even if your attempt kills me, at least I will still be free from the chair."

Heracles nodded, grabbed me, and started pulling. Since my buttocks were for all practical purposes part of the chair, it was not long before the rending of my flesh became agonizing. I had to bite my lip to keep from screaming. My eyes blurred with tears.

I felt something within me clutching at the chair, as if my own soul were trying to hold me captive. Whatever it was fought Heracles at every step, clinging to the chair as if its life depended on it. At times, my mind was so torn that I felt as if I were two people locked in an endless wrestling match.

I hung on as long as I could, but eventually, I passed out. When I awakened, I was lying on the ground. On the ground! Heracles had succeeded!

He was standing over me, watching me with concern. "Are you all right?" he asked.

"Better," I said. My voice was still hoarse from all the screaming, but I could make myself understood. My buttocks throbbed dully, far less than I expected—especially when I looked over at the chair and saw what looked like flesh still sitting on it. My flesh, though I tried to deny it. A shudder passed through me. Maybe it wasn't flesh. It was hard to tell with blood all over it—and all over the ground. So much blood! Could there be any left in my body?

Pirithous was still sitting in his chair, but his eyes were as focused on me as Heracles's. Why was he still trapped?

"Heracles, you've forgotten Pirithous."

Heracles opened his mouth but didn't speak.

"I gave permission for Heracles to rescue you," said Hades. "But not Pirithous, for his sin was much greater. He must stay."

I tried to get up but found I couldn't.

"You need to rest a little," said Heracles. "Persephone came and administered a salve to heal your wounds, but it does not instantly replace the blood you lost. Don't try to—"

"But what about Pirithous?" I croaked. My voice was muffled not only by hoarseness but by tears. "Can nothing be done?"

I saw motion behind Heracles. It looked as if multicolored flower petals were swirling in the wind. Then it pulled out from behind him, and I saw that it was a she, a woman so beautiful she could only be a goddess. She was the only thing I had seen in the underworld whose colors were not muted by pale but merciless light. She looked younger than Athena, almost girlish, though with goddesses, one could never tell by looks. But I did not need to know her age to recognize her. Aside from Hecate, there was only one goddess who could easily enter the Underworld, indeed who had no choice but to enter it at times—Persephone. To look upon her was to behold the beginning of spring. Even in this dead place, I could imagine new leaves, with that special green color that they alone possess. I could visualize young buds, ready to burst into bloom.

"Goddess, I thank you for your mercy. But please, help my friend."

Persephone shook her head. "His sin is too great." She spoke the words without conviction. Dazed as I was, bleary-eyed as I was, I still noticed that her lips kept moving.

"His punishment will not be eternal." I wasn't sure whether I heard her or had suddenly developed the ability to read lips. If her words were audible at all, they were as quiet as a light breeze whispering through falling leaves. Either way, she didn't wish Hades to overhear her.

"It's all right," said Pirithous, who didn't sound as if he thought anything would be all right ever again. "I deserve no better. But Theseus, on your way back to Athens, can you stop at Larissa and check on Polypoetes?"

"I will see to it that he is well cared for," I said. Of course, I was visualizing him as an infant, but who knows how many years had passed. He could have been a grown man by then.

Persephone smiled at me and departed in a rustle of flower petals. The room became much darker once she left.

"Heracles, it is time to go," said Hades. "I cannot bear to think of my poor Cerberus in chains any longer than necessary." As was often the case with Hades, his tone, in contrast to his words, sounded as if Cerberus's fate were a matter of indifference to him.

"And there is Hermes to consider, waiting to guide you out. He has other things to do, you know."

"Can I come with you?" I asked, trying to rise and again failing.

"I'd say yes if I hadn't already captured Cerberus," said Heracles. "But Hades is right. It would be cruel to keep the poor beast chained any longer than necessary. As it is, I have a long trek to Mycenae before I can return him. Besides, Hermes will bring me out at the Cape Taeneron entrance to the Underworld. You would have to pass through Spartan territory to return home. From what I hear, that route might not be… wise for you.

"Stay here and rest until you are more yourself."

"But…how do I get out?"

"The Larissa entrance is still there," said Hades. "You may go out the way you came. I will seal it once and for all as soon as you have left."

"Farewell, then, Theseus," said Heracles. "Perhaps our paths will cross again."

"I hope so," I said, forcing a smile. "Maybe I can save you next time."

Heracles smiled at that. Hades came as close to laughter as he probably ever did. Then they were gone.

I managed to stand enough to hobble over to Pirithous. "Will you be all right when I have left?"

"I'm not all right now," said Pirithous. "But it is as it is. Here is where our paths divide. I cannot go—and you cannot stay. You know you cannot."

"I will make sure he has company," said a voice behind me. I turned and saw Caeneus standing there, looking exactly the same as he had at the ill-fated wedding feast.

"You're...still alive?" I asked.

"Very much so. It's not clear to me how long I will remain that way. Hades is surprisingly vague about that. But someday, I know I will die, and when that happens, Poseidon will see to it I end up in the Elysian Fields.

"In the meantime, I cannot climb back to the mortal world. I'm not sure why, though Hades has explained it to me. Now that I know Pirithous is here, I can keep him company."

Caeneus tried to hug Pirithous—not the easiest thing to do since Pirithous was still trapped in his chair. Then he turned back to me.

"If I were you, I'd return to the surface while you still can. One thing I've learned around here is that anything can happen."

I bid them goodbye and felt a little better about leaving Pirithous. At least now, he would not be all alone.

I had a moment of fear navigating the labyrinthine corridors leading from our prison to outside Hades's palace—and from there, the way out. I didn't remember the route we had taken so long ago to get in. I would never have found my way in to begin with if Hades had not led me. How could I possibly find my way out?

Just as I was beginning to think that I would wander through empty, cavernous hallways until I died, Hades walked around the corner. I jumped at the sight of him. His eyes glanced in my direction, but his face remained expressionless. With one hand, he beckoned me to follow him, and I did. What choice did I have?

It did not take him long to lead me out of the maze and close to the Larissa exit to the Underworld. To my surprise, someone else was there as well. His winged sandals, the way he hovered in the air rather than standing on the ground, and the magic that flashed from his serpent-entwined staff, made me certain it was Hermes, who, among other things, had just been Heracles's guide out of the Underworld. But why had he come here? I didn't need his guidance to climb back up the hole. And why was he enveloping Hades and me in magic?

"Thank you for guiding me here, my lord Hades. And greetings, my lord Hermes. What brings you here?"

"I have something for you," said Hades. He held out what looked like an enormous fang on a dark chain, possibly adamantine.

"I humbly thank you," I said, taking the bizarre trinket by the chain.

"It is a tooth Cerberus lost during the battle with Heracles. Don't worry—it will grow back."

I hadn't been worried, but I was smart enough not to say anything. I just nodded.

"I have cleansed it of any poison. It is safe to wear it around your neck."

I took the hint and slipped it on over my head, though it was about the last thing I wanted to wear. What was going to be next, rings made from human bone? The chain felt cold against my skin.

Hades started doing the same thing Persephone had done a while earlier—speaking some of his words aloud but whispering others. His whisper was like the faintest scraping of bone against rock in the darkness.

"Let this token remind you of how close you came to being trapped here forever. *It is attuned to the powers of the Underworld. It makes excellent protection against certain forces, particularly witchcraft.*"

"I will wear it always," I said.

"See that you do. *Do not try it against a certain goddess, however. It will not be strong enough against her. I will try to distract her from coming after you. Some people are not as smart as they think.*"

Hades gave me the barest hint of a smile. It vanished so quickly that if I had blinked, I would have missed it.

"I too have a gift for you," said Hermes. "You have suffered much in your life—too much. The curse of Myrtilus will no longer trouble you or your sons."

He flicked the caduceus in my direction, and I felt invisible bonds I had never sensed before. They faded away, and I was free. After having no hope for so long, it was strange to feel it again.

"I do not even know how to thank you for such a gift," I said.

Hermes smiled. "I hear bitterness in your tone, but I forgive it. Do not forget, however, that all the curse did was create circumstances. It was you who shaped how those circumstances affected you."

"I have sinned many times," I said. "If I were feeling bitter, it would be about my behavior, not Myrtilus's or yours."

"Wisely said," replied Hermes. "*Now say no more,*" he added in a whisper like distant lyre music. "*My magic has shielded us from prying ears. Once I am gone, it will shield you no more. Never speak of what Hades and I have whispered to you.*"

"*Thank you for the wise advice, and I will speak of it to no one,*" I whispered back. No human ear could possibly have heard me, but both gods nodded. Then Hermes flitted away almost too fast for my eyes to follow. Hades turned and moved away much more slowly, as if he were carrying the whole weight of the Underworld on his back. Perhaps he was.

FREEDOM AND WITCHCRAFT

NOT WANTING to linger in that gloomy realm, I hurried to the shaft, found the handholds, and began to climb. It took longer to get to the surface than I would have liked. But when I first saw the sunlight, I found myself holding my breath in awe.

I emerged at midday and blinked at the brightness of the sun, which I hadn't seen for…how long? I had descended into darkness in early fall. Looking around me, I saw wildflowers around the hole, a sure sign of spring. That meant I'd been in the Underworld for six months—unless this was the following spring or the spring after that. I had no immediate way to know.

One thing I did know was that when Persephone came to heal me, she returned to the Underworld during the part of the year she was normally free of it. But before I had time to ponder what that might mean, the men guarding the hole noticed me and rushed over, thinking their king was about to emerge.

I had no choice but to tell them briefly what had happened. Their expressions shifted from hopeful to glum in seconds.

"Your king bid me check on Polypoetes before I return home. Could a couple of you escort me to the palace? Uh, but before that, can you tell me how long it's been since your king and I descended."

"Six months," said one of the guards. I was already prepared for that news by the wildflowers. I thanked the gods it had not been six years.

The guards said nothing else. But two men did step forward and gestured for me to lead the way.

My return to Larissa caused much more of a stir even than my emergence from the ground. I hadn't realized how many of the Lapiths could recognize me on sight, and all of them knew I had ventured to the Underworld with Pirithous. The guards helped me navigate my way through the anxious crowds to the palace. But even then, I was not just able to check on Polypoetes and leave. Instead, I was ushered to a meeting with Pirithous's council, to whom I had to recount the sad tale in greater detail.

"Our king was vague on the details of his journey," said one of the counselors, a man whose dignity reminded me of Alexius. "We had no idea that he intended to make Persephone his wife, nor that he would be gone so long."

"The second part was not his idea," I replied. "He intended to be back in a few days, weeks at most."

"Then he was a fool," said a much younger counselor. He looked more like a warrior than an adviser. But the Lapiths were more devoted to war than the Athenians, so it made sense that the council would have at least as many fighters as thinkers.

"It is not right to disrespect the king," said the older counselor, glaring at his younger colleague.

"And he may return at any time," I said, thinking of Persephone's words.

"That is all well and good for you to say," said the younger counselor. "But this is not Athens, where the king can be gone for months and leave the government in the charge of *bureaucrats*. We are a society of warriors and need our king back to lead us into battle. It is only a matter of time before our enemies realize our weakness and take advantage of it."

"Then go into the Underworld yourself and take up that question with Hades," I snapped. The man had already made me dislike him.

"Forgive my colleague," said the older counselor. "You understand that our ways are different from yours. Among us, power is intended to be held directly by the king. We exercise the royal authority in his name, but our people grow restless with that arrangement. However, they have no legal remedy. They cannot challenge Pirithous for the throne, for he is not here to answer the challenge. They cannot challenge his heir, the person who would normally run the kingdom in his absence, for Polypoetes is still an infant.

"At some point, if we do not have a present king, they will rebel."

"Anyone who does so will answer to me," I said. "I promised Pirithous I would keep his son safe."

"You are a great warrior, Theseus, but there is only so much one man can do. If Pirithous returns soon—"

"I am more than just one man. I am the king of Athens, after all, and can summon an army if needed."

The older counselor raised an eyebrow. "Do you not know—but how could you, having been in the Underworld these last six months? You rule Athens no longer."

Since I'd been gone half a year, this news should not have surprised me, but I felt my blood freezing in my veins.

"Sparta has conquered Athens?"

The old counselor shook his head. "Athens is still free. From what I have heard, Tyndareus decided against all-out war to rescue his daughter —the daughter you abducted, is that not so?" His eyes bored into me.

"Yes, it is, though if I had to do it over again, I would never have taken the girl. But if Tyndareus did not make war, how am I not still king?"

"The Spartan king sent Castor and Pollux, together with a small force, to attack Aphidnae, where their spies determined you were keeping Helen. Catching the deme unawares, they took Helen, as well as your mother and our king's sister."

"My mother—" I began, alarmed.

"Is well," the old counselor hastened to assure me. Tyndareus might have conceived a harsher fate for her, as well as Physadeia. Helen argued on their behalf, quite eloquently I'm told. Your mother and Physadeia, instead of being formally enslaved, were given to Helen, not as slaves but as servants fulfilling an obligation. If all I have heard is true, your mother had grown used to caring for Helen. I suppose she is still in a sense a captive, but in captivity of the lightest possible sort."

"But how did Physadeia end up in Aphidnae?"

"She said it was to visit your mother, though since they have never met, I doubt that explanation. I think it more the king's sister was too nervous to remain here. You see, Pirithous had made promises to her related to her marriage, though the nature his assurances, I don't know."

It was fortunate that in the account of Pirithous's fate, I hadn't mentioned what he had promised his sister. The council was agitated enough without being told the truth, which would no doubt have made them feel even worse about their imprisoned king.

"Whatever those assurances might have been, with Pirithous gone, many in the council wanted to marry Physadeia to a man of their choice, a warrior who could claim the right to act as king until Pirithous returned to us.

"When we heard she had been captured, we tried to ransom her, of course, but Tyndareus said she would remain as his guest. Without our king to lead us, we couldn't very well go to war with Sparta, so for the moment, Physadeia's status remains unresolved. I suspect both she and your mother, though well-treated, are hostages to ensure that neither the Lapiths nor the Athenians go to war against Sparta."

"Thank you," I said. "You have reassured me somewhat. But none of this explains how I came to lose my crown."

"You're right. It seems Castor and Pollux stopped by Athens on their home with Helen and their captives. They demanded a meeting with the council and used it as an opportunity to denounce you and demand your replacement.

"Theseus, I must speak plainly with you. Some of your decisions had not been popular, but particularly your seeming abandonment of Athens to a possible Spartan attack. Having already suffered a war against the Amazons on your account, they had no desire for a war against Sparta. So they deposed you, with only a few dissenting votes. Then they named Menestheus, another descendant of Erectheus, as king in your place."

A terrible thought struck me. "And my sons? What of them?"

"It seems a counselor named Alexius, one of those dissenters, spirited the children out of Athens with him. Whence he took them, I know not. It is said Alexius has found a secret sanctuary for them somewhere. At least, there has been no report that either one of the boys was captured."

I was both comforted and alarmed. My mother was a hostage, however honorably held. In all likelihood, Tyndareus would never allow me to see her again. I might yet see my sons, but searching for them could draw the attention of my enemies, of whom there were now more than I had realized.

No, I would have to take satisfaction that they were safe. I could not expect to see them again. I still had family, yet I was now effectively all alone, with no place to go.

I thought of assuming the acting kingship of Larissa. Though such a thing would be irregular, even by Lapith rules, I doubted anyone would challenge me to combat.

But no, I didn't think a borrowed throne among an alien people would make me happy. Caeneus, Pirithous, and Hippodamia were the only Lapiths I knew well, and all three of them were in the Underworld in one way or another.

There was, however, one thing I could do to make it more likely that Pirithous would have a throne to return to.

"I would see Polypoetes. But first, I need to ask you about the witches."

There was a nervous rustling in the chamber. "What of them?" asked the older counselor.

"Pirithous has commissioned me to drive them out of Larissa."

The older counselor sat up straighter. "What proof have you of this?"

Of course, I had none—because Pirithous hadn't told me to do that. It was Hades who had hinted at it, but I couldn't say that. I knew one thing, though—after his recent experiences, Pirithous wouldn't want witches anywhere near his son. I might not be able to help—or even see —my own family, but I could still do something for his.

"We were in the Underworld, and neither of us had any paper upon which he might write an order. But doesn't the situation speak for itself? I'm not saying your king has never been at fault. I'm not saying I've never been at fault. But haven't the witches encouraged him in his worst mistakes? He told me himself that witches encouraged the trip to the Underworld that left him trapped. Surely, you are not blind to how often their advice miscarries. Perhaps those miscarriages are not accidental."

A thin, sickly-looking counselor shuddered during that last sentence. "Be careful what you say. What if you're wrong? The witches now support our government. What if they were to turn on us?"

I stared at him long enough to make him look down at the table in front of him. "Have you forgotten you are Lapiths—brave warriors all? It is not like you to accept the subtle slavery these witches impose on you as they manipulate your actions from the shadows."

"What do know of it, *Athenian*?" said the younger counselor, making the word sound like an insult. "Do you accuse us of being cowards?"

"I accuse you of nothing," I said, using my calmest voice. "But you are being manipulated. When I was in the Underworld…I heard things. You are being used as a steppingstone in the witches' plan to control all of Greece."

I wasn't sure whether mentioning Hecate would have made them more outraged or more frightened. Nor was I sure whether mentioning her would violate the secrecy Hades expected me to keep. Now was not a time to take risks.

"What do you propose?" asked the older counselor. "That we fight the witches?"

"That you let me deal with them. Call a meeting here, and I will greet them. Authorize me to ban them from the city, and I will be responsible for making sure they leave."

"Will you accept responsibility if the plan fails?" asked the older counselor.

"The failure will be on my head."

Muttering buzzed through the chamber. The counselors, many of whom were younger and more warlike than their Athenian counterparts, glanced at the one young counselor who had argued with me. Some of them eyed him suspiciously and whispered with each other.

"Theseus is right," said one of these younger counselors, a man who would have looked more at home on the battlefield than in the council chamber. "I have never trusted these witches. Who among us has?"

"They are too powerful to oppose," said the sickly counselor. "The agreement that we have now keeps the peace with them."

"But at what price?" asked the counselor who had just spoken. "Control of our destiny? We were not born to be slaves, nor to be the toys of witches." The passion with which he spoke reminded me of Pirithous.

Several others spoke, mostly in favor of doing what I wanted. The sickly counselor shuddered more violently.

When the time came to vote, most of the counselors sided with me. But before the older counselor could announce the result, the sickly one rose, turned to face his colleagues, and shed his borrowed form. In the place of the man who looked as if he were dying stood a young, strong woman, staring defiantly at the council.

"You have no authority to renounce the alliance your people have with us," she shouted. "Reconsider this action at once, or face the consequences."

"These men are Lapiths," I said. "They do not fear your magic—as long as they have a sword at hand to counter it."

Given the mixed reactions, I wasn't sure all the counselors would have agreed with me. But my words, once spoken, took on a power of their own. No counselor would want to be the first to claim that Lapiths were not fearless.

"Then I will demonstrate to them why they should fear it," she said. I felt her magic, pulsing and fatal, flow in my direction, but it didn't touch me. Deflected by the power of Cerberus's tooth, it passed harmlessly around me.

The witch's eyes widened as she realized her attempt to strike me dead had failed. Just in case, I was not about to give her the opportunity to try again. I drew Hephaestus's club, so long unused, which had frightened even Medea, and swung it as fast and as hard as I could. The witch, unable to defend herself fast enough with magic, fell as the club crushed her skull.

"The gods are with me in this!" I shouted. Well, at least Hades and Hermes were, but I was pretty sure the others would have supported me against Hecate as well if they knew what she was up to. "You saw the witch's magic fail against me, and you saw the price she paid for her ill-considered attack. I am the way whereby you can rid yourselves of them forever.

"We will invite the witches here as you have asked," said the older counselor. "But if they come, they will doubtless be prepared for you."

That *if* turned out to be more prophetic than the counselor knew, for not a single witch showed up. When the one who had infiltrated the council didn't report back, they must have realized a new danger menaced them, even if they did not yet know what it was. Well, no matter. I could not allow them to lurk nearby and attack the Lapiths as soon as I was gone. But where could I find them?

There was no way to know with certainty where in the forest they met at night to perform their rituals, but this night, when there was an unprecedented threat, there was only one logical place for them to choose—the entrance to the Underworld carved out by the body of Caeneus. There they could be closer to their mistress, Hecate, and draw more effectively upon whatever power with which she chose to endow them.

Carrying orders from the council, I ran to the spot as fast as I could. Unfortunately, I was slowed by crowds in the streets. People were agitated by strange omens I suspected were being manufactured by the witches. Nonetheless, I couldn't very well strike down anyone who got in my way. As a result, the sun had already set by the time I reached the hole.

Where were the guards? Even as the question formed in my mind, I tripped over one of them. By the light of the rising moon, I could make out their forms, all sprawled around as if they had fallen where they were standing. Fortunately, they were still alive. Their breath was slow and rhythmic, as if they were sleeping, but I couldn't awaken them. Perhaps that was just as well. None of them shared my immunity to witches' spells.

The light was suddenly brighter. I looked up and was shocked to see that the moon looked far too big. I had heard stories about the ritual called drawing down the moon, which was used to amplify the power of witches, but I thought such tales were exaggerated, at the very least.

In the unnaturally intense silver light, I could see witches standing around the hole—many of them. I could count at least fifty. A lot of them were probably not very powerful, but at least a few of them must be to "bring down the moon," even if its growth in size was just an illusion of some kind.

I rose, club ready to smash through their lines. That was when I heard snarling. From among the trees, black dogs surged, their eyes glowing in the moonlight. There were more of them than there were witches, and the hounds looked larger than they should have, as well as fiercer than any animal which was not mad should have looked. I could not charge the witches without defeating the dogs first.

They bared their teeth in eerie unison. The fangs were unnaturally white and looked more than strong enough to rend my flesh.

If the dogs were also illusionary, they would dissipate like mist the moment they touched me. But if they weren't, I doubted my talisman would protect me from those fangs.

I thought about little Polypoetes in his cradle and realized I had to try. I couldn't let the witches continue to be a threat.

The moment I started forward, the dogs bounded in my direction. With my shield on my left arm and my club in my right hand, gripped as firmly as I could manage, I swung at them as soon as they were in range. I dropped three of them in one stroke, but then they were upon me, surrounding me, snapping and clawing.

They were physical. I felt their every touch and even their every breath. But they must have been somewhat augmented by magic, for they fumbled when they tried to attack. Claws scratched shallowly, if at all. Fangs seldom broke my skin. They came nowhere close to tearing chunks off of it as I had feared.

Even so, there were so many of them that I made poor headway. For every one I killed, more sprang from the between the trees that ringed the groves. My arm already felt weary, and I was only a few steps closer to the witches than when I had started.

The moon looked even bigger, and the light was now almost blinding. I could just barely keep my eyes open.

The witches had no trouble keeping *their* eyes open, and I could feel the way in which their power expanded as more and more moonlight poured into them. Were they trying to build up enough magic to overcome the protection Cerberus's tooth afforded me? Or were they trying to accumulate enough to twist Larissa the way Medea had twisted Athens? There was no way to be certain. But unless I stopped them soon, they might lash out at the Lapiths even if they couldn't directly attack me.

The drawing down the moon ceremony had to be pretty close to over by now. The witches would make their move then. I had to make mine first.

If I'd had magic of my own, I would have known what to do, but how could I interfere with the spell by nonmagical means if I couldn't reach them?

Neither my sword nor my club was fashioned correctly to be good throwing weapons, but I had nothing else. Taking advantage of a momentary lull in the dog attacks, I dropped my club, pulled out my sword, and hurled it at the nearest witch. It spun in the air, and the hilt bumped one of them in the back. She staggered, but her concentration remained unbroken.

I bashed a couple of dogs with my shield, grabbed up my club, and threw it with as much force as I could muster. It struck one of the witches hard enough to knock her unconscious. As she fell, the moon-light flickered but didn't dissipate. I'd have to do more if I wanted to disrupt the accumulating power, but I was all out of things to throw. I was also reduced to fending off the dogs with only my shield. I couldn't keep up with their ever-growing numbers this way.

I needed help—but to which god could I turn? I was afraid that praying to Hades would somehow tip Hecate off. The logical choice would have been Athena, but she hadn't appeared since I told her not to kill Pirit-hous. Poseidon tended to help much more often when I was near to or on the water. Persephone had rescued me when I least expected it, but she was probably above ground again, and I had no idea where. I couldn't invoke her by striking the ground, as one usually did with Underworld deities.

The moonlight recovered from its momentary halt and continued to brighten. I needed an idea—and fast. Perhaps I was thinking too much of myself. Which gods might be invoked to help defend the Lapiths?

Ares had fathered Ixion but hated me, so I knew praying to him would be useless. Apollo had fathered Lapithus, the first king of the

Lapiths, but Apollo was Artemis's brother, and she might very well still hate me. Even if she did not, Ixion's brother had tried to burn down Apollo's oracle at Delphi, and the god had shown little interest in the Lapiths since then aside from his solitary intervention against the centaurs.

Desperate, I flung my shield at one of the witches. Without waiting to see whether or not it hit its mark, I turned and ran. The dogs came howling after me. I climbed the nearest tree to evade them. They surrounded the base, looking up at me and barking as if they were rabid. I would not be able to go down the way I had come up.

I hadn't had much experience climbing trees, but I was more than strong enough to do it fast. I also had good enough balance to swing and jump from one treetop to another. The dogs followed my movement, but they couldn't climb well enough to do more than that.

However, keeping the dogs at bay would do little good if the witches could complete their ritual. The moonlight was blazing around them like a silvery conflagration that looked able to melt the walls of Larissa if that were their desire.

They were so focused on their magic that they seemed to forget I was nearby. The barking dogs moving ever closer to them should have been a hint, but they didn't pick up on it. Their eyes were like tiny moons as they chanted in a language I didn't recognize.

Now without weapons, my only hope was the talisman Hades had given me. It had done its protective job so far, though I had no idea whether even it could withstand the level of magic the witches could now deploy against me. But how would it be as a weapon? There was only one way to find out.

I had finally reached a tree close enough to drop on one of the witches, who were so congested below me that the dogs couldn't get around them. I took the chain from around my neck and gripped the tooth like a tiny dagger. Then I flung myself toward the closest witch I could find.

Cerberus's fang was a little small for a weapon—but I couldn't have asked for a sharper one. It ripped into the left arm of the witch I fell upon. She screamed, blood gushed, and silver magic abandoned her with explosive force. I punched her in the face and moved on to my next target.

The witches nearest me couldn't help but notice me now, but the spells they flung at me were not as strong as I expected. They were trying to conserve power for some larger purpose. The talisman was no longer around my neck, but as long as I kept touching it, it seemed to ward me against the spells, silvery and dark at the same time, that they hurled at me.

The dogs, still snarling to get at me, didn't attack the witches, but, jostled by the canines, some of Hecate's minions were clearly distracted, and the silver energy dulled and flickered. The moon's abnormal size also began to shrink. Either the illusion or the connection with the moon that underlay it had begun to fray.

Even so, the odds seemed hopelessly against me. The witches couldn't attack me directly, but when they realized that, they could easily hurl the energy they had accumulated at some other target. They could curse the Lapiths, maybe even collapse the city of Larissa. And even if I felled enough of the witches to make that impossible, there were also the hounds to consider. They seemed reluctant to shove past the witches, but once enough witches were removed from their path, they would break through and overwhelm me.

I saw more and more of those moon-silver eyes glancing toward Larissa. The witches were thinking about lashing out.

I knew little about witchcraft, but I suspected that, as in all human activities, there had to be a leader. Thank the gods it wasn't someone as powerful as Medea, but surely someone was leading the ritual. If I could overcome the leader, perhaps that would disrupt the ritual.

One of the witches shifted the rhythm of the chant and perhaps the words as well. It was hard to tell in an unfamiliar language. The power gushing from the hole suggested the witches were summoning Hecate herself. If she appeared, I'd be doomed.

But I'd noticed which witch it was that seemed to order the change of course. Shoving others aside, I lunged at her, Cerberus's tooth extended.

Just before I collided with her, she vanished, and I fell, smashing into the ground. She must have been an illusion.

A mist rose from the hole, and the dogs howled in unison, greeting their mistress. I scrambled to my feet and looked around for the leader's real location, but I couldn't see her anywhere. Perhaps the illusion had shown me a different witch than the leader, maybe even a nonexistent one.

The mist began to coalesce into a silver figure. From having met Hecate, I knew the rising image wasn't really the goddess. The witches were using their power to create a double of her. Or perhaps they thought it was Hecate. But I could sense it was weaker.

Without waiting for them to finish, I charged the silver image, which looked in my direction and blasted me with a spell that shined like moonlight in the middle of a dark cave. The magic slipped around me. No, this wasn't Hecate at all.

I swung the tooth through the image's head, which exploded in a shower of silver sparks. The rest of it dissipated like mist in a high wind. Some of the witches shrieked. The dogs whined and trembled.

Holding the tooth over my head, I yelled, "I don't want to kill you, but I will if I have to. If you want to live, leave this land at once—and do not return!"

As if to punctuate my words, the ground shook, and the hole leading down to the Underworld crashed shut like the mouth of a wild beast closing on its prey. No doubt Hades was belatedly closing that entrance to his domain, but the witches had no time to divine the truth. As far as they could tell, I had closed the hole myself. They fled, though they retained just enough composure to gather up their wounded first. The dogs followed their lead and vanished into the night.

Putting the tooth back around my neck, I walked quickly past the guards, who were starting to wake up, and then walked as fast as I could back to the gates of Larissa. The gate guards recognized me, and one escorted me to see the members of the council. Despite the lateness of the hour, they had remained to see what would come of my mission.

"The witches will not trouble you—at least for a while. As for me, I will be on my way as soon as I have said goodbye to Polypoetes."

"The infant is asleep," said the older counselor.

"I will try not to disturb him too much, but I have protection I must bestow on him. It will prevent him from being used by the witches the way his father was."

After a little muttering, the council allowed me to see the child. A guard escorted me to his room, where a nurse was watching over him.

"Who are you, who comes so late?" she asked me. "This has been a foul night, and if you be some—"

"I am no night horror, lady, merely a friend of the lad's father who comes to him with a gift."

"This is Theseus, a friend to all Lapiths," said the guard. "The council has allowed his visit."

The nurse stepped aside, though she continued to eye me suspiciously.

The baby was sleeping soundly, unaware of how close his people had come to total ruin. As I looked upon him, I felt power surge through me, but only for a second. Was it the tooth or something else? I couldn't say. But vague feelings about the future crystallized, as if I had been granted a momentary vision of a tiny part of destiny—just a speck, really, but enough.

Polypoetes did not awaken when I lifted his little head and placed the Cerberus tooth medallion around his tiny neck. I had been worried Hades might be angered when he discovered I had broken my pledge to him and given the powerful artifact to someone else. I was worried about that no longer. Even if I had still feared his wrath, though, I would have given the child the protective tooth, anyway. Polypoetes would need it more than I. My own story was near its end. His was just beginning.

"What is that ugly thing?" whispered the nurse. "It is not suitable for a baby."

"It is a talisman that will guard the infant against all spells cast by witches, now and until the end of his life."

"How can you be sure of that?" she asked. "For that matter, how do I know you are not a witch in disguise?"

"The council will vouch for me," I said. "As for the first part, I just fought against every witch in Thessaly—and won."

The nurse didn't seem much moved by my words. Doubtless, she had heard a lot of bragging in her time. She looked at the guard, who nodded. Then she looked reluctantly back at me.

"The talisman may stay—tonight. Tomorrow I will seek the advice of the gods."

"I can ask no more than that," I said. I bent down, kissed the baby on the forehead, and left the nursery.

I had not glimpsed exactly what awaited the son of Pirithous, but I knew I would never see him again.

PREPARING TO GO

I MANAGED a couple of hours of sleep in one of the unoccupied rooms of the palace. I rose before first light, reclaimed my horse, and prepared to leave.

In my uneasy dreams, I remembered that I had not stopped to recover the sword and shield given to me by Aegeus. Nor had I picked up the club fashioned by Hephaestus. When I rode back to the grove, there was no sign of them, though the guards assured me no one had been there. Likely, the witches had snatched them up on their way out.

At almost any other time, the loss of such fine weapons would have disturbed me, particularly the ones bestowed upon me by my father. But now, they seemed as if they were part of a life that wasn't mine. And things that had happened two days ago now seemed more like dim memories from two decades past.

From Larissa, I traveled southwest, living off the land as best I could and being careful not to get too close to large cities. My reputation was not what it had once been, and I wanted to avoid any place that might have any connection to Sparta or to Athens. Around Trachis, I veered southeast. I risked a close pass by the devastated Thebes, a city nearly destroyed by the evil of its earlier king, Laius. He had drawn a curse upon his family from the lips of my ancestor, Pelops, and had earned the wrath of Hera as well. After two bloody wars, the city was now in the hands of Argos. My folly had brought Athens terribly close to being in the hands of Sparta. But looking from a distance at Thebes, I could see little of the destroyed buildings. Nor could I see how underpopulated Thebes was after the prophet Teiresias had managed to get most of its citizens evacuated. The fires that would have darkened the sky above the city with their smoke had long ago been put out. If I wanted to, I could imagine Thebes undamaged and at peace.

If I wanted to, I could imagine myself as I had been when I first set out into the world to meet Aegeus. Ah, possibilities stretched out infinitely in all directions. Yet now, they had shrunk to one narrow road.

I turned away from Thebes and rode on, this time to the northeast. I passed over the narrow isthmus that joins Euboea to the mainland. I maneuvered between Chalkis and Eretria, not wishing to stop in either and completely unaware that these cities were where Alexius had hidden my sons. But even if I had known, I wouldn't have dared stop. Someone might have seen. Their hiding places might have been compromised. I could never have taken the chance.

I headed instead to Kymi, a small port town from which I planned to sail to Skyros. Why Skyros? I could not yet have said. Through Pittheus, I had inherited some land there, but this much I knew—I was not going there to make a new home for myself.

Near the gates of the city, I felt as if I were being watched. I trotted off the road and looked around. I saw nothing, but I still felt eyes upon me.

Just as I was about to start riding again, Athena appeared right next to me. Despite myself, I jumped.

"Foolish man! Riding unarmed over such a long distance! And where is the talisman…someone gave you?"

"I bestowed it on Pirithous's son. He will need it far more than I."

Athena's stern expression softened a little. "Always Pirithous! But I cannot fault you for wanting to protect his innocent son. May his reign be better than his father's."

"Pirithous was a hero," I said, though I was so tired that I didn't make the words sound as convincing as I wanted to. "He had his faults, but then so do I."

Athena sighed. "I must agree with you—on both counts. Yet I would not have you think I was still angry with you. The truth is that you were right to stop me from killing Pirithous."

I couldn't help raising an eyebrow. "I am grateful for your words, but I don't understand why you changed your mind."

"I have had more time since to study the pattern of fate," she replied. "Though you sacrificed much to follow Pirithous into the Underworld, without that trip, we would never have learned...certain important facts."

"I had no idea how long I would be gone," I said. "Had I known the peril into which I placed Athens, I would never—"

"You might have, anyway," said Athena. "But in that, too, you were fortunate. Though you are unpopular in Athens now, the reforms that brought people closer together kept the city from dissolving into civil war. Menestheus was crowned peacefully, and though he will never be the king you might have been, he is at least competent. Thanks to the foundation you laid, Athens continues to grow and prosper. Your sons are safe and well, as is your mother."

"And I suspect your watchful eye is part of the reason for that."

"It is...a little bit. But I did not come just to confirm what you already knew. Why do you go to Skyros?"

"Pittheus owned a little land there. It seemed a good place to retire."

Athena's gray eyes widened. "This is the first time you have ever lied to me."

"Everything I said was true."

"But it was not the whole truth, was it? You must have heard the rumors about King Lycomedes. He is jealous of heroes."

"Idle gossip."

"Industrious truth. He will not like someone as famous as you settling on his island. Going there seems...suicidal unless you intend to kill him and take Skyros for yourself."

I shook my head. "You know I would never murder my way to a throne."

"Then you do intend to use him as an instrument to end your life?"

"I cannot explain why, but I know I am meant to go to Skyros."

Athena frowned in a way that would once have frightened me. "Do you think your death is what is needed to atone for your sins? Do not surrender to your guilt. You have made mistakes. What mortal does not? What god does not? Yet, as I have told you, your mistakes were not as costly as you feared. Perhaps you have torn open some of your old wounds. You think of Hippolytus, do you not?"

"How could I not? I see his mangled body every day." I spoke with more passion than I thought I had in me. "I should have trusted him! I should have at least investigated. But no, I believed Phaedra—"

"Who had given you no reason not to up to that point."

"Neither had Hippolytus!" Tears were trickling down my cheeks, but I didn't try to wipe them away.

"Just as your Underworld journey can be viewed in more than one way, so too can the story of Hippolytus. Artemis, it is time."

I thought I was beyond being surprised at this point, but when Artemis appeared next to Athena, I froze. Surely, the divine huntress still wanted nothing to do with me—yet she looked at me without a trace of hatred. Perhaps there was even a hint of kindness. I didn't know what to make of her.

"When I left with the body of your son, I carried him straight to the throne of Zeus. I begged my father to give life to Hippolytus again, but the king of gods was unmoved by my pleas. Hippolytus had neglected all the other gods, not just Aphrodite, and so my father would not grant my wish.

"I could not accept that decision. Instead, I went to Asclepius, the son of Apollo, and a great healer. He had learned the secret of bringing back the dead, though he also knew not to use it. His refusal was gentle, understanding—but it was still a refusal, and I would have none of it.

"Since he was Apollo's son, I could not threaten him with death, so I tried to tempt him instead. I offered him gold, more than enough to build the greatest temple to Apollo the world had ever seen. I told him it would be a great sanctuary for the sick, a way to heal even more people. Asclepius hesitated, but finally, the thought of doing so much good overcame him for a moment. He took the gold and raised your son."

For a moment, I felt as if time had stopped all around me, as if the universe was too small to contain such news. "You mean, Hippolytus—"

"Wait until you have heard the whole tale," said Artemis. "Yes, Hippolytus was alive again, but I had to flee with him at once, for I knew Zeus's wrath might otherwise destroy him. I swept him away to a grove near the town of Aricia in Italy and disguised him as a stag so that, at least from a distance, even the eyes of Zeus might be deceived. Lest another tragedy be visited upon him, I persuaded the nymph after whom the town was named to watch over him and see to it that he didn't fall victim to a hunter. Then I returned to Olympus, prepared to face whatever punishment Zeus decreed.

"By the time I returned, however, Zeus had already executed justice —but not upon me. Instead, he had burned poor Asclepius to ashes with a thunderbolt for daring to raise the dead. Even worse, my dear brother, Apollo, enraged by what he saw as Zeus's unjust murder of his son, tried to get revenge by killing the cyclopes, who help to forge Zeus's thunderbolts. As they are immortal, he failed, but Zeus, angered by the attempt, condemned Apollo to spend some time as a mortal.

"All of this suffering—and all because of me, because I acted without thinking. When you condemned Hippolytus, you did the same. Theseus, I can hardly fault you for doing what I myself did. It was at that moment I forgave you. It is why I am here now to help Athena convince you that your life is worth living.

"Just as your mistakes led to some unexpected good, so too did mine. Many of the gods argued Asclepius's case before Zeus, pointing out that he had done much to ease mortal suffering and that his one mistake should be forgiven. It took a while, but Zeus relented. Not only did he bring Asclepius back to life—annoying Hades in the process— but he even went so far as to make him a god, so that mortals would always have his help in easing their suffering. He is forbidden to ever resurrect a mortal again, but otherwise, he is unfettered by his past.

"But then Zeus turned to me, and I feared—"

"That he would demand the life of Hippolytus in exchange for that of Asclepius?" I asked.

"Fear not, for that is not what happened—but I confess it is what I feared. I should have known Zeus would have made that demand before resurrecting Asclepius if he were going to at all. Instead, Zeus showed mercy, not only assuring me that Hippolytus had nothing to fear from him but offering to make Hippolytus a god."

"Hippolytus is—"

"You interrupt too much, but yes, he is now a god. I think Zeus saw in him an opportunity to tempt me to relinquish my virginity. I had no intention of doing that, for my love for your son is of spirit, not flesh, but I let my father dream for a moment.

"To avoid the jealousy of the other gods, whom Zeus feared would start demanding the resurrection of every single mortal child, friend, or lover any of them had ever had, Zeus did insist that Hippolytus change his name to Virbius and that he live among the Italians—a small price to pay for godhood, especially considering I could still easily visit him.

"But fate had one last card to play. I changed Hippolytus back into a man, and Zeus granted him godhood, just as he had promised, but I forgot one thing. The charm I put upon him to resist Aphrodite's wiles expired with his death, and I neglected to restore it.

"It was not long before Hippolytus fell in love with Aricia, whom I had made his protector. I could not be angry with him. It is the nature of men. Charm or no, it would have happened eventually. I could no longer hunt with him, but I don't regret bringing him back—even into the arms of another woman."

"So now you know," said Athena. "The son whose death wracked you with guilt lives, is happily married—and is a god. He is far better off than he would have been if you had never caused him to be killed. And he is right here, come to affirm all that we have said."

Hippolytus appeared just as abruptly as Athena and Artemis had. It was clear it had not taken him long to master the powers of a god.

He looked just the way he did right before his death—not surprising, since he was now ageless. But as a mortal, he had been calm, almost to the point of detachment. Now he embraced me warmly, and I felt his tears on my shoulder.

"How long…how long I have waited for this day," he said. "Father, I have missed you so much. I have Zeus's permission to be here, but I cannot come to Skyros with you. However, you could come to Italy with me. I have spoken to Aricia, and she would be overjoyed to have you as our guest."

As if on cue, a beautiful woman who had to be Aricia appeared right next to Hippolytus. In her arms, she carried a baby a little younger than Polypoetes.

"See here, father of my husband," said Aricia in a musical voice. "Here is your grandson, whom we have named Theseus after you."

I took the offered child in my arms. He looked up into my eyes and laughed. I fancied that in his unformed features, I could see my own face, and perhaps even Poseidon's.

I kissed little Theseus's forehead and handed him back to his radiant mother. "I could never express in words how much it means to me that you are not only alive but prospering in ways I could never have anticipated. And your offer fills my heart with joy. But I cannot accept it. My destiny lies elsewhere."

I had never seen Hippolytus look so downcast. "But…but Athena tells us going to Skyros will cost you your life."

"But death is not the end," I said. "You have proven that yourself."

"If you are thinking that Zeus will make you a god as well—" began Athena.

"Goddess, I look for no such honor. And I cannot even tell you why I go to Skyros. But there is a reason why I must go. Something will be far worse if I do not."

"There have been indications that we may be facing a great disaster within a generation or so," said Athena. "None of us have yet discerned all the details, except that events are coming that will pit not only man against man but god against god. But how could your going to Skyros prevent such a cataclysm?"

"Not prevent necessarily." I said. "I can't claim to have heard a divine voice or had a vision. I can give you no details whatsoever. All I have is a feeling."

"Inspired by…someone?" asked Athena.

"If I thought that, I would go with my son and his family to Italy and never look back. I suppose I could be deceived, but this feeling blossomed within me while I still had the…artifact. It was when I stood near the cradle of Polypoetes, I think. And someone was occupied elsewhere then, or so it seemed."

Athena nodded. "Your assumptions are accurate. And there have been rare cases of mortals with no earlier prophetic gift suddenly seeing a small part of the fabric of fate. But because you have seen so little, you could be wrong. Know that, once you set foot on the island, none of us will be able to stop what you will set in motion."

"I know, and I would not ask you to. On this quest, I must go alone."

Athena and Artemis both looked as if they accepted my decision. It took Hippolytus longer, but eventually, even he yielded.

"Someday we will meet again, though," he said, hugging me for perhaps the last time. "Fate could not be so cruel as to separate us forever when we have only just been reunited."

"May it be as you have said," I told them. Then he was gone. They all were.

I mounted my horse and got back on the road. But I was not as grim as I had been earlier. Instead, I was smiling. That at least they had been able to do for me.

The voyage to Skyros was an extremely short one, for the distance was not great, the sea was calm, and the wind was favorable. Apparently, Lycomedes had a good spy network, for he was waiting for me at the dock with a small welcoming committee. The king was all smiles and greeted me as if I were a brother he hadn't seen in years.

I caught his expression a couple of times when he thought I wasn't looking. He was eying me like a predator watching its prey. I wasn't worried, though. It was the reaction I had been expecting. Nor did I decline when he offered to give me a tour of the island. I didn't hesitate even when the rest of his entourage gradually fell away, leaving us alone.

As we started up a path leading to the top of a cliff, I must admit that I hesitated for a moment. I thought about Hippolytus and his family. I thought about my two sons, growing somewhere in secrecy. I thought of my mother. Then I put those thoughts aside and kept walking. Even then, I didn't know why I was following this path and not some other. I only knew that I had to.

"You must see this view," said Lycomedes, beckoning me forward. "On a clear day like this, I swear I can sometimes see Lesbos from here."

I stifled a laugh. One would need the vision of a god to see Lesbos from there, and whatever else Lycomedes was, he was no god. Nonetheless, I walked forward, clear to the cliff's rocky ledge, and feigned interest in the view. What I could see was a large expanse of water, rippling gently from tides and wind. The sunlight sparkled on the water, making it look inviting.

I didn't even flinch when I felt a rough hand give me a hard shove. I had been expecting it. Nor did I scream as I fell. Instead, I felt oddly at one with Aegeus, who had fallen over grief for me and whose death had haunted me until this very day. Now, at long last, I would be reunited with him.

I struck the water hard enough to be knocked unconscious, but somehow, I remained aware, though I felt no pain. I felt the cold of the water and tasted its saltiness. I didn't feel as if I were dying. What I did feel were strong arms embracing me. What I heard was a whisper pulsing in the surrounding sea.

"Son, how I wish I could have done more for you. But I never stopped loving you, no, not for an instant!"

It was not Aegeus's voice, but Poseidon's. As if in a dream, I saw my life as Poseidon wished it could have been. I saw an alternate childhood, spent walking with the god by the seashore, while close behind strolled my mother and Bellerophon, united before it was too late. My young manhood remained much the same, except that Dionysus didn't take Ariadne away from me. She became my wife and gave me many fine children. Because Dionysus never scrambled my brains, I didn't forget to change the sails this time, so Aegeus never fell from Cape Sounion. I had many more happy years with him. When he did die, more than twenty years later, I became king of Athens, which I ruled successfully until I myself died at a very old age.

"That was a pleasant vision, Father. Thank you for it. It would have been wonderful to spend time with you, to see my mother married to Bellerophon, to have more time with Aegeus. But Ariadne would never have become a goddess. How could I have denied her such an opportunity? And Pirithous—would we never have met? And to never love

Antiope, to trade the children I actually had for others—perhaps, Father, some parts of my life were better as they were."

"So wise! No wonder Athena speaks so highly of you."

I don't know exactly when I died or how long I rested in the arms of my father.

But I did know one thing. My mortal life was at an end—but my adventure was just beginning.

TRIAL AND ERROR

THANATOS, Death himself, chilled the water with his shadowy presence and chilled me with his touch. My death was now official. I could no longer feel my father's arms. I was pulled from the depths by a stronger force than I could resist. The moment I broke the surface of the water, I spotted Hermes, hovering above me and smiling.

"I didn't expect to see you so soon, Theseus. But I'm glad to see you so calm."

"My death wasn't unexpected," I said. Suddenly, I was floating next to Hermes.

"I'll see to it that you reach the Underworld," said the god, still smiling. He must have had a lot of experience with calming the dead who didn't start out so tranquil. Something about his face made me feel even more relaxed.

I stayed by his side as he flew me to Cape Tanaeron, the nearest entrance to the Underworld. After flashing across the bright blue sky with the sun shining on my back, the sudden descent into darkness took me a moment to adjust to.

"Almost there," said Hermes, taking my hand and pulling me along.

When my feet came to rest on solid ground, I stood before a broad, dark river. Though it flowed lazily past, I sensed that no man—or ghost, perhaps—could survive a swim across it.

"There is Charon," said Hermes, giving me a gentle push in his direction. "I would walk you over, but I have much to do, and it must be done quickly."

I felt a sudden breeze, and when I glanced toward him, he was already gone. Much to do indeed! I wondered if some horrible battle called out to him, if the riverbank would soon be thronged with thousands of the newly dead. I shuddered and hurried toward Charon.

As I drew closer, though, my steps slowed. I had met gods before—many of them, if I thought about it. I had even stood face to face with the cold and unfeeling Hades, as well as the dark and forbidding Hecate. Yet in his own way, Charon was more dreadful than either.

The tales said he was born in utter darkness from the coupling of Night and Erebus when the universe was young. That made him older than Hades, older even than Hecate. And while most gods looked young or at least like vigorous people in their middle years, Charon chose to look old. His face, pale and bloodless, was so thin that, from a distance, it could be mistaken for a skull despite the unruly white beard that grew from his chin. His body, almost skeletal, was clothed in filthy rags.

Despite his decrepit appearance, there was no mistaking the power that radiated from him, cold as ice and hard as rock. Nor was there any mistaking the implication of the adamantine hammer that hung from his belt. His job might be considered a menial one in human society, but he would perform his duties relentlessly. No one would pass this point without his permission.

He said nothing but thrust out his clawlike hand, waiting for the necessary obol. Did I have it? For a moment, I visualized what it would be like to be trapped forever on the wrong side of the river, doomed to watch others move on to an afterlife that I could never share. Then I felt the coin in the palm of my right hand. Poseidon must have slipped it to me without my even noticing. I dropped it into Charon's waiting palm, being careful not to touch his flesh that I couldn't help thinking would be unimaginably cold and hard. He gestured for me to enter the boat. Then he rowed me across the river without a single word.

As soon as I exited the boat, I felt six pairs of eyes on me.

Cerberus, large as a horse and deadlier than the wildest of beasts, trotted over to me. As he approached, I saw that his three canine heads were wreathed in manes of poisonous snakes and that his tale was a snake as well. I marveled at how Heracles had been able to capture him.

He was supposed to let the spirits of the dead pass unharmed, but he seemed inordinately interested in me. Since I had no hope of fighting him, I stood as still as I could and waited.

Cerberus sniffed me all over, spending more time on my upper chest and neck than on anything else. He must have picked up the scent from his own tooth. But, having failed to find it, he eventually turned and walked away, growling just a little, perhaps from frustration.

I walked slowly through a cavern that opened out into a space I'd seen before from a different angle. In the distance, I could see the dark marble palace of Hades. Much closer, the Fields of Asphodel, covered with pale flowers unlike their earthly counterparts and filled with shambling ghosts, captured my attention.

I was a ghost now, too—I knew that. Yet there was something different about these men and women. They seemed to wander aimlessly, mindlessly.

"Behold those who lived indifferent lives," said an unfeeling but familiar voice. Hades had appeared nearby, his cold eyes examining me as if I were a bit of broken stone he had just stepped on by accident. "Neither good nor evil, they were left here to wander. Over time, their sense of self wore away, until they became as you see them now—mere shadows of their former selves."

"And is this to be my fate?" I asked. Somehow, I managed to keep my voice steady.

"Are you neither good nor evil?" asked Hades.

"I fear I am a little of each. Is that the same thing?"

"Once, I might have said yes," replied the lord of the Underworld. "But these days, Zeus has...persuaded me that we should do things a little differently. Just recently, three judges have been appointed to determine the fates of the newly dead. Eventually, they will review older cases as well, but for right now, they await you."

Hades pointed to a spot that seemed empty of everything but flowers a moment before. But now, three figures sat on high thrones, regarding me with interest.

"All three were sons of Zeus in life. To your left is Aeacus, king of Aegina, son of Zeus and the nymph Aegina, known for his fairness. To your right is Rhadamanthus, son of Zeus and the beautiful Europa, known as a just judge throughout the Aegean islands. And in the center is an old friend of yours, Minos, another son of Zeus and Europa, who drafted the famous law code of Crete."

I froze. How could Minos judge me fairly? I had started him on the way to his downfall. He didn't look the same as when I had known him, though. Unlike the other two, who retained the form of dignified older men, Minos looked very young, much as he must have been when he first became the ruler of Crete.

"Come forward," said Minos. "Come forward and be judged." His voice was neutral, but did I detect the hint of a vindictive smile on his lips? Either way, I couldn't get my feet to move. It was as if they had sunk into the stone beneath them.

"You need to stand closer," said Hades. "See where the stone has a golden glow about it? That is the power of Aletheia, Truth herself, infused into the stone by the skill of Apollo and Hermes. Any who stand upon the stone will be able to tell only the truth."

"Come forward," Minos repeated, looking a little annoyed.

"He is not the Minos you know." The voice was not that of Hades this time. There was feeling in it, as well as thunder. Looking to the right of the judges, I saw a god wreathed in his own power, dignified and strong. A quiver full of sparkling thunderbolts hung on his back.

I fell to my knees.

"Rise," said Zeus, his voice gentle, yet loud enough to echo from distant walls.

"I had no idea you intended to grace us with your presence," said Hades. His emotionless tone made it difficult to tell whether he was honored or annoyed by a surprise visit from the king of the gods.

"I thought it wise to observe our new experiment a bit. I told you I might." Zeus turned to me. "If it is Minos who makes you tremble before the judgment, fear him not. My son died with the weight of many sins upon him. He could never have reached the Elysian Fields on his own merits, and I have grown tired of placing mortals there simply because they are related to me. Henceforth, places there must be earned by virtue, and divine ancestry is no guarantee."

"However, Minos died before the new system was in place. Consequently, I struck a deal with him."

"Over my objection," said Hades.

"But not in violation of your rights," said Zeus. "Such exceptions as I make are always allowed by the covenant between us. In any case, given the vastness of the human population, we needed assistance in the administration of justice—three judges renowned as lawgivers, as judges, or both, who would sit in judgment on mortal souls and determine their fate in the afterlife. Aeacus and Rhadamanthus had led suitably virtuous lives for such an honor, but Minos had faltered in his later years. So I offered him a choice—wandering in the Fields of Asphodel or serving as one of the three judges.

"He chose the second and was given enough of the waters of Lethe to strip away his most recent, sinful memories and thoughts. Restored as the virtuous lawgiver you see before you, he must work his way into the Elysian Fields through the administration of justice. He no longer remembers his animosity toward you, Theseus, but even if he did, he would not act on it for fear of losing his own place in the desirable afterlife."

"Come forward," said Minos for the third time as if he had not heard any of Zeus's comments. This time, I stepped closer without hesitation, being careful to position myself on the golden stone.

"Theseus, you stand before us that we may determine the afterlife that you deserve," said Minos. "If you are evil enough, you will be consigned to the Place of Punishment. If you are good enough, you will be allowed entry into the Elysian Fields. If you are neither good near evil, you will be left here. However, in the last case, you may ask us to grant you reincarnation."

"Reincarnation?" I remembered what Dionysus and Ariadne had told me, but she was an exceptional case back then. Was the opportunity now universal?

"It is a relatively new possibility," said Minos. "King Hades, with the advice of Queen Persephone and of his nephew, Dionysus, and with the agreement of the council of the gods, has decreed that mortals may have their memories wiped away by the waters of Lethe, return to the living realm, and be reborn, that they might live better lives if given another chance."

I glanced at Hades, whose face was unreadable. Dionysus had not been as mad as I thought. He had accomplished a major change in the nature of the afterlife. How many gods could claim such an achievement?

"Thank you for explaining," I said. "I am ready to be judged."

"And so you shall be," said Minos, looking down at what appeared to be an enormous scroll. "Let us begin with the good."

The former king of Crete recited my achievements, nodding as he read each one. He didn't even flinch when the Minotaur came up.

"Were those the end of the story, you would qualify for the Elysian Fields without question," said Minos. "But just as you have accomplished great good, you have also inflicted great evil on the world."

I listened as calmly as I could while Minos dissected every one of my failings. After hearing them all again, I would have consigned myself to the Place of Punishment.

"This is a strange case," said Rhadamanthus, stroking his beard. "The evidence weighs equally on both sides."

"Do the virtues and sins then cancel out, making him fit only for the Fields of Asphodel?" asked Aeacus.

"There is a difference between being mediocre and being both very virtuous and very sinful at the same time," said Rhadamanthus. "It does not seem fair to treat the two situations in the same way."

"If that is the case, it would seem that the only logical sentence would be reincarnation," said Minos.

"Your honor, may I speak?"

Minos nodded. "It is only fair that the person standing in judgment be given an opportunity to explain himself before the final sentence is determined."

"I'm not sure I can. What I have done, I have done. I have no excuses to offer. But precisely because of that, I don't see how reincarnation will benefit me. Without my memories, but still being otherwise the same person, how will I be able to do better?"

"A question I have often asked," said Hades. "Reincarnation in this fashion is like bringing back a lion in the foolish expectation that it will somehow be transformed into a lamb."

"What do you ask of us?" said Aeacus? "Do you want to reincarnate with your memories intact? If so, we cannot do that."

"And yet it has been done," said Rhadamanthus. "Years before we were judges, Hermes made his son, Aethialides, one of the first mortals to reincarnate—and with all his memories intact."

"That was a special case," said Hades. "You cannot employ it as a precedent here."

I noticed movement and glanced away from Hades for a moment. Standing behind the judges, but still partially visible, was Hecate, her eyes filled with burning hatred for me. Her unexpected appearance was an evil omen if ever there was one.

"Yet was not the whole purpose of adopting this new system to make assignment to the afterlife less arbitrary?" asked Zeus.

Hades's eyes were cold as he looked at his brother. "Would you send a mortal back to Earth with such secrets as Theseus knows? What if he tells other mortals what the Underworld is like?"

Zeus's laughter echoed through the cavern. "Mortals have discerned the basic details long ago. Theseus knows nothing that any half-decent storyteller does not already sing of. Still, your argument is not without merit in the general sense. If all mortals were to return to Earth with full knowledge of previous lives, they might do better—or the extra knowledge might help them to do worse.

"Let us put aside that discussion for the moment, however. There are witnesses who wish to speak about Theseus's character."

"I don't recall this being discussed," said Hades. "Who are these witnesses?"

"Unimpeachable ones," said Zeus. "Various members of our own family, in fact."

"You brought other gods here without my consent?" asked Hades, his eyes glowing with wrath that didn't show in his voice. "This is an affront to my power as king of the Underworld."

"It is no such thing," said Zeus. "If you read the agreed-upon rules governing this court, you will see that provision is made for witnesses.

Gods are not excluded from that provision, though they may not venture further into the Underworld without your consent. Under normal circumstances, they would have to venture this far to ask for permission to visit, would they not?"

"My king, there is such a provision in the rules," said Minos.

Much to my surprise, Hades looked at him and scowled. "I must read future agreements even more carefully than I have in the past. Very well, if the witnesses are here, let us see them."

I turned to look myself, and the air behind me wavered for a moment. Then I had to close my eyes against the brightness. Just how many gods had been assembled as witnesses?

"This is unseemly," said Hecate. "This is not Olympus. The gathering of so many gods who are not part of the Underworld order could be disruptive to the proper operation of the place."

"You were not originally an Underworld goddess," said Hermes. "Nor, for that matter, was Persephone. Nor was I an Underworld god. Yet the place has not collapsed after all these centuries of our presence. I venture to guess it will not collapse from a short visit by other gods."

"Proceed!" said Hades, waving his hand impatiently. "Proceed, and let us be done with this!"

A look passed between Hades and Zeus. From where Hecate was standing, she couldn't see it, but I could. I wasn't sure what it meant, for it was brief. But an old memory flashed into my mind, vivid as the day on which it happened. I thought of Pirithous and Caeneus, arguing in front of the centaurs. Though the tension between them was real, the argument had been contrived to fool the centaurs.

More was happening here than I could figure out with certainty. It appeared that the gods could mask their true feelings as easily as mortals could.

Minos squinted at the supernova of witnesses. "I cannot make out who is here."

"If your honor is agreeable, I will call the witnesses," said Zeus.

Minos glanced quickly at his fellow judges, who both nodded. "You may proceed."

What else could he have said? The judges might have theoretical power, but comparing them to Zeus was like comparing ants to elephants. It was hard to imagine they would stand up against Zeus or even Hades if they disagreed with him.

"Athena, my daughter, come forward and give testimony."

"A goddess as friendly to Theseus as Athena is hardly an impartial witness," said Hecate. "If we are to proceed with this fiction of a court, at least it ought to *appear* fair."

"Potential bias of witnesses is not an issue here. Once Athena stands upon the golden part of that stone before the judges, she can only speak the truth," said Zeus. Hades glanced at Hecate, eyes unreadable, then turned his attention to Zeus.

"Perhaps I should make myself more familiar with the procedures to which I agreed," said Hades, eyes fixed unblinkingly upon the king of the gods. Zeus handed him a scroll even longer than the one that had contained all my deeds. Hades gripped the top of it and began to read.

Athena had waited during the brief exchange between Zeus and Hades came forward. Now that it was done, she stepped forward bearing her spear. Her breastplate was decorated with the aegis of Zeus. She looked more prepared for the battlefield than for the courtroom. And a whole army could not have possessed the power she did. Could the rock really compel her to speak the truth as it could a mortal?

"Why does she wear the aegis?" asked Hecate. "Where are the enemies into whom she wishes to strike fear? Is this not an attempt to bias the judges, all sons of Zeus, by reminding them of her connection with Zeus?"

"As if anyone would ever forget that connection," said Hades, looking up for a moment from the scroll. "Proceed, Minos."

The former king of Crete turned to Athena. "We are ready for your testimony, Goddess."

"I have seen much of Theseus's life, and I could speak at length of his heroism. But I will not, for your honors know full well all he has accomplished. Instead, I have come to urge you to consider not only his acts but their context. Though Theseus has erred, sometimes grievously, yet his motives were often purer than his deeds would suggest."

"But should not his deeds speak for themselves?" asked Minos. "Is it not his acts by which we should judge him?"

"But may not the circumstances of those acts alter them?" asked

Athena. "If a man kills another without cause, that is murder. But if that same man kills another to defend himself, the act is no longer murder. What preceded the act changed its nature."

The former king of Crete nodded. "In that sense, you are correct."

"Then let us speak of specifics. Theseus started a needless war with the Amazons, but why did he do it?"

"Because he chose to pursue an Amazon queen for his wife, knowing full well that her people would never accept such a violation of their customs," said Rhadamanthus. "Is that not true, Theseus?"

"It is," I said. "Though I did hope that I could persuade them to make an exception."

"Theseus's guilt makes him less of an advocate for his own cause than he should be," said Athena. "His plan to win Antiope was not just to satisfy his own lust or even to gratify the depths of true love. It was because he wanted a strong partner, a queen who could help Athenian society see that women are as capable as men."

"But are women the equals of men? No kingdom in the mortal world operates on that assumption," said Rhadamanthus.

"Is gender that important, your honor? If so, does that mean the goddesses are inferior to the gods?"

Rhadamanthus had been a brave man in life, but he turned pale under Athena's gaze. "I didn't mean—"

"I know you didn't," said Athena, smiling. "But the thought must then give you pause, for if being female is not a barrier to excellence in the divine world, why should it be in the mortal one?

"But let us put that issue aside for the moment. There is at least one kingdom in which the laws assume the equality, if not the superiority, of women—the Amazon kingdom. It is this very kingdom whose traditions Theseus is accused of violating. But if their traditions are in are some way inferior, then why was it a sin for Theseus to disrespect them?"

"Because the disrespect led to many deaths," said Aeacus.

"That was the choice of the Amazons, though, was it not?" asked Athena. "They chose to pursue Theseus over hundreds of stadia to take back Antiope, who went with him willingly in the first place. If their traditions were not respectable, then the war they fought against Athens was an act of unjustified aggression, and Theseus was simply defending against it. If the defense of one's kingdom is a sin worthy of banning someone from the Elysian Fields, then there will be no kings who will ever reach it from this point on."

"Your arguments are challenging," said Minos. "But it is not our function here to decide whether or not the Amazon way of life is appropriate."

"No, but it is your function to decide whether or not Theseus is worthy of the Elysian Fields. For that purpose, it doesn't matter what you think of the Amazons. If you admire their ideals, then you must admire Theseus's desire to spread the notion of female worth to Athens. If you deplore their ideals, then you cannot blame Theseus for acting against those ideals."

"You have given us much to think about," said Rhadamanthus. "It may be that, at least in this case, Theseus is not to blame."

"Athena is trying to obscure the truth," said Hecate.

"I cannot," replied Athena. "The rock I stand upon forbids it."

"Nonetheless, you have found a way. But even if not, you are more advocate than witness. It is a cardinal principle of Greek justice that a man must plead his own case."

"Hecate, perhaps I am confused," said Hades. "I didn't remember you had been appointed as a judge here."

"I was not, but—"

"The rules are clear," said the king of the Underworld, his voice cold as the far north. He waved the scroll he was holding as if that would enable Hecate to read it. "The mortal who is the subject of this inquiry may speak at the appropriate times. Witnesses may speak when called. The judges may speak. Zeus and I, under whose authority this tribunal operates, may speak. No one else, even a god, may be heard here. If you wish to be a witness, wait your turn."

It was clear from Hecate's expression that she was not used to being forbidden to do anything, even by Hades. Nonetheless, she didn't argue, though she glared at him in a way that would have driven a mortal mad with fear.

Minos glanced uncertainly over at Hades, then back to Athena. "It does appear that there is a fine line between testimony and advocacy. Perhaps testimony should be limited to the facts."

My heart skipped a beat. Yes, I knew I no longer had a living heart, but my spirit felt the same as if it were still enclosed in flesh. I had no idea what else Athena might want to say, much else what the other gods planned to say. If I had to advocate for myself, I wouldn't know how to question the witnesses.

"Are gods not knowledgeable about the human soul?" asked Athena. "And if we are, are we not permitted to share our knowledge with the court?"

"Let us see where the remaining testimony takes us," said Rhadamanthus. "We can always disregard that which seems out of place."

The other two judges nodded, clearly eager to have some plan to avoid ruling on the issue. I would not have wanted to be sitting in one of those chairs. How could mortals, even those given authority by the gods, argue with their own deities?

As if the proceeding wasn't nerve-wracking enough all by itself, I noticed that Hecate had disappeared at some point and began to worry about where she'd gone. She'd shown enough interest in my case to make it unlikely that she no longer cared what was happening.

When Athena finished, Zeus called Hera—a surprise, considering I had never met the queen of the gods.

"Too often, men care little for their wives," said Hera. I gave her credit for not glaring at Zeus while she spoke. "By undermining marriage, they undermine the foundation of society—the family unit. But not so Theseus. Some of his choices might have caused problems. That I will not deny. But he was fiercely loyal to the women he married. Not once during any of his three marriages did he dishonor his marriage bed by committing adultery."

I looked at the judges to see how they were taking Hera's testimony. Rhadamanthus, as long-lived as his brother, had only one wife as far as I knew—Alcmena, mother of Heracles, whom he married after the death of her first husband. He had always been faithful to her. Not so Aeacus, who had only one wife but had children by two other women. And definitely not so Minos, who had children by three women other than his wife. The tales said he would have taken other women to his bed far more times, but Pasiphae used her magic to put a stop to such behavior.

All three of the judges looked serene during Hera's discourse. Of course, Minos remembered his earlier, virtuous self, not the adulterer who seemed ready to break his father's record.

They had a harder time retaining their self-control when Aphrodite came forward and stood upon the rock of truth. It may have been hard for her not to be alluring, but she seemed to be deliberately as charming as possible. If so, no one ventured to rule her out of order.

But what could she have to say in my favor? And, given what she had done to Aegeus and Hippolytus, did I even want her help?

"Honorable judges, I have not always been on good terms with the family of Theseus," she said as if reading my mind. "But Theseus himself I generally had the highest respect for. Though he had reason to dislike me, he never rejected love. Indeed, his life was, in part, a quest for it. And despite all the ill-luck he had in that area, he never once cursed me for it, though I'm sure he wanted to."

That sounded a little like damning with faint praise, but Aphrodite wasn't finished yet.

"He did once call me a liar when I told him how his wife, Phaedra, had an unnatural desire for his son, one that, despite my encouragement, she could have resisted. I cursed him to be in a situation in which he too would feel desires that could lead to disaster, but that he would have a choice, just as Phaedra had. Thus, I hoped to show him the truth of my words."

"The kidnapping of Helen," said Minos. "We see that in the records. It could have led to war quite easily, just as his choice of Antiope did."

"It was worse than that," said Rhadamanthus. "He took Helen without her father's consent or hers. Antiope at least was willing."

"Ah, so it appears," said Aphrodite. "But just knowing the facts, as Athena has pointed out to you, is not enough. You must know why he did what he did. I was watching him during that time, and, much to my surprise, he made the right choice."

"Kidnapping Helen was the right choice?" asked Aeacus. "How could that be true?"

"He decided not to abduct Helen after all. He told Pirithous—"

"Ah, yes, that one!" muttered Hades, scowling as I had never seen him do.

"He told Pirithous he would not go along with the abduction. But then Pirithous forced his hand. You see, the Lapith king had tricked Theseus into an oath that obligated each of them to help the other take a daughter of Zeus in marriage."

"To the oath, I bear witness it was sworn," said Zeus. "The records will include it, also."

"But the situation was even more complicated than that," said Aphrodite. "Theseus had reason to question the soundness of Pirithous's mind. Not only was the Athenian king reluctant to break a solemn oath, but with everyone else magically asleep in Tyndareus's palace, even if Theseus refused to help, Pirithous could have abducted Helen on his own. The only way to stop him might have been to kill him. Can we be surprised that he declined the double sin of oath-breaking and the murder of a friend?

"I have never seen a mortal do so well at making the best of a bad situation," the goddess continued. "Yes, he took Helen—because he had no choice. But he pledged to her never to force her into his bed or into marriage. He even promised to return her to her father if, after a short time, she continued to refuse his affections. Has any abductor in the history of the world ever behaved in such a fashion? He treated Helen so well that I think she might have grown to love him in time, despite all her protestations—and that would have been for the best."

"Without the consent of her father?" asked Aeacus.

"Despite Tyndareus's feelings and the...irregular way in which Theseus handled the situation, I believe he would have been ruled by his daughter's wish. I am not prophetic in the way Zeus and Apollo are, but I have a feeling for the future of romances. I sense a darkness in Helen's future, a great evil that may prove to be far worse than a potential war between Athens and Sparta, though I do not know the details. Had Helen and Theseus married—and I believe that such an outcome might have come to pass—she and countless others would have been spared much pain."

"But Theseus had no way of knowing that," said Minos.

"True, but it was his kindness toward Helen that made such a favorable outcome possible. In fact, I will go so far as to say it might have been likely, had Pirithous, once again holding Theseus to the oath,

435

not dragged him off to the Underworld to seek the hand of Persephone."

For the first time since I learned of Aphrodite's curse on Aegeus, I realized I had only been seeing part of her. In truth, she was as complex as love itself. Like lust, she could be destructive. Like infatuation, she could be fickle. But like true love, she could create, just as it was said that primal Eros began the process of creating the whole world. She could draw men and women together, making them more than they would ever have been singly. She could bring joy to the present and hope for the future. How had I been so blind to all of this before?

"If we accept the testimony we have heard so far, there are two major sins for which no one has yet accounted," said Minos. "The effort to steal the lawful wife of Hades is the most serious of the two."

A chill ran up my spine. The other sin must be my murder of Hippolytus. Not so long ago, I had learned that the consequences of my action had been reversed by the gods, but I could not have known that. At the time I killed my own son, I thought I was consigning him to the Underworld. If, as Athena had argued, the context was important, it would give me no comfort for the slaying of Hippolytus. I would be barred from the Elysian Fields for sure—and richly deserve it.

"Your honors, I can speak to that issue," said Persephone, emerging from the glowing throng of gods.

"As can I," said Hades. I could hardly have been more surprised if Hecate herself had stood upon the rock of truth in my defense.

Aphrodite yielded her place to the king and queen of the Underworld, who stood side by side upon the rock.

"My king, did you yourself not condemn the actions of Theseus in this matter?" asked Minos. "Did you not imprison him and Pirithous alike? Why now do you give testimony in Theseus's favor?"

"Most men are much alike to me," said Hades. "And those whose spectacular sins make them stand out are far too willing to find excuses for their actions.

"Theseus, however, is not a maker of excuses. He accepted my judgment with uncommon humility. It was for that reason that I allowed Heracles to try to free him. There is no question he sinned—"

"But his sin lay in honoring an oath and in trying to protect a

436

friend," said Persephone. "That is why I was so willing to heal him after Heracles rescued him from the chair. But what most amazed me about Theseus was that, once freed, he almost didn't leave because he didn't wish to condemn his friend to a solitary existence. How many mortals would have been willing to make such a sacrifice?"

"Very few, from what I've seen," said Hades. "Though seeking to marry an already wed goddess is an extreme example of hubris, the sin was Pirithous's. Theseus, as my queen has pointed out, was trying to do what he could to protect the Lapith king from the consequences of his own foolishness."

"It appears what we at first thought was a grave sin may be much less grave," said Rhadamanthus. "But there is yet one sin for which no explanation has been offered—Theseus's misuse of a wish given to him by Poseidon to murder the king's own son. I cannot imagine what explanation could possibly wash away that sin."

Neither could I. Despite being comforted by Hippolytus himself, I continue to brood over what I had done. I wished he was at my side to comfort me again. He might be better off than he would have been if I hadn't killed him, but that good fortune was not my doing. Was I truly worthy of the Elysian Fields, or was I fit for the Place of Punishment and nowhere else?

VERDICT

"The witnesses have not all testified yet," said Hades. "Some, it appears, will not be necessary, but there is one you must hear." He and Persephone stepped out of the way—for Hippolytus, the very person I had just wished to see. For some reason, it never occurred to me he would be among the gods who testified on my behalf. It's hard to adjust to one's son being a god in the first place.

Hippolytus looked as I remembered—like his human self, only more radiant. Despite the relative newness of his divinity, he seemed calm even though surrounded by half of Olympus and facing three intimidating-looking judges.

"Your honors, it is true that my father wished for me to die. He has never denied that. But it is important to keep the facts in mind. He believed that I had raped his wife, my stepmother. He had the evidence of her suicide and a letter in her own hand as evidence of my crime. Men have been executed for less—and people have called it just."

"But Theseus did not investigate. He simply called the power of Poseidon down on you," said Aeacus.

"He acted rashly, but understandably. Normally, the victim in such a case cannot speak on his own behalf. I am fortunate to be able to do so. I will tell you now what I told him some time ago—I forgive him. With all my heart, I forgive him. Is it not true that in most Greek cities, a victim has the right to excuse the offender? If so, then I should be able to exercise that right here."

Poseidon, dripping saltwater as if he had just risen from the sea, came forward and stood beside his grandson. "I, too, forgive the murder of my grandson. I was unable to cleanse Theseus of the blood guilt myself, so I sent Palaemon to do it. He acted in my name and under my authority. A man cleansed of blood guilt by a king—let alone a god— may not be prosecuted unless it is by the family of the victim seeking vengeance. But who among the family of Hippolytus seeks vengeance? Not a soul. Could they all be present, they would all stand with him in forgiving Theseus.

"Can there be a sin when the sinner is repentant and has been forgiven by gods and mortals alike? I say there cannot be."

"Judges, what say you?" asked Minos. "Have the charges against Theseus been adequately refuted? And, if they have, do his heroic acts justify allowing him entry to the Elysian Fields?"

"I say—" began Aeacus.

"Wait!" yelled a familiar voice from some distance away. "There are more witnesses desiring to be heard."

Hecate stepped forward, her expression as black as her gown. Behind her stood a mob of ghosts straight from the Fields of Asphodel nearby.

"What is the meaning of this?" asked Hades, his normally unfeeling façade cracking enough to show the raging anger beneath. "Why did you bring the souls of the dead here without my permission?"

Hecate squinted at him as if she had never seen him before. "You have never objected when I borrowed a few dead for my purposes. Why would you object now?"

"If they came from the Fields of Asphodel, as it seems they must have, judging by their faded appearances, what testimony could they have to offer? Their memories must surely be as faint as their physical presence." Hades stepped forward, as if to block the ghosts from the rock of truth.

"Look at them closely, lord of the Underworld," said Hecate. "Each has had a little water from the well of Mnemosyne. Their memories are restored now."

It was hard for me to see from where I was standing, but they did look more alert than I would have expected.

"What kind of testimony do they wish to give?" asked Minos.

"These are the many people who died because of Theseus," said Hecate. "They have a right to be heard."

Looking more closely, I could see Phaedra standing near the front of the line. She didn't look in my direction. But Molpadia, standing right behind her, did. Her face was twisted by hatred.

"The rules of this court do not allow for the testimony of witnesses from among the dead," said Hades.

"But do they exclude such testimony?" asked Hecate. "Unless I am mistaken, the answer to that question is no." Then she pointed to Hippolytus. "And if someone who, by an accident of fate, is now a god, but was dead before that, is allowed to testify, then on what principle should the testimony of the other dead be excluded? Judges, what say you?"

"On principle, such testimony could be allowed," said Zeus before the judges had a chance to respond. "However, before they do, I think it only fitting that you, Hecate, stand upon the rock of truth and tell us all for what reason you oppose the admission of Theseus to the Elysian Fields. Your reasons must be weighty to cause you to go to so much trouble."

"My king, my testimony would serve no purpose," said Hecate. "It is these individuals who have been wronged by Theseus. It is they who should be heard."

"And have you not been wronged by Theseus as well?" asked Zeus. He turned to Hades. "Did I not hear something about Theseus opposing Hecate's witches—and more than once?"

Hades nodded. "You did indeed, and I think it would be most... enlightening for Hecate to reveal why it is that witches were so active in Thessaly. What was it that you wanted to accomplish there, I wonder?"

More than once, I had wondered why Zeus and Hades had gone to so much trouble to create a tribunal ultimately dependent on them if their only purpose had been to allow me into the Elysian fields, a function the gods themselves had performed for centuries. Much else was going on beneath the surface of this inquiry.

Hades met my eyes at that moment, and I thought he might have winked at me. But perhaps I just imagined it. It had been so fast, and it was a gesture so unlike Hades.

"We can discuss the witches after the dead have testified," said Hecate.

"Perhaps it would make more sense to hear from all interested gods first, and then from the dead," said Minos. "That seems a more organized way to proceed."

"And would you keep even your own daughter waiting?" asked Hecate. Phaedra stepped forward so that Minos could see her clearly. She had no magic of her own, yet I sensed magic about her. The gods nearest her tensed. They could feel it, too.

"My...daughter?" said Minos, as if he had never heard the word before. Of course, he had only the memories of the young, upright Minos. Phaedra had been born after that.

A wave of magic splashed from Phaedra to Minos before even Zeus could intervene. Suddenly, the judge looked older, and his eyes widened in recognition.

Whatever Zeus and Hades had done to him to repress his memories, Hecate had used her own magic, coupled with the waters of Mnemosyne, to reverse it.

Minos was once more the man who craved revenge against me.

"What have you done?" roared Zeus. The sound of thunder echoed throughout the Underworld, and the walls shook.

Hecate looked confused. "I noticed that Minos was having memory problems of some sort. Surely, you didn't mean for him to be so... reduced when you sat him upon a judge's chair. All I did was restore him to normal."

"I call Phaedra as the next witness," said Minos, glaring at me as if I had ruined his life—which, from his point of view, I probably had.

"Remember our agreement," said Zeus.

"Was there some prior understanding between Zeus and the presiding judge?" asked Hecate in a remarkably good imitation of innocence. "Does not that invalidate these proceedings?"

"He is bound only to rule justly," said Zeus. "He is not bound to reach a particular verdict in the case of Theseus."

"No, I am not," said Minos. "Nor have I ever been. But Hecate makes a good point that the people Theseus has harmed deserve to be heard. Do you deny my fellow judges and me the right to hear witnesses?"

I doubted Zeus was often at a loss for words, but he hesitated a little before speaking. "You may call whom you wish. Just make sure that you do not allow Hecate to manipulate the proceedings."

"I begin to suspect that it is you who wish to manipulate the proceedings," said Hecate. "Perhaps after Phaedra, you yourself should stand upon the rock of truth and tell us to what end you manipulate them."

"It is not for you to question me," said Zeus. His voice was loud enough to crack the cavern ceiling above our heads.

"It is just that you have at times offered testimony from the side-lines," said Hecate. "Confirming that Theseus was under oath, for example. If this is, in truth, an attempt to do justice to all after death, then it must have consistent rules, correct? There cannot be one rule for you and one for all others."

"You are right," said Zeus with surprising mildness. "The process is new, and, though I helped write the rules, I sometimes forget that they are there.

"However, you also have offered testimony from the sidelines." He held out a hand to her. "Come, Hecate, powerful among goddesses. Come, take my hand, and stand by my side on the rock of truth. Together, we will explain ourselves."

I couldn't see all the gods, but the ones I could see appeared to be readying for battle. Athena's spear flashed even in the dim light. So did Poseidon's trident and Hades's bident, both capable of generating massive earthquakes. In the case of Hades's weapon, it was said it could also kill with a single touch, though probably a god would only be harmed.

Hecate took a step back. "Forgive me, my king, for going beyond the bounds of propriety. I withdraw my accusation of you."

It must have been clear even to the corrupted Minos that, whatever else Hecate might have wanted, she profoundly *didn't want* to stand on the rock of truth.

"And do you also withdraw your request to have all these ghosts testify?"

"I do," said Hecate in a tone reminiscent of someone trying to draw a knife out of her own flesh without the aid of a surgeon.

"Nonetheless, I wish to hear them," said Minos.

Zeus stared at Minos, and one of the king of the gods' hands twitched as if it were eager for a thunderbolt. "It is your right…but tread carefully."

"Phaedra, tell me how you came to be married to Theseus."

"Your son and heir, Deucalion, arranged the match."

Minos's eyes narrowed. "Much has been made here of how great a husband Theseus was. Did he ask your consent, or did he just take you as he would have property?"

"He ascertained that I desired the marriage with all my heart."

Minos looked visibly displeased with the answer. He opened his mouth to ask another question, but Phaedra started talking before he could.

"Hecate asked me to come, but I am not a witness against Theseus. Far from it, I can testify that he was always a loving husband and father —to my sons just as much as to Hippolytus. If he erred in any way with me, it was believing my posthumous denunciation of Hippolytus. If I had the power, I would take back those words, but I cannot. The Place of Punishment would have been a fitting place for me, and but for the mercy of Zeus, that is where I would be. I am more responsible for the death of the excellent Hippolytus than Theseus, even if his sin were to be multiplied by a thousand times."

Hecate must have needed Phaedra for the memory magic she worked on Minos. It was clear she hadn't bothered to check Phaedra's testimony in advance. The goddess's face was white as bone now, an even sharper contrast with her black robes than normal.

However, Minos was not to be so easily deterred. He called witness after witness. Molpadia spoke at length on how I had undermined the whole Amazon way of life, as did some of the other women who died in the Attic War. Minos looked almost gleeful, but I was more worried about the other judges. Aeacus and Rhadamanthus looked more and more doubtful as ghost after ghost detailed the wrongs I had done to them in exhaustive detail. As the proceedings continued, the color returned to Hecate's cheeks.

Both Zeus and Hades disappeared for a while. I hoped they were finding some way to defeat Hecate's strategy, though I wasn't sure how they could. What man, denounced by the ghosts of all his enemies, wouldn't sound terrible? Listening to the testimony renewed my own feelings of guilt.

Hecate had been clever enough to find a selection of the Lapith dead, men who blamed me for their king's folly. Though what they spoke was not the truth, they believed what they said, and consequently, the rock of truth did not compel them to speak differently. Together, they painted a damning picture of me as an overindulgent friend who led their king astray.

But were their words altogether false? Perhaps if I had turned down Pirithous's invitations, if I had refused his suggestions more often, some of the ghosts now haunting me would not be dead. Perhaps Pirithous himself would not be a prisoner in the Underworld.

"These witnesses have given us much to think about," said Rhadamanthus. His face was grim, and he didn't look in my direction.

"Agreed," said Aeacus. Their terseness, so different from their earlier reactions, chilled me. But I couldn't complain, no matter what their verdict was.

"There are two more witnesses to be heard," said Zeus, returning at last with Dionysus and Ariadne.

I hadn't seen Ariadne since I took the Athenian crown. Naturally, as a goddess, she was as beautiful as ever. She smiled at me as she stepped toward the rock of truth. So did Dionysus—and I was relieved to see that his smile betrayed no hint of insanity.

Minos looked annoyed. "This has already been a lengthy proceeding. What have these two to say that has not already been said?"

"Forgive me, son," said Zeus. "But you seemed so interested in seeing Phaedra that I would have expected you to be happier to see your elder daughter."

Minos made a point of not looking at Ariadne. He had not forgotten her long-ago betrayal.

Hecate's eyes widened. "No, this is a—"

Ariadne, too, had been wrapped in strange magic. I guessed some combination of the waters of Lethe with a spell of Hermes, who had taught Hecate underworld magic in the first place. Just as a wave of magic had flowed from Phaedra, so now one flowed from Ariadne. It washed over Minos, who looked suddenly younger and more confused.

"My daughter?" he asked, an eerie echo of what he had said about Phaedra.

"You will not remember me," said Ariadne. "I was born after the 'better self' that you now are had started to fade. Nonetheless, I love you and hope that you are proud of me, for I have, as you can see, become a goddess."

"No parent could want more than that for a daughter," said Minos, smiling uncertainly.

"The presiding judge is under an enchantment," said Hecate. "The whole proceedings are corrupted."

"The presiding judge has been restored to a pristine state, unbiased against Theseus," said Zeus. "Come and stand with me on the rock of truth, and we can both explain what we have done to Minos—and why."

"I withdraw my objection," said Hecate. I lost track of her in the shadows, though I was sure the other gods could still see her.

"Uh, daughter, what is your testimony?"

"I could reiterate what a wonderful man Theseus is, but it is my husband, Dionysus, who has something new to add."

"In your records, you can doubtless see that Theseus was murdered," said Dionysus.

"Yes, by Lycomedes," said Aeacus. "But that is a mark against him, not for Theseus."

"But what if I were to tell you Theseus died as a martyr?" asked Dionysus. "Though not normally a prophet, he sensed a very, very small part of destiny shortly before he died. Despite an offer to live to a happy old age with his son and family, he went to Skyros on purpose, knowing he would die there. He also knew that, if he did not, the pattern of fate would be badly disrupted."

"Disrupted how?" asked Rhadamanthus.

"He did not know, and that is the wonder of it—he sacrificed himself without even knowing who or what his death might save."

"There is nobility in that," said Aeacus. "I don't think any of us would deny it. But if we do not know what his sacrifice saved, it is hard to judge its merits."

"The secret of that I do not know," said Dionysus. "However, Zeus has seen the truth of it. He told me that Lycomedes had learned from an oracle that a hero would one day come to Skyros and cause him much grief. The king, determined to avoid his fate as mortals so often are, resolved to kill the first hero who set foot on the island. Theseus, in his willingness to create a better future, became the first hero to visit the island. But he was not the hero referred to by the prophecy."

"Who was that hero?" asked Aeacus.

"He is not a hero yet. He is not even born yet, though he will be soon enough. He is a descendant of yours, Aeacus. His name will be Achilles."

Aeacus looked shocked. "You…you are sure of this?"

"He is sure of nothing," said Hecate. "He repeats what Zeus has told him. Let Zeus testify to the truth of it."

"If you will stand with me on the stone of truth," said Zeus, once again extending a hand to her. "But if you do not reveal why you so hate Theseus, then I see no need to reveal my reasons for wanting him placed in Elysium."

Hecate looked back and forth between Zeus and me. To my surprise, she took a step toward the stone of truth…then another…and another. She moved slowly but deliberately.

My heart was beating too fast. She must have figured out how to trick the stone. How else would she dare to approach it? But if she could trick it, why approach it with such a so slowly, as if she were still reluctant?

I looked in the direction of Zeus and Hades. Zeus looked surprised but also pleased. Hades wore his usual, unemotional expression. But did his mouth turn just a little upward in the slightest smile I had ever seen? Perhaps.

As Hecate continued her painfully slow walk toward the stone, I could feel her gathering power. Though children of gods were evidently more sensitive to such things than average mortals, I was not sensitive enough to tell what she was doing, just that she had enough magic enveloping her to dwarf even what the witches of Larissa had commanded when they drew down the moon.

The gasps from the nearby gods suggested that they had noticed what Hecate was doing. How could they not? But their inaction suggested they had no more idea what she was doing than I did.

Shadows spun a web around her, obscuring her from view. When they parted, Hecate stood on the stone of truth. She looked calm, as if she had never tried to avoid standing there. But magic crackled around her, intense as an electrical storm but dark as night, though it did not prevent me from seeing her any longer. What was its purpose?

"I am ready to testify against Theseus," she said to the judges, who looked every bit as puzzled as I felt.

"Before you do that, you must stand on the actual stone, not hover above it," said Zeus. He sounded calm, but his hand rested upon a thunderbolt.

Hecate looked back at him, painted across her face an expression as innocent as Hippolytus had in life. "What do you mean?"

"Hecate, you are taller now," said Zeus.

"I changed my form a bit. What of it?"

"It is not your form we see, but an illusion," said Hades, pointing his bident in her direction.

She *did* look taller, but I noticed something even more suspicious. I could not see the glow of truth beneath her feet.

"There is no illusion here," said Hecate. "You are just trying to confuse the judges. I stand upon the stone of truth. No one can deny that."

"You stand cloaked in the power of Apate, night-born Deceit herself," Hades replied. "The others may not be able to see it, but you can't fool me with any power that makes its home in the Underworld, even an elder one. Dispel the illusion!"

"There is no illusion. Will you allow me to speak, or will you prove this court is a fraud by refusing me."

Hades nodded. In the blink of an eye, he and his brothers formed a circle around Hecate. Bident, trident, and thunderbolt were all aimed at her heart.

"Triple power against the triple goddess," said Hades. This time, his

447

smile was big enough that I could not be imagining it, though it was still cold. "Remove the illusion, or we will remove it for you."

"Would you do violence upon me to keep me silent?" asked Hecate. Looking around, she said, "I know most gods spurn me, but surely, I have a few friends left among you who will come to my aid."

I squinted against the glow and looked at the gods as closely as I could. Some looked confused, but as far as I could tell, only a goddess who looked like an older Persephone stepped forward. She must have been Demeter, whom Hecate had aided in the search for Persephone.

"Brothers, lay not one hand upon her," said the goddess of the harvest. "She is no felon and should not be treated like one."

"We do not need to lay any hands upon her," said Hades. "We don't even need to strip away the illusion surrounding her person. We need only do this."

He nodded again, and Hermes and Apollo stood before the judges. The messenger's caduceus flared, reinforced by the golden light of truth from Apollo's hands. Their power was answered by a burst of light from the stone of truth—which was at least two feet away from the spot where Hecate was standing. No, not standing—hovering. The glow from the stone also revealed that she was not actually touching the ground but floating a short distance above it, just in case.

"Behold, Hecate has attempted to deceive this court," said Zeus.

"I did no such thing," said Hecate, looking at Zeus as if she would kill him. "I intend to tell the truth. But it ill-befits my dignity as a goddess to be *compelled* to do so.

"Enough!" said Zeus. "My brothers and I order you to depart from this place, silently and with no further attempt at magic.

Hecate, so powerful moments before, looked both smaller and weaker. Her anger hadn't weakened, though, nor had her determination. She looked to Demeter, and my eyes followed her gaze. But the nature goddess, mouth set in a hard line, shook her head. Scowling, Hecate vanished into the shadows.

Zeus turned back to the judges, who were still staring in the direction in which Hecate had just disappeared. "Pardon the goddess's unseemly interruption. But she has not delayed us too much, and if it pleases the court, I will deliver my confirmation of what Dionysus has said."

Minos stopped studying the shadows and looked at Zeus. "Please come forward and bear witness, as you have said."

Hades, Poseidon, Hermes, and Apollo all stepped out of the way. Zeus put both feet upon the stone of truth that Hecate had been so desperate to avoid. "What I told Dionysus is correct. A time will come when Thetis, mother of Achilles, will wish to hide him on Skyros. As fate is now woven, Lycomedes will do the goddess this favor and conceal the boy she wants to protect in disguise among his own daughters. By the time he discovers who Achilles really is, he will not be able to kill him without risking the wrath of Thetis. But had Theseus not sacrificed himself, Lycomedes, still looking for the hero who would bring him much grief, would have been warier. He would have figured out that Achilles was the son of Thetis and therefore, a probable hero. He would have killed Achilles soon after the boy arrived but made the deed look like an accident. Thetis would have seen through the deception and destroyed the king, but that would not have brought Achilles back.

"The loss of Achilles would have been more than the loss of one hero. A great war that is to come would have become even more catastrophic than it must already be. Even worse, Achilles would never father a line that is destined to produce a hero so great that he will unite the Greeks and conquer their greatest enemy at the time, a mighty empire created by the Persians.

"Every word of this is true, as the stone bears witness."

Zeus stepped down and smiled in the direction Hecate had left. I imagined her watching from the shadows, fists clenched but able to do nothing.

Minos looked to his right and to his left. His colleagues both nodded vigorously.

"It appears that we have reached an agreement. Theseus has erred, as men do, as even the gods do, for error is a part of life. Yet his virtuous acts far outweigh his sins. We hereby grant him a place in Elysium."

EPILOGUE: DAWN

MILTIADES STARED AT THESEUS. There was no doubt that it was the ancient king of Athens who sat next to him and who had told him a tale that filled his heart with hope and wonder.

"When you first appeared, you suggested that perhaps you were here to atone for some of the wrongs you committed in life. You are too humble, for it seems the gods themselves have placed the seal of their approval upon your deeds."

Theseus smiled, but just barely. "I would like to think so, but even after so many centuries, I cannot be certain. You must surely have perceived that some of the gods used my trial as a way to trap Hecate, who was eager to punish me for my interference. Just as they hoped, she made her evil plain enough that even her allies would not be able to excuse it. I have a hard time imagining that they would have emptied the halls of Olympus to support me if they had no other purpose in mind."

"Athena would have come," said Miltiades. "And Poseidon. Perhaps others would have come as well. I think you do not appreciate yourself enough."

"I appreciate the number of times I changed the course of destiny for the worse," said Theseus. "The Amazons are no more. I helped start their decline. And the Lapiths also have vanished forever."

"That was surely more the fault of Pirithous than yours. And what about the great war Zeus spoke of. That must have been the Trojan War, right?"

Theseus nodded. "You know the story well enough that there is no need for me to explain it. It is the conflict Aphrodite caught a glimpse of and thought that my marriage to Helen might avert. And it is definitely the great war that Zeus spoke of at my trial."

"The king of the gods himself testified that it would have been far worse without Achilles…without your sacrifice."

"It was certainly terrible enough, even with my sacrifice. Eris, they say, motivated it out of anger over not being invited to the wedding of Peleus and Thetis, parents of Achilles. But that Hecate had a hand in it, I have little doubt. The gods, knowing what she was plotting thanks to that one indiscreet conversation with me and motivated further by her attempted perjury, united to keep her restrained. So she worked in the shadows to tear apart that unity, to get the gods to take sides in the war between the Trojans and the Greeks.

"If you think about it, it would have taken both an elder power like Eris and a goddess with authority in every realm like Hecate to bring the other gods so near to anarchy. How else could anyone explain why goddesses as powerful as Hera, Athena, and Aphrodite should lose their sanity over something as frivolous as a beauty contest? In truth, it's hard to imagine Athena even entering such a thing. Yet they did, and all three tried to bribe Paris, the human judge Zeus appointed to keep himself out of the fray. That was bad enough. But then, for Hera and Athena to be so angry that Paris had chosen Aphrodite as the most beautiful that they swore vengeance not only against Paris but against the city of Troy as well—a city for which Athena was one of the patrons? Nothing short of insanity can explain that.

And what about Aphrodite? She had foreseen a dark fate hovering over Helen and had tried to avert it. Yet she didn't hesitate to bribe Paris with the love of Helen, even though she knew Helen was already married. Paris had a wife as well, whose heart was broken by his betrayal. Even worse, Aphrodite knew perfectly well that in order to choose a husband for Helen without risking retaliation from the other suitors, Tyndareus had made all of them swear an oath to defend the rights of the chosen one. That gave Menelaus, the man Tyndareus selected, the ability to demand the support of all the Greek kings when Paris took Helen away with him. By encouraging that relationship, Aphrodite made massive bloodshed inevitable. So many men died...so many heroes, some of them children of gods. Even Aphrodite's lover, Ares, the most bloodthirsty of gods, was moved to tears by the death of one of his sons. Yet Aphrodite, who had always before brought out the more peaceful side of Ares, stirred up the worst war the Greeks had ever known.

"The gods have their flaws. Even they would admit that now. But it was so out of character for those goddesses—and so out of character for the other gods not to realize what was afoot—that it seems as if they were all wrapped in some kind of mental fog.

"Nor did the carnage begin and end with mortals. When god fights god in battle, it is a dark day indeed. Such conflicts might have split the gods irrevocably. Caught in a civil war among gods, how could humanity have survived?"

"But it didn't come to that...because you changed the destiny of Achilles, preserved his life, and somehow, that changed everything. What other man can say that?"

"You have a persuasive tongue," said Theseus. "Though I wish the war could have been avoided altogether—as several times it nearly was—yet at least peace came eventually. With it came a feeling in my heart that maybe, just maybe, I really had made the world a better place. Certainly, subsequent events brought me comfort, little as I might have deserved it.

"Demophon and Acamas, my two sons by Phaedra, fought bravely at Troy. Once the war ended, they made arrangements to take Aethra back with them to Athens. Helen, whom she had served well all those years, was happy to let her return home. Demophon became king of Athens and ruled well, just as I would have hoped.

"In the Elysian Fields, Aegeus was waiting there to greet me, just as Athena had promised long ago. I was a little more surprised when I was reunited with Antiope, whom Artemis had sponsored for a place there long before Zeus and Hades created a tribunal for that purpose. We live there as husband and wife. Visits by gods are very restricted in Elysium, but Hippolytus, because he started out as a mortal, can visit more often. He comes as often as he can, and together we are the family we would have been in the first place, if only the world were a perfect place."

"That family grew even further when the long-suffering Aethra finally joined us. Not long after, Bellerophon, fresh from a redemptive reincarnation, was united with her at long last. Over the years, the worthiest among our descendants joined us as well."

"What of Pirithous?"

Theseus smiled. "Persephone kept her word, though it took years— I'm not sure exactly how many. But eventually, I was reunited with my friend. By that time, the judges had addressed some of the backlog accumulated before they took office, and Hippodamia was there as well. Even Polypoetes was there. Having lived free from the manipulation of Hecate and her witches, he became a good king to the Lapiths and fought with distinction at Troy. Unfortunately, when he died, Cerberus's tooth was misplaced, and the Lapiths entered their final decline."

"And what of Hecate?" asked Miltiades.

"She schemes even to this day, but as long as other gods keep an eye on her, she can accomplish little. The son of Zeus who is destined to become the next king of the gods has yet to be born, so that elaborate plan of hers has so far come to nothing.

"From what I understand, her witches still exist, but Zeus has gradually put more and more restrictions on how much direct help the gods can give mortals. Thus, the magic she bestows on them is far weaker than what it once was, and despite all the goddess's schemes, they are confined mostly to rural Thessaly. Most cities ban them now, even there, though they are careful not to ban the worship of Hecate."

"Is that why one hears so little of relationships between gods and mortals these days?" asked Miltiades.

Theseus nodded. "The gods have not lost interest in mortal affairs, but they intervene much more subtly than was the case in my time. Gods seldom take mortals to their beds and produce human children. Nor do they become personal tutors, as Apollo used to sometimes teach music, Athena weaving, and so on. Even the hunting parties of Artemis are no more. It hurts my heart to see the divine presence fading away.

And yet perhaps it is for the best. A woman like my mother will never again be forced to be the mate of a god, after all. And Pirithous, for all his faults, showed that one didn't need to be the son of Zeus to perform like the son of Zeus. I would like to think his example might have been in the mind of Zeus when he urged the gods to pull back. How else would one ever know for sure what greatness mortals could achieve on their own?"

"What of the prophecy about a descendant of Achilles who will one day unite the Greeks and conquer the Persians?"

"That has not yet come to pass, as you well know," said Theseus. "But I have faith in Zeus that it will."

Theseus looked at the tent flap. "Dawn is breaking. So, knowing what you know, will you let me lead the troops into battle?"

"It would be our honor to be led by you...my king." Athens was done with kings by then, But Miltiades didn't think it would hurt anything to acknowledge Theseus by his ancient title.

"Well then, let's get to it," said Theseus, rising. Against the sunlight, his glow was not as obvious, but he was still translucent. Miltiades didn't think the troops would mind.

* * *

In 490 BCE, the Athenians and Plataeans defeated a numerically superior Persian force at Marathon. Much later, Plutarch wrote that the victorious Greeks had been led into battle by a phantom of Theseus, dressed in full battle gear. The victory improved Greek morale enough to enable the Greeks to drive the Persians back, both in this invasion and a subsequent one.

In 329 BCE, the armies of Alexander the Great crushed the last Persian resistance. Through his mother, Olympias, Alexander claimed descent from Achilles. More subtly, he sometimes implied that his father was Zeus, though he never repudiated his generally acknowledged father, Philip II, through whom he claimed the Macedonian throne. In any case, he died six years after assuming control of the Persian Empire, in 323 BCE. He had been fond of pointing out similarities between his life and that of Achilles, but he was not expecting to die young—just as Achilles had.

AFTERWORD

ADAPTING Greek myths into novels for modern readers is always challenging. The original sources, both Greek and Roman, were written over several centuries by many different people for a variety of different audiences and purposes. The resulting body of literature, though often beautiful, is also inconsistent, sometimes downright contradictory.

The situation is complicated by the loss of many of the early stories. By one estimate, only about ten percent of ancient Greek literature has survived. Some of the stories referred to in other texts have vanished completely. Others exist only in summary form. The result is the surviving works often assume knowledge that we, as modern readers, no longer possess and present some myths in such a compressed form that they are difficult to appreciate fully.

A further complication is that ancient Greek and Roman values were in some ways far different from our own. Particularly noticeable is the tendency to treat women as property, to accept slavery, and to allow for a far broader range of justifications for taking human life.

Consequently, while mythology textbooks designed for scholarly use have the duty to present the myths exactly as they were, warts and all, novelists may well take a different path, as I did in *Fateful Pathways*.

First, I tried to work out the inconsistencies among the various versions of the Theseus story, much as the ancient mythographers tried to do. My basic technique was to select details from the different versions that created a coherent narrative. For instance, the tradition I followed made Theseus much younger than Heracles, but there is another tradition that makes them almost the same age, adding Theseus to the heroes who sailed with the Argo and fought the Calydonian Boar. The version with the older Theseus forces his supposed coming of age to occur after he'd already performed a huge number of heroic feats, making his need to prove himself by fighting isthmian bandits harder to understand. That's just one of numerous points at which the details are inconsistent and needed to be reconciled.

Second, I tried to make the material relatable to a modern audience. I did this by honoring the basic premise, that Theseus is a hero, and presenting him in a way that would make him heroic by modern standards, though still having flaws, just as we all do. For example, that was one reason I selected the version of the story in which Dionysus takes Ariadne from Theseus rather than the one in which Theseus abandons her on the beach at Naxos for no particular reason. That's also why I found honorable motives for some of his actions, such as the abduction of Helen, which would be hard for a modern audience to accept at face value. (Ancient literature often presents action without really discussing motivation. Fleshing out those details is part of the transformation from ancient myth to modern novel.)

In the process of reconciling contradictions and adapting to a different audience, I incorporated some Greek ideas that didn't develop until long after most of the Theseus stories were first written. Students of mythology will notice that Hecate, who is regarded as a benevolent goddess by early Greek writers such as Hesiod, is presented here in the darker way she often appears in much later literature. The Thessalian witches are also a staple in later Greek literature but not part of the original Theseus story. Similarly, Orphism, which included the idea of reincarnation and a reborn Dionysus as a spiritual focus, doesn't appear in any of the ancient stories about Theseus.

As far as Hecate and the witches are concerned, Medea, undeniably a witch and a priestess of Hecate, *is* part of Theseus's story. Bringing Medea back into the story a little later makes more sense than having her, after wreaking havoc throughout Greece, go peacefully back to Colchis to reconcile with her father, who in the most common version of the story, forgives her for betraying him and butchering her brother. Bringing in Hecate and her witches is a natural complement to Medea's presence as an antagonist, and it also serves as an explanation for some of Pirithous's excesses. Like Theseus, he was regarded as a hero by the Athenians, but from a modern standpoint, making Pirithous a hero would require some explanation for his erratic behavior. Divine and sometimes magical manipulation is part of the ancient Greek tradition in general, and it seemed as good an explanation as any.

Reincarnation served the purpose of reconciling some details, such as the problems with Ariadne's chronology and the seemingly unmotivated insistence by Dionysus on having Ariadne for himself. It also provided a way of explaining the gradually changing nature of the Underworld. No ancient Greek author that I've read ever exactly said that the Underworld changed over time, but the fact that three sons of Zeus, who lived long after people had started going to the Underworld and yet were its judges, demonstrated that some aspects of the place must have been changeable. The changes I suggest in *Fateful Pathways* approximately reflect the way the Greek view of the afterlife changed over time.

You'll notice that there is a pattern here. Even when I deviated from the way in which the original writers told the story, I tried to draw, when possible, on ancient Greek ideas documented elsewhere. For instance, Aegeus did have a conflict with Aphrodite, but no surviving myth says she prevented him from having children. However, there was obviously some problem, and Aphrodite did prevent the much more evil Glaucus from having children, so I took advantage of that precedent.

I also took advantage of hints in the original literature. For instance, Aethra obviously isn't portrayed in ancient myths as the feisty feminist who appears in this novel. However, she does dedicate a temple to Deceitful Athena, which suggests some degree of attitude. And Aethra would certainly have had reason to fight for consideration for women if such a thing had been possible in her society.

Other elements are drawn more purely from my imagination, though I tried in such cases to use them to create a consistent picture to which a modern reader might more easily relate.

There is no evidence in the original myths that children of gods could necessarily sense each other, though such evidence of divine kinship helps explain Theseus's rapid acceptance of Pirithous as a friend.

No ancient myth makes Castor and Pollux low-level shapeshifters. I did that to reconcile the variations in their reported ages, and shape-shifting does play a role in a number of other Greek stories. Since the gods were able to shape-shift freely, there's nothing inherently improbable about sons of gods (or half-sons in the case of Castor and Pollux) having a lesser form of the same ability.

No ancient myth describes Theseus as having momentary prophetic flashes. I used that as an explanation for Theseus being so easily murdered by the far less powerful Lycomedes. If Theseus let himself be killed, the story becomes more understandable. Though not as common among the gods as shape-shifting, prophetic powers are widespread enough among them and common enough among their children to make it credible that Theseus might experience prophetic inspiration occasionally.

Most significantly, no ancient source reports judgment being passed on Theseus in the Underworld, though the idea is consistent with ancient Greek belief. No myth preserves the details, but Theseus, like every other mortal, would have faced judgment after death. The use of such trials for political maneuvering is not mentioned in any myth, either, but the gods certainly did maneuver politically on other occasions.

I hope you enjoyed my effort to present the Theseus story, even though you might have presented it differently if you had been the one making the decisions. Any lover of Greek mythology will have a vision of how Theseus should be. In that respect, we are no different from the ancient Greeks, with their multiple competing versions.

ABOUT THE AUTHOR

As far back as he can remember, Bill Hiatt had a love for reading so intense that he eventually ended up owning over eight thousand books--not counting e-books! He has also loved to write for almost that long. As an English teacher, he had little time to write, though he always felt there were stories within him that longed to get out, and he did manage to publish a few books near the end of his teaching career. Now that he is retired from teaching, the stories are even more anxious to get out into the world, and they will not be denied

For more information, visit
https://www.billhiatt.com

OTHER BOOKS AND BOOKLETS BY BILL HIATT

Spell Weaver Series

(Shorts set in the Spell Weaver universe are inserted where they belong in the storyline but are not numbered.)

"Echoes of My Past Lives" (0)

Living with Your Past Selves (1)

Divided against Yourselves (2)

Hidden among Yourselves (3)

"Destiny or Madness"

"Angel Feather"

Evil within Yourselves (4)

We Walk in Darkness (5)

Separated from Yourselves (6)

When Parallels Collide Series

(A continuation of the Spell Weaver series, set several years later)

The Serpent Waits (1)

The Dragon Bares Its Teeth (2, expected in 2021)

Different Dragons

Different Lee (1)

Soul Switch (2)

Blood Is Thicker Than Runes (3)

Soul Salvager Series

Haunted by the Devil (1, also includes *The Devil Hath the Power*, originally published separately)

The Inner Worlds Trap (2)

Mythology Book (hybrid mythology text/young adult urban fantasy)

A Dream Come True: An Entertaining Way
for Students to Learn Greek Mythology

Novels Based on Greek Mythology

Fateful Pathways: A Story of Theseus

Anthologies

[The name(s) of the piece(s) by Bill Hiatt are in parentheses following the anthology name.]

Anthologies of the Heart, Book 1: Where Dreams and Visions Live
("The Sea of Dreams")

Flash Flood 2: Monster Maelstrom, A Flash Fiction Halloween Anthology
("In the Eye of the Beholder")

Flash Flood 3: Christmas in Love, A Flash Fiction Anthology
("Naughty or Nice?" and "Entertaining Unawares")

Hidden Worlds, Volume 1: Unknown, a Sci-Fi and Fantasy Anthology
("The Worm Turns" and "Abandoned")

Great Tomes Series, Book 6: The Great Tome of Magicians, Necromancers, and Mystics
("Green Wounds")

Education-related Titles

"A Parent's Guide to Parent-Teacher Communications"
"A Teacher's Survival Guide for Writing College Recommendations"
"Poisoned by Politics: What's Wrong with

Education Reform and How To Fix It"

Made in the USA
Las Vegas, NV
09 November 2021

34048827R00258